BEYOND REVANCHE

GERRY DOCHERTY

Published by:
Trine Day LLC
PO Box 577
Walterville, OR 97489
1-800-556-2012
www.TrineDay.com
trineday@icloud.com

Library of Congress Control Number: 2022934857

Docherty, Anthony (Gerry).
Beyond Revanche: The Death of La Belle Epoque—1st ed.
p. cm.

Epub (ISBN-13) 978-1-63424-402-2
Print (ISBN-13) 978-1-63424-401-5
1. Fiction – World War I. 2. Fiction – Conspiracies -- History -- 20th century.
3. Fiction – World War, 1914-1918 -- Causes. I. Docherty, Anthony (Gerry). II.
Title

First Edition
10 9 8 7 6 5 4 3 2 1

Distribution to the Trade by:
Independent Publishers Group (IPG)
814 North Franklin Street
Chicago, Illinois 60610
312.337.0747
www.ipgbook.com

To Those Who Dare Think For Themselves

GLOSSARY

Action français: a far-right monarchist political movement. By 1914 it was the most effectively structured nationalist movement in France. Anti-German and pro-war.

Adams, Professor Ephraim: professor of history at Stanford University in California. Chosen personally by Herbert Hoover to oversee the vast tonnage of records, initially concerning the Commission for Relief in Belgium but expanded into virtually every pre - war piece of evidence about the origins and execution of World War I, which were transferred half way around the world to Stanford University immediately after the war.

Air raids over Paris took place in the early months of the war but became a desperate fact of life in Paris from March 1918 until the Armistice of 1918. The city was badly damaged and civilian life shattered.

Auberge is an inn.

Phillipe Berthelot: French diplomat credited with undermining peace efforts in 1914 by secretly encouraging the Serbians to continue upsetting the Austrians.

Boches: a derogatory French word for Germans. Translates roughly as cabbage-heads.

Bolivar Metro Station was built as part of the Paris Metro in 1911. It carried trains on line 7. Used as an air-raid shelter, it saw the worst case of civilian death in an air raid in Paris when, in sheer panic, 76 people were crushed or suffocated while the bombs were falling above.

Briey: an industrialized part of Northern France / Alsace with vast quantities of coal and iron. Centre of French steel production industry which lay a few kilometers from the frontier between France and Germany. Questions will always be asked about the French decision not to attack or dismantle the steel production which fed the German army.

Henriette Caillaux: French socialite and wife of former prime minister, Joseph Caillaux. On 16 March 1914 she shot dead Gaston Calmette in his offices. Her subsequent trial was one of the gravest travesties of justice in pre-war France.

Joseph Caillaux: Minister of Finance in 1914. Had been prime minister 1911-12. Known as a leader of the peace movement during the war.

Chateau Monthairons: built in the mid nineteenth century. Barely 13 kilometers south of Verdun, it served as an elegant army Headquarters.

Calmette was the editor of the French newspaper, *Le Figaro*, and he targeted the Caillaux family history to create maximum damage before forthcoming elections in 1914. He was on the point of publishing private love letters from Joseph Caillaux to his first wife when Henriette intervened.

The Caudron G.4 was the first twin-engine aircraft in service in numbers with the French Air Force. It was used to carry out bombing raids deep behind the front line, but it was comparably slow and increasing losses led to its withdrawal from day bombing missions in the autumn of 1916.

Comedie-Francaise on the Rue Richelieu was founded in 1680. It is the oldest active theatre company in the world.

Comité des Forges or Foundry Committee was an organization of leaders of the French iron and steel industry. It took a protectionist attitude on trade issues, and was opposed to social legislation that would increase costs. It was influential, particularly during the First World War, when it made vast fortunes from the armaments industry.

George Clemenceau was prime minister of France twice. Known as a hard man he is sometimes referred to as the "Father of Victory". Hated by the left, especially the miners whom he crushed in a 1906 strike, he was fearless in criticizing other French governments until he himself took over in 1917. Shot by would-be assassin Emile Cottin in 1919.

Emile Cottin: an anti-war French militant who attempted to assassinate Georges Clemenceau in February 1919. Hated the prime minister for his harsh treatment of striking workers. Initially condemned to death by a military court but had the sentence commuted to ten years after loud and persistent protests. Died in the Spanish Civil War.

Committee for the Relief of Belgium was set up under the auspices of Herbert Hoover as Chief Executive of the food relief program for Belgium and Northern France. Believed to have also supplied food to Germany and thus played a major part in sustaining the war beyond 1915. Most of the produce was paid for by Britain and France in the main.

Deuxième Bureau: France's most prestigious policing department, involved in counter-espionage and the protection of key political figures during WWI.

The Dreyfus Affair was a monstrous attempt by the French Army to imprison an artillery officer for spying for Germany. Dreyfus was Jewish and an easy target for the powerful anti-Semitic. After a retrial and immense journalistic pressure from Emile Zola and socialists like Jean Jaurès, he was eventually proven innocent.

The Élysée Palace is the official residence of the President of France

Estaminet is a small cafe-pub selling alcohol, often found in poorer quarters or out-of-the-way country places.

Pierre-Etienne Flandin: a French conservative politician who served as a military pilot during the First World War. He was prime minister from November 1934-June 1935. Involved in bombing of Briey.

Gaugin, Paul René: the grandson of the world famous artist Paul Gaugin, important figure in the Symbolist movement as a painter, sculptor, printmaker, ceramist, and writer.

General Joseph Gallieni was brought back from retirement at the start of the war. Left behind by the government which had retreated to Bordeaux, he defended Paris from the onslaught of the German armies in September 1914, and ordered many of his own troops north to stop the German advance.

General Guillaumat: chief of Adolphe Messimy's military cabinet. Ended the war as commander of the Fifth Army. Involved in the decision to bomb Briey.

General Joseph 'Papa' Joffre served as commander-in-chief of French forces on the Western Front from the start of World War I until the end of 1916 when he was promoted to Marshal of France. Loved by his troops.

General Adolphe Messimy was a politician and general. He served as minister of war during the outbreak and first weeks of the war but insisted in returning to his army post and commanded a brigade at the Battle of the Somme. He was a brave and decisive leader, awarded the Croix de Guerre. Returned to politics in the 1920s.

General Robert Nivelle was promoted to commander-in-chief of the French armies on the Western Front in December 1916. Aided by his fluency in English, and his confidence with French and British political leaders, he was responsible for the Nivelle Offensive. When it failed to achieve a breakthrough on the Western Front, a major mutiny in the French army occurred and around half of the French Army refused to take part in further offensives for several months. Nivelle was replaced as commander-in-chief by Philippe Pétain in May 1917.

General Philippe Pétain, known as the Lion of Verdun, was by the end of the war Marshal of France.

The Gotha G.V. was a heavy bomber built for the Imperial German Air Service during World War I. Designed for long-range service it was used principally at night.

Célestin Hennion was head the Prefecture of Police in Paris. He was responsible for the reorganization of the service and the introduction of the flying squad, the Brigades du Tigres. He was considered one of the most influential French pioneers of modern policing.

Myron Herrick was previously Governor of Ohio. He subsequently served as U.S. Ambassador in Paris from 1912 to December, 1914 and again from 1921 to 1929. Although he was at the end of his first tenure in 1914, he assumed responsibility for some ambassadorial business covering those nationals from other countries who had been left behind in Paris.

Herbert Hoover was a former mining engineer whose close ties to the British elite gave him entrance to the upper levels of that society. Friend of Foreign Secretary Sir Edward Grey. Backed too, by President Wilson and his Wall Street supporters. Deeply involved in food supplies and international payments for these. Later 31st President of America.

Hoover was also the principal architect for the removal of all evidence of foodstuff importation and distribution through the Belgian Relief Fund, though some called it the American Relief Agency, at the end of the conflict. His organization procured and transported vast quantities of food into Europe and distributed it. How much went to Germany? Evidence removed. Profits? Audited by a company of Hoover's choice. The records of governments, companies, deals and distribution disappeared from Europe alleged to be kept safe in Stanford University in California. Few had any idea that this was happening in the 1919-20s and even now the records of what was precisely taken remain sketchy.

Hotel-Dieu on the Ile de la Cité is the oldest hospital in Paris, reputedly founded in 651 AD.

Jusserand, Jean Jules: the French Ambassador in Washington from 1903 - 1924. He was by the side of the American president Woodrow Wilson during the Versailles Peace Conference which began on 18 January 1919, and culminated in the signing of the Treaty of Versailles on 28 June, establishing peace in Europe, but not for long.

Lloyd George began the First World War as Chancellor in the British government, became the powerful Minister of Munitions in 1915 and then Secretary of State for War in 1916. He was head of a clique which assumed power in Britain under his prime-ministership in December 1916. Friend and associate of Basil Zaharoff.

Edward Mandell House, known as Colonel House, was the right-hand man of President Woodrow Wilson in the White House. Was never in the army and his rank of 'colonel' is entirely dubious. Mandell House was complicit with the English ruling elites and had access both to Prime Minister Lloyd George and King George V. He had close and dark associations with the great banking institutions on Wall Street.

Alexander Isvolsky was the Ambassador of Czar Nicholas II in Paris in 1910. He strengthened Russia's bonds with France and Britain. He is alleged to have funded President Poincaré's successful election in 1913. A warmonger.

Jean Jaurès was possibly Europe's most outspoken anti-war figure and legendary publisher of the daily newspaper L'Humanité (Humanity). An antimilitarist, he spent his last days travelling across Europe desperately trying to stop the war. Jaurès was assassinated in Paris on the night of 31 Just 1914, the day before the First World War began. He remains one of the main figures in French 20th Century history.

Jean Longuet, depute editor of L'Humanitè, was the grandson of Karl Marx.

The Grand Prix de Paris at Longchamp remains France's greatest horse-race and apex of the equine season. On 28 June, 1914 the race to the finish line was between Maurice de Rothschild's Sardanapale and his cousin, Baron Édouard de Rothschild's La Farina. The Austrian ambassador to France left the race meeting on hearing about the assassination of Archduke Ferdinand.

Mobilization: General mobilization was the last step before an all-out war. In 1914 it was recognized that the next step was a full declaration of war. Thus when the Russians mobilized the Kaiser tried desperately to convince the Czar to recall his troops, but when the Russians continued, he was obliged to declare war.

Montmartre is a historic district of Paris. It is primarily known for its artistic history, and as a nightclub district. Near the end of the 19th century and at the beginning of the twentieth, many artists lived in, had studios, or worked in or around Montmartre, including Amedeo Modigliani, Claude Monet, Pierre-Auguste Renoir, Edgar Degas, Henri de Toulouse-Lautrec, Suzanne Valadon, Piet Mondrian, Pablo Picasso, Camille Pissarro, and Vincent van Gogh. Nightlife included La Cigale and the Moulin Rouge. Remains very popular with tourists.

Mutilés is the French word for disfigured or mutilated. In the context of our story, it also has the sense of a disabled war veteran

Raymond Poincaré was President of France from 1913-1920. He was strongly anti-German in his attitudes, and used the Franco-German Alliance to build towards war in Europe. He visited Russia in 1912 and 1914 to strengthen the Czar's resolve to hold fast to war against Germany and his visit in July 1914 had exactly that effect

Quai d'Orsay: Ever since the mid-19th century, this grand mansion has housed the Ministry of Foreign Affairs in Paris, and is the headquarters of the French Diplomatic Service.

Quai des Orfèvres sits on the island Isle-de France in the middle of Paris not far from the law courts called Palaise de Justice and Notre Dame Cathedral. No. 36 is the headquarters of the Deuxième Bureaux.

Rothschild, Baron Edmond: was a French member of the Rothschild banking dynasty. He was an intrepid supporter of early Zionism and played a pivotal role in the development of what became the State of Israel.

Sacré Coeur: The stunningly white travertine-stone that sits on the summit of Montmartre in Paris, towering above the city. It was scheduled to be opened in 1914 but the war intervened and it was eventually consecrated in 1919.

St. Gervais: a stunning parish church on the north bank of the Seine dates back into the middle ages. On 29 March 1918, a German shell, fired from long-range fell on the church, killing 91 people and wounding 68 others; the explosion collapsed the roof during a Good Friday service.

La Santé in Montparnasse is one of the most famous prisons in France, with both VIP and high security wings.

William Sharp: Ambassador of the United States in Paris. Appointed in June 1914 but didn't take up post until December 1914. Remained in Paris for the duration of the war until April 1919.

Spanish Civil War 1936-1939 was a bloodbath in many quarters between the different forces of the left (anarchists and communists) and the right (Nationalists and Falangists). The war reached over to the Balearics in September 1936 and the narrative of this story follows that path. The town of Ibiza was indeed bombed.

Spanish Flu raged across the world as a pandemic in 1918-20. It did not originate in Spain. Probably brought from America by one of the first waves of army volunteers, it was an unusually deadly influenza pandemic caused by the viral H1N1 influenza. Lasting from February 1918 to April 1920, it infected an estimated 500 million people – about a third of the world's population at the time.

The Taxi-cab army has assumed a much more grandiose legend than it probably deserves, but the Taxi drivers and companies from Paris greatly assisted the movement of many troops forward from the city towards the battle to defend the capital in September 1914.

Toul: Rhine canal (known as the Canal de la Marne au Rhin). The borders between France and Germany in the North East were served by a network of canals and rivers which boosted the industrialization of the area. Toul was an important junction with one major system running north to Verdun and Briey and a second flowing due west, crossing the river Meurthe at Nancy where a second major artery carried barges to Strasbourg and the Rhine.

Tour de France remains Europe's premier international cycling race testing stamina and endurance over Alpine tracks and main road routes. In 1914 it was won for the second time by the Belgian champion Philippe Thys barely one week before the First World War began.

Vespasienne: the green circular public urinal which was literally a part of the street furniture of Paris at the time. Often adorned on the outside with posters for forth- coming theatrical events

Marcel Villain was Raoul's elder brother. He served on the Western Front as an aviator

Raul Villain, the assassin, always claimed to have acted on his own. His back history is as we record it. His internalized thoughts are of course, fictional, but trace a genuine timeline. His childhood traumas, association with right-wing politics, arrest, trial and consequent life are as accurate as modern research permits.

Wendel, François: Before the war began, the Comite des Forges appointed François de Wendel as its president, the man dubbed by the socialist leader Joseph Caillaux as 'the symbol of the plutocracy'. Deputy to the National Assembly, acknowledged as a maître de forges (iron master) from a dynastic line of iron and steel producers, Wendel became a Regent of the Banque de France. Francois was deeply anti-German and a strong supporter of Raymond Poincare and his Revanchist party.

Wendel, Henri – After the war of 1870, Henri remained behind in the annexed section of Lorraine as a subject of the new German Empire in order to keep control of the family's extensive industrial interests there. Indeed he quickly reoriented his political loyalties and was elected to the Reichstag as a Representative for Lorraine from 1881-1890.

Wendel, Charles: elected to the Reichstag in Germany from 1907-1911. Thus the Wendel family retained both its political and economic interests on both sides of the border, with Francois in the French National Assembly and his father and cousin in the Reichstag. Together they owned the mines and factories, the plants and smelters in and around Briey.

Zaharoff, Basil: the Merchant of Death, international arms dealer. Said to be the richest man in the world in his lifetime. Of Greek or Turkish origin, he became a naturalized Frenchman. Awarded Grand Cross Legion of Honour (France) Knight Grand Cross of both the Order of the Bath and Order of the British Empire. (Great Britain) Personal friend of President Poincaré and Prime Minister Lloyd George. Sometimes called the Mystery Man of Europe.

FRENCH SWEAR-WORDS
Trou de Cul – Asshole
Merde– Shit (or an equivalent)
Putain – Whore, Bitch but generally a stronger swear-word
Bâtard – Bastard
Bâtard Lèche – Bastard crawler or bootlicker
Cretin – Dumbass
Mère de Dieu – Mother of God (much less of a swear)

PROLOGUE

JANUARY 1914

"That's her, behind the Fabre Line cruiser. She'll come across its wake and make for the canal any moment now."

They had tracked the small twin-masted steamship from the moment it left Bastia. Bathed in an innocence warmed by the mid-morning Corsican sun, *La Pierre Cartes* had sailed northeast with the accustomed ease of a frequent traveller. Onboard the worn wooden craft, powerful binoculars swept fore and aft, port and starboard, alert to anything unusual. No one cast a second glance in the ship's direction. In its heyday, it carried passengers from Corsica to France and back in a three-day turnaround, but now there were other purposes which offered handsome profit. La Pierre Cartes had been transformed into an empty husk where hidden cargoes replaced second-class cabins. Its contraband was precious brandy, and wholly illegal.

As the vessel swung into Marseille's canal Saint Jean, dominated by the formidable La Joliette fortress, bareheaded Corsican foot soldiers hidden inside the hold, clutched their weapons and listened once more to Carlo Vesperini's final instructions … for a third time. He was rightly nervous. This was his first time in charge of the family's "trading mission" and his future depended on quick success.

Onshore, the special task force watched in silence, weapons at the ready. Concentrating. Captain Rougerie gave his final order; "Keep low, everyone. Vincent, take your men through the left-hand alley and out-flank them. Do not fire unless forced to. The rest of you follow me. Above all, keep them trapped in the canal."

There was an unaccustomed quaver in the captain's voice. Life was cheap in these parts. He had little confidence in instructions from city politicians, but his team knew the drill. These Corsicans were bandits to a man and woman, slippery as moray eels and just as dangerous when cornered. Political pressure demanded action. But no more bloodbaths. There had been too many, apparently, though politicians rarely ever meant what they said in public. The swoop had been secretly approved at the highest level and the plans had been carefully and thoroughly rehearsed. No one was to know in advance. There would be casualties, but it would clear the vermin from the streets.

Vincent Chanot led his squad through the narrow alleyway along the fish factory wall to conceal their advance from the Corsicans. It was their first action together. They were young, inexperienced, and excited; fear would have been a better shield.

A weathered fisherwoman sat pipe in mouth in a makeshift hide close to the far edge of the factory, lost in her own world of harsh work and harsher insults. She glanced briefly towards the four men hugging the sidewall as if it was their mother's apron. Her brief respite from the tedium of endless slicing and boning was not to be interrupted by wasted greetings to strangers.

Instead, her attention was drawn towards the steamship as it slipped into the canal for it rode heavy on the calmer water. Suspiciously heavy.

The police squad had just broken cover when mayhem exploded from two sides. Gunshots cracked from above, ripping into the steamship's starboard structure. Splinters raked the unprotected deck, but the Corsicans reacted instantly, firing blindly at anything that moved. Dockside, unsuspecting cafe patrons reeled in shock. Those already on the narrow quayside had little cover from a vicious indiscriminate crossfire. Vincent dived below a wooden handcart, which offered scant defence, but hid him from the immediate line of sight.

"Fire at the starboard portholes," he screamed above the deafening explosions. "They're using machine guns."

A fresh burst of murderous hail turned in their direction, isolating a father and child who had been crawling towards a tethered sailing boat. Vincent raised his right hand and tried to direct them towards the factory. Man and boy broke cover, father half crouched, bending over his ten-year old in a protective shield. The detective grabbed the youngster and pulled him down. His father sank to his knees and hit the handcart wheel with what remained of his head.

It took time to work out what was happening. Vincent's team were trapped between two armed groups, one safely positioned on the castle walls, the other, bewildered by the attack, fighting for survival on the vulnerable steamship.

"Look out! They're firing on us from above,"

Vincent half turned to look as more bullets zipped around his head like angry wasps set on self-destruction. Why were these people shooting at them? Nothing made sense. Across the canal, two figures emerged from the front hold in a desperate attempt to escape, the tarpaulin shade above them already in tatters.

"Don't let them get away," Vincent roared as he set his sights on the fleeing Corsicans. Something slipped from the arms of the taller smuggler and splashed into the sullied waters. The figures steadied themselves to dive after the package, but a stream of bullets seared through one torso cutting it in half. Then silence. Smoke billowed from the port side, gifting the Corsicans unexpected cover. Bursts of sporadic gunfire confirmed there would be no surrender. Bright orange flames broke through on the starboard side, licking the deck above in a gentle arc.

The traumatized boy lay by Vincent's side, gasping for air and drained of all understanding. The boy was in shock, face scraped by the sharp quayside dirt, innocence lost in a nightmare that would haunt his dreams forever.

"I'll come back for you," Vincent promised, but it was an empty gesture born of good intention to salve his conscience.

"Papa ... Papa," the frightened youngster sobbed, knowing full well that death stared back at him from his father's lifeless eyes.

Vincent tried to reassert his authority. "Back, lads ... we'll try to cut off any stragglers at the other end of the alley." No one moved. He looked back. His colleague's head jolted forward angrily, blown apart from behind, shot from the fort wall. Murdered by an unknown assailant. A second was clutching a wound in his midriff, his lifeblood slipping into drains more used to fish-gut than human entrails. The man gulped for air. His mouth formed words that might have been a prayer, but stopped forever at "Amen."

The third sat in silent shock, his back against a plane tree, drinking in the enormity of his injuries. Both legs were bleeding from machine gun wounds. Vincent knelt beside him and tried to stem the flow by binding a torn roadside rope tight above his right knee. The fisherwoman, whose half-hidden shelter had given her privileged protection, pushed him aside and took control of the wounded officer.

"Arsehole" she spat in disgust

Vincent ran towards the burning ship through the billowing smoke, blinded by his own inadequacy. The unit captain, Rougerie, lay close to the single gangway, his team around him in a roll call for hell. They had been caught in the crossfire as they approached the steamboat. Their guns lay beside them, unused. Ambushed. Unquestionably.

His own team had been wiped out. Bennet, Toutain, and Verany were their names, but he never knew who was who. More bodies bobbed on the surface of the canal. Vincent crouched at the water-side unable to speak, unable to think. The ancient Roman towers of Marseille's iconic green and white-striped Cathedral broke through the thick, foreboding smoke, mocking both the living and the dead. It looked like the bastard child of a forced marriage between a Byzantine immigrant and a Roman refugee, but it loomed over the carnage in self-important mockery. No God worthy of worship would have permitted such callous slaughter.

A flesh-colored toy bobbed slowly in the water. Almost lifelike, it had lost an arm.

"Oh, Christ." Vincent dived instinctively into the rancid canal and struggled to lift the small body out of the slime. Only then did he realize. He howled to the bare fort walls and his horror reverberated over the battlements and echoed into the unsuspecting city. Behind the child a woman torn in two floated, arms outstretched, as if she was trying to catch the infant in an innocent game of chase. Sirens rose and fell. Voices spoke words that made no sense. Transfixed, he sat in the solitude of shock as life moved cautiously around, trying to dissect the unimaginable.

"It was just a baby," he told the police officer who coaxed him from the canal-side by insisting he had to see a doctor. It was a lie.

The police car swept him, head in hands, past the Saint-Esprit Hospital, which looked more like a luxury hotel than a place of healing, straight to the Town Hall. Of course, they were taking him to his grandfather, the Depute Mayor Chanot. Politics.

"Vincent." He was greeted with open arms. "Vincent." The old man's voice was edged with annoyance. It felt like he was about to be scolded.

"Grand-père," he mouthed. Still breathless in confusion, he shivered involuntarily.

"What happened?" No kiss to the cheek. No familial warmth. Vincent sensed he had done something wrong.

The depute mayor's balding grey head, formal black morning coat, sharp-nosed features, and tight-lipped mouth gave him an eagle-like appearance, as did his predatory eyes. He bid the room empty itself of officers and staff with one stern nod towards the door. He would speak to his grandson alone.

"Vincent, sit down. Can I get you a drink?" He made to ring a bell on his desk but his grandson shook his head.

"Bad business, this. Bad business. It would appear that your squad was caught in a Mafia ambush near La Joliette. Wrong place, wrong time. Most unfortunate."

"No. That's not what happened. … We were supposed … but …"

"But what?" his grandfather rasped with such venom that Vincent thought he had stood on a reptile.

"That's not what happened," he repeated slowly, looking to his grandfather for the comfort of understanding.

The depute mayor's eyebrows met in disapproval. "Are you saying that the chief of police is lying?"

It made no sense. They'd been monitoring the illegal traffic in brandy from Corsica. It was a secret operation, the result of months of surveillance. At least it was supposed to be secret. What they walked into was a carefully planned ambush, not a surgical strike to round up half-brained smugglers. This was certainly not an unfortunate coincidence. Vincent tried to work out what had happened, but words and questions leaped over each other to add to the confusion.

"People knew what was happening. People in high places, here in the Town Hall, in police headquarters. It was a set up. We were ambushed. We were sacrificed." He looked up again for reassurance but saw instead a brooding anger. Did his grandfather think he was lying?

Depute Mayor Chanot physically distanced himself from Vincent. His grandfather, the man who had taken him into his home when his widowed mother died of pleurisy, took three steps back and cut an invisible umbilical cord. He looked sharply from side to side to reassure himself that they were alone, marched directly into Vincent's space, put his hands on his shoulders, and fixed his glare on the young man's ashen face as if he was a practiced hypnotist.

"Nonsense, you're in shock. You don't know what you're saying, Vincent. I thank God you were spared this morning … but you cannot go about speaking like this. People will misunderstand. If you made such allegations in public, the fallout would be catastrophic … for our party, I mean. If you, you of all people, my grandson, raised ridiculous suspicions …"

He never finished the sentence. A flunky burst into the room as if summoned telepathically. He ushered the depute mayor towards the interior window and whispered urgently in his ear. The old politician gasped.

"Two women and a child were shot dead in the affray, Vincent. You need to know that they were Carlo Vesperini's mother, wife, and child. Witnesses claim that they were shot dead by the police as they tried to surrender."

5

Merde. Vincent closed his eyes and relived the moment. He had. He had told his team to shoot at the people escaping overboard. The baby. The woman. Just floating in the canal. Vesperini's family. Christ. He was responsible.

"But we didn't know who was who. How could we? It was a double ambush. There were two targets, the Vesperinis and us," Vincent reasoned.

"Nonsense. Absolute nonsense." The depute mayor dismissed his explanation.

Anger pumped through Vincent's veins like a deadly poison, but for now, compliance was his best option. Grandfather would insist that he was right. It was always so. And if he had killed Carlo Vesperini's mother, wife and child, he was dead. Mafia families were not to be crossed by the living. Vincent Chanot lifted his head and faced a grim and short future.

Depute Mayor Chanot thought otherwise. "Wait here. Don't move. Speak to no one." He reached the door and spun round in an afterthought. "When were you assigned to that unit, Vincent?

"Yesterday."

"Ah."

And he was gone, leaving his grandson in a guilt-ridden hell. The broken porcelain child bobbing in the water. How? The carnage that had erupted when they'd broken cover. It made no sense. The captain and his unit spread-eagled in death, mowed down by machine guns as they approached the ship. Why?

The depute mayor must have been gone for the better part of half an hour. Vincent sat mute, all senses seized. Broken. His grandfather returned as he had left. Swiftly.

"We will say that you were killed in action. I've made arrangements. Trust me. You are a good detective, Vincent. France will need your service in the days and months ahead, but it will be much safer elsewhere. For you, I mean."

Vincent shook with anger. This wasn't about his safety. What had happened had another purpose; served another agenda for political reasons. It didn't take him long to work out that his survival was more than a slight inconvenience. But who was pulling the strings? His own grandfather was certainly one of the political elite. But who else? Who ran this city? Politics and power were much more important than a grandson. If he hadn't appreciated the cost of bitter disillusionment this morning, by nightfall he did.

"You will change your name, Vincent, and leave Marseilles. Start a new life. It's the only way acceptable to them. I've arranged new papers for you and a respectable post in Paris. Start again. You're young, you're resilient, but you must go now."

When the train from Marseilles pulled into the Gare de Lyon in Paris, Vincent still could not fathom who his grandfather meant by "them." Corsicans, Mafia, their own police force, politicians, or others? How far did this go? He was trapped in a conspiracy inside a conspiracy and his grandfather's solution was his exile.

And he was no longer Vincent.

THE ROOTS OF DESTRUCTION

I ran across the road and onto the sand, picking up speed; not sparing a look backwards. One minute was all I needed to get around the first rocks and they would not know where I had gone.

Slam. I fell down head first as I ran. Then the noise of a gunshot carried forward into the soft beach. The shock of pain blasted through me and then subsided. The sand was warm and accepting, I heard my neighbors' shouts and the soldiers' reply, but it took some moments to understand.

A gruffer voice spoke in a matter-of-fact way. "He's not dead, Sir. Should I shoot him in the head?"

You coward, I thought. I'm unarmed and cannot move, yet you would shoot me in the head? You coward.

Listen to me please, my friend. I have to tell it as it was.

I used to believe my mother the most beautiful woman on earth even though I have no true memory of her. There was once a faded photograph in my father's study but I don't know what happened to it. She haunted my dreams for many years, pleading with me to help her, but it made no sense. She left me at the age of two. Or was it four? Still, it wasn't her fault, it was his, of that I am certain. A son knows.

My father told me he was important, many times. Praise for me did not fall naturally from his lips, save a simple recognition that I was clever. My brother was said to be strong, dependable, honest, helpful, good at games, and at ease with the ladies. There seemed to be an endless lexicon of affection with which his hallmark was stamped. But I was only clever. That was his word, clever. I wore it first as a badge of distinction, proud as Lucifer and every bit as deceitful. But as the years progressed, his praise lost value like outdated currency until I merely "used to be clever." I remember the first time he said that. The parish priest was in my father's study and, though I was an altar boy, he offered no objection. "Used to be clever." How that stung. Me? I was the one who spoke in flawless Latin and knelt before the raised sacrament. I knew how to fire the incense in the thurible and swing it with unerring precision. Perhaps I was clever then.

He told me that I had no personality, no worthy attributes, no sense of conviction. At best, I might be a dreamer. I was dubbed a wastrel, a butterfly who flittered from one idea to another. From clever boy to inconsistent, inconsequential loner. He told me I was scared of my own shadow, too fragile of nature to risk a fall, but not fit company for the brave and the daring. As with all he said, it was rot. An illusion he invented to salve his own conscience. What I still don't understand is why.

My father.

I'm tired. Very tired. May I sleep now, just for a short while? You will stay won't you?

Part 1

FIN DE SIÈCLE

1

MARCH 1914 – LA BELLE ÉPOQUE

It started with a phone call to the prefecture. Like a thunderclap from an otherwise seamless sky, the day literally exploded and no one saw it coming.

Mathieu Bertrand was seething, angered that his so-called colleagues thought it funny to leave him behind like a glorified office boy. Let him know that he didn't belong. Well, sod that. He didn't choose his transfer. He hadn't even chosen his new name. It had been ordained between Marseille and Paris at a level beyond objection. Even if they had asked him along, he wouldn't have gone for a drink. Bastards treated him as if he was a liability imposed by the prefect of police. Their obvious dislike offended him, but he wouldn't let it show.

His new colleagues, though the word had to be taken at its broadest classification, raced around the capital in their new-fangled Panhard and Levassor motorcars, the self-declared elite, claiming to be the cutting edge of crime detection. The Tigers. They loved that name. Some claimed they were the best of the best. Whether it was true or not, their reports read well, though anyone can write a report with fancy, self-promoting prose.

The phone rang four times in the adjoining office. Let it. So what if it was a diamond robbery in the Place Vendôme or a bank job on Rue St. Denis? He had filing to complete. Important they had said, laughing as they grabbed their hats and headed out. Perhaps he should polish the floor while he was at it? *Bâtards.*

The dingy office smelled of tobacco and stale policemen with evidence aplenty of half-eaten sandwiches and cigarette stubs. Captain Girard's desk sat furthest from the door with assorted files and notes strewn carelessly across the top, left no doubt for someone else to put in order. His wastebasket was filled to the wicker-brim and the overspill lay on the wooden flooring as if it knew it would have to wait there patiently for some time. Directly in front, two smaller desks displayed very different personalities. Lieutenant Dubois's reflected a precision to detail. Not a pencil out of line nor a loose paperclip disturbed the immaculate order of a well-trained operator. His desk looked as if it had been polished daily, and his established sense of order was at odds with the rest of the room. To his left, second lieutenant Guy Simon's desk was festooned with notebooks, newspaper cuttings, and record sheets. He had covered the wall beside him with pictures of the Tigers posing for the photographers beside their motor vehicles; with the chief of police, with the minister of the Interior, with the mayor of the city. Mathieu's first impressions were clear; these guys loved themselves. And as for the chief, Commander Roux? He hadn't even found time to introduce himself.

The telephone restarted on the desk behind with an impertinent urgency that demanded attention. Mathieu should not have touched it.

"What?"

Nothing made sense. A voice screamed alarm and a list of barely intelligible words.

"Say that again." The same words were repeated at a higher decibel.

"Look, I'm in the office on my own. What do you expect me to do? Commander Roux and the team have left…"

A torrent of abuse followed, but the gist of the threat as he understood it was, "Get Roux. Find him and tell him personally."

"But I don't know where he is." Was that so difficult to understand?

"Roux. Now. Immediately. Find him and give him my message. Get him to the *Figaro*…"

"Boulevard Haussmann? And who do I say this message is from?"

"*Crétin*. Get Roux. Right now."

The officer at the front door knew where they'd be. He looked Mathieu up and down as if he was the village idiot. Didn't everyone at the prefecture know that the Tigers drank in the Café Clichy every Friday evening?

Struggling with his jacket, Mathieu powered down the street, a man on a mission, almost colliding into the high-rooted elm that overstretched itself above the paving.

"Haussmann, *Figaro*, Gaston Calmette, black car." He knew there were other equally important phrases. "Scandal, political nightmare, outrage." Mathieu dodged past the kiosks, the fresh budding trees, the strolling bourgeoisie, and the glitterati out to see and be seen.

"Haussmann, *Figaro*, Gaston Calmette, black car, gun," he muttered to himself.

From a distance of one hundred meters, it was obvious that a major hurdle lay ahead. On such a pleasant March evening Café Clichy patrons adorned the pavements like early spring flowers. Cherry blossom hovered over daffodils; peony, iris, lily, nasturtium mixed with the occasional rose, but failed to smell as sweet. Men in bowlers and straw hats hovered at the entrance, flattering the ladies, conveniently forgetful of matrimonial vows. The main door was a melee; a rugby scrum comprised of beer, wine, spirits, and assorted bodies. There was no option. It was barge right through. No time for nicety.

"*M'excuse.*"

Putain. He ducked under the outer edge of the first phalanx and squeezed into the well- patronized hostelry. Inside was even more impenetrable. Groups huddled together around the bar blocking those still desperate to place their first order. Table service had been suspended. Packed satin booths hugged the mirrored walls, which added to Mathieu's confusion. He was lost in a sea of unrecognizable faces duplicated in the resplendent mirrors, and for a moment, despair replaced his anxiety. From his left he heard a booming voice. It was the commander.

"...and then the minister's face went beetroot."

Laughter.

He was at a corner booth, standing tall, entertaining his troops, cigarette in one hand, brandy glass in the other. Rumor whispered he came from aristocratic stock, and he held himself upright, straight-backed and unbending. Commander Bernard Roux was an imposing presence. Save for a trimmed moustache, his face was close-shaven with arched eyebrows and elongated nose. His teeth were perfectly white yet the fingers on his right hand were nicotine stained, discolored by a life-long addiction to his weed of choice. His bespoke three-piece suit had been fitted with care and his waistcoat sported a fashionable fob watch. He had been gifted with the ability to treat people as he himself wished to be treated. The corner booth hung on his every word.

"May I speak with you, Sir?"

Conversation paused mid-sentence. Men of consequence winced. In that moment Commander Roux had no idea who had spoken to him.

"I have to speak with you, Sir. Urgently."

Vague recognition dawned. The commander nodded towards his audience and laughed. "Did anyone tell the new boy we can't be disturbed after half-past six?"

A chorus of reassurance dutifully claimed that they had.

"Back to the office, young man. We'll discuss this later." He turned away, keen to finish his story before he forgot how it ended. The commander was fast approaching that dangerous and embarrassing age.

"Sir, you have to know..."

13

Useless. Mathieu was appealing not to Roux's ear but to his back. He struck so quickly that no one around the booth had time to react. Spinning the commander around, he shouted into the prevailing noise.

"Outside, now. This…is…serious."

An eagle eye stared back in warning. "It had better be."

The commander handed his drink to the nearest officer and literally propelled Mathieu backwards through the crowded café into the street. An onlooker would have presumed that the doorman was ejecting an unsavory client.

"This had better be good. Spit it out."

"Henriette Caillaux, *Figaro*, Gaston Calmette, black car, gun."

"Say that again."

"Caillaux, Gaston Calmette, *Figaro*, black car, gun." This time he added, "Scandal, political nightmare."

"Where?" The pointed question put Roux back on his front foot. He understood what it meant and took control. Immediately.

"Boulevard Haussmann, *Figaro* offices."

"Right. Go."

Commander Bernard Roux, head of the Flying Squad, friend and intimate of politicians and government officials alike, moved to brush past Mathieu Bertrand but the newcomer took one step from the pavement and stopped a taxi in its tracks, opened the door, and pushed Roux inside, bellowing to the driver, "Haussmann, Figaro offices. Double-time."

It took Commander Roux a second to realize what had happened. Too late. He turned and pointed back towards the café. "What I meant was, go get the car."

"Which car?"

"Our Panhard, the one back there at the corner. Never mind, the boys will follow."

His *boys* had already spilled onto the street, uncertain why their commander was disappearing down the boulevard in a taxi. For one moment, Mathieu thought that he was going to be thrown out but Roux did a double take. Between Rue Clichy and Boulevard Haussmann, he learned more.

"The minister of finance's wife has entered the *Figaro* newspaper offices with a gun in her possession. Apparently, she's still there and whoever placed the emergency call needs you to know, Sir. It's you he asked for. Repeatedly. I don't think he wanted the local police involved."

"You don't think?" was the commander's curt reply, eyebrows arched in condescending amazement but there was a change in his tone which bordered on approval.

"You do appreciate there will be hell to pay if she threatens him … or worse?"

The new junior officer nodded, but had no idea what the commander was talking about.

"You're Bertrand, are you not? The new boy I was instructed to accommodate?"

"Mathieu Bertrand, Sir. From Marseilles."

"I thought it was Vincent." He seemed puzzled.

"It was," Mathieu said to himself, but shook his head in sad denial.

"Well, Mathieu Bertrand from Marseilles, if we are too late, you may have landed us in the biggest bucket of pig shite this side of St. Petersburg. And I fear we might be."

He shook his head in a manner which made Mathieu feel he had made an elementary mistake. Not just a rookie, a stupid rookie. "Henriette is, as you know, the wife of the minister of finance and darling of the coiffured classes. But she and her beloved Joseph have many enemies hell-bent on ruining his chances of ever becoming president of France. It's an open secret that Gaston Calmette, editor of the royalist newspaper *Figaro* has a shovel-full of dirt on Joseph and intends to use it."

Roux shifted his position to look again at the young man whom he had made no effort to acknowledge since he was ordered to find a place for him in the Flying Squad.

"What you have to understand is that Calmette is threatening her husband's career, and by default, Madame Caillaux's position in Parisian society. If she has thought this through, carefully…"

He paused, sat further back in the taxi, and lit a Gauloises.

"*Putain.*" Mathieu Bertrand sensed disaster.

"Precisely."

2

MARCH 1914 – THE FALLEN ANGEL

enriette Caillaux stood erect, close to the door of the editor's suite, as if frozen in defiance, instantly recognizable in her dark fur-collared long coat and wide-brimmed hat with large back-flowing feather fetchingly curving behind. She was La Belle Époque personified, at least in her own head. Everything that France had to offer the world in terms of impeccable style could be witnessed in this one-woman icon of beauty and class. Every item in her wardrobe had been made to measure by her chosen designer, and patronage was her ultimate gift to the up and coming artiste. Her hair had been styled this year by Cierplikowski in his salon at The Galeries Lafayette. Like most of the well-heeled upper class that frequented his outrageously expensive hairdressing salon, Henriette knew him as "The Little Russian," though he was of Polish extraction. *Antoine de Paris* was his more vulgar trade name.

Her relationship with the socialist politician Joseph Caillaux had been the topic of much criticism even before they both divorced their original spouses. But no one needed to ask what she saw in the man. He was a living legend whose political decisions were more contentious than any other elected official in the Third Republic. Three years ago, he had been prime minister. A successful eighteen-month spell promised hope of even greater office ahead. He might yet be president of France.

Shameless enemies now threatened that dream. Joseph, as minister of finance, was under attack from the gutter press which constantly tried to undermine his ambitions, none more so that the gutter-master himself, Gaston Calmette, editor of the *Figaro*. He had taken possession of some intimate letters written years ago by Joseph to his whimpering first wife, and promised to destroy his career by publishing them. Such detail was common knowledge among the whispering classes. Aware of her well-pampered background, Mathieu knew that she had thought this through, carefully.

Had he considered his own upbringing, Mathieu might have realized that being raised in his grandparents' exclusive villa served him well, not in terms of ingrained prejudice or overbearing selfishness, but rather in observing the kind of man he was determined not to be. The small boy left on his own to wander the great rooms of privilege became the invisible observer of the cruelty of his mother's older sister egged on, as she was, by his grandmother. Servants were dressed down in public; tradesmen had their reputations trashed. What he never fully understood was that his grandfather knew of the cruelty, heard the screaming and the beatings, yet did nothing to stem the abuse.

Mathieu vowed that he would never treat fellow humans with such callous contempt, and as he looked across the editor's office, he recognized that contempt standing before him. The *Figaro* sub-editor held Henriette Caillaux by the arm, but she made no effort to resist the citizen's arrest. She stood staring at the man she had shot as if she was carved in marble. Certain. Her whole demeanor screamed, *Let that be a lesson to you. I will not be scorned.*

Gaston Calmette sat slumped on a chair by his desk, and someone, a doctor perhaps, was administrating superficial aid. His breathing was shallow, his pallor grey, but at least he wasn't dead. Mathieu looked carefully at the weapon lying at Madam Caillaux's feet. *Mère de Dieu*, it was a .32 Browning; the assassin's gun, spring-loaded and deadly. Fear rose from the pit of his soul. The Browning was a semi-automatic death sentence. How had she acquired such a weapon? In a moment of petrifying clarity, Mathieu realized that they had been sucked into a scandal. Was that why the telephone caller had been so insistent that Bernard Roux be warned in advance?

He looked back and heard the commander ask, "Was it a clean shot?" The doctor gently lifted back the chair cover he was using to compress Gaston Calmette's injuries. Three clear bullet wounds punctured the shaken body, as if it had been stabbed three times by the Fallen Angel herself.

"She shot him three times?" There was an edge of disbelief in Roux's voice.

"She fired five shots from point blank range, Sir. Five."

Mathieu struggled to make sense of the scene. Madame Caillaux had clearly shot Calmette as he turned to greet her. She must have hidden the weapon inside her hand muff, then thrown both to the floor. It was clear that her act of retribution would resolve itself into an uncomplicated full-blown murder within a few hours. Yet she had not tried to flee. She had fired the gun, thrown it to the ground, and waited to be caught in an act of supreme arrogance. Both his aunt and his grandmother had bathed in that conceit of self-righteousness which besets the privileged. These people actually believed that they had every right to ignore the law of the land. They frightened him then, and Henriette's immediate future frightened him now.

Angry voices could be heard outside. Word had spread along the boulevard like rabid contagion. The gathering mob smelled blood, but it wasn't the editor's. Mathieu moved to the commander's side and whispered, "We need to get her out before anyone realizes how few we are." Roux agreed with a curt nod and, as if occasioned by a prearranged signal, the off-duty Tigers pushed their way into the room and made straight for the commander.

"Dubois, call the prefecture and alert the minister of justice. Tell him we are going to move her to the station at Faubourg." The local police station had not been built to defy a mob, and Dubois' reaction betrayed his surprise.

"Temporarily?"

"Obviously." He turned to the captain. "Girard, do make sure that the minister of finance is informed immediately, and tell him where she'll be. Simon, get hold of a friendly face and find out how we can get her out of the building without being ripped apart."

"Not much chance of anonymity with her dressed to kill," Girard quipped. No one smiled.

Though she remained stationary, caught in her own moment, Henriette Caillaux was no alabaster Madonna. As she began to re-engage with a hostile world, Henriette gained confidence. Perhaps the ringing in her ears was beginning to soften. She looked directly at the wounded man and smiled. Shock gave way to euphoria. She looked over towards the stricken editor with a conceit of triumph which she could not hide, as if she had shown that rat the consequences of impugning a lady's honor.

Mathieu spoke slowly and calmly. It would have been counterproductive to intimidate this woman. She held her posture like the heroine she imagined herself to be; Danielle in the Den of Lions, no doubt. Surrounded as she was by a hostile press with an army of photographers desperate to shoot her least flattering side, Henriette betrayed no outward fear. It was as if she were a higher being caught by a minor distraction which would disappear of its own accord, leaving behind no consequence of worth. Realizing that some common person held her arm, she pulled away, bristling at such impertinence. Henriette Caillaux had no notion that she was now, and would forevermore be, a criminal. Mathieu read her changing body language carefully and stood directly in front of her in a manner which was neither threatening nor submissive.

"We have to get you into a police car and out of this place immediately for your own safety." His upbringing in Marseilles had included an appreciation of political and social propriety.

"Certainly not." She shuddered as if she had been offered a glass of cheap table wine.

Of all possible responses, this was the last Mathieu expected.

"I beg your pardon?"

"I am going nowhere in a police car. I have a limousine standing ready on the street. Patrick will drive me to the police station."

"Patrick?"

She threw a look in the direction of the question as if it had come from a certified imbecile.

"My chauffeur. I came here in my own limousine and I will leave in it. Call Patrick, would you?"

Mathieu swallowed the temptation to overreact. She really did fail to understand that, having fired the gun, she no longer called the shots. What she held to be dignity was in fact arrogance. Encouraged by her own voice, Henriette deigned to explain herself. As if reading from a prepared statement she continued, "Because there is no longer justice in France…"

"Shut up."

Two simple words, spoken with venom by one of the *Figaro* journalists, stopped her in mid-sentence and she began to appreciate the vulnerability of her situation.

"She won't get into a police car?" Captain Girard was incredulous. In forty years of service he had never heard such arrogance. "Caught in the act of attempted murder and she expects to be given special treatment? M'lady needs to be brought down a peg or two."

Commander Roux cocked his head and raised an eyebrow to invite other views.

"That's what I'd do, Chief, and let the *Figaro* boys photograph her struggling down the stairs." Guy Simon was far from impressed but this was not a time for self-indulgence.

"She's in shock," Mathieu reasoned. "She's arguably unstable. Getting her out of here safely is in everyone's interest. There will be enough political shit flying about to drop the whole police force in the *merde*, so keeping her calm right now is in our best interest. Let's go with her for the moment. The wagon can take her to prison later."

The commander looked at Mathieu, surprised not so much because he thought to comment, but because he understood the predicament with such clarity.

"Do it," he ordered.

Pascal Girard instructed Guy to find the limousine—not a difficult task since it was the largest vehicle in the Boulevard—and order her chauffeur to bring it to the main entrance. As unit captain, Girard led from the front and Mathieu kept close to Madame Caillaux all the way down the stairs. She made no further protestations but her every step dripped contempt. The commander brought up the rear and tried to block a pack of *Figaro* photographers who suddenly realized that a unique photo opportunity was already half way out of the building. Other loyal employees began to shout and gesticulate from the top of the stairwell, at which point the assistant commissioner of police burst through the entrance, took one look at Henriette, saluted her, and made directly for Bernard Roux.

"What's going on here? Are you out of your mind, Commander?" he rasped. "I should have been informed immediately."

"Carry on, gentlemen. I'll update the Assistant Commissioner." He stared down at the intruder, wondering how he had heard about the incident so quickly. "Do you think we should go somewhere more private, Assistant Commissioner, or shall we let the *Figaro* journalists hear our plans?"

At 2:00 A.M. in the morning, in the black emptiness of suspended time, Gaston Calmette succumbed to his wounds. He passed from editor-in-chief to the subject of a fulsome obituary in his own newspaper. Madame Henriette Caillaux had successfully promoted herself from assailant to murderess.

3

March 1914 – Confirmation

Commander Bernard Roux read the contents of the folder on his desk and rubbed his nose. The trouble with a healthy moustache was that it itched, mostly at the wrong moment in company which required the highest level of decorum.

Seated in front of him, Mathieu felt he was back in his headmaster's office about to be chastised for something he hadn't done. Roux had that effect, intentional or otherwise. Behind him a vast painting of Napoleon at the Battle of Austerlitz filled the wall, breaking sunlight dispelling the darkness over which the Emperor had triumphed. Its magnificence filled every Frenchman's heart. This was a copy of the priceless original which hung at Versailles, but the symbolism of General Rapp presenting the Emperor with captured enemy standards could not be denied. *Vive La France.* If Bernard Roux had chosen this backdrop carefully so that the visitor to his office would think that his men were the standard bearers for justice and he was Rapp, Mathieu felt like the dying soldier draped over the broken gun carriage. His time was up.

"Bertrand, you were appointed to the Tigers on a temporary basis at the request of Celestin Hennion, the Prefect of Police. Your grandfather is known to him, I understand."

Mathieu squirmed at the mention of his grandfather.

"You appear to have been involved in some rash, inappropriate action which necessitated your speedy removal from the great port of Marseilles. Am I right?" Roux looked over the parapet of papers he held in his hand and reached for the Gauloise resting impatiently on the ash tray.

What? Mathieu stopped breathing for a moment as the implication set fast. Was that how the story read? Had the official version of the ambush at Joliette been translated into a fiction of rash and inappropriate police action? That was ridiculous. He looked at Bernard Roux and realized that his question was serious; the man genuinely had no idea about Mathieu's real background other than his grandfather knew the prefect of police. He had been told a lie, which by default meant that he was not one of "Them."

"Is that what is says, Sir," was Mathieu's only response, spoken quietly with a darkening voice, not so much a question as a comment.

Roux looked at him again and breathed deeply. He had made his decision. "Well, I don't like having any member of my team chosen for me. Not even by the prefect of police. I don't care who your grandfather is or what happened in Marseilles. I choose my own team. Me. When the Tigers were created as a rapid response unit, he gave me a free hand to pick the best available in Paris. That being so, I only agreed to take you on a temporary basis because of your record, not your grandfather's, however important he might be."

Mathieu set his jaw to absorb his impending dismissal and feigned disinterest. "Sir."

"And so far you have interrupted my evening, disobeyed my instructions, physically thrown me into a taxi, pushed me into political quicksand—because I'm now the senior man in the Calmette murder inquiry—made your own decisions inside the *Figaro* office without any reference to me or anyone else, and acted as if you knew what you were doing. That is so?"

Mathieu looked at him, unsure. If Roux didn't want him, so what? He was who he was, experienced but bruised. He hadn't asked for the transfer. It had been imposed "for his own good."

"I had thought that a six month trial period would be sufficient. In all fairness, I gave you that space to prove your worth. It would just be a waste of time." Roux shook his head and opened a packet of Gauloises. "And I hate time wasting." He handed over a piece of paper. "Sign that."

Before Mathieu had time to read or reply he added, "I'm appointing you to my team immediately. *I'm* appointing you. Not anyone else. You are my choice, Sous-lieutenant. Mine. Never forget that."

Mathieu opened his mouth but no words formed. He literally didn't know whether to be pleased or dismayed. Roux took the momentary silence as assent and sealed his approval with a bold drag on his Gauloises.

"Unfortunately for us, your first case is Calmette's murder and Henriette Caillaux's trial. I say "us" because the file has landed on my desk, and although we know she murdered him in cold blood, everyone involved with her on that day has to be interviewed and their stories checked. That will be your job." He took Mathieu into the main office and made public his decision.

"Gentlemen, I have brought Sous-lieutenant Bertrand into our fold on a permanent basis. My decision. I want you to know that." He slapped

Mathieu on the back as if the gesture went in tandem with his apostolic blessing, and retired to his office, digging deep in his pockets for his next Gauloises.

Captain Girard smiled and nodded his approval as if to say it would have been his decision too. He crossed to Mathieu and offered his hand. "Welcome aboard, Sous-lieutenant, but now I have a problem. Who does the filing?" Lieutenant Paul Dubois remained at his desk but threw a cursory wave in Mathieu's direction. Guy Simon stared at the form in front of him, unmoved.

Raoul's Story

WE WHO LOVE FRANCE

I am a Frenchman who dreams of France. My heart pounds with its gallantry. Images of the noble dead spin 'round again from distant history. A tricolor, draped loosely over bruised and bloodied bodies, shines bright in its blue, white and red glory, though time has faded detail. There is a magnificence of spirit in the past. La Gloire. The ancient truths that rooted France to honor. God, the Church, the King, and the purity of an unadulterated nation. We have to restore these still.

I knew the tide of history must ebb and flow, and that the flow was with me like a mystic force. But it had to be encouraged, championed, empowered to help the people understand the error of those malignant socialist intellectuals. I can feel the power still. It is an energy of purpose. Have you ridden such a tide? Perhaps not. I have, my friend. I am a thoughtful man, well-read, educated. What would you expect of a boy who was, from his earliest years, deemed clever? I saw what they intended, those left-wing bastards who tore religion from the State as if they were the new high-priests of a pagan rite. Without the order and certainty of our Kings, the guidance of our national faith, a frank rejection of the impurities of Jewish and agnostic influences, what will France become? This had to be stopped. This malignancy. Rooted out. This was the true priority. All else, self-indulgence.

Do you recall the Dreyfus affair? What nonsense. A Jewish army officer sold secrets to the Germans and was rightly disgraced and imprisoned. The socialists claimed that he was framed, and several trials were held over a number of years. They wanted to destroy the good name of French Justice. They intended to undermine the army. Of course Dreyfus was guilty, but with the backing of other nameless wealthy Jews and that disgusting rag *L'Aurore*, a stinking nobody was acquitted and the army made to look racist. One of them was Emile Zola, the author; the other was Jean-Jaurès, the journalist and politician. More about him later, I promise you.

We who love France, care. We know that France cannot survive with any dignity if these vermin are allowed to take control. Murderers. Cold blooded murderers. That Caillaux woman was typical of their lawless impertinence and poor Calmette, the helpless victim. I belong to the Action française Oh come on, you've heard of Action française? They are the true spirit of France, like me.

I was badly injured at Gaston Calmette's funeral. That was back in March '14. Never forgot it. Can still feel the bitter wind and rain that battered down on thousands and thousands of us, mourners and demonstrators, outside St. Francis's church in the Rue Ampere. The streets of Paris had begun to fill from an early hour, despite the uncharitable weather. Newsboys sold specially printed editions of up-to-date revelations about the Caillauxs with such speed that they set up a relay to feed the frenzy for more scandalous information. Every latest edition was followed by another, until by noon, the rolling presses printed the final morning edition. Seats inside St. Francis's had been reserved for the Good and the Great only. We were proud to be outside, soaked to the skin, like Gauls of old, sworn to protect our heritage. Like you, my friend, I'm sure that you, too, are a soldier at heart.

The procession from the church to the cemetery outside the old fortifications at the end of Avenue Clichy was a testament to the bleeding heart of loyalty. So many wreaths and crosses. Carriages heaved with unrestrained emotion. The actress Sarah Bernhardt sent a personal message of condolence to the chief mourner, Calmette's brother, a military doctor. Action française and those of like sympathy, filed in behind the family on a prearranged signal. Two, three, perhaps even four thousand of us. Paris would not forget the murder of a loyal son of France. We were aware that there was a substantial police presence, glaring in silent provocation. They wanted it. They were prepared for it. A riot. And it would be our fault, of course.

The ceremony of committal was as brief as dignity could permit. So wet; so windy. It was a blessing for us all that the Monseigneur, his storm-stained beretta literally dripping from his face into pools in the sodden grave, shortened the prayers, closed his missal, and headed back to the warmth of St. Francis. There were no speeches. No diatribes against the Caillaux murderer. There was no need. The funeral party, including the prime minister, may well have been forewarned, for they fled the scene with undue haste. Not a soul lingered. Within what seemed like seconds, it was the police against us. But it was not as we expected. The bastards were ready. Behind the old fortifications, hidden in corners of the partly dismantled city walls, armed reserves had been amassed in secret. We could not see the mounted Republican Guards, infantry of the line, or the municipal troops carefully placed in the ruins. Napoleon would have been proud of such tactics.

We stood in no particular order until, at a prearranged signal, the street merged into one dense column marching towards the gates of the city. We broke into a run, followed by the gendarmerie, laughing to ourselves that they were already too late to stop us. Such innocents. A phalanx of police, swords drawn, broke from hiding and blocked the way. A chant of "Caillaux assassin" thundered in their faces and we charged into the mayhem with black loaded sticks. The collision was of Donnybrook proportions. The free-for-all threatened to degenerate into full-scale riot. A shot was fired into the crowd by an officer in plainclothes who had become isolated from his colleagues, and the mob swarmed around him. One stout blow opened his skull. The mounted troops and police reinforcements charged to his assistance from the protection of the walls, forcing us into prearranged channels. Like most around me, I had no wish for martyrdom, but chance intervened. A Republican Guard must have caught me from behind and banged my head with his sword-butt. I remember falling on the slippery stone and then no more.

Well, I can tell you the truth. You will not betray me. To be honest, there was no Republican Guard, but, pressed from behind I did slip and bang my head unceremoniously on the lethal cobbles.

"Help him up. Keep him moving." I heard the words, but was lost in my own confusion.

"Can he walk? He's wounded. Bleeding hard." Hands grabbed my arms and lifted me from the treacherous cobbles.

"My God, I've been wounded," Panic and joy. Was I a hero or near death? Or both?

"Go left. Quickly."

I let myself be led down a passage away from the murderous clamor. Friendly voices expressed genuine concern, but it was not until I caught sight of my blood-smattered face in a café mirror that I appreciated the extent of my injury. An ugly tear split my forehead above the hairline. All being well, I would carry this mark of honor proudly for the rest of my life.

"Sit there for a while." Someone pushed a glass of red wine into my shaking hand. A cold cloth compressed the cut.

"How do you feel?"

How did I feel? Happier than I had ever felt. More complete than when the Bishop's smack confirmed my right of passage into the Catholic Church. More meaningful than any membership card or secret handshake. Henceforth I would wear proof of my loyalty to Action française before me.

"I'm fine, my friend, fine. It's just a scratch. Nothing compared to the wounds of poor Calmette, eh? Let us salute the memory of our dear colleague and vow to rid France of the cancer of socialism and left-wing appeasement."

"Bravo, Raoul, Bravo"

Looking around at the faces of those who had dragged me to safety I knew that I had found my purpose.

But how did they know my name?

4

JULY 1914 – CONFIDENTIAL

"Sous-lieutenant Bertrand," the commander bellowed. "Bertrand. Move yourself."

Roux had returned from a long morning meeting at the Ile de la Cite with the Prefect of Paris Police. Mathieu heard his shout above the routine office clamor but it lacked annoyance so he ambled towards the blue fleur-de-lisle tiled corridor, his mind clear and his conscience clearer.

"Poor bugger, left alone in the office in your first few days here and you get saddled with the Caillaux nightmare for the next four months." Guy Simon seemed genuine in his sympathy but there was a resentful irony in his statement. Both men were sous-lieutenants, but Mathieu Bertrand's previous service in Marseilles gave him seniority. Guy's military experience and time spent with the Tigers earned him the right to act as if he outranked Mathieu. It stood to reason. Mathieu was last man appointed to the group, and had the least experience of the Parisian underworld. Guy told him this to his face but Mathieu did not respond. His colleague was right on one point. If anything went wrong, the mess would end up in his lap. That was certain.

Guy was small in stature, with a thick neck and exaggerated torso. His shirt bulged across his chest yet there was hardly a trace of fat on his body. His bright eyes and stub of a nose left a bull-like impression on those he confronted—and confrontation was his most natural trait. Mathieu was aware that he had met small men before who seemed incapable of projecting anything other than aggression to compensate for their lack of height. Life for Guy was a constant competition which he intended to win.

The shrill telephone bell on Captain Girard's desk intervened.

"Yes?" He listened with studied attention, his face reflecting no emotion. "Very well. Don't let anyone touch the body." Girard rose smartly, donned his jacket, adjusted his bow-tie, took a pistol from his drawer, and headed for the door. "Right, gentlemen, another mangled body bobbing in the canal. Let's see what state this one's in." Mathieu hesitated, caught between the boring certainty of yet another review of trial evidence or charging through the city streets in the Panhard to a crime scene which suggested that a serial killer was on the loose. Third floating cadaver this year. Every one smashed beyond recognition.

"Not you, *mon ami*." Guy's eyes glowed behind a sardonic smile. "The commander wants to speak to you. Remember?"

"Shut the door behind you, Bertrand." Commander Roux drew heavily on his Gauloises, indicating with a nod of his greying head that Mathieu should sit down. He paused before rising to the window, and stared out at the Paris landscape without seeing a single feature of his beloved city. A second deep inhalation of the rancid-smelling tobacco followed in almost desperate haste, as if time was pressing him close to a perilous precipice. His suit, unusually rumpled, reflected his spirit; his well-groomed moustache, normally cut with elegant precision looked unkempt. He sighed, glanced at the floor and then at Mathieu. Troubled. Deeply troubled.

"Sir?"

He paused again before stubbing out his cigarette. "We're going to war with Germany."

Mathieu leaned back in his chair and looked the commander in the eye. In the space of his five brief months in Paris his appreciation of Bernard Roux had become almost familial. He knew the man did not waste words, swallow shallow rumor, or repeat half-baked gossip. Yet he could not stop himself saying, "With respect, Sir, we've been going to war with Germany every summer since I can remember."

A brooding silence spread an aura of impending trouble. Bernard Roux, fifty-seven and counting, father and grandfather, looked at Mathieu, stubbed out the cigarette, and craved a glass of Cognac to steady himself.

"Yes, I know. And every time war has been forecast I've said it was nonsense. In 1911 when Joe Caillaux was prime minister, every newspaper heralded the coming war. Never happened. Caillaux sought conciliation rather than war. No matter what the English said in London or the Russians in St. Petersburg, he had the courage to stand against the warmongers. Now we have a president hell bent on war." He went to the door, opened it, glanced down the corridor, and locked them inside his office. Unprecedented.

Mathieu tried to take stock of the situation, but it did not make sense. His inner voice knew that it must be true. The commander licked his dried lips, unaware that his reaction presaged his despair.

"I have to unburden myself, Mathieu, and since I value your judgment, you have to share this with me. No one must know. No one. Not even along this corridor. Not your family. Not your friends. No one."

"Of course," he replied, and a second later his brain registered another phenomenon. Bernard Roux had just called him Mathieu. *Merde.* "How do you know, Sir? I don't question what you have just told me, but how can you be sure?"

"You understand, no one hears of this." It was a statement, not a question. "When I was at headquarters with the chief of police this morning, we were interrupted by the minister of war. I left the room of course, but Celestin handed me the text he had been given so that I could check the instructions we will be obliged to enforce. He has a habit of doing that. Sharing information with me. I thought, years ago, that it was a test of loyalty, but he confided recently that one of his fears was that, should he drop dead, no one would know the secrets he held. I share that fear, Mathieu." He paused briefly to allow reflection. "Anyway, these instructions are to be sent to the mayors in every city, town, and hamlet. They will be instructed to summon anyone who owns a horse or a car, and secretly forewarn them that they must stand by to have it requisitioned. I don't mean one horse or one car. Every single one of them."

"Oh," was all that reached Mathieu's lips, though his mind was racing through a range of possibilities.

"They are preparing a General Mobilization. Call-up papers have been prepared. Standing regiments are on alert. The Army have planned exercises close to the German border and, most disturbingly, the president, the prime minister, and the minister of war will leave immediately for a state visit to the Czar at St. Petersburg. They are taking the newly commissioned battleship *France* through the Baltic and are scheduled to arrive in Russia on 20th July."

"They'll miss the trial." Mathieu's comment bordered on sarcasm.

"They plan to miss the trial. Furthermore, the official line from the Élysée Palace is that it is courtesy visit of no particular importance."

"So why?"

"Now you're missing the point." The commander lit another Gauloises. "Everyone's missing the point. While the French nation is focused on the most sensational murder trial of the twentieth century, their president and prime minister will be focused on ensuring that the Russians are ready for the war they intend to launch against the kaiser. You know that Poincaré and his die-hards live only to avenge themselves against the German victory forty-odd years ago. For stealing Alsace and Lorraine. I promise you, as soon as the czar's resolve has been stiffened and those agitators are back on French soil, it will be war. President Poincaré and those who support him have a plan. A secret plan. Believe me, there have been meetings between the minister and Army high command in England and Belgium. This is not an exercise. But he will not move until our Russian allies commit themselves to his plan. The English are important, too. I know about their secret agreement. Already our entire fleet has moved into the Mediterranean to shut it down completely. The English have guaranteed to protect our coast along the channel. What comes next is war."

Silence filled the space between them with an awkward hesitancy. Roux turned back to the window and Mathieu bowed his head, troubled and uncertain. He crossed to the window beside the commander and looked out over the glistening rooftops of Paris. A light smattering of rain caused a strange bluish hue on the slate canopies from the semblance of sunshine which struggled into the frame. There was a promise of better weather to come, but no guarantee. Every word the commander said would have been nonsense had it come from a lesser man.

"I'm flattered, Sir. I am. But won't the others be affronted if I'm the only one in whom you confide?"

"Of course they will, if they ever find out. But they won't because you know when to hold your tongue. You're diligent, confident, and you understand how to deal with difficult situations. I don't know what life was like for you growing up in Marseilles, but living in a household consumed by politics has taught you lessons money couldn't buy. You instinctively dealt with the traumatized Caillaux woman without overreacting. You solved the problem by removing her from the scene without the attendant hysteria others would have caused. Pascal Girard is tired. I know that. He understands the Paris in which he grew up, but his mind rarely strays beyond the city boundary. The only future he can talk about is retirement. Dubois is a good detective, too, but he has no concept of flexibility. Guy Simon would want to fight with anyone and crack a few heads in the passing."

There was more to be said, but Roux was still weighing his options. "Mathieu," he sighed in a breath so heavily laden with sour nicotine that it could have satisfied a battalion of smokers, "my judgment tells me to trust you, and I know for a fact that you are not leaking information to other interested parties."

Ah, so there was a leak in the department's security. "How do…?"

"Don't ask."

Guy Simon broke the spell. He almost broke his nose too when he attempted to walk through the locked door. The team was back. To their disappointment, local police had dealt with the incident in the canal and they didn't want the Tigers around to steal the headlines.

"Give us a moment." Roux tried to be cheerful.

Guy almost insisted. "Six-thirty, chief. Café Clichy." It was as though the whole world should understand that the evening drink claimed precedence.

The commander softened his approach. "Be with you shortly. You go ahead." As the others trundled past the closed door, Roux turned, searched for the most appropriate phrase, and stared so hard that Mathieu thought someone was standing behind him. He picked up a file from his desk and reread the first page.

"Mathieu, I should have checked. You're single aren't you?"

"Yes. Is that important?"

"Yes and no. But it makes the job easier when you have to stick with a case day and night for months at a time. That poisons relationships. Married ones."

He checked again. "Still living in Rue Pasteur?"

"In a boarding house. Clean, comfortable, and all I can afford."

"Fine." He placed the file back on the desk and got to the point.

"Your grandfather?"

"My grandfather? Surely you know all about him already. My grandfather considers me to be a political embarrassment." Mathieu found it difficult to capture his sense of injustice. "He more or less exiled me from Marseilles because I told him the truth about a set-up which cost the lives of seven policemen."

"Eight."

"Eight?"

"Dennis Benett died three days after you left Marseilles. His death certificate claims it was from blood poisoning."

"Benett with the shattered legs? Dennis Benett? I didn't know his christian name. I didn't know any of their…" Mathieu left his words to linger as his world spun slower and backwards to a nightmare of uncertainty. He didn't know the Christian names of the men who were slain by his side on the scorched canal basin that day. They died in a pitiless massacre in which he too ought to have perished. And he didn't know their Christian names. He knew nothing about them at all. Dennis Benett. Was he married? Did he have children? What of the others?

Roux saw the pain on Mathieu's face and continued his short lecture in a very matter-of-fact way. "You know that the Republican Party used the massacre to gain votes at the election, and as you know, they are fiercely loyal to President Poincaré."

Mathieu buried his head in his hands and confessed his confusion. "I distrust them all; and I don't understand who THEY are? Where THEY are? Politics is a cover for a bigger bag of thieves than the mafia."

Roux laughed and added his own philosophy. "Politicians are like a gaggle of blind geese, squawking around, all talking at the same time, unaware that their masters have already decided which to eat at Christmas and which to keep 'til Easter."

Mathieu had never heard a more succinct analysis.

The commander inhaled automatically. "What about here in Paris? Did you have an association with either side?"

"Of course not. I hate politicians. The power-brokers amongst them believe they have a monopoly on patriotism and expect everyone else to be likeminded."

"Especially Action française. Your grandfather for one."

"My grandfather is a member of Action française?" Mathieu felt his lungs constrict until the pain forced breath back into his body,

"I checked his standing with a contact in the Bureau's intelligence department. He was being investigated by a special unit headed by the same Captain David Rougerie who was shot dead in the ambush at La Joliette. We won't ever be able to prove it, but that's probably why the ambush took place."

"But I…" Mathieu let the sentence hang while he absorbed the implication. His grandfather had been prepared to sacrifice everything, Mathieu included, to protect his political career. *Bâtard*.

Roux read his consternation. "We don't think he knew you had been transferred to Rougerie's unit until after the event."

"We?"

"Hennion, and a few other interested parties. And you are right about power-brokers. They have allies everywhere, protected by even more powerful friends at every level of decision-making and influence. These are dangerous and ruthless criminals who will never be held accountable for their crimes." He glanced at his pocket watch and stood up. "Look at the time. We'd better join the others at the Café Clichy. We can talk en route."

Outside the trees swayed in a gentle wind and the heat of the day gave way to the slightly cooler warmth of early evening. It felt good to cut free from the stifling office, but Mathieu was still troubled.

"Why are you telling me this?"

"Because you know how the system works and your judgment is sharp." The commander stopped to light yet another Gauloises and caught Mathieu's arm, instinctively drawing him slightly closer lest they be overheard.

"But listen to me. We need to be careful. Over the next few days and possibly weeks, we, you and I, will be closely involved with some of these so-called power-brokers because of the political sensitivities of the bloody Caillaux case. You have to keep what you learn close to your heart. Now is not the time to draw attention to our fears. It's important that when we do go to war, our team continue to tackle all the vermin which will crawl from the woodwork to feed off rich pickings. In times like this you either lead or follow, and when it comes to police work, I want us to stay close to the real decision-makers. We are not without friends. Not at all. But we have to be very, very careful."

Riddles again, Mathieu thought. Who were our "friends," who were the real decision-makers?

"Tomorrow, I want you to go over all of the evidence for Henriette Caillaux's trial. I know you're prepared. I know that you have checked and rechecked everything, but we can't afford a mistake, and her bloody lawyers will be ready to pounce if we have a cedilla out of place."

They headed to Café Clichy with little interest in further casual conversation. Mathieu's powers of concentration had been shattered by the commander's news. Suspicion quickly found voice in the crowded café.

"What's going on then?" Guy prodded quietly, sipping his vin rouge through thin, taut lips. "Behind closed doors, the two of you. What's the story?"

"The commander is paranoid about the trial. He's under pressure from all angles to keep the scandal localized. Minimize the fallout. Make sure that we can't be blamed if anything goes wrong."

"Hardly a reason to lock this office door," Guy huffed dismissively. "Something's wrong."

He turned away, unconvinced. It would have been so easy to tell him in confidence, tell them all, but a shrug of the shoulders was all he could offer.

Mathieu shrank back into himself, feigning interest in the conversation, and caught his own image in the great wall mirrors for which the café was famous. His suit looked threadbare, faded in patches and barely acceptable for the workplace. He definitely needed a haircut. As a youngster he had hated the curls which insisted on making him look like a choirboy, but these had matured into more acceptable black waves, thick and unruly. He liked the fact that his eyes still sparkled and his moustache, which had taken so long to grow into place, made him appear older than his twenty-three years. But living in Paris came at a cost and his skin was definitely paler than it had been in the Mediterranean clime. At almost six foot in height he stood literally head and shoulders above the other Tigers, and, immodest though it was to admit, his physical appearance was still as daunting as it had been during his army service with the artillery reserve. But those clothes…

"Snap out of it, Bertrand. It's your turn to buy." Pascal Girard was never one to stand on ceremony. Heavy shouldered, the former boxer looked forward to retirement. Life was not good. He had married late and found relationships difficult. He bore a scar which cut across his left temple and disappeared into a receding hairline. Bullet or sword? No one knew for certain. He had paid his dues to France and the least the young whipper-snapper could do was buy drink. What else kept him sane?

"Of course." Mathieu beckoned towards the waitress hovering close to their stall. She smiled at him, pleased to be asked. Mathieu noticed she had a beautiful face, like Renoir's painting of the girl in the low-necked green dress. Her cheeks were pink under heavy eyes that spoke of hard work and struggle. Yet they flashed in defiance. Her auburn hair had been combed-through carelessly by her own hand while watching her reflection in the mirrored wall. But her smile. He always remembered the first time he saw that smile. They called her Agnès.

"Again, Monsieur?"

* * *

"Again, Monsieur?"

This time the question was laden with resignation. Georges Formentin could hardly believe he was expected to repeat his story again. As salesclerk for the elite weapons and gun shop Gastinne-Renette, poor Formentin had suffered dozens of enquires, interruptions and useless questions from all sorts over the last four months. His normal routine as guardian of the historic dueling pistols, ancient blunderbusses, high-powered hunting rifles, and immensely expensive pearl-studded made-to-order handguns, had been disturbed on a daily basis since Henriette Caillaux swanned into Gastinne-Renette's inner sanctum and announced herself as if she was the reincarnation of Marie-Antoinette. Perhaps she was. He told Mathieu this when first interviewed.

By the third interview, Formentin thought her a she-devil; a cursed interloper who had abused his hospitality and ruined the company name. Gastinne-Renette, 1812, armorer to the Emperor Napoleon. Was there a prouder heritage in France? Yet Henriette Caillaux was about to drag the proud emblem of dueling excellence into the courts in a miserable, clear-cut charge of premeditated murder. He ushered Mathieu into his side office and shut the door lest any customer overheard his disclosure.

"It was mid-afternoon. She breezed through the door and marched up to my counter without so much as a by-your-leave, and said, 'I am Madame Caillaux and I want to see a revolver,' claiming that she needed a small weapon to carry on her person. She and Monsieur Caillaux were apparently due to leave for a trip to his constituency in the country, and she felt that in the current climate of antagonism towards government ministers, she should be armed. Of course we all knew that Joseph Caillaux held an account with us, so his wife had open access to our stock."

"She presumed that you would know who she was?"

"Monsieur, she is a Caillaux." His look betrayed contempt. "To continue, I offered her a thirty-two caliber Smith and Wesson, but she struggled to operate it confidently. On her insistence she was taken downstairs to our basement firing range and I instructed Monsieur Dervillier to help her. The gun was simply too awkward for her to fire safely. She bruised her finger and whimpered pathetically. We brought her the .32 Browning automatic, and she immediately liked its flexibility. Madame Caillaux held it in her hand, thought it more comfortable, and indicated that she wished to purchase it."

"She then asked you to load it for her, did she not?"

"Yes."

"And you obliged?"

"Sir, you are well aware that I did not. Company policy clearly states that no employee may load a customer's gun on the premises. I have repeated that every time your officers have asked."

"But you showed her how to load the gun."

"Yes," he sighed. How often must he repeat himself? "I demonstrated how to remove the clip from the bottom of the gun, fill it with six bullets, and snap it back into position. Even when loaded the gun could not be fired until the first cartridge was racked into the chamber."

"Just to recap, Monsieur, Henriette Caillaux consulted you in regard to a .32 Browning on the afternoon of 16 March, was personally tutored on the process of loading the gun, and subsequently purchased said gun."

"I've told you and your associates this four times. You really are wasting my time."

Mathieu's head snapped up from his notebook. "Associates? Other police officers have been here? Before me?"

"Surely you knew? From the Deuxième, they said. The general manager called to instruct me to assist them. They went down to the basement and fired several shots. Quite alarming it was."

Strange. Mathieu said nothing but thanked Formentin and reported back.

The commander shook his head in resignation. "They're checking us out. Want to make sure of every aspect we've covered for the trial."

"Who?"

"Ah ... If we knew that, we'd probably know more than was healthy."

Bernard Roux's apprehension spread throughout the prefecture and reached Mathieu at a low ebb. He was exhausted by the endless demands emanating from the prefect of police. He reviewed his notes, reorganized the dossiers of evidence, despite the fact that there was no mystery. Nothing needed to be proved, save how much political interference and judicial sleight of hand could be brought to bear on the jury. But a storm was brewing behind the apparent calm. It could blow everything off course. The commander's last words to Mathieu as they left Café Clichy on the night before the trial chilled the young man's stomach.

"It will not be a court drama, trust me. It will be a pantomime; a pantomime which will concentrate attention on the scandal, while in the corridors of power, secret steps are already underway to propel us all to hell. The more unpopular the right wing press can make the Caillauxs, the easier it becomes to paint him as a German-loving traitor who wants to stop war. You do understand, Mathieu? This trial will be about sensation and showmanship, and behind that façade, it will be about politics. There will be no winner. It's not about justice. It's a smokescreen to keep the people from listening to the anti-war brigade."

Mathieu lowered his voice and asked in vain, "And we can do nothing?"

"It's already too late."

THE CHOSEN ONE

I drank hard from the chalice of commitment and dried my lips to leave no stain. At last I understood what it was to be chosen. I was a modern-day Templar about to set off on crusade. In the cool of the vaulted wooden ceilings, I found refuge from the trials of the day, safe in the unassuming home of the Jesuit Order in Paris, my beloved Saint Pierre de Montmartre.

Here, they say, Saint Ignatius Loyola took his sacred vows that led to the founding of the virile Society of Jesus—the Pope's foot soldiers. No sign now of the ruinous disgrace of the Revolution which desecrated and destroyed the old church and built a telegraph tower in the midst of its apse. Revolutions are but passing fancies and my spiritual home was rebuilt with massive Roman columns and, eventually, stained-glass windows. Frankly, I disapprove of the new limestone Basilica of Sacré Coeur which has been constructed beside my ancient church, so that it now dominated Paris, enveloping Saint Pierre as a swan would its cygnet. This is my secret place. In my heart, still.

Have you a secret place in which you can shelter, my friend?

I sat in the still of its ecstasy, head back against the wooden pew, a living statue, breathing deeply to smell the lingering incense from an earlier celebration. All the perfumes of Arabia may not have solved Lady Macbeth's proverbial problem, but she had not experienced the heady draught of incense which infused my mind and body like an opiate.

"May I be of assistance, my son?" A hand on my shoulder.

Startled, I recoiled from the touch.

"What the…?" I almost shouted at the black shape before me, but the priest made no move. Why would he? This was his parish. It was his church. Or so he assumed.

"Can I help? Do you wish to go to confession? You have been immobile for a good half hour, which is long enough for any prayer."

Confused in that moment, I shook my head. The priest nodded gently. "I'm over in the far confessional if you have a change of heart."

"Thank you, father."

With a swish of his black soutane, he disappeared into the privacy of other people's sins, though only a few elderly souls had need of his earthly judgment. I waited in the shadow of the great columns, seeking reassurance. This time I startled my prey when he stepped out from his seat of forgiveness.

"Father, may I have a word?"

We slowly walked down the central aisle to the great door which commanded a spectacular view across the Seine to the Eiffel Tower. Some modernists apparently admire the latticed monument to French engineering but I thought it soulless, like the late author Guy de Maupassant who lunched there every day because it was the only place in Paris from which Eiffel's monstrosity could not be seen. We, both priest and Patriot-Templar, absorbed the view of a wonderful but immoral city which had to be brought to its senses. Our eyes could only see sin.

"Father, tell me, would you kill for God?"

The priest looked at me in astonishment. Was this a theological hypothesis or a genuine question?

"No man has the right to take the life of another," he paused, "unless…"

"Unless?"

"Well there are circumstances of war, of self-defense, of the protection of the innocents…"

"Would you kill for God?"

"I hope never to be in such situation."

"Would you?" I stamped an insistence on the question by raising my voice and facing my would-be mentor. I changed tack. "Would you kill for France?"

"What is this talk of killing? We are not in confessional. Take care what you tell me."

"I'm not telling. I'm asking. Would you kill for France? Catholic France?"

Pity and confusion wrung a frown from Monseigneur Richard. He had to consider his answer. My question clearly troubled him.

I looked into the priest's face for some sign of confirmation. Perhaps the concept was too contentious for the clerical mind. A true Jesuit would have approved any action to protect the church in France. And it was not simply about religious belief. I was talking about the body politic. About the future of France. I had recently heard a discussion at Action française where a senior surgeon from the Hospital Hotel-Dieu had likened our task of liberating France from cretinous socialism to his own professional dilemma. Did the patient require urgent intrusive surgery to save his life, or should he take a conservative line, make some minor cut, and keep his fingers crossed that all would subsequently be well? Intrusive surgery. Those words resonated within me. I heard Gregorian chant, sensed hot incense, weighed the power of clear resolve against constant dithering, and knew that I was being called to action. This was war. It was. Inner voices dispelled older doubts. I'd found my vocation. It was to be intrusive surgery on the body politic.

And what of Madame Caillaux? She had not hesitated to kill. Her trial was imminent. I could hardly control my anticipation of the witch's conviction. Indeed, why were the authorities prepared to waste money? Thousands of francs on an unnecessary process. Feed her to the guillotine. Have you ever heard of a clearer act of premeditated murder? Justice was demanded. Had she been some lady of the night from the Pigalle or an impoverished immigrant starving in the eighteenth arrondissement, she would have been dealt with summarily.

But Henriette Caillaux? Five-star treatment. Best of everything. Ate with her husband in the commandant's own office. Haute cuisine brought from the most exclusive restaurants. Visitors every day. Two nuns were allocated to look after her, and her personal maid stayed by her side. The ordinary prisoners slept on stone floors and survived on thin oatmeal broth. How I wished that Saint Lazard had remained a leper colony. That would have been a fitting home for Madame Henriette Caillaux. Her jaundiced body parts disintegrating before her eyes. In the Music Halls, songs were concocted to ridicule the assassin, but such was the power of the Caillaux name, that the police had intervened to stop the fun. Typical of a feckless France. The case against her was uncomplicated. She was charged with voluntary and premeditated homicide. Should not be a long affair.

What do you think? Over in a day? Two at the most?

Monday 20 July, 1914 – The Trial

B ernard Roux's premonition proved an almighty understatement. From start to finish the trial of Henriette Caillaux was pure farce. Justice and law in the Third Republic earned its reputation as an irredeemably inconsistent oxymoron.

Mathieu met the commander at the Café de Deux Ponts between the Pont Saint-Michel and the Quai des Grands Augustins. As was his way, he arrived ten minutes early and chose to draw breath beside the meandering Seine. He hung over the side wall as if pondering a quick dip in the water, but the river was almost as low as his spirits. The heatwave would soon bring a shortage of water and a significant rise in the crime rate. *It won't be the only crisis this summer*, he thought to himself.

Mathieu rested his forehead on the warm grey stone and breathed deeply again. The immediacy of the trial ought to have driven Roux's secret from his mind, but they both found time each day to trace events elsewhere as if, by careful watch, they would find fault with the undercurrents steering Europe to war. But the secret timetable kept pace with the president's sacred plan.

"Croissant and coffee, or just coffee?" Bernard Roux's voice boomed above the traffic. There he was, dressed immaculately in his black suit, tailored waistcoat, and shoes polished to within a fraction of reflection. His top hat rested on the red-checkered tablecloth, upturned, doubtless to accommodate his black gloves. You might have mistaken him for an Advocate.

"Coffee's fine, thanks. My stomach couldn't face food at the moment."

"Please yourself." He beckoned the waiter and ordered croissant, cheese and thinly sliced ham, and two coffees. Bravado or what?

"It's going to be hot over there. Outside and in."

The Palais de Justice stood firm across the Seine, its magnificent gilded gates enclosing the three-sided courtyard which created boundaries that French law had not fully defined.

"It'll be fun and games, be assured, and the whole damned lot of them will use the occasion to promote themselves. Henriette Caillaux may be the accused, but it's French society which is in the dock."

Mathieu sighed. The commander had repeated the same warning on a daily basis for the better part of a month.

Roux pulled out that morning's edition of the sports newspaper, *L'Auto*. It had sponsored the Tour de France, a cycle race around the coasts and borders of the country, and its coverage was unsurpassed. Like the weather, the 1914 Tour had begun to heat up. The Belgian champion, Philippe Thys, was considered favorite for a second win in a row. His main rival was his popular Parisian teammate, Henri Pelissier. The contest that day, a 325 kilometer race from Geneva in Switzerland to Belfort near the German border, included some tricky mountain twists. The French champion certainly thought he had a chance to win the stage. *L'Auto* concurred. But anything could go wrong, and frequently did. During the third stage from Cherbourg to Brest, the entire peloton took the wrong turn. Embarrassment bordered on national humiliation. After they had ridden for 30 kilometers in the wrong direction, the riders reached the first check point one hour late. The race had to be restarted. No one was impressed by the stupidity of the marshals, least of all the competitors.

Mathieu studied the detailed route map on the front page and solemnly agreed. "This'll suit Pelissier. Today could be his big breakthrough." He traced his fingers along the circuit as if he could feel the undulating course. Mathieu was ever hopeful; that was in his nature. A serious French contender and a close race was good for the nation's self-belief, and the paper's circulation. Roux shook his head. Was this boy the supreme optimist, or not?

"Believe me, the Belgian will lead the rest of the pack around these streets on the final day. No question. A Cognac against two beers says I'm right."

"Done."

Commander Roux brushed flakes of heavenly croissant from his waistcoat. Whatever the consequences, a warm croissant was worth the risk of tell-tale crumbs. No man would ever be damned because he ate a croissant. It was, for Bernard Roux, one of life's maxims. But his indulgence had drawn his attention away from the crowds who headed across the St. Michel bridge.

"Notice something?" His attention had been drawn back onto the street. It was as if word had passed from lip to lip that a great spectacle was about to begin. Like the populous of Rome, excited by the prospect of a good day's killing at the Colosseum, the people exuded a strong sense of anticipation. Would Henriette be thrown to the lions or gladiators hack

41

each other's reputation to shreds? Might the charioteers ride to the rescue, or the Emperor conclude events with a determined thumbs-down? One thing was certain. They smelled blood.

Both sides of the bridge had sprouted vendors as if they were early summer mushrooms, selling newspapers, journals, fruit and vegetables. Was that man buying a rosette? Why would anyone want to purchase flowers at this time of day? The detritus of cloth-capped society mixed freely with the top hats, bowlers and boaters. There were, too, huge wide rimmed concoctions of fashionable lace, feathers, plumes and ribbon. The pavements strained. Charabancs, some motorized, some still horse-drawn, vied with each other for space to disgorge their occupants. Across the boulevard the mighty Notre Dame Cathedral stood ignored. Even the legendary Quasimodo would have failed to turn these excited heads towards God.

A strict regiment of municipal police officers guarded the courtyard gates. All passes were carefully scrutinized, though Bernard Roux and Mathieu Bertrand had no need to provide documentation. The commander acknowledged a salute and lead Mathieu smartly across to a side-door. The Palais de Justice had been bedecked with tricolors and red, white and blue flower arrangements, spruced up for the benefit of high society. It was a truly theatrical backdrop to international self-flagellation.

Ahead a melee of journalists exchanged rumor and gossip, keen to find a fresh angle with which to keep their readers spellbound. Headlines bounced around the world, some indignant at the frivolous French, some basking in their own moral high ground. Yet another Parisian scandal. Marvelous. Typical of the French. Completely without morals. The Americans thought themselves above such vulgar distraction and their obvious disapproval was tinged with disdain for the Caillaux family. This was the journalistic métier of the moment. Theirs was the pen that would report, analyze, synthesize, and deliver the final verdict. But it was a charade which held the illusion of importance. In the sum of what transpired it was but one of several smokescreens behind which real evil prepared to strike. Justice descended to the depth of La Grande Theatre. *Take your places, please. Stalls to the right, Sir. Private box, upstairs, Madam. The show is about to begin.*

The conduct of the court added to the spectacle. Procedures were so lax that authority disintegrated into a free-for-all. Defendant, witnesses, lawyers, and the presiding judge took advantage of the occasion to color events in their decidedly jaundiced views. At times Mathieu could not work out whether the speaker was addressing the all-male jury, political allies, vested interests, or the greater world beyond. He gave his testimony with a confidence he had not expected to display, responding to both sets of lawyers with a clarity which brooked no objection. His job was to establish the facts. The circumstance of the arrest, the subsequent conduct of Madame Caillaux, and her reaction to the charges. He must have sorely disappointed the vultures from the press. They had already stripped the flesh from factual evidence and picked over the bones for four tedious months. No one had come to hear his evidence. This was a one woman show.

Directed by the best legal minds which a millionaire could buy, Madame Caillaux held her head high as she declared her actions to have been an uncontrolled crime of passion. Her every move was recorded. If she sniffed, some saw regret, while others wondered if it was mere scorn. Did you hear her voice? Was she close to a breakdown or play-acting? When she turned to face the jury, was she flirting or simply explaining her feelings? Not a single flicker of her eyebrows, subtle turn of her neck, clasp of her gloved hand, or purposeful pose went unnoticed. Each merited a comment. The home-based editors and journalists understood their appointed role. When she fainted, the gasps from the gallery echoed like a Greek chorus.

As she began to portray herself as a passionate heroine whose actions had been motivated by love for her husband, the tragic broken woman who could not be held accountable for the overwhelming emotions which dictated her reaction, it was clear that her defense lawyers were deconstructing and reframing the assassination into a crime of passion. The conservative press had screamed guilty before the trial began and scorned her every claim. She was not an emotionally distressed woman or a violently wronged female. Surely every sane person could see through her measured pretense? An expert was employed by *L'illustration* to analyze her dress in court. He concluded that it betrayed her emotionless personality which deserved no sympathy from the jury. In contrast, the daily newspaper *Le Matin* praised her modesty, her discreet sense of appropriate dress, her obvious distress at the mayhem she had apparently caused. She was indeed the epitome of a vulnerable lady. But then, *Le Matin* had long supported Joseph Caillaux.

As if to underline the distinct irrelevance of fact, the evidence taken in court from the two policemen was brief and to the point. Bernard Roux cut an impressive image of the law in action but his clarity was met with a yawn from the president of the court and a curt, "Yes, yes," from Henriette

Caillaux's lawyer. Mathieu was treated with equal disdain when he took the stand but even the press pack were disinterested. Calmette's murder inside his *Figaro* office had been reported in great detail by the newspaper itself. No one from her defense team sought to question what had taken place. Just as he was about to step down, one of her extensive legal team rose smartly to his feet and feigned a sudden interest in Mathieu's view of the events.

"How did Madam Caillaux appear to you when you first saw her?" A smirk crossed his tight-mouthed lips. Instinct warned Mathieu to think carefully.

"She was in shock, standing…" He got no further.

"Ah." A wry smile slithered across the lawyer's face. "Madam Caillaux was in *shock*." He accentuated the final word as if it proved some point. The legal inquisitor preened himself like a sly crow spying an easy morsel, but Mathieu anticipated his next move.

"Everyone in the room was in shock. It's what happens when an assailant fires a gun close to you. Madam Caillaux was no more and no less in shock than everyone else, with the probable exception of the man she had shot." Mathieu was not to be patronized by some lawyer seeking to put words in his mouth. "If a person fired a gun in this courtroom, I can assure you that everyone here would be in shock. It is neither remarkable nor unexpected. That is not what I think, it's what I know." He set his jaw and moved his head imperceptibly towards the crow as if to advise he should take flight. Silence. It took the president half a second to thank Mathieu and dismiss him from the witness stand.

"Good man," was all that Roux whispered as his junior officer rejoined him, but to Mathieu it felt like his boss had embraced him with approval.

The commander established his own routine for the duration of the trial. First, breakfast at the Café-Bar Saint Michel. Roux certainly loved his croissants, followed by a tasty Gauloises. His assistant stuck to coffee. They analyzed the progress of the Tour de France as if it was the highlight of the day. To Mathieu's delight, the Parisian favorite Pelissier had won the stage which ended in Belfort, but he could not best Philippe Thys overall. Even after the Belgian champion incurred a thirty-minute penalty when his cycle wheel broke and he was forced to buy a replacement on the last day, his lead proved unassailable. Years later Mathieu realized that the 1914 Tour had started on the 28th of June, the same day that Archduke Franz Ferdinand and his wife were assassinated in Sarajevo. By that time, historians had decreed that the murder of the heir to the Austrian Empire was the cause of a world war. He knew it was a lie. A lie so monstrous that it would be taught as fact for a century. No one wanted to know the awful truth. Perhaps they never would.

They ambled back from the Café-Bar reluctant to step back into the sweat-filled furnace of the court. Roux energized himself with a healthy Gauloises. That's how he described it.

"A moment, Commander." They turned to find one of the diplomatic advisers from Quai d'Orsay pressing his way through the gate. "The minister would like a word."

"Which minister?"

"General Messimy. He is in the left-hand room off the Gallerie de Presidence."

"Wait for me in the corridor, Bertrand." No familiarity was ever displayed in public. What did the minister of war want? Not good, whatever. Messimy was a soldier first and politician second, and he had served as war minister once before, just days before the crisis between France and Germany over Morocco in 1912. They said there would be a war, but Joseph Caillaux had smoothed the ruffled feathers and a strained peace was maintained. Messimy was known to have a low regard for the kaiser. What was he plotting? It was the perfect place to hold a secret meeting right in front of the world's press. Absorbed as they were with the gossip and tittle-tattle of a salacious trial, no one stopped to question why the minister of war and the most senior policemen in the city were engrossed in their own meeting. Mathieu paced up and down the corridor, aware that the trial had resumed. Five minutes dragged into an hour. Several minor officials from the war office and the diplomatic corps acknowledged him with a nod as they came and went from the meeting room.

Stern faced, Bernard Roux finally left his unscheduled audience, throwing Mathieu a look which said, *Say nothing.* The two policemen strode towards the courtroom but did not enter the inner sanctum of French justice.

"I need a seat," Roux said, meaning that he was desperate to taste a Gauloises so they veered off into the side garden.

"Apparently the president needs to have regular reports about the trial sent to him by diplomatic channels, and they want us to provide an objective view every day."

"Can't some civil service lackey from the war office do that?" Mathieu reflected Roux's annoyance. "We've our own job to do."

"I'm afraid you've just been volunteered." He pulled a long drag on his Gauloises and looked away.

"They seem to trust you implicitly. Your grandfather was mentioned in passing, and ironically they have assumed that you, too, can be trusted with matters of state."

"But…"

"Don't waste your time. It was me or you and I'm not trundling along there to hand in a report." He saw Mathieu's lip curl upwards. "It's one omnibus stop along the river, my friend. Break up your day."

And it did. It more than did.

Because he arrived at the Quai d'Orsay with information which had to be coded before being sent by diplomatic telegram and forwarded firstly to Russia, and then, as the week progressed, to the presidential party on the battleship *France* as it steamed down the Baltic, the secret brotherhood of trusted insiders assumed his loyalty. Mathieu's became a familiar face to diplomats and civil servants in the Quai d'Orsay where the all-knowing Benoit Durfort decided to adopt him as a friend.

"Ah, Mathieu Bertrand." He greeted the commander's messenger as if he was a well-loved sibling. "How safe are we all today on the streets of Paris?" Public opinion may not have mattered to him, but it exercised the president's mind so he feigned interest. Mathieu detested him.

Durfort was of aristocratic descent, connected by blood to a remnant of the ancient regime which had survived the Revolution. He treated Quai d'Orsay as his natural abode and cherished its splendor with proprietorial interest. He walked the great corridors as if they belonged to him, finding fault only with those who were not granted audience as his favorites. Benoit Durfort dressed in the nineteenth century and undermined the twentieth. His inability to consider the feelings of those around him added to the difficulty of working for him. Underlings were barely tolerated in his world. His long skeletal fingers were tipped with sharp feline nails which he drummed noisily when irritated, and little irritated him more than the kaiser and Germany. He was a hatcher of plots, a minder of secrets, a devious influence on those who would hold power, but from the outset, Durfort liked Mathieu.

"What nonsense today in the Palaise de Justice? Should the guillotine be sharpened for the Caillaux bitch?" Benoit Durfort punctuated his conceit with a high-camp giggle. The commander's handwriting appeared to defeat him on a daily basis, drawing Mathieu uncomfortably close to the scented fop.

"And what does Monsieur Roux mean precisely when he notes that Henriette Caillaux appeared to be distressed by the proceedings? I hope she is thoroughly distressed, the harlot."

Mathieu had never been tasked to work with a more self-obsessed creature and he let Commander Roux know. "He has this need to impress how important he is," he complained to no effect, "and he makes my skin creep." Bernard Roux was not moved. He had long known the bloated ego that was Durfort and had no intention of reacquainting himself with a man he despised.

"His indiscretion is boundless. He has shown me copies of telegrams between the president and the kaiser, he talks about the English foreign secretary as if he was a best friend, and assumes that I know precisely why the president is currently in Russia. Of course it's not the President, it's 'Raymond.' It took me three hours to realize that 'Alex' was the Russian Ambassador, Izvolsky."

Roux chortled to himself with such force that his moustache appeared to take on a life of its own, dancing a pacy jig above his trusty Gauloises, but when he tried to suppress the laughter a deep painful cough rasped his throat. Mathieu thought his boss was having a fit. Once he had regained his composure, the commander agreed. "As you say, he's not to be trusted but let him confide in you. He's a mere undersecretary, but believe me, he is a protected species. He wouldn't treat me that way but your youth and openness unquestionably attracts him. Play to his vanities. Pretend you're impressed, but don't get too close."

Mathieu nodded. He now knew every word spoken by Bernard Roux was truth. "Everything I see and hear proves you are right. We are organizing for war. It's scandalous."

But Paris was agog with a different kind of scandal. Mathieu had expected the voyeurs who hung around the Palais de Justice to thin out as the trial unfolded, but public interest was stoked by scurrilous revelations, open squabbles, and barely veiled political self-interest. Inside the building, the atmosphere became febrile. Lawyers berated each other; advocates sweated. Judges fell out. Honor was allegedly impinged. The government ought to have moved the entire proceedings to the *Comedie-Française* on the Rue Richelieu. For a start, it would have been more comfortable.

There was one compensation: lunch. Lunch in the small but well-provisioned Bar-Bistro across the Pont Au Change became a daily respite. No matter what, Mathieu managed to make it back in time from the Quai d'Orsay. Bernard Roux knew how and where to eat. The proprietors greeted him by name, and he returned the compliment. Having survived his initiation at the Quai d'Orsay on the opening Monday, Mathieu allowed the commander to treat him to a respectable plat de jour. On Tuesday, after Joseph Caillaux had impressed the court, they ate a succulent rabbit stew in a red wine sauce. Wednesday witnessed the spectacle of Henriette presenting herself as a vulnerable, sensitive, dutiful, and loving wife. It may have turned the stomachs of more conservative diners, but the steak au poivre, washed down by a palatable wine, proved a worthy compensation. Thursday's excitement in the Palais de Justice, as Caillaux's former wife took to the stand, required a lighter lunch; a salad sufficed. But Friday's farcical performance over the infamous letters for which Gaston Calmette was shot drove the duo to serious drink.

"Enough," Roux decided. "We have suffered enough. I have had my fill of so-called honor, reputation, and virtuous women." They pushed their way through the crowded street, across the river and north to familiar territory. "We've spent the whole week listening to pathetic excuses from a pampered harlot who brings disgrace to our nation. She may have millions of francs in the bank, live in a luxury we will never comprehend and pursue a hedonistic lifestyle behind the closed doors of her indulgent villa, but she is not a good person. Believe me." He snorted menacingly. His stride widened. Bernard Roux was a man on a mission and it would only be accomplished when they reached the Café Clichy.

"Oh." He stopped short and turned to Mathieu. "You'll be mindful you owe me a cognac."

The bloody Belgian had won the Tour de France.

A LEADER IN WAITING

My sense of justice has always been acute. So has my instinct. I treasure my own code of honor. I do.

Standing at the gates of the Palais de Justice with its grand colonnades and nineteenth century facelift, I gloried in the thought that though Marie-Antoinette had been imprisoned on this site before being condemned to the guillotine, the indignity of this regicide would shortly be redressed by Henriette Caillaux. Yet, surrounded as I was by a large group of my friends, I sensed a problem. Every morning a cohort of Action française supporters lined up behind the cordon of municipal police and gendarmes to hurl insults at everyone associated with the Caillauxs. What amazed me was the number of her supporters who massed on the other side. Were they paid agitators? No Frenchman worthy of the name would surely associate himself with these socialist murderers.

Caillaux had proved to be an enemy of France. His previous willingness to submit to the kaiser's demands had weakened our nation and made us a laughing stock in Europe. His misdeeds as minister of finance were an affront to decency, but still Joseph Caillaux hung onto his ill-gotten post until she put paid to his reputation and career. But it was insufficient. Action française would take care of such traitors. Now his wife Henriette had been disgraced, his filthy affairs spread across the civilized world like a sexual disease. That was it. The Caillaux clan were a cancer which must be removed. The Paris sewers, though too good for them, had work to do.

"Murderer! Murderer! Liar! Thief! Thief!" A chorus of phlegm shot across the gilded gateway as Joseph Caillaux's limousine glided to a halt, Patrick at the wheel. Bodyguards leapt forward to clear a passage as Caillaux exited towards his supporters, removing his top hat as if in salute. Joseph smiled broadly, raised his walking stick, and bowed almost imperceptibly. I shivered as the enemy turned towards us and extended the same confident smile. His eyes were cold and friendless. His moustache groomed to perfection. Was he looking at me? Did that bastard actually smile directly at ME?

"Die Caillaux!" I heard myself yell. And meant it. "Prepare to follow her to the guillotine!" To my surprise the packed throng around me took up the cry. "Die! Die! The guillotine's too good for your likes!"

"Off with her head…and yours!"

"Lock them away and lose the key!"

"Guillotine them both!"

The thrill of leading orchestrated abuse fired me up. Each day I prepared a new insult for Caillaux. It became my ritual contribution.

"Callous Caillaux" became "Shameless adulterer" and then "Treacherous lecher." I particularly liked that one, and gave it a second airing. Hearing my insults reverberate around the courtyard made me proud. I felt like a leader.

Are you a leader, my friend? I think not.

A firm hand patted my shoulder just as Caillaux disappeared into the Palais de Justice on the fifth morning. "Raoul?" the fresh-faced enquirer beckoned. "Raoul, be careful. This way." I let myself be drawn into the crowd. It was always more comfortable there. I recognized the man from Action française meetings, though we had never spoken. He sported a bowler hat which struggled to fit over his curled black hair and a suit so sharply pressed that it cut a passage before him.

"What's wrong?"

"We're being watched. Plain-clothed detectives. Keep your head down and follow me."

I did as advised, turning my gaze to shoes, boots, and cobbled road. We picked up pace. I was about to ask where we were headed when a sleek green Renault EF Torpedo, its engine purring, braked hard at the curb. Maurice, the fellow's name came to me just as the rear door opened, beckoned me forward.

"Quick, before they realize we've gone." The thrill of conspiracy increased my heart-rate. The last time I had felt that kind of joyous fear, I had just escaped the clutches of my brother's friends. They intended to beat me for betraying them to our teacher. They had no business stealing from the orchard. Thieves. Every one of them.

"Keep your head down. We don't want you arrested."

"Arrested?" Why would the police want to arrest me? Oh dear. I was decidedly uncomfortable despite the luxury of the Renault's brown leather upholstery. My rescuers smiled knowingly.

"Because they have orders to waylay important members of the A.F. Several of the lads were picked up this morning and held for a couple of hours."

"So they couldn't protest at the Palais de Justice?" I filled in the rest of the story as they probably hoped I would.

"Precisely. I'm Conrad, by the way." He extended his hand and grasped mine firmly.

"Raoul." I nodded seriously. "And you are Maurice, I believe."

"Yes. We met that night you were assaulted by the police. After poor Calmette's funeral."

"Right."

"I'm Theo," the driver added without turning his head. The Renault sped effortlessly down Boulevard Saint Michel, past the Sorbonne, the Luxembourg Gardens resplendent in their July finery, almost empty, too early yet for the ambulant bourgeoisie. We cruised across Montparnasse towards the Catacombs and the Porte d'Orleans. Theo slowed down.

"We've given them the slip."

"Well done, Theo."

He drove round in a circle before announcing, "We're here."

We climbed out onto the Rue Friant, checked up and down the street for spies before I was hustled up two flights of stairs into a well-appointed apartment.

"Raoul." A middle-aged gentleman rose from his window seat and greeted me enthusiastically. "Very pleased to meet you at last." He had the aura of breeding. Erect, confident, his words implied a positive familiarity which disarmed me immediately. He bore a short-cropped beard which must have required daily attention, and his waistcoat was of deep purple satin. Thin rounded spectacles sat comfortably on his nose, and while his smile appeared genuine, it may have been well-practiced. A manservant appeared from the kitchen with a tray of coffee and small patisseries which were laid before us as an offering.

"Sit down, please, and thank you for agreeing to meet with me."

It took a second before I realized he was speaking directly to me.

"I understand you have suffered for the cause, and want to be directly involved. Action française has need of strong men like you, which is why Maurice was sent to keep you from the clutches of those who would put you in prison. I'm Charles, by the way."

There was no proffered hand.

"And before we begin, this meeting never took place. You understand? No one must know about it. Ever."

What followed stunned, frightened, and excited me in like measure. Here I was in a select meeting of the inner core of A.F., as an equal. A "strong man." Sufficiently important that they had to keep me from the clutches of the police. I could not fathom why the gendarmerie might throw me in prison, but then I had lost faith in law and order in Paris. Every right-thinking person had.

"Who constitutes the greatest danger to our nation?"

"Caillaux and his associates?" I anticipated that his would be the approved response. I was wrong. Slowly stirring a single silver spoon into his coffee, Charles smiled at my ignorance. I reckon he had counted on it.

"No, my friend, not Caillaux. His power was effectively snuffed out when his brute of a wife gunned down Gaston Calmette, may he rest in peace." Charles blessed himself and the others followed. Ah, we were all Catholics. Fine.

"The enemies of France, the enemies of our people, are the peddlers of peace and conciliation." He leaned forward as if someone close by might be eavesdropping. "On pain of death, you will never repeat what I am about to tell you." Charles's voice became gravely guttural. This was more than a mere whiff of conspiracy.

"Of course, you may depend on me."

"I need to be certain of that. We all do." If there was some underlying threat, it was unnecessary.

"I would give my life for France," I promised.

"May it not come to that, but we will all face sacrifice in the near future." Charles cleared his throat, adopted a stiff-backed position, and drummed his fingers on the table as if buying time to make a final decision. He inhaled a long slow breath before choosing to continue.

"We will be at war with Germany within the month. Possibly sooner. France is prepared. Presidential directives have been drawn up. The army is ready. General Joffre is straining at the leash."

"But the president is in Russia?" Instinctively, I knew I was wrong.

"President Poincaré is currently en route from St. Petersburg. He and Prime Minister Viviani will be at their desks by Wednesday at the latest. The directives were prepared long before they went to visit the czar."

My jaw dropped involuntarily.

"So why?"

"Poincaré knows that now is the time to strike back at the Boches. This is our one chance to regain the stolen provinces, if the czar fulfills his treaty obligations. Have no doubts that is why the president is dedicating such precious time to this visit. We can catch Germany in a pincher movement, and crush her from the East and West. Raymond Poincaré went to reassure Russia that all was ready. And the czar has been reassured."

The immensity of this statement swept through me. Adrenaline pumped surprise and delight into my veins. It was to be. And soon.

"Our problem lies with the internationalists; the syndicalists, the rabble intellectuals who would call a halt to action across Europe. Jaurès here in Paris, that damned Polish Jewess, Rosa Luxembourg, the bastard Kier Hardie in England. If we let them rally their pathetic workers, organise mass meetings and general strikes, demand that armies lay down their weapons, it will be disastrous. They will have to be eliminated, one way or another."

He paused for effect. I nodded in obvious approval as if to infer that I fully understood what he was saying.

"Action française cannot stand back. We must be ready. It is a point of honor."

The discussion did not end there, but my mind teemed with possibilities. Here, I was a hero. Here, I had friends and colleagues. Like minds who respected me. I was a soldier for Action française. And they wanted me.

6

July 27-28, 1914 – Verdicts

Over the weekend, a few newspapers ran stories of trouble in Europe. Distant trouble. Stupidity, really. The Austrian Archduke and his wife had been assassinated a month back, and hints began to emerge about Serbian complicity. Serbians? Who cared about those murdering peasants? The Austrian government demanded that while Serbia investigated what happened they should allow Austrian investigators access to the inquiry. Naturally, all of Europe appeared to have immense sympathy for the Archduke's family. Austria could hardly let such a blatant murder rest unresolved.

President Poincaré heard of the tragedy while he was at the races at Longchamp in the Bois de Boulogne. Everyone who mattered in Paris society was there for the annual Grand Prix festival of French excesses. Nobility, diplomats, millionaires, politicians of power, and those who had temporarily lost it, displayed their elegance amongst the vibrant June flowers and Longchamp's iconic old windmill. The latest daring fashions flaunted by the mannequins caused muttered comment from the more restrained ladies of wealth. Their black and white satin and lace ensembles with dazzling pearls were themselves a statement. Dead-black was fashionable. Henriette Caillaux had not been forgotten.

The president was informed of the Sarajevo slaying at a suitable junction between the third and fourth courses of his splendid dinner. He did not leave the table. It was sad news indeed, but the Grand Prix had been exhilarating. In crowded stands which boasted Prince Kinsky, the Raja of Puddikkottai, a host of English Lords, eminent French Barons, and the multi-millionaire arms procurer Basil Zaharoff, the magnificent chase from the turn of the home straight to the winning line between two Rothschild three-year-olds had been breathless. Baron Edmund de Rothschild's *Sardanapale* edged ahead of his cousin Maurice de Rothschild's entrant, *La Farina*, by barely a neck. Who would want to leave a garden party more sumptuous than that at Eden?

One calendar month later, the trial of Henriette Caillaux ended. Bernard Roux fretted. His thoughts strayed beyond the city limits; beyond the borders of France and Germany towards darker regions in the Balkans where an earthquake threatened to split Europe's fragile peace. Demands from Austria for an acknowledgement from Serbia that the wrongdoing had to be avenged threatened an escalation into a full-blown storm which would involve Russia, Germany, England, and the Balkans. What had started as a requiem for the Archduke Ferdinand was rapidly descending into the Dies Ira of Europe's Armageddon. Bernard Roux summoned his Tigers to meet at the Café de Deux Ponts for breakfast. They had to know what lay ahead.

Guy Simon bounded along the quayside. "This is a nice change for us office boys, Commander. Are we here to celebrate Madame Caillaux's death sentence?"

Roux raised his eyebrows. "Perhaps," was his laconic response. Mathieu had asked him to consider sharing his secret with everyone on the team. Whispers had begun to leak through government departments that France was gearing up for war. He had almost blurted out the truth twice. Once in the Café Clichy and once in the office. Pascal Girard and Paul Dubois arrived in tandem. "Well, here's a first. Breakfast paid by the commander. Celebrations, then?"

Bernard Roux rose to greet them formally, dispelling the air of jocularity. His handshake was firm, his face, firmer. "Gentlemen." His chill soured the frivolity.

Mathieu waited and watched from the other side of the street before crossing to join them. He brought his own gravitas to the table and chose not to join in the usual banter. Coffee was served and the Tigers smelled bad news. "What's wrong? Have we messed up?" Pascal Girard sensed trouble.

The commander looked at this men with unexpected sadness. "I don't know if it will come as a complete surprise…" he drew on a sympathetic Gauloises, "but, unless something dramatic intervenes, by this time next week we are likely to be at war."

Guy tried to soften the moment. He smiled, relaxed and positive. "Do you really think so, Sir? Someone in the Quai d'Orsay starts a rumor and before you know it…"

Roux turned eyes of stone towards Guy Simon and petrified them all. "I've seen the order for general mobilization. That is the final step before a declaration of war. You are aware of that." Each found a different level of gasp. Guy's had a short intake. Pascal's included a low moan. Paul Dubois broke wind softly. "Mathieu and I have used the time wasted on this charade of a trial to follow what is really happening. President Poincaré and his diehards have set everything in motion."

"No. We would know. We would all know." Pascal Girard was not having it. He was six weeks from retirement. War was not on his mind. Mathieu knew that it was, however, on the president's agenda, and also the czar's. The English? They were certainly involved, but everyone knew the English. They said one thing and did the other. The coffee sat untouched. Mathieu watched their reactions carefully.

The commander continued. "You've read about the Austrian demands to Serbia and all the commotion which is now going on. What you don't know is that the Serbian reply to the Austrians was written here in Paris in the political division at Quai d'Orsay and circulated for approval to the other countries involved in the plans. This whole mess is being orchestrated through Paris, St. Petersburg, and London. They want the Balkans to explode so that they have the excuse they need for war."

Mathieu underlined the facts. "Benoit Durfort, that two-faced slimy bastard of a diplomatic nonentity, takes great pride in detailing the duplicity which is behind all this."

Pascal Girard was immediately agitated. He knew Durfort. Paul Dubois's reaction was solemn. What he heard confirmed his every fear. "London? So the English are involved, too? This is bad news, Sir."

Guy Simon caught their attention by spreading his arms across the table as if it were an altar.

"Coffee anyone?" Mathieu had expected him to be taken aback, but Guy was perfectly calm. They ate their breakfast in silent thought, each wondering what it meant for their future.

The commander took one sip of his bitter coffee and fixed his attention on a low-flying swallow winging across the shallow river. Its slick blue-black form swooped and dived in balletic turns, oblivious to the poisonous war that man was concocting.

"Once the newspapers have had their fill of the Caillaux verdict, the coming war will be all-consuming. You know what it's like. War is popular until you start to lose." Roux's pessimism was tangible. He was consumed by a horrific deja vu. He rose to go to the Palais de Justice, a croissant in hand in case hunger pangs descended later.

Ever the optimist, Guy insisted, "But if we have England and Russia on our side, the Germans will be crushed."

"That's what they reckon," was the best Mathieu could offer.

"You need to know, gentlemen, because one way or another we will have our hands full. I don't need to remind you all. Not a word."

55

The partisan crowds outside the great courtyard bayed at each other in mutual contempt. Inside the legal teams rehearsed their parting shots for the benefit of a jury that had already made up its mind. The prosecution case maintained that Henriette had deliberately, and with premeditation, murdered Gaston Calmette because she and he agreed that without a bullet to his heart, Calmette would ruin Joseph Caillaux's career. He could have done the deed, but she knew that she had a better chance of being found not guilty. Because she was a woman. The prosecution counsel played the Catholic card by pronouncing her a moral degenerate for whom marriage meant nothing sacred.

Not so, claimed the defense, brilliantly and dramatically led by Maitre Labori. In a different era he would have been a peerless director of stage or screen. Henriette collapsed into her husband's loving arms as arranged and reacted on cue, better than anyone might have anticipated. Labori produced a report from the Paris faculty of medicine which implied that Henriette was governed by subconscious impulses which demonstrated a split personality. It was, he instructed the jury, a female weakness. She had killed out of a feminine drive to preserve her sexual reputation. If the jury at that point swiveled on the cusp of either argument, Labori added a telling plea. He reached beyond the court and begged the jury, and all Frenchmen for whom the tricolor was sacred, to preserve their anger for those enemies who had appeared at the borders to threaten the very survival of the Gallic way of life. Brilliant. Utterly masterful. Maitre Labori earned every franc of his fabled fee.

The jury retired from the claustrophobic chamber at five minutes to eight in the evening. Word spread across the city like a dust storm in Algeria. It was on everyone's lips. Hot and acrid opinion divided Paris. All other rumors were buried in the shifting sands of ill-informed prediction.

Unable to resist the will to be part of the dramatic cast, the jury of citizen magistrates returned to the stage after twenty-five minutes. They sought clarification on points of legal consequence. What length of sentence would Madame Caillaux receive on the two counts brought before the court? Suitably reassured, they retired again. Half an hour later they were back. This time it was to declare their decision. Months of bitter accusation and counter accusation came to an end within one judicial hour. Hundreds of thousands of reams of newsprint had been churned out detailing every possible angle for the better part of four months. Duels had been fought over the case that very morning. Injured parties would take much longer to heal, yet the jury had decided in less than sixty minutes.

Commander Bernard Roux stood impassive, certain of but one fact. Whoever lost would cause a riot. Judge Albanel bowed to the court and addressed the foreman of the jury. " Is Madame Caillaux guilty of voluntary homicide against Gaston Calmette on 16 March?"

"Of course she was," Mathieu murmured to himself.

The foreman differed. "Before God and before all men, the decision of the jury is NO."

"What?" Mutterings of anger and anguish turned to a growl as the second, by that time utterly superfluous, question was put.

"Was the said homicide committed with premeditation and criminal intent?"

"No."

Commander Roux watched Judge Albanel smile to himself before attempting a closing gesture. A roar erupted from the body of the hall as if two tribes gave simultaneous vent to their deepest war cry. Joy or anger boomed from every quarter in a cannonade of disbelief. Journalists raced each other for the exits, pushing, pulling, threatening violence, and throwing inconsequential blows and insults at each other. Mathieu and Bernard Roux stepped into the well of the court to add weight to the police presence, ready to hold back angry protestors, but the disbelieving horde turned and raced outside to bay their outrage over Notre Dame, the Sacré Coeur , and Eiffel's tower, to a waiting world like wounded wolves gathering their clan.

So ended the one woman show which had held Paris in thrall while all across Europe the bankers and arms dealers, the empire grabbers and warmongers aligned their forces with political and military expediency. Henriette Caillaux enjoyed one week on center stage while behind the scenes the legions of the damned gathered in the wings for years of retribution.

THE WRATH OF INJUSTICE

I was incensed. Beyond words.

I tried to punch a gendarme who had started to shut the gilded gates fronting the Palais d'Injustice. Granted, there were at least four others in advance of my useless swipe into the ether of corruption which surrounded the trial, but I swear that no one was more outraged than me. No one.

More than the constant bullying at school, more than my father's barely disguised condescension, more than my brother's contempt, the Caillaux verdict crushed what remained of my confidence that all would come right in the end. Chants of "Ass-ass-in, ass-ass-in" rent the Parisian twilight. Clenched fists pumped the air like traction engines warming to their task. The roar was manic. A surge of power thrust me forward. Crushed against the courtyard gate I was trapped between burning anger and blind indignation, hardly able to breathe. My head spun. Not guilty? Not guilty of voluntary homicide? Not guilty of premeditated criminal intent? Logic was affronted. It was a nightmare, surely?

It was impossible. Henriette Caillaux bought a gun with the sole intention of killing Gaston Calmette, waited on her prey like a weathered predator, and struck down an unarmed man. She planned it. She chose to murder in cold blood. The police arrested her with the weapon. She never denied her action. Yet from a jury of twelve citizens, all male, all reputedly sane, eleven declared her NOT GUILTY. France was a laughing stock. How they must have sniggered in Berlin at the stupidity of Parisian justice. No wonder they considered us soft and flimsy, spineless and gullible. The patronizing English were delighted at yet another example of French farce. For Palais de Justice, read that obnoxious theatre, the Palais Royal.

My anger boiled in the Lake of Fire. I was incandescent. Burning with emotional rage. My being was filled with an inner certainty. Have you seen the holy pictures that they sell outside Catholic churches to the Faithful? Paul of Tarsus falling from his horse, struck down by a shaft of all-consuming revelation, reborn as a messenger to spread the word of God? He was gifted inner certainty. Or any of the glorious martyrs who were burned at the stake, their fate decided, glowing with the certainty of everlasting life after the horrific death before them? Halos alight? Now I knew. I would become the true avenging angel. I would wield the heavy sword of justice. Because I knew what injustice was. I would be a martyr for France.

Tears ran freely. I remembered how in my childhood father had unaccountably beaten both my brother and I, for allegedly laughing during mass. We were taken into the study and thrashed. Me first. With every stinging stroke I screamed my innocence.

"It wasn't me, it wasn't me, Papa. I don't even know Pierre Monette!"

"It was him," I cried, desperately pointing to my stone-faced brother in the hope that the beating would stop. But there was no justice. "They made a joke about Claudine Therbault's breasts resting on the pew. I couldn't help looking."

The smacks increased in intensity. "Im-pure-thoughts-in-church." With each syllable father's wrath found fresh expression. It hurt. Deeply. Such undeserved pain.

Left heaving on the floor, I failed to see my brother's contempt. But I felt it.

"It was you," I sobbed outside. "Why didn't you tell him? It's not fair. It's not fair."

"You should not be here," a voice from behind insisted. It was Conrad, and behind him, Theo. "We cannot afford to have you arrested, Raoul. You know that. Monsieur Charles will be displeased. Come with us. The lads will manage without you this time." They grabbed my shoulders unceremoniously and pulled me away from the railings.

"It wasn't my fault. It's not fair."

As they hustled me through the ranks of outraged young men, seething for his kind of justice, I felt no reassurance. I wanted instant retribution for Caillaux's crimes. Instead I was dragged to safety when my first wish was to embrace danger; preserved, though I sought martyrdom. I felt that I was being punished, denied the pleasure of immediate vengeance, while others were free to spill their blood for the honor of France. "Why me? Why do I always end up the victim?"

7

July 28-30, 1914 – Targets

A brooding darkness settled on the center of Paris, like a gathering storm rolling out of the Palais de Justice from which the heavens might or might not open. Heavy clouds sagged through the growing gloom, promising a downpour but delivering only a claustrophobic haze. As every policeman knew, a thunderous rainstorm would have cleared the streets but nature declined to oblige. By eleven o'clock order seemed to have prevailed.

Watching carefully from a vantage point on Boulevard Haussmann, the chief of police voiced his optimism. "I think the worst has..." He hadn't finished his sentence before a shot rang out and the forces of good and evil squared up to each other with serious intent. It was as if a bugler trumpeted a charge. Street fighters from both sides exploded in justified outrage, and the boulevard was swamped by hate and retribution.

What had been a barrage of insults became a barrage of missiles. Gendarmes clashed with the Action française legion, emboldened by Corsican sailors recruited for the fight. It degenerated into a free-for-all, combatants splitting and reforming, police officers regrouping and arresting as they could. The Prefect knew who would be blamed if the grand boulevard was held hostage to the raving mob. Him. Mounted reinforcements were brought in to clear the streets. Two bloodied young men lay prostrate on the steps of the *Figaro* office as if frozen in adoration of the martyred editor-in-chief. We watched them fall under the blows of anonymous gendarmes. As the battle ground moved forward, the two inert figures stained the proud doorway from which so much anti-Caillaux propaganda had flowed. The irony did not go unnoticed. The murderess, free to walk away unharmed, the victim's supporters dragged to the Hotel-Dieu hospital across from Notre Dame for life support. And they called it justice. Would either of those men walk again? Nothing in life is fair.

Next morning there was only one topic in the prefecture. War. Looking back it seemed to Mathieu that someone had finished a novel, returned it to the library shelf, and begun to read another more violent story, without pause. Caillaux was old news. The previous night's riot hardly mattered, though his colleagues were far from convinced despite the evidence which Roux had disclosed before the verdict declared Caillaux innocent.

"Europe is smoldering. Small grass fires have been set alight. It is happening around us. Austria and Serbia might have gone it alone, but they won't because the Russians have promised to guarantee the Serbs their freedom. They've declared Serbia their Slavic brothers. And who is treaty-bound to Russia?" He looked round the room, not for an answer, but to make his point stick fast. "Us. We are."

"But treaties only apply if our allies are invaded. If Germany declares war against Russia ..." Guy Simon felt the grounds for his certainty beginning to slip. "The kaiser's not so foolish."

"Poincaré is." Mathieu spoke with an authority that wasn't to be challenged. "Poincaré is."

The chief interrupted them abruptly. He had been with Celestin Hennion at the central prefecture since 9:00 A.M., assumedly to be congratulated on last night's success. His face betrayed a different story.

"Shut the door and sit down." Not a good start. He wandered to the window then reached back to his desk for a compensatory Gauloises. Mathieu couldn't look him in the eye.

"You have to get into your heads the fact that we are sitting on a keg of gunpowder, and the fuse has been lit. We have perhaps one day, or two at the most, to avoid Armageddon." He dropped his eyes and inhaled sharply. "It may be too late already." Dubois and the captain visibly stiffened. They wanted to disbelieve him, but said nothing.

"Tomorrow, General Joffre will be permitted to deploy his battalions from Luxembourg to the Vosges. The only stipulation is that he must keep them ten kilometers from the German border so the Germans can't see our buildup. He's not at all happy. Joffre wants full mobilization. Now."

"*Merde.*"

"Christ," Girard swore loudly. "So we can't stop this madness."

The chief pursed his lips. "Trouble is that half the country wants revenge on Germany. Wants war. The army does, for sure. However, it gets more complicated." It felt as though there might be a slim sliver of hope, as if there was something they could do, despite what had been said. "Our Intelligence believes that the extremists in Action française have created a hit-list of people who remain a danger to them. Who might yet stop this damned stupidity. Of course the Caillauxs are number one target, Joseph in particular. Stories have been bandied about that he has sold out again to the kaiser and will try to stop our boys going to war. It's nonsense. He's locked up at home and politically friendless. Second is the editor-in-chief of *L'Humanite*, Jean Jaurès, who has been warning for days that unnamed power-brokers are driving all Europe to war for their own ends. Jaurès may be printing rubbish, I don't know, but the little I do, frightens me. He could be right. Someone is pulling the strings at the Ministry of War and the Foreign Office is out of control. They have their heart set on war. Telegrams flow from Quai d'Orsay to every embassy in Europe on an hourly basis. Jaurès has upset his enemies in a big way. They want him dead." He paused to draw long on his preferred drug. "And that means they genuinely fear him."

"He's just a newspaperman and minor politician. What can he do?" Guy was not impressed.

"He could bring a hundred thousand trade unionists and socialists onto the streets to refuse to fight against their fellow workers in Germany and Austria."

Guy's laugh had a hollow ring. "That's not going to happen."

"Probably not…if they've taken us so far down the road that no one can stop war." Bernard Roux hadn't finished. "And to make matters worse, the socialists have a new bogeyman, one Basil Zaharoff."

"Who?" the name meant nothing to Mathieu.

"He's a wealthy philanthropist." Guy Simon knew who they were talking about, but he minimized the mystery man's importance. "Is he not financing our Olympic team for 1916?"

"He's the most important arms dealer in the world," Roux corrected Guy's trivia. "He's a Rothschild prodigy. A personal friend of the president. He owns banks and industrial firms. He deals in the cannons and shells, the guns and bullets, France needs for the coming war. No Zaharoff, no point of starting a war."

"Never heard of him," said Dubois, as if that diminished Zaharoff's standing.

"When you have a fortune like his, the papers don't splash your imperfections across the front page. For a start, he probably owns half the press. Look, we need to think clearly here. Paris is still seething about Henriette Caillaux. Another riot could blow up anywhere in the city, and we don't have the resources to deal with several outbreaks at once. These named citizens must be protected. From the president's point of view, they rank in this order: Zaharoff, Caillaux and, at the very end of the queue, Jean Jaurès."

"But surely this should be left to another department. Our task is to combat organized crime."

The chief was not to be beaten. "This could be the biggest organized crime in history, believe me." He had the last word and lit another Gauloises, formally ending the discussion.

* * *

Doubting Dubois was sent off to the exclusive Avenue Hoche, a few hundred meters from the Arc de Triomphe, where Monsieur Zaharoff lived in grand luxury. From street level the chandeliers on the first floors of his villa at number 53 hung like exorbitant Christmas trees, dripping perfectly cut glass and promising even greater excess inside. The captain and two gendarmes announced themselves at the front door to a man who looked like a no-neck Turkish bullfighter resplendent in bespoke livery, his French as flawless as his manners. He identified himself as Monsieur Zaharoff's valet.

"I shall indeed, Sir, alert Monsieur Zaharoff to your timely concerns. If it is your intention to remain on guard in the avenue, someone from the kitchen will bring you sustenance."

"Oh, three coffees would be much appreciated," Dubois responded immediately.

"Would that be Turkish, Persian, North African, Yemeni, East African, or Columbian, perhaps, Sir?" A distasteful inflection rested on the word Columbian. Dubois's instinct was to avoid that choice. "Roasted, roasted and ground, pounded or roller ground?"

"What?" Dubois struggled to keep up.

"And would you like your coffee boiled, steeped, or filtered? The three policemen looked blankly at each other.

"Cream, milk, iced, or plain?"

"Can we have three normal coffees? Just ordinary. Whatever that tastes like here." Dubois did not want to appear ungrateful, but enough was enough.

"Very good, Sir."

"Actually," came a voice from behind, "could my coffee be iced?"

"Certainly, Sir. Any sugar? We can offer—"

"Just as it comes would be fine." Dubois closed the conversation and turned back, glowering at the iced coffee. Now they all knew what real wealth meant.

Guy Simon was sent to liaise with the Caillauxs. Clearly Mathieu would not be welcome. As a former prime minister and finance minister, Joseph was a target for any right-wing critic, but the anger generated by Henriette's acquittal had driven reason and fairness from any sentence which included their surname. Death threats swirled around. Their private residence was surrounded with cars and charabancs like a circle of wagons in a Wild West circus show. Policemen from different branches of the constabulary were in clear evidence. Ugly crowds chanting hostile slogans and promising vile retribution on both Joseph and Henriette had been driven away. A trickle of friends and colleagues constantly came and went, but their reassurances were empty. Caillaux was seen as a threat to the unity of a France which stood strong against the hated Boches. The air had been poisoned by a very potent nerve gas.

Back at the prefecture Guy Simon gave a short report. "They should get away from Paris while they can." He was adamant. "It's crazy to live here in full view of the lunatics. It's a red rag to a bull."

Roux nodded his agreement. "For as long as they stay, they'll attract the mob." He picked up the telephone and called the minister of the interior.

Mathieu and the captain made their way to Rue Montmartre through the crowded boulevards and side streets, the colors and smells of Paris wafting before them in the sunshine. An urchin in a tattered shirt cycled past, in front of him a converted pannier laden with fresh baguettes. They could taste the smell of freshly baked bread reach out to tempt them. Hastily pasted advertisements for this week's performances at the *Moulin Rouge* promised alluring half-dressed cabaret dancers. Old posters from the *Folies Bergere* hung limply from the local pissoir, poised on the corner to relieve the troubled. The bold promise of a jolly weekend in London adorned an advertising board, advising the cheapest route from the Gare St. Lazare. Cars shared the broad streets with horse drawn carts, though they parked at any angle without thought for animals or humans. Such beauty and elegance. Such promise and passion. Would it survive the war to come?

Pascal Girard explained that *L'Humanite* was a left-wing daily newspaper, owned and controlled by the socialist Jean Jaurès, a depute in the National Assembly and accomplished pacifist. Its circulation was widespread and crossed international borders. According to the old captain, Jaurès was an acquired taste. If your politics veered to the right, he was the devil incarnate. He had championed the Jewish army officer Alphonse Dreyfus when he was wrongly convicted of selling secrets to the Germans some twenty years before. Little else fired the anger of Action française than anything they could damn as Jewish. Shameless in their prejudice, they continued to claim that Dreyfus was a spy and the left-wing press, his patsy. Jaurès thus bore the badge of Jew-lover; it was a badge he cherished.

No matter what was eventually proved in court, the Action française held on to their myth as an act of faith. Girard found the inconspicuous entrance to the newspaper at 142 Rue Montmartre, crushed between a café-bar and a shoe shop.

Inside was a hive of concentration with a deep intensity of purpose. Deadlines approached and could not be bypassed. The captain looked around for the famous and fearless editor but no one seemed more important than any other. Jaurès himself was not on this floor.

"Jean Jaurès?" His question hung in the air briefly and was lost in a clamor of industry. No one answered. "Can we speak to Monsieur Jaurès, please?" Girard bellowed. "We must speak with him. We're from the prefecture."

One of the older compositors looked up, sweat glistening from a rugged face which wanted to concentrate on the precision of its art. He wiped his stained hands and grimaced, reluctant to change his focus. " He's on his way to Brussels. Back tomorrow." The two men were forced to shout against the prevailing gale of technology.

"He needs to know we are very concerned about his safety."

"Monsieur, we all are. Today is no different from any other day."

Raoul's Story

A TASK OF HONOR

Of course I was not afraid. Concerned? Yes, but not afraid. I was frogmarched once before, a memory I had kept behind tightly closed vaults. And then it began to seep through a keyhole in my mind and grease forgotten dread. What unlocks these buried thoughts? I wanted them obliterated, but they have the power to unleash themselves into the uncontrollable night.

I remembered a hood placed over my head so that I could not see my assailants, but as they banged me through the barracks, out behind the hateful gymnasium, I knew who they were. I was not deaf. I was none of the names they chose. Warmth streamed from my bladder despite my best intention to appear strong.

"Dirty bastard's peed himself," was followed by a whack to my head.

"Let me be." My semi-confident appeal to their better natures proved a waste and had no effect. "I didn't mean to."

I trembled involuntarily. "I didn't mean to tell the sergeant about the wine. He made me. He tricked me."

"Yeah, you didn't mean to, you lying shit. Just as you didn't mean to fail in the route march last week. Every fucking time you let us down, we all pay. Now it's your turn."

The first kick struck my leg from behind, just under the knee, and I collapsed into the hard gravel. Furious fists pummeled my prostrate body. Tears and snot almost choked me, writhing in pain, arms blindly flailing to protect me from the unseen enemy.

"Remember this you fucking coward. Remember. The boys won't forget. You'd be better off away from here. We'll be back…when you least expect us."

They left me in the silent chill growing ever colder under a clouded moon. Knuckles, scraped and bloodied by the boots that had stamped their authority, slowly untwisted so that I could use my hands to remove the filthy hood. Crawling, wounded like a back-broken cockroach, I hauled myself into the barracks. Ah, my bed was warm, but wet. I slept in their urine, willing myself to accept and forget. I accepted, but could never forget. They are probably all dead now, but in the sweat of a lonely night, I do remember them.

But this was different. The strongmen protected me. Maurice, Conrad, and Theo. Their grasp, though over firm, held me safely. And still I recognized fear. Did they think I was a fraud? Did they think I don't mean it when I say I'm going to kill Caillaux and Jaurès?

"I will kill them. I will."

"Silence, Raoul. Not another word!"

I hadn't meant to speak out loud.

"Where are we going?"

"Raoul! No questions. What you don't know cannot be beaten from you."

The unfortunate phrasing punctured my sense of wellbeing and darker doors reopened. Not far north of the station, we came to a cul-de-sac, Passage Ruelle, so close to the track it might have been a siding. Maurice pushed open a featureless faded blue door and we climbed up narrow stairs to a third floor apartment. Yet again, I found myself confronted by Charles, in whose presence they all assumed the lower rung.

"Matters have become critical."

No one sought elucidation.

"We are almost there. The army is in place, our plans have been well considered. Mobilization is on hold and the Russians have begun to move towards the German border." You could sense Charles's hesitation. He was about to say, "but."

"But one last obstruction will have to be removed. Permanently."

"Caillaux?" I heard myself ask.

"Not Caillaux, no. He is a spent force."

"Jaurès? Jean Jaurès, the Jew-lover?"

Charles turned to Raoul, his eyelids narrowing, like a raptor whose attention had been drawn to a minor morsel. "The same," he said, opening a thin dossier which lay on the table. "I see you were well considered by your superiors in military service. Good. You are a confident marksman, it says here. Very good." Charles leaned his obvious approval in my direction. I couldn't remember any positive feedback from my miserable military service, but nodded dutifully. Praise from Charles was not to be questioned.

"Did you mean what you said about killing Caillaux and Jaurès, my friend?"

"Of course." I was determined to do that. All I needed was the means. "I meant every word. I see it as my mission."

Knowing looks crossed the room. Judgments were made, although whatever Charles decided would be unquestioned. He approved.

"Maurice has a present for you. Take it home. Destroy the box. No one can connect you to us or us to you. Jaurès must be dead within 48 hours. If you cannot do this, we will be very disappointed. Listen well, Raoul. You carry the mark of a soldier of France on your forehead. You have clearly been chosen for greatness. When you do the deed, and it must be done, dispense with the evidence as quickly as possible. We will be watching you, like your guardian angel. If you are arrested, say nothing. Nothing. Blaming someone else would be a death sentence. You know what happens to men who blame others. They are punished. Silence will confirm you as the hero you are. All of Action française will stand by you. But only if you are silent. If you dare to betray the cause, you will die a most painful death and be cursed by the heroes of France. Raoul, do you understand?"

I looked at him with swelling tears. My mouth quivered. My heart pounded with pride. I was the chosen one. My guardian angel had descended from the heavens. Of course I understood.

Maurice gave me his present, saying pointedly, "This is from us. Do what must be done in our name." An enormous sense of sanctity filled my spirit. I held the sacred present in both hands, as if it were a sacrament.

"For Jean Jaurès. His time has come." I almost chanted my promise.

Charles raised a symbolic glass of red wine and replied, "For Action fran-çaise, whose time has also come. Maurice, take our champion to the metro and make sure he is protected." They bowed to each other like co-celebrants in a mystic charade and I was shepherded from Charles's presence. The audience was over.

It all happened so fast. So many instructions. So much responsibility. Do this. Have that. Go there. Alone in my lodgings I opened the box and looked in wonderment at two pistols. I held them in my hands. Felt the weight, counted the bullets, personalized the butts.

Did you ever meet your guardian angel? No. Of course not. You don't have one. I had three. I felt strangely hot. "I am a champion, you know."

Yet caution intervened. What if I died in the attempt or was betrayed? Anything was possible. I wrote a will, not to be opened until my death, and took it to the one man in the world I trusted absolutely.

Thank God.

8

July 30, 1914 – Jean Jaurès

"**D**o we have a file on Jean Jaurès?" Pascal and Mathieu returned to headquarters empty-handed.

Commander Roux looked up from his desk and asked, "Official or unofficial?"

"There are two?" queried Pascal. He paused for a second, looked at Mathieu and asked, "Why?"

Roux went to his locked filing cabinet and removed two slim dockets. He carefully laid one on his desk and opened the other. "Jean Jaurès, Socialist Member of the National Assembly for Tarn, historian and philosopher, founder and editor-in-chief of the daily newspaper, *L'Humanite*, leader of the French section of the Socialist International, anti-militarist, campaigned against the three year service law, working class hero… that kind of thing."

Mathieu looked at Jaurès' official photograph pinned to the opened file. He'd never given thought to the politician as a person and would have struggled to recognize him in the street. Not tall, medium at best, but sporting a heavy torso, Jaurès looked like any affluent Parisian. His round head and bristling hair lent him an air of moderate distinction but the ruddy, weather-beaten face framed in a short grey beard housed a disarming smile. Underneath the photo was a handwritten description penned by someone of different political persuasion.

"Did you read this?" Mathieu laughed. "It says here that Jaurès 'has a healthy appetite which often spreads onto his formal attire, bearing the evidence of previous dinners.' Unnecessarily sarcastic, don't you think?"

"Anytime I've seen him in the National Assembly," Bernard Roux added, "his pockets were stuffed with books, notes, and pamphlets. Made him look scruffy. But, in fact, he is generous, kind, speaks extremely well, and people love him. He is idolized by the younger socialists. You won't find that in the file."

They didn't.

"However, this," he held up the second file, "is entirely different, compiled by the political section which serves President Poincaré." Roux handed it to the lieutenant, unopened. Clearly the commander was familiar with its content. "Before you read it, be aware; Jean Jaurès is seen by many important and powerful Frenchmen as the enemy of France. And he is the enemy of their kind of France because of his outspoken criticism of the establishment. Action française hate him with a vengeance, but no less than the Russians. And if he is right, I can understand why. Read it. You first, Pascal, then you. We'll discuss it after lunch."

There were the usual comments about Jaurès' links to the Dreyfus affair and Jewish-sympathizers, articles from newspapers about his involvement in international socialism, details and copies of reports and minutes of the Socialist Party of France, and records of meetings with socialists from all over Europe. But it was the Russian content which caught the eye, largely because much of it had been underlined for effect. On the first page, Jaurès' most recent appeal to workers in Russia to go on strike in protest against President Poincaré's visit had *traitor* scrawled across the whole article. There were cuttings about his drive to unite the workers of France and Germany to stop war. Down the side, someone had added, *Must be stopped.* He had insulted Isvolsky, the Russian Ambassador in Paris, mocking him as a poisonous mosquito that had infected every court in Europe. One piece referred to the "sinister co-operation" between Russia and France. The letter to which it was originally attached had been removed. There were papers from President Poincaré's 1913 election which claimed that his funding had been sourced from Moscow. Scandalous if true.

Finally, a handwritten note contained numbers and letters 29 14 52 18 36 B 30 8 05 11 49 P.

"Your thoughts?" The commander put them to the test. Lunch had been sufficient though not excessive.

"Sir, do the prefect of police and the minister of justice know you have this information?" It was a bold query, but Mathieu knew the commander expected searching questions.

"I believe so. It came from their offices. Why do you ask?" He took refuge in a fresh Gauloises.

"Because the information has been gathered by two different sources for different purposes?"

Pascal agreed. "Has to be. But why?"

"What are these purposes? Seems unlikely to me." So, Roux agreed with them. He had left thinking space inside the conversation. Both men knew he was testing them.

"The first file contains nothing of particular importance; the second is relatively recent and concentrates on our Russian allies." Captain Girard tried to think beyond the obvious..

"Odd, that."

"Why odd?"

"Odd that you were sent two files. Odd that one of them reads more like a list of reasons for eliminating Jaurès right away."

"When you break it down the second file shows that certain people want him dead. The president? We know how anti-German he is. Bitter about Alsace-Lorraine. Fair enough. But Jaurès is saying that his election was funded by Russian money. That's rot, surely?"

If he was looking for a reaction from Roux, Mathieu was disappointed. Two drags of his Gauloises later, the commander urged," Go on."

"So the Russians would want him out of the way. Especially Ambassador Isvolsky."

Pascal Girard pointed to the obvious. "So does Action française and every other right-winged warmonger. Let's face it. They all want Jaurès dead."

"And the numbers on the note? Crack that and I'll buy the drinks." A rare promise indeed from the canny commander. Now there was a challenge. They had till 6:30 P.M. to solve that mysterious equation.

Pascal Girard sat at his desk in studious concentration. He had that look on his face usually reserved for choosing winners at Longchamps. Mathieu tried to concentrate, but numbers meant little to him. His thoughts centered on the Russian, Isvolsky. He should be further investigated. But where to start?

"Time." Pascal Girard broke the silence.

"Nearly five o'clock."

"No, the numbers. Time. Look at this."

Mathieu scurried across to his colleague's desk. A report sheet was covered in figures , with combinations reading backwards and forwards, additions vied with subtractions, arrows pointed to possible solutions but had been heavily scored through. Alphabetic substitutions appeared here and there, to no avail. The indecipherable had been made even more incomprehensible. He appealed for the answer.

"OK, let's take two sets of numbers. What do you make of the sequences 14 to 36 and then 8 to 49?"

"Nothing."

"I've already told you. Time. If these sequences are in hours and minutes, then you have 2:52 P.M. – 6:36 P.M. B and 8:05 A.M. – 11:49 A.M. P. See? Both sums total exactly 3 hours and 44 minutes."

71

"How is that likely?"

"Because, my young friend, the difference between the two sets is identical. If we are dealing with the sixty minute clock, it's a journey between two fixed points at an identical rate."

Pascal was half way up the corridor to the commander's office before Mathieu warned, "What about the rest of it?"

Too late. He followed his jubilant friend, keen to see what next transpired.

"So?" queried Commander Roux.

"Not sure yet." Pascal paused to make room for possible enlightenment. "If these are times, what takes 3 hours and 44 minutes?"

"A damned good lunch?" The chief actually smiled at his own joke.

"No, it's a fair question." Girard kept unpicking locks. "And if these figures indicate a time differential, then the numbers 29 and 30 might be dates?"

Bernard Roux broke the habit of a lifetime. He stubbed out a half-finished cigarette and launched himself at a pile of reports stacked neatly to his left.

"Of course!" he agreed, pulling one out, close to the bottom.

"Well done, Pascal. We've solved it. Look, boys, look. Jean Jaurès went to Brussels, B, on the 29th, that's today, catching the 2:52 from Garde du Nord. He will return tomorrow, the 30th, to Paris, P, at 11:49. Excellent. Well done. Great teamwork!"

Mathieu had to insist that he had not contributed anything to the solution, but Girard resigned himself to a share of the glory. Pronouns always betray management thinking.

"But why? Why would a police file identify Jaurès' travel arrangements in code?"

It was Mathieu's turn to unlock another door. "Unless it's not a police file."

Roux smiled. Caught. He would have told them eventually, but Mathieu was sharp.

"Quite right. It's not. Either someone in the Ministry secretly wanted us to see this or a clerk inadvertently shoved two files into one folder, and both were sent here. Doesn't matter which. Jaurès has enemies in the highest offices of the land, and they are tracking his every movement, but he also has at least one friend who needs to stay anonymous."

The captain dropped his head into his hands and groaned. "They are going to kill him when he gets back from Brussels."

"We can't be certain, and we certainly can't share this information." The chief drummed his fingers on the desk. "At 11:49 tomorrow, you will meet Jaurès from the train and stay with him all day."

"That guarantees very little."

"I know, I know. We'll just have to do our best and try to stay one move ahead of the pack, whoever they might be. But in our favor, they don't know we've worked it out."

"*Merde.*"

Raoul's Story

THE CHAMPION OF JUSTICE

Though it may be somewhat immodest to admit it, I looked the part of a man about town. Not overdressed but smart. Monied without flouting it. For once in my life I felt stylish, as if my new clothes cast a charm around me which announced a person of substance. Class even. When I caught a glimpse of myself in the freestanding mirror at the exclusive outfitters in Rue du Faubourg Saint Honore my first thought was, Would that my brother could see me now.

Maurice had insisted that he purchase a stylish suit. "We cannot have the champion of Action française dressed like a working man. You must look the part to be the part." Maurice was clever with words. "Don't worry about anything. Nothing can go wrong. This is your time."

Old apprehensions dared to surface as we approached the outfitters. The attendants would take one look at me, shake their heads, and throw me out onto the street. Surely they could see beyond appearance? Not so. Maurice was greeted like a long lost cousin and we were guided into a private dressing room. He took charge. Two-piece suit, leather shoes, shirt, gloves, and stylish straw hat. I said nothing. I watched it happen around me, distanced from reality. Tape measures flashed with military precision across head, shoulders, waist, calf, and knee. The distance between collar and lower back assumed an importance of surgical acuity. A brief meeting was called to agree how the jacket might hang. Off the peg? Possibly, sir, but that has never been our style. A few adjustments, I think, and we will have precisely what you want. Breathe in. Breathe out. Chest measurement, followed by neck size, produced a perfect shirt. And I simply stood still, like draped royalty in a distant epoch.

"He'll wear it to go." A guardian angel can be so masterful.

A different man strode down Rue du Faubourg. A classier man. A man of outward confidence and determination. A man on a mission.

"A certain gentleman promised you a very special meal today. Follow me." Though I had no recollection of such a promise I did as I was bid, but struggled to keep pace with Maurice. Two brief metro journeys brought us to the high level station on Quai de Grenelle, built on the former tax collection barrier on the left bank of the Seine. Though it was an architectural accomplishment in itself, with cathedral-like arches of renaissance beauty, the traveler's eye rarely dwelt on the station. There was a rival attraction.

"I've never seen the Tower Eiffel from this angle," I conceded. "It's…it's stunning." There before us, in close-up, was the symbol of Paris in a new age, an iconic structure which I had learned to dismiss, simply because it was modern.

"Wait till lunch." Maurice appeared to enjoy the moment. I was calm, confident and composed, as was the instruction.

I lunched in the Eiffel Tower, you know. Just me. On my own. My guardian angel had a number of tasks to complete but booked a table for one under the name Bonhomme. Can't remember what I ate, but it was haute cuisine. Small portions of elegant delicacy. The views were awe-inspiring. So unusual to see Sacré Coeur from this height, stunning in the hot midday sun, whiter than purity itself.

Maurice sat in the cooler gardens below, in the shade of the Champs de Mars, reading L'Echo de Paris. Its front page headlines carried a story about a soldier who had been reprimanded for daring to say that politicians who wanted to return to a mere two years compulsory military service instead of three were either imbeciles or traitors. The second made mockery of a German offer to act as an intermediary between Russia and Austria-Hungary and included a claim that the German army had already mobilized in secret.

"Good news?" I asked hopefully

Maurice folded the newspaper into his pocket and punched me gently on the arm. "Not as good as tomorrow's." His conspiratorial grin was infectious. "Let's walk back along the river. I want to make sure that you fully understand the plan."

It was unbearably hot. Ask anyone about those days at the end of July and they will talk about the heat. We sat by the Seine in the shade of an awning and drank iced orange. Maurice repeated the plan…again.

"Jaurès has returned from Brussels. Did you read about it? Photographed with his arms around the Boches delegate to some socialist conference. Calling on all workers across Europe to go on strike. Bastard has an interview scheduled for this afternoon with the prime minister, but will be back in his office in the evening. You will take revenge on this insult to France by gunning down Jaurès as he stands, just as Madame Caillaux slew poor Calmette. Say nothing. Take both your revolvers. March up to him and fire as many rounds as you can into his body and make good your escape. We will be nearby. The workers will be so shocked that they will rush to him, not you. Down the stairs and into the street. Don't run. Walk smartly across to the metro at Bourse and take the train to Saint-Lazare. We will follow and meet you outside Lazare on the Cour du Rome. Have no fears. We will be with you. Watching."

I had no fears. Fear had left me. I had been born again as a champion of justice.

9

July 31, 1914 – The Last Supper

According to *L'Humanite* the meeting of the International Socialist Bureau in Brussels had not gone well. Representatives simply didn't understand the disastrous abyss over which Europe was teetering. Yes, the assembled leaders had debated what they could do to avert war, but pessimism ruled the day. They were preaching to the converted. The rest of Europe had fallen under the spell of nationalist self-interest. Rosa Luxemburg and Kier Hardie tried to rouse the mass meeting in the evening, but even they struggled. Jean delivered an impassioned speech with his arm extended symbolically around his German colleague's shoulder, insisting that the French wanted peace. A vast crowd of enthusiastic Belgians roared approval.

The train pulled into Gare du Nord just before midday. Mathieu and Pascal stood in the center of the exit from Platform 7 searching every face that passed. Trouble was, almost everyone disembarking was in a rush. Let that train be minutes late and the rush becomes a torrent. Middle-aged lawyers, shirts already damp from the relentless heat, shoved past shop assistants. Matrons with overdressed children tried valiantly to protect their brood. Holidaymakers, slowed by heavy luggage, stopped abruptly to check the city map, unaware that it was upside down. Youths with the strength to do everything at the double dived between fast-paced locals, all heading briskly towards the metro entrance. Nuns, swathed in black robes and white wimples, gathered like giddy sharks in a strange cesspool, feigning any need for help, safe in the knowledge that some good Catholic would come to their aid.

A human tidal wave rushed towards the two policeman, broke either side, and disappeared into the cavernous station. Mathieu tried to hold his head stiff and let his eyes absorb the onrushing passengers. Pascal's head spun from side to side. Was that…? Time and again he thought he had spotted his target, but no. When the rush thinned, an aged residue slowly descended onto the platform, bones creaking silently, the pain of minor ailment and joint erosion, borne with considerable fortitude. Lastly, Jean Jaurès stepped down, laden with packages, briefcase, and assorted papers, his suitcase dragging behind, well-bruised by years of mistreatment. A porter ran to their assistance; man and baggage. Clearly he had been waiting patiently for this hire.

"Monsieur Jaurès, pardon my intrusion," Mathieu interrupted the editor-in-chief and his helper. "We must speak with you." He paused to show his identity card and stressed the immediacy of his quest by adding, "Urgently."

"Do I know you, young man?" He paused to think. "We have met. But where?"

"Sous-lieutenant Mathieu Bertrand, Monsieur. I think we met briefly at the Palais de Justice. The Caillaux trial."

"Ah, the young policeman. I recall now. You were one of the first to give evidence and the only one, let me assure you, who did not use the occasion to promote his own importance. Well done. The rest was an embarrassment to Justice. Shall we sit here?"

Jean Jaurès pointed to an empty bench on the platform. "Tell me, what is this urgency?"

Pascal cleared his throat. He was the senior man and felt the need to assert his status. "Monsieur, we have reason to believe that your life is in danger."

"Ah." Jaurès nodded, and looked beyond them both, as if he had a second sight. "Indeed."

His features unmoved, his passive acceptance of a truth he had known for many weeks, bore no sign of fear. "It is the world we live in, my friends. If I reported every death threat I've received this year alone, little else would be done. Do you know of a particular threat?"

The policemen looked at each other. They had not considered how much they could share.

"Sir," Mathieu made his decision, "I know you will not betray the confidentiality of this information. We have seen a file, an unusual file, which appears to have been created by a person or persons unknown. Could be military, could be political."

"They might even have Russian connections," Pascal Girard interjected.

Jean Jaurès nodded. "Ah, the ubiquitous *they*."

"Whatever and whoever, we believe that they are stalking your every movement. They want you dead." Mathieu looked around as if he might catch an unwary assailant. The platform had emptied.

Jean Jaurès rose to his feet, his dignity intact. The good that Mathieu had read about this man stood before him. He was indeed the peoples' hero, if in want of some personal grooming.

"I know. I know, and I thank you. I cannot run from this." He put his hand on Mathieu's right shoulder and touched his soul. "Yes, I have to live with this possibility every day, but the truth is," and he paused, face saddening, the light in his eyes dimming, "*you* are in far graver danger than I am. Before the week is out we will be at war unless people start to listen and do something about it. Take to the streets. Refuse to obey the call to war, because, when war comes, your generation will be sacrificed. We are all in danger and my death is no less likely than yours."

Mathieu winced. He knew that war was coming, but hadn't considered its consequence. It took Jean Jaurès to do that. They watched him saunter along the platform, talking all the while to the porter as if best friends. At the platform exit he turned back and shouted, "Thank you for your concerns, gentlemen. Take care."

Commander Roux summed up the situation at their Friday morning meeting. Caillaux was still in Paris but out of the public eye. His days in the limelight had gone. Zaharoff was cocooned in his exclusive apartment on Avenue Hoche guarded day and night by his own liveried staff. Doubtless he was wheeling and dealing in the merchandise of death. Good times beckoned. Jean Jaurès was back at work feverishly trying to avert an international disaster. Effectively little had changed.

"Well, that's not quite true. I have been informed from the Élysée Palace that Monsieur Basil Zaharoff has been ennobled today as a Commander of the Legion d'Honneur." Roux almost spat his contempt onto the floor.

"He's not even a real bloody Frenchman!" Dubois stamped his foot in exasperation.

"Naturalized. I told you already." But the chief shared Dubois's annoyance. "Fuck Poincaré. War tomorrow, so let's reward the arms manufacturer today."

Mathieu squirmed. Under normal circumstances no one would have dared swear in the commander's presence, far less swear at the president. "Our problem is Jaurès, and he won't hide behind anything or anyone."

"You're right. Try to stay close to him. We know they have him in their sights. But we don't know who *they* actually are." Roux shrugged his shoulders and opened his arms as if to say, *what else can we do?*

"What did Jaurès call them?" Pascal grimaced. "Ubiquitous? Don't even know what that means."

Roux had contacted Jean Longuet, the sub-editor of Jaurès' newspaper, and insisted that his men accompany Jean Jaurès anywhere outside his office. It didn't take the policemen long to appreciate his talents. Longuet possessed a powerful intellect, which others attributed to his grandfather, Karl Marx. With windswept strands covering a receding hairline, Jean Longuet looked through short-rimmed glasses, down an aquiline nose to a moustache which curved upwards, leaving barely a hint of smiling lips. To the left of his shaven face a minor mole broke the symmetry of his features. What made Longuet different to everyone else on Jean Jaurès team was the political telepathy through which they communicated. And the trust. Jean Longuet told Mathieu over a cup of passable coffee that he worked with *L'Humanitè* so that he could learn from the master himself. Jean Jaurès.

That last day of July was crammed with opportunities for Jaurès to spread his anti-war, anti-militarist gospel. He was the man of the moment, consumed by a single purpose. Stop war. Phone calls had been placed with Prime Minister Rene Viviani who agreed to speak with him in the early evening. Mathieu and Pascal accompanied the two Jeans to the Quai d'Orsay where the editor of *L'Humanitè* begged his prime minister to use his influence to bring pressure on the Russians not to declare war on Germany. If Russia showed restraint, there was yet a chance of peace. Viviani made unspecific promises to try to avoid the coming war, but Jaurès was not deceived.

Mathieu took the opportunity to catch up with Benoit Durfort when Jaurès was with the prime minister despite his dislike of the preening snob.

"Mathieu, what a pleasant surprise. To what do I owe this honor?" Durfort all but stroked Mathieu's hand and smiled his approval with a fawning obsequious gesture which assumed that "his favorite policeman" would sit by his desk. "Coffee?"

"Apologies but I haven't time today. Had to escort Jean Jaurès to see the prime minister and return him home safely."

Durfort's upper lip curled into a scowl like an oily carp which had bitten Mathieu's hook.

"Ah, poor Rene. He is obliged to meet the riff-raff. I hope that Jaurès doesn't upset him. He and Raymond came back from St. Petersburg with such high hopes. We are only days away." He leaned over his desk and lowered his voice lest the furniture hear his scurrilous secret. "The czar has agreed. But keep that to yourself."

"Of course." Mathieu remained on his feet, hands braced on the back of the gilded Louis XIV chair, mind racing. So it would be war.

"Jaurès is wasting his time. Man's a fool and a danger to France. He'll get his comeuppance."

"What do you mean, Benoit? Have you heard … rumors?"

"There are always rumors, my friend." He tapped the side of his right nostril with an over-accentuated flourish, as if he was acting in a Moliere comedy. "But, take my advice. Don't stand too close to the socialist traitor. That might be safer."

The taxi back from Quai d'Orsay weaved its way at top speed through crowded Parisian streets crammed with weekend revelers. Jaurès joked about being killed by the driver, but Jean Longuet thought otherwise. "It won't be the driver, he's a good trade unionist and a socialist. They all are, taxi drivers." That was Paris in a nutshell. The people were either all for you or all against. No one held the middle ground.

Mathieu and Pascal reported back to Bernard Roux who was even more alarmed when he heard what Durfort had said. "I hope you haven't plans for this evening, gentlemen, because we have to be vigilant beyond vigilance."

* * *

The editorial team at *L'Humanitè* was back on duty by eight o'clock with Jaurès at the helm conducting a well-tuned and talented ensemble. He had explained in the taxi earlier that he wanted to make a gesture so powerful that politicians across Europe would be forced to rethink their stated positions. In his head, he imagined a special edition like Emile Zola's famous *J'Accuse* headline which undid the plot to keep Alfred Dreyfus in prison. But how?

"Who's for dinner? Eat first; work later. We need a break. Do you wish to join us, Messieurs?" Jaurès had agreed to Roux's insistence that the police stay close to him for his protection, but insisted that his routine would not be compromised. "I haven't eaten all day."

While technically true, everyone knew that Jean Jaurès had snacked his way through the day. More accurately, he hadn't eaten a proper meal since breakfast. He donned his coat, unnecessary in the heat of the evening, but Jean always dressed properly for dinner. They trooped downstairs to Rue Montmartre and walked two paces into the Café Croissant next door. Allegations that Jaurès had chosen the building to house his newspaper offices because of its proximity to a good restaurant were never fully proven. What did it matter? Mathieu and Pascal stayed out on the humid, heaving street, moving from corner to corner, sometimes together, sometimes on their own, cranking their necks in search of anything suspicious. Unfortunately they had no idea who or what that might be.

Indoors, it was even less comfortable. Though the windows were wide open to any wisp of fresh air, the café's fans could only recycle the humidity. Jaurès led the way and chose the long marble-surfaced table to the left, calling, "Bonne soir, Jules," to the waiter with the familiarity of a long-standing client. There were twelve of them in total, and the editor assumed his usual position in the corner, his back to the window on the street. Le Croissant was their local eating place, a home away from home. None of the regulars paid attention to a group they knew well, a familiar crowd that waltzed in and out all day. The menu was appetizing and reasonably priced. The *Filet de Daurade*, sublime.

Any pretense at bonhomie failed to lighten the somber mood. The gravity of the situation in Europe weighed on them all. On the spirit-stocked wall behind Jules, his pride and joy, a wooden Eruner wall clock with a home-painted image of the Eiffel Tower, ticked ominously towards a point of no return. It was almost 10:40 P.M. Jaurès began to apportion tasks to each listener as they hung on his beautifully deep-carved voice. He threw half-considered ideas across the table.

"Can the English be trusted?"

"No."

"Was Sir Edward Grey genuinely trying to bring opposing forces to peace talks in London?"

"Kier Hardie thinks it's a charade." Jaurès tore at a piece of *petit pain*, unable to wait for his starter. "I'm beginning to think that our best chance rests with Woodrow Wilson in America."

"Can we speak to the American Ambassador?" was the logical question.

"They've just appointed a new man called Sharp, and the former ambassador is eager to get away. Don't know how willing he would be to get involved."

"We have to try every avenue. No pessimism. Not tonight. Contact the ambassador. Ask if I can meet with him tomorrow."

A man rose from his table and approached Jaurès, his hand reaching into an inside pocket.

"Ah, Citizen Dolie," the editor interrupted the gathering to greet a long-time acquaintance who brandished a child's photograph before him. "How perfect. This is a wonderful likeness." Everyone's uncle turned to have a better view of his friend's daughter caught in her red bonnet by one of those new color prints. How proud Monsieur Dolie looked.

"Charming. Is she…"

Raoul's Story

THE ASSASSIN'S CREED

P atience is not my virtue. It never was. I wanted to go immediately and slay the dragon, but I had to wait. They said so.

When I returned to my room I resented the poverty into which I had fallen. A champion should not dwell in the poorer quarter of Rue Leon above a poster-stained tabac. The proprietor was loud and offensive, so I timed my return to avoid his obnoxious ranting that I was behind with the rent. Yes, I had money in my pocket but I was ill-disposed to part with it. Let foul-mouthed Henri Boucher wait. Of course I would pay, as all gentlemen should, but in my own good time.

The room was sparsely furnished. An uncomfortable bed which must have seen service with one of the survivors of Napoleon's Old Guard was propped up against the window. A rudely varnished wardrobe whose front hung open displayed a shirt I washed some days ago and a jacket with threadbare cuffs. The rag on the floor once posed as a rug. Worst of all, the smell from the near-by tannery was overpowering in the heat. Foul, as if a rat had crawled into the skirting boards and died, festering the very air which choked me. I hated that room. How good it would be to leave, never to return. To walk away from the dreary shabbiness of a life worth forgetting and be reborn as a national hero.

I reached for the revolvers. Maurice and Theo had instructed me never to carry guns in the street in daylight. I must wait till later. But there, in the solitary confinement of my cell-like poverty, I retrieved them from behind the wardrobe and stroked the precious cold steel. My proficiency in loading and unloading a revolver is the one skill I learned in my short military career. I took a silver-coated knife, stolen from a kitchen two years ago, and began, mindlessly, to scratch initials on the butt.

I was inspired and started to sing La Marseillaise, softly at first but the power and sense of euphoria I drew from the pistols took control. I became the great tenor Leon Escalais, with the orchestra and choir from L'Opera. Magnificent. Harmonies blended with triumphant horns and vibrant strings. The chorus implored "Marchez, Marchez, Qu'un sang impure." By the glorious third verse, as the anthem peaked, the drum rolls urging the brave legions to die for France, tears burst from my glazing eyes. Heart pumping furiously, I found new meaning in "Tremblez vos projects parricides." Feel fear, you who have murdered our people. Cymbals crashed, feet stamped in time to the military beat. Trumpets burst in clarion call as the entire orchestra pounded with national pride. Eyes closed, I could see the vast tricolor blowing over the Arc de Triumph beckoning me. The bass reverberated, so loud, the room began to shake.

I will do this. I want to do this. For France. For my people. Herr Jaurès must die tonight. Clever, don't you think; Herr Jaurès. Boches-lover? I wanted to do it there and then. I was ready. But I had to wait. The thumping grew louder.

The harmonies were interrupted by a dissonance which had no place in my score. The rhythm broke and I found myself standing in the midst of my shabby room. Henri Boucher was thumping on the ceiling of the tabac below, yelling insults at my patriotism.

"Stop that racket, you cretin. Stop it. Stop."

I would have liked to see Boucher's face in the morning. But what if he stormed up the stairs and caused a scene? A gun in each pocket, I scurried from the tabac, never to return.

I caught the metro. I was early, but time had ceased to matter. Everything paled bar the immediacy of now. Now was the time. I changed lines at Villiers, as instructed, but in my haste stood on the wrong platform and travelled north. Merde. I feared I would be late. Miss my opportunity. Back to Villiers. Changed lines again. It was all too much. Confusing, exhilarating, I knew they would be waiting for me. Worried. They should not have worried. I would never let them down. Ah, Sentier. The flat-roofed electric underground train pulled into my destination and I clambered up the stairs to street level. A maimed veteran offered some flowers, cloth cap drawn over tired face. The cardboard sign by his side claimed that he was a victim of the Boxer Revolt in China, but he looked too young. Industrial accident more likely. I looked back to check if the would-be-vendor had lost both legs and slipped on the edge of the gravel area marked out for pétanque. Quick dust-down. No one saw me, surely. Checked my pockets. Guns intact, I picked up the pace. Don't run. Don't attract attention. I remembered.

Rue Montmartre was crowded. Visitors mingled effortlessly with local tradesmen. Though I was warned not to make eye contact with anyone, I had to ensure that I wasn't walking into a trap. Surely not. It was already well after nine o'clock in the evening, I could see that lights were burning at number 142, inside *L'Humanitè*. I stood for some moments in the refuge of a shop doorway, feeling tension in the atmosphere. Little did these people know that they were by-passers on the edge of history. "I was there," many would claim proudly, as if they had paid for front row seats at L'Opera, not wandered through Montmartre on a Friday night, ignorant of everything that would come to pass.

A face in the crowd turned toward me, eyes sweeping the thoroughfare like a spotlight at sea. I thought I recognized him…but from where? Uncertain, I pressed against the door, not daring to move. That face again? Was it one of the policeman at the Palais de Justice? A detective? No. Couldn't be. I was surely imagining shadows. Even so, I waited fully five minutes and crossed the street into L'Humanitè's offices without raising my head. Madam Pernaud, the concierge, was brushing the stairs. She made no move to let me past.

"Yes? Can I help?" She was the stout gate-keeper, and reveled in her power to control.

I froze. I must admit I always had difficulty in dealing with assertive women. Always.

"Can I help?" Her tone was more like a final demand.

"Ehm, Monsieur Jaurès?"

"Yes?"

"Can I speak with him please?"

"Not here, Monsieur,"

"Pardon?"

"He's gone for dinner. Don't know when he will be back."

She had dealt with hundreds of interlopers over the years. It was no contest. Brush in hand, chins bulging, bosom raised in defiance, she glared at me with a look that said, Thou shall not pass.

I backed into the street and turned towards the Rue Croissant. Such a tourist-trap name, Rue Croissant. I glanced at the café-restaurant next door and stopped breathing. Jaurès was sitting there, at the open window, his back turned away from the crowd outside. Head bowed, I walked on for fifty meters, hands in pocket, disinterest personified. How had I managed to miss the devil-incarnate sitting in the window like a prize exhibit. I knew that this was it. This was the moment. Now. Now or never. A flood of adrenalin surged through me, defying resistance. I felt the gun in my left hand warm to the touch. It was ready, too. Go. Five steps, draw gun and…

The noise ricocheted from every angle of Rue Montmartre and Rue Croissant like a cannonade in an echo chamber. I ran.

10

July 31st-August 1, 1914 – The Death of Reason

Mathieu was on his feet faster than the first fluttering pigeon. His iron-backed chair bounced on the pavement, shocked to find itself abandoned to such violence. The crowd's collective attention began to turn down Montmartre in slow-motion surprise, but the only words he heard were his own.

"*Non. Non. Non.*"

He and Pascal had been sitting at a café-bar on the corner of Rues Saint-Marc and Feydeau, still taking turns to amble down Montmartre every ten minutes to ensure that no known undesirables were hanging around. It was a hopeless task. The narrow old streets were thronged with weekend tourists, holidaymakers, city-dwellers, and rural visitors. It was a time of youth and pleasure. Bars and cafés jostled to accommodate the crowds who had come to eat and drink-in the atmosphere. Paris glowed with the health of nations. Alive. Exuberant. Noisy. Full of its own importance. To be in Paris was to be at the center of culture, style, and all that was new. Unless, of course, you survived in the thankless shadows of society's underclass. But who cared about them?

In the midst of this tumult they were more on duty than on guard, lulled into the boredom of resignation that assumed they had wasted their day and their time; that nothing would happen. Jean Jaurès had been seated in Café Croissant for more than an hour and not one person had noticed him. Over the years he had grown to be part of Montmartre, one of her sons. There he sat in the bosom of his adopted mother, enjoying her patronage, nurtured by her many blessings, until…

Both shots shattered the back of Jean Jaurès' head and blew the world asunder. He was thrown violently forward onto the table as the window space exploded behind him. No last farewell. No longer *L'Humanitè*. His disciples were aghast. The shock of disbelief was followed by confusion, screams of horror, and gasps of piercing pain. Panic filled the café and spilled into Montmartre. Inside and out, the moment made no sense.

Jaurès' defiled body had been thrown onto the marble tabletop, untidily set, bathed in lingering stench of cordite. Incredulous, his colleagues tried desperately to make good the irreparable damage. A sub-editor grabbed a handful of serviettes to soak up the blood as if it could be poured back into his friend. Droplets of grey matter began to slip down the table leg to the floor. A doctor rushed to Jean's side, his hands trembling, the savagery marking him for life. He hesitated to touch the statesman's neck in search of a lost pulse but found none. He shook his head in sorrow.

"Gentlemen, Monsieur Jaurès is dead."

All hope evaporated, though in truth there was never hope. The great man had been murdered in cold blood before their very eyes. Transfixed in misery, someone began to sob, so deeply, so passionately, so honestly, that the table shook. Within seconds the sobs reached biblical proportions. The enormity was utterly incomprehensible.

Though those around the table had frozen in horror, one of the company's print workers, Robert Tissier, was standing by the door. Nicknamed "the greyhound," Tissier had been a member of one of the Paris gymnastic clubs in the 1880s where his prowess as a sprinter meant that the mainly bourgeois members tolerated his inclusion in their well-heeled ranks. He looked like a greyhound, grey of head and still sleek of body. His fellow workers were frequently annoyed by the rate at which he constructed a flawless print plate. Speed pumped though his veins. Even at work he needed to run between machines as if the hand of time was eternally set against him. When the gunshots rocked Café Croissant, he reacted like it had been a staring pistol and was first into the street, walking-stick in hand. Mathieu charged towards the screams from the direction of Saint-Marc, but the assassin was already on the run. Others joined the pursuit and the gunman fired a third bullet in their general direction. No one flinched. The runner had memorized the escape route dictated to him by his guardian angels, and dropping the revolver from his right hand, he charged towards the metro station on *Bourse*, down Rue Reaumur and across the side street at Rue Leon-Cladel. The killer tried to increase his stride but his new shoes caught on the uneven cobbles. He slipped as he reached the corner and Tissier was upon him. One swipe of the walking stick disabled the assassin's left knee and he collapsed.

"*Bâtard lâche*, you cowardly bastard." Howls of anguish rocked the wary cobbles.

Mathieu, barely a second behind, pushed Tissier away and stood over the prostrate body, arms outstretched trying to reason with a wolf pack set to rip out the murderer's throat.

"Stand back. Police. We've got him, we've got him. Back, I said." A flurry of kicks were directed towards the gunman, but with Mathieu obstructing the prone body, few hit their target.

"He's killed Jean. Killed Jean Jaurès."

"Shot him in the back. The greatest man in France."

Mathieu hauled the assailant roughly to his feet. Where were the reinforcements?

"Murderer!" a worker screamed into the assassin's face, spittle projecting with venomous intent.

"Cowardly fucking murderer." Other voices threatened instant retribution.

The policeman dragged his quarry towards boulevard Reaumur where the streetlight offered a moment's respite. Anonymity melted under the bright lamps, but with the crowd incensed, they did not care. Blind anger fueled the fires of an unreasonably hot night.

Captain Pascal Girard was the oldest man in the prefecture. Neither the brightest nor the most convivial, but experienced and streetwise. He had not followed Mathieu towards the gunshots, but turned in the opposite direction. Pascal grabbed two gendarmes who had been watching the crowds from the opposite end of Rue Montmartre, aware that something had happened further down the street. He flashed his identity card and spoke with the authority it carried.

"Find a telephone, call Commander Roux of the Mobile Police unit, and tell him what's happened."

"What?"

"Jean Jaurès has been shot." He swung round to the other and shouted, "Get into the van and drive like France depends on it."

"*Bourse*," he rasped in annoyance when the gendarme looked at him blankly. The streets of Paris were imprinted in Pascal's brain. He calculated the probabilities of an escape route and followed his instinct. "Get onto Rue Reaumur as fast as you can. Officer in pursuit of possible murderer." The police wagon swung onto the tree lined boulevard beside the Bourse and Pascal Girard smiled to himself. "Clever boy. Got them under the street light." The wagon braked to a screeching halt beside the assailant and the policeman, still fending off the screaming mob. From the baying crowd, someone handed Mathieu a gun.

"He threw it away."

"Thanks, Monsieur. I'll…" But whoever it was, disappeared.

The crowd continued to gather around them, outraged at the news. Some had seen Jaurès' lifeless body though the café window and sought instant retribution. The captive was hauled into the van without ceremony and driven from immediate danger. Once inside, his attitude rapidly changed. Was it self-pity? Mathieu held him tight in an arm lock, aware of his own anger, part directed at his prisoner, and partly at himself. If only he had stayed close to Café Croissant. An alternative world can be built on *if only.*

"You don't have to hold me so hard. I'm not going to run away," the murderer complained.

Pascal had an urge to slap him hard. So he did. The prisoner's response surprised them.

"Would you take the revolver from my left pocket, please. It might go off."

Startled, the two policemen held him down and Pascal removed a second gun.

Helpless, the disbelieving diners in Café Croissant stared at their lifeless friend in the horror of real time. He was no more. Taken from them in mid-sentence, the violence of his murder so extreme that reality turned to absurdity in a flash. Forlorn hope numbed the room. Then the clamor from the street poured in though the open window and cries of indignation and disgust filled the room. An unforgivable crime had been committed in their presence. There was no way back. No alternative ending to the tragedy. A debilitating paralysis followed the shock. What to do? What would Jean Jaurès have done?

"My friends," the depute editor's voice rose above his ever-loyal comrades, "we have a paper to print." His voice broke, his bravery challenged by a bursting heart. He tried again and found the words. "Clear the front page: we have a tribute like no other to construct. The government ignored him in life. We can still make them listen through his death." Brave words. They needed to hear brave words but in the hearts and minds of each of his colleagues Jean Jaurès' legacy became their most treasured possession. A man had been killed, but his ideal could live on. They could make that happen, surely? The details, every moment of the dastardly event filled the pages of the morning edition of *L'Humanitè*. The front page of for 1st August 1914 read **Jaurès Assassiné**, and all hell was let loose.

Commander Roux reached the police station before the wagon swung into the courtyard and instantly doubled the guard. He knew that Jaurès' assassination would already be widely known. Only the plague spread faster than bad news.

"Bring him into the interrogation room immediately, and keep outsiders away."

Raoul Villain was shoved into the cramped space they called a room. It was as sparse as his own above the tabac. Probably little more than two cells knocked into one. He stood before Bernard Roux and raised his head. Was that defiance or resignation? They would soon find out.

"Sit down on that chair," Commander Roux ordered, asserting his status. The words really meant *I am in charge and you will do as I say.*

The assassin cut an unexpected figure. Tall, blond, and elegantly dressed, he looked like a dancer at the *Moulin de la Galette*. His carefully groomed moustache, short-cut hair, expensive suit, pleated shirt with collar and cuffs, straw hat, and polished shoes placed him in a league of upper-class gentlemen. His possessions included two nickel-plated revolvers. The first he had thrown away during the chase; the second, of course, he had surrendered. Sixty-five francs were found inside his jacket pocket, but no wallet. Nothing in his appearance fitted with the image the Tigres had expected.

"Name?" Roux howled directly into the suspect's face, causing him to shudder.

He coughed and bowed his head. "Raoul Villain."

Dubois punched him in the ribs. "Don't get fresh. What is your proper surname."

"Villain."

The commander intervened. "Leave that for now. Tell me what happened tonight?"

A sense of self-assuredness raised itself into his reply. "I killed Jaurès. I slew the enemy of France." He made it sound like David versus Goliath.

Roux nodded encouragingly. "How did you do this?"

"I saw him in the café at the open window and killed him."

"Explain how. Precisely how."

Villain appeared to grow in confidence, as if he was beginning to enjoy the audience. "I saw Jaurès through the open window, moved aside the curtain with my left hand, and fired two shots at him with the revolver in my right hand." So cold; so precise.

"Why?"

Villain had not expected to explain such an obvious question. "We have to punish traitors."

"Ah, so who was with you?"

"Pardon?"

"You said 'we.' You certainly did not do this on your own, monsieur. Who else was there?"

Villain took stock. His face betrayed confusion. Guy Simon slipped into the room and stood behind Raoul Villain. He had the pistols in his hand, but only his colleagues could see them. The interrogation continued unabated.

"And in a crowded street, you had time to carefully move the window curtain before shooting the unarmed man in the back of the head? No one saw you. No one shouted a warning?" Mathieu ought not to have interrupted, but the chief kept his gaze firmly fixed on Raoul Villain.

They tried a frontal team attack.

"If you had to move the curtain, how did you recognize the back of Jaurès' head?

"Where did you purchase the guns?" Guy added. "Nickel-plated, I see. Expensive, eh?

"Is that a new suit?"

"Where were you running to?"

"What was your plan of escape?" Questions were fired with such rapidity that Villain's head spun round in shock. His face betrayed his confusion. Suddenly, he wasn't so sure of himself. Mathieu watched the assassin try to steady himself as if he realized for the first time that he was on the point of stepping into a trap.

"Were you told to say nothing?"

Alarm visibly registered, eyes widened, brow furrowed as if to ask, *My God, can you read my mind?*

Roux softened his voice reassuringly. "Were you given instructions, Raoul? Were you forced to do this?"

His eyes darted from Roux to Dubois and then Mathieu, while inside his head he struggled to find an answer. You could almost hear him trying to work it out. *They're being nice to me. Be careful.*

Dubois picked up the wad of notes which had been taken from Villain's jacket. "Where did you get these francs from?" Again the silence of confusion.

"Do you know how much money you have in your pocket?" Girard asked. It was a simple question.

"No, er, yes, of course. Yes."

"Which?" Everyone in the room knew that had the commander left, Dubois would have resorted to the straightforward process of beating the truth out of him. Instead, Bernard Roux repeated

"You said that you were given instructions?"

Though he had refused to answer the question previously, Villain's reaction was edged with panic. "No, No."

The commander repeated his question "Who gave you instructions? You said you were given instructions." The commander's voice was raised. Angrier, ever more assertive.

The prisoner swung round shaking his head vehemently. "No, I didn't. I meant that I know how much money I have."

"And how much is that?" Dubois closed his fist round the notes, forming them into a paper knuckle-duster.

"Em," Villain struggled to remember, "six …"

"…hundred?"

"Less. Much less. Not six hundred."

"Where did you buy your revolvers?" Guy Simon planted a firm hand on his shoulder. Villain shuddered. The interrogation never broke stride.

"A suit from Hermes, or is that a fake label?" Mathieu observed with apparent interest. "We'd all love to have enough money to buy our clothes at Hermes."

Dubois leaned forward and roared, "How much have you spent today?"

The commander pursued his own line. "Who forced you to do this?"

"You are a member of Action française." The captain drew the statement from the ether. It blindsided Villain and punctured what was left of his bravado.

"Yes. Why wouldn't I be? It's not illegal, is it?"

It was the manner in which he admitted the fact which struck them all forcibly, almost as if they found the link he had been denying.

"You know people in Action française? Important people?" Mathieu slowed the pace down to calm the assassin.

Villain's confusion ran ahead of his capacity to think. "They didn't tell me what to do. I did it myself."

"So who did, Raoul? You can tell us. Who put you up to killing Jean Jaurès for France?"

"I don't know names …"

The door burst open and the assistant prefect of police stormed in. All except Villain stood to attention, as shocked as they were surprised. God's right hand man had descended once more from on high and stood once more in their presence. He glared, not at Villain, but at the commander.

"I was told you were bringing him to headquarters. In fact, you were instructed to," he shouted angrily, flecks of spittle flying in all directions. His jowls shook in uncoordinated fashion as if trying to catch up with the rest of his face. "You appear to think that you can do as you like, Monsieur Roux. Well you can't."

Roux shrugged in apparent surprise. "Dear me, my apologies." His lack of sincerity was obvious. "I suspect that there has been a failure in communications. Were you aware of this, Captain Girard?"

"No, Sir. Bertrand and I simply brought him to the nearest police station. Here. For protection, Sir."

Assistant Prefect Guichard looked contemptuously in their direction and sneered. "Well, he's coming with me. Right now. Immediately." The commander didn't even blink.

Raoul Villain did not know whether to object or go quietly, but was glad that the interrogation had been interrupted. He needed more time to think.

"You. Out," was Guichard's two word instruction to him. "And I'll take your notes on the interrogation. This is politically sensitive. The minister will want to read these." He scooped up all of the paperwork. "Whatever has been said in this room falls under privileged information, and must not be subject to further discussion." He turned on Bernard Roux and scowled. "I will be in touch in the morning."

"Very good, Sir." Each word was punctuated with an implied insolence. There was no likelihood that the chief would allow himself to be patronized. He, too, knew people in high places. The door slammed shut, and the Tigers sat in silence. Rank would hold its sway.

"Damnation, we almost had him." Roux kicked the wall behind him in exasperation. "Look everyone, I know it's late but spend the next ten minutes putting every word you can remember on paper. Legally, we are allowed to keep our own records."

"No need," said Mathieu, picking up his own very detailed notes from under the table. "He said, and I clearly heard him, that he wanted all the notes on the table. Mine were on my knee. It's how I take notes. They fell to the floor when I stood up."

"Tut tut." Bernard Roux smiled.

"He didn't ask for these, either." Guy Simon took a pair of nickel-plated revolvers from behind his back. "I, ehm, was examining evidence when we were interrupted. This one, the Smith and Wesson, has been fired twice."

The guns were placed on the table for all to see. Pascal picked one up as if it was delicate crystal. "Look at the butt. He has carved the letter C into its surface." He checked the second. It, too, had been marked, this time with a J.

"Jesus Christ?" asked Mathieu.

Roux shook his head. "Try Jaurès and Caillaux."

"Jaurès and Caillaux. Member of Action française. Has lots of money, but doesn't know how much. The bloody suit was from Hermes. And he did it alone? No way." Pascal's frustration was clear.

Bernard Roux agreed. "We will have to get to the bottom of this immediately. Time is the enemy."

The door crashed open again and a gendarme interrupted in a much more respectful manner. "Excuse me, chief. You have an urgent call from a Lieutenant Dubois."

"*Merde.* Zaharoff." Bernard Roux almost ran to the telephone. "Dubois, what's happened? Has Zaharoff been shot, too?"

"Chief? This is bizarre. Twenty minutes ago a squadron from Army Headquarters appeared out of the dusk and surrounded the building. I went out to ask what they were doing and was promptly arrested. ME! Arrested! We were ordered to leave the car at gunpoint. Gunpoint."

Paul Dubois was clearly upset. "I tried to show them my police credentials. Not interested. Then more armed men arrived. Looked like a special team. They overpowered the valet at the door. He put up a fair struggle and about a minute later they were back outside. The avenue has been cordoned off. Residents have been told to stay inside. What the hell is going on?"

"Calm down, Dubois. Take a long slow look at everything around you and phone me back in five minutes."

"We've been ordered out," Dubois spluttered.

Roux put down the phone and took a moment to think. The others had followed him into the corridor for enlightenment.

"Zaharoff's residence has been surrounded by a squad from Army HQ. Why?"

"Tip off? He's a target for the left-wing. And now they know that Jaurès has been assassinated." Pascal tried to put together pieces of this complex jigsaw puzzle.

"Why is this foreigner so important that the prime minister makes him a member of the Legion d'Honneur, Grand Croix, no less, and then decides that he has to have more personal protection than any other citizen in France?"

Mathieu knew. "It's war, my friends. And he is the merchant of death. Citizen Zaharoff."

"No one's put a bullet in his head, then." Pascal was tired of the nonsense.

"Dubois will not be pleased," Guy Simon guessed.

"Oh, he isn't. I forgot to say, they arrested him." The commander was beginning to appreciate the humor in the occasion.

"What for?" Pascal Girard was incredulous.

"Being Dubois?"

"Fair enough."

They trooped out, tired and in need of sustenance. Bar Clichy would still be open at this time of night. They deserved a drink.

"Chief, a moment, please." Mathieu was examining the Smith and Wesson, mindful that it had been handed to him in the dark. "Guy says it has been fired twice, and so it has. But I've a problem with that."

"Yes?"

"Villain, or whatever his real name is, fired three shots."

THE LOYAL SON OF FRANCE

Anxiety raised its ugly fears and swam in the darkness of doubt. Every night. I began to hate the night. It was a time ill at ease with itself so that thoughts took free reign and refused to be called to heel. So much to remember. So many instructions on what not to do. And doubt is a subtle enemy. It requires no reason or proof. What if they let me down? What if I'm left high and dry, alone? What if I cannot do this? Why, in the middle of the night, do we revisit old doubts? Before, I was certain. Afterwards...

The police were nasty. Trying to trip me up. Trying to put words in my mouth. So sly. Insisting that I was instructed to kill Jaurès. That is a lie. I said I would kill him, and Caillaux, and I am half way there. One out of two. The man who led the rebellion against a three year military service, the man who voted against our president going to Russia last week, Herr Jaurès, is dead.

And I have a new friend. Such a surprise. When the assistant prefect climbed into the back of the police van and instructed the others to leave us alone, I thought he was going to beat me to death. But no. He leaned into me and whispered, "Did you give them any names? Charles needs to know."

Charles? He knew Charles. He had links to Charles...Assistant Prefect Guichard was one of US! Who would have thought?

"Nnnno, no. Nnno names. I've told them nothing." I was shaking. Must have been the heat.

"Good." He patted me on the shoulder. "Take me through your instructions."

"No names. Did it myself."

"Right?" He wanted to hear more. "What about the clothes and the money?"

This worried me. "They've asked awkward questions about the money."

"Say you found the money in the street and you were going to hand it in but spent a little on some new clothes. Don't worry. You are protected. You have many friends, and they are already very pleased with you."

He took me by the shoulders and looked directly into my eyes. That confused me. I didn't know whether he was going to throttle me or kiss both my cheeks.

"You did it. You took out Jaurès. Do you have any idea how jubilant they are in the Ministry? In the president's office? In the prime minister's? In the Russian embassy? You have dared to remove, by clinical means, the one remaining obstacle to war. You. Raoul Villain, the hero. All of France will soon know who you are."

I hadn't thought of that. All of France? Including my father?

"Do you think that you could warn my father before he reads about this in the papers. He gets very anxious at times, and I think he will be angry if I don't warn him. He lives in Reims."

"Yes, yes. I'll see to it later tonight. But first you have to listen to me very carefully. You will be interrogated by a commissioner. Not one of us, so you must say nothing. And when I say nothing, I mean nothing. Answer no questions. If they ask you your name. Nothing. If they raise any of the points that were discussed tonight, say nothing. Understand?"

"I think so."

"Look. It is very simple. Act dumb. Recognize no one. Give the court reason to believe that you are a complete simpleton. All of your records have been altered. School, army, college, work, visits abroad, everything. You will say nothing. If it appears that your advocate is making a fool of you, forget it. We are all part of the same team. To save you, we can call on hundreds of loyal citizens who will swear blind that you are not in control of your senses.

That wasn't much consolation. What did it mean, not in control of my senses? Why should a hero be protected by lies?

"But…"

"Charles says that if you stray form the chosen path, all will be lost. Are you the savior of France or just a wastrel?"

"No, Charles knows I am a loyal son of France."

"Then you must act like one."

"I will."

I promised…and I did. The police wagon stopped on a corner and the assistant prefect took his leave with a stiff salute in my direction. His grim face had lost all personality. He had turned back into a pillar of society. I was passed on to another officer, rougher and less educated. The assistant prefect never spoke to me again. He died at Verdun, I was later informed.

96

11

AUGUST 1, 1914 –
UNANSWERED QUESTIONS

Afalse dawn broke over Paris that Saturday morning. Mathieu slept fitfully in the wake of the late night tragedy, saddened more than angry. He rose wondering if he had slept at all. Yet another cloudless sky promised opportunities to come, but he knew that darker horizons swirled in the stratosphere. The streets were almost empty. A pretense of calm rested over the city after a night of miserable tension. The world seemed to hold its breath. The birds had not risen to announce the day. Perhaps they knew that peace was an illusion; that this new day held no promise.

First into the office, Mathieu took the opportunity to review the notes from the previous evening. What worried him most was a feeling that the facts had already been compromised. The assistant prefect's sudden arrival had taken everyone by surprise; everyone save the commander.

It was evident now that Roux had rushed to interrogate Villain because he knew that other government agents would react fast. Fresh reports had been compiled during the night and left on the commander's desk. Such rapid intelligence smelled of careful preparation. Villain was a member of Action française. Mathieu had assumed that. One source claimed that he was also a member of the Camelots du Roi, the thugs who organized mob violence in Paris. Hardly likely. He had given himself up too easily. Army records all stamped and dated showed that he had been discharged from the 94th infantry in Bar-le-Duc in 1907, and a police file recorded that before his military service he was considered a very serious young man. Villain had been educated by the Jesuits. His school diploma ranked him in the top twenty students out of forty-four. He had visited London, Athens, and Ephesus in the Ottoman Empire. He had lived in Paris for the last four years. Where? It didn't say. His source of income? Nothing. So Raoul Villain was well educated, well-travelled, and of religious disposition. One report inferred that Raoul Villain was an imbecile, slow of mind, enfeebled. Interesting. When was that profile concocted? No date.

No signature. But Mathieu recognized the quality of the paper. He felt its smoothness. Was this from the prime minister's office, the War Office, or Quai d'Orsay? Nothing made sense. New clothes, two revolvers, cash in his pocket. Villain could not have been acting on his own. Mathieu studied his notes again. The final lines read:

"*They didn't tell me what to do? I did it myself.*"

prompted – "*I don't know names…* "

Villain's version of events in Montmartre was not credible. He was not alone. Never.

Mathieu was summoned to the phone downstairs by the duty officer. "It's the boss. He's at headquarters. Wants to speak to you."

"Chief?" He was puzzled.

"Sous-lieutenant Bertrand, I require your attendance here immediately." His voice was strangely officious.

"At HQ?"

"Yes. And bring all the notes you made last night. All of them. Is that clear, Bertrand? Problems."

Something was up. Roux's final word was almost a whisper. The charade of apparent anger was no more than playacting. Someone else was in that room. Someone else was listening. Mathieu could sense trouble.

Bernard Roux stood at the entrance to the prefecture in Isle de la Cite, agitated, despite the Gauloises—clearly unhappy. The sentries in their guard boxes hardly glanced in his direction. Why provoke a prowling senior officer? Flicking his cigarette stub to the ground, he pushed Mathieu back into the taxi as soon as it arrived so that no one outside could hear.

"General Messimy knows that I colluded in withholding evidence. I don't know how. Celestin Hennion also knows, but is on our side. Something ugly is happening, but do NOT contradict Messimy. Remember who he is. Oh, and that asshole Guichard is upstairs, too, trying to look important. Humor him."

So the minister of war and the prefect of police were waiting along with Assistant Prefect Guichard, whose instructions he had chosen to ignore. Felt like judge, jury, and firing squad had gathered for some live sport. Mathieu found it difficult to keep pace with Roux as they climbed the elegant Louis-Napoleon stairs. If he was dismissed, there would be plenty of vacancies in the army soon. He tried to console himself, but there was little joy in his strained black humor.

They were ushered into the luxury of nineteenth century imperial France. The second floor reception room was more of a grand hall than an office. It boasted vast, mirrored, and finely papered walls with luscious purple drapes which reflected the excesses of that time. At the far end, close to a marble fireplace, a huddle of high-level influence listened carefully to instructions. Before them on a lacquered table lay an array of plans which were being shoved around the flawless surface.

"For that reason," the larger central figure spoke not to his comrades, but to the room, "we have to remain one step ahead. Communication centers have to be policed. I want subtlety, not brute force. Unity is the order of the day. Keep promoting the president's new mantra. This is a sacred union of all Frenchmen forged to protect France."

Bernard Roux and Mathieu stood in silence until the prefect of police realized that his men were present.

"Ah, commander, and this is Sous-lieutenant Mathieu Bertrand, formerly of Marseilles, I understand." He beckoned me forward as if I was being presented at the Royal Court.

"May I introduce General Adolphe Messimy, minister of war, a gentleman whose immense importance in this moment of national crisis cannot be overstated."

The general turned his attention towards the policeman as if he was inspecting an errant corporal from his own regiment. Formally dressed, with high collared shirt and deep blue tie, he looked more like a bank manager than minister of war. A shiny black bowler hat sat on the table, upturned, with leather gloves peering over the edges. Sparse hair failed to cover a wide dome which had not required a comb for many years. His half-moon glasses stared over a good sized nose, but there was a sparkle in his eyes which defied his apparent abruptness. His huge handle-bar moustache had been carefully waxed that morning but would likely require further attention as the day progressed. Military men never consider themselves out of uniform even when dressed in a morning suit.

"Citizen Bertrand, you appear to have become quite a personality in a very short time. First you arrest Henriette Caillaux, and then you apprehend the assassin Raoul Villain. One such foray into the limelight ought to have been sufficient. Two in five months is immoderate." He enjoyed his own witticism. "You have brought us a missing document, I understand." His hand extended to accept the file. "What compelled you to disobey Assistant Prefect Guichard's instruction?"

"Stupidity, Sir." He held the general's eye and then looked down, submissively.

"Ah," Messimy almost smiled, "I see a great deal of that all around me, every day, present company excluded, of course." He read Mathieu's scribblings in silence.

"You have underlined the words *'I don't know names'* several times. Why?"

Silence.

From nowhere, Mathieu heard himself say, "I was unconvinced by the prisoner's ramblings, Sir."

The General paused briefly and smiled. "Excellent, perfectly excellent. Well done, young man." Messimy snapped shut the file and nodded his dismissal. He turned to Hennion.

"Yes, Celestin, that one has a future."

"Sir?" Assistant Prefect Guichard failed to grasp the general's conclusion.

"Did you not hear? He says that Villain was rambling. Of course he was. Off his head. No inference of others involved. The officer has clearly informed us that Raoul Villain was rambling. Mad as a lunatic in the Bicêtre asylum. Probably end up there. Thank you, gentlemen. That is reassuring. Brings closure to any further consideration of the matter."

The assistant prefect glared in Mathieu's direction like a hawk whose prey had scurried down a rabbit hole. Too bad. The judge, having misconstrued the evidence, had declared Mathieu's innocence. The jury concurred and the firing squad stood down, disappointed, and marched into the velvet curtains. As Mathieu and the commander reached the gilded door, General Messimy had an afterthought. He fixed a warning in Mathieu's direction.

"A moment, young man. This is no place for disobedience. Especially now. Disobey *me*, and I will have you shot; and if it is for stupidity, I'll shoot you myself."

Roux picked up his pace as they descended the staircase, urging Mathieu to move faster. His body language said only one thing. Gauloises. Now.

"You know I didn't mean …" Mathieu got no further.

"I know. Of course you didn't mean to infer what the general has said. But believe me it would have been a stroke of genius if you had. The powers that be want this to go away, at least for the moment, and now that you have corroborated their version of events, it will."

Their taxi slowed to a halt behind a lame horse whose cart was laden with barely edible vegetables. Under the relentless heat they would be useless by lunchtime.

"We have a problem."

"I'm sorry?"

Roux interrupted once more. "Not you, idiot boy, not you. Someone in the prefecture told Guichard about your notes. He tried to berate me earlier, before the general arrived. He began with the phrase, 'I am informed that...' No one outside that interrogation room knew you still had your notes. If he was informed, it was from the inside. Not me. Not you. This leaves us with the embarrassment of suspecting Simon, Dubois, or Girard."

"Surely not." Mathieu was unconvinced. "Surely not."

They sat in silence as the taxi edged past the stricken cart horse. "What did you make of the interview?" mused Roux.

"There was one item on Messimy's agenda. He wanted to know if we intended to investigate Raoul Villain further. To pursue our belief that he did not act alone."

"Correct. Hennion told me that the government was caught out by the murder last night. They knew Jaurès was in danger, but not that the assassin would strike so quickly. At one stage the president and prime minister considered recalling three cavalry divisions from the border regions in case the workers took to the streets today. Someone steadied their nerves. Not certain who. Might have been that Russian ambassador or one of the other real power-brokers. In the end Poincaré decided to keep some cavalry in reserve, and use the press to tell their version of the story first. Have you read today's paper?"

"No."

Bernard Roux took *L'Humanitè* from inside his jacket and handed it to Mathieu. "Bottom of the fourth column, front page."

Printed there was an open letter to Jean Jaurès' wife.

"Why did the president of the republic send Madame Jaurès a letter of condolence in the middle of the night?" It made no sense to Mathieu.

"In which he urges national unity, please note," Roux added, thinking aloud. "And have it delivered to the newspapers in time for publication this morning. And why make it public?

"He wants to keep the socialists on-side. United against Germany." Mathieu tried to help.

Roux nodded rhythmically. "Understandable of course. But his speed is almost indecent."

"Neither the Élysée Palace nor Quai d'Orsay are noted for quick responses to anything. That I have learned in my short career." Mathieu had

101

watched the diplomatic corps take twenty minutes over a decision on whether or not to have coffee. "Do you think they prepared this statement in advance? Ready for the event because they expected Jaurès' assassination?"

Bernard Roux looked straight ahead towards the river, letting the question hang like rotten meat in an abandoned abattoir. "Look at the next letter. From the prime minister. Note that it is to be copied and printed on official posters all over France today."

Mathieu concentrated. Tried to put any quick conclusions to one side. To see the flaw in his chief's unspoken accusation. But it was Prime Minister Viviani's letter which provided the evidence of state collusion: *The assassin has been arrested. He will be punished. Have confidence in the law. Stay calm and united.*

"It's official, then. The assassin. Singular. Raoul Villain. No one else. They have not only decided that the prisoner is guilty, but that he is a lone wolf."

Roux shook his head disconsolately. "The people of France have been informed that there is no need for further investigation. That's what it's all about. They have effectively closed down any discussion on Jean Jaurès' murder. No need for further investigation."

"And our notes on Villain before Guichard burst into the room?" Mathieu need hardly have asked.

"Gone forever. As will we be if we continue our inquiries, and all on the same front page which carries the first news of the great man's death."

"Can they do that?" Mathieu's question betrayed an innocence as yet unshed.

"They already have, and you will be quoted as having said that Villain is a rambling imbecile. According to the minister of war, you confirmed in the presence of the prefect of police, his assistant, and your own commander, that Raoul Villain is an imbecile. And everyone agreed."

Mathieu closed his eyes and wished he was somewhere else.

Guy Simon burst into the office at half past four in high excitement, brandishing a wad of yellow public notices. "Just been delivered … we've to ensure that they are plastered over every public place, railway station, street corner, and theatre." He held out a large poster from the Ministry of War announcing, GENERAL MOBILIZATION. All reservists are to be called up, starting tomorrow.

Mathieu could hardly pretend surprise. He had heard part of Messimy's discussion that morning, but the miserable deception annoyed him. Germany, threatened by the massive Russian mobilization on its eastern border, was on the point of declaring war against the czar. It was a carefully orchestrated trap. If Germany moved against Russia, France would support its ally in St. Petersburg. If the kaiser waited, the Russians would be upon Berlin before his armies could be mustered. What else could he do? The president had just come back from Russia. His bags were barely unpacked, but he insisted categorically that the subject of war had not been discussed. Liar. In his eyes, there was surely never a better chance to crush Germany. It beggared belief… Jaurès, not cold in his grave, and the war he tried so hard to oppose, became unstoppable. Did no one sense a connection?

They did not.

The Clichy Café-Bar was alive with jubilation. Guy was genuinely happy. Happy? He was ecstatic. Such a change from the comparative calm when the commander had first told them all that war was coming.

"The Russians will take them from the east and we will drive in from the west. The race for Berlin has started." He danced around the floor like an overexcited Dervish.

"Tell you what, I'm not going to miss this. I am going to be there." Guy's beer sloshed onto the carpeting as he raised his glass to *la victoire*. The lounge responded with the blind excitement of untested youth. Cheers and bonhomie filled their jars. The ensemble gave voice to a passionate rendition of *La Marseillaise*. Men bellowed their patriotism from atop the tables, standing rigid to attention hats in one hand, glasses in the other. Protest was useless. Waiters garnished the presentation with a hearty two-part harmony.

Bernard Roux sipped his cognac and tried to find hope in his heart; joy was impossible. He knew enough to doubt conventional wisdom.

"You do know that the Germans will be no pushover. I lived through the war of 1870 . It was just like this at the start." He recalled the initial hysteria. It had died along with hundreds of thousands of Frenchmen. Did no one remember?

Mathieu looked deep into his beer, but found no consolation. Agnès saw the sadness in his face from across the room and read the pain as if it were written in longhand. She pushed her way closer to his side.

"Why?" was her first question. "What are they doing to us?

Her presence warmed him instantly. He gazed into her soft features and wanted to be lost in her spirit. Here was goodness and common sense. He had lived in a world of men since he came to Paris, a world of intrigue and petty jealousies, of politics and dishonesty yet with Agnès he felt he could leave that aside. They had both recognized something different in each other, but the few months of their brief encounter had left their feeling to smiles, nods, occasional pleasantries, and unspoken feelings. Mathieu put his arm around her so he could smell her touch and she pressed closer to him.

She whispered to his heart. "And us? You and me? Whatever happens we will be part of it, too." It wasn't a question. The future had suddenly lost its certainty. In the midst of this general euphoria Mathieu abandoned his reserve. What did it matter who saw them? He kissed Agnès with modest delicacy, unsure why, in the midst of so much apparent joy, he felt so happy and so sad. It was a kiss which held no promise; no condition; no wasted words.

"We will…" He tried to find a promise, but she touched her finger to his lips.

"We will see." That beautiful woman. Agnès the good was also Agnès the wise.

Part 2

THE AGE OF DESTRUCTION

No Denial

I did it. Me. I released every loyal Frenchman from the bonds of servitude. My name was being written in the annals of glory as I spoke. On August 4th 1914, my bravery opened a new chapter in French history. I did that. Not on my own, but as far as the world will ever know, me alone. I lay on the hard cell cot and saw myself accepting the Legion of Honor, Grand Cross from a grateful President Poincaré, bedecked in a tricolor. Of course.

They used to celebrate the abolition of serfdom in 1789 on August 4th. Fine, if you consider the Revolution a noble achievement. Otherwise forget it. They buried Jean Jaurès on 4th August 1914. Huh. That was an opportunity missed. All the socialists and traitors, all the peace-mongers and international worker-types turned up. We should have shot them. There and then.

But wait. The news of news. The reason for my being. The German ambassador returned his papers and left France for Berlin on 4th August 1914. War was declared. Our war of liberation for Alsace and Lorraine was underway. Revanche.

Some judge had tried to interrogate me on the night I was rescued from the police after they tried to confuse me, but I knew I had to keep quiet. I said nothing, as instructed. It was fun really because I answered every question in my head…but said nothing.

"Your name, Monsieur?" Pen in hand, he waited.

I looked blankly in his direction and smiled.

"Address?"

Find out, if you can, I said to myself, turning to count the number of persons in the room.

"Did you kill Jean Jaurès as he sat with his back to you…"

I have to admit I broke my vow at the stupidity of the question. "Yes, of course I did," I shouted at him. "He was a traitor to France. Don't you know? Everyone else does."

I recall my inquisitor was taken aback.

"You admit murdering Monsieur Jaurès?" His mouth fell open like a sea bass on a bed of ice in the Marche Bastille. I am partial to sea bass baked in salt, so the look was far from offensive. I didn't bother replying. This trumped-up fellow asked me to read and sign what he had written. He called it a declaration. I looked away and shook my head, as contemptuously as I could.

"Will you sign your admission?" He was getting angry. I smiled again and said nothing.

"Very well." He was shouting by then. "You will be charged with voluntary homicide. Take him to the cells."

So they carried me to La Santé. As prisons go, this must be the best. I was given a large cell to myself, and could receive visitors in a special room which led into Rue Messier behind the prison walls. I was forbidden to tell who did visit me. You would be shocked, believe me. I could hear the crowds cheering in the background. Was it for me? Have you ever heard crowds cheering for you? An unfair question, my friend.

One of the warders slipped me a copy of the Figaro. He winked and whispered, "The war is underway. The people are cheering our troops in every town and village across the land.. They've forgotten Jaurès already." He pulled me into a corner. I thought he was about to strike me, but no. He had a message. "They are going to examine you in a special court. I have to remind you to say nothing...except that you killed him. No names. You know that, don't you?"

I nodded. I was never sure about that man. Might have been another trick. I had to stay alert.

Apparently it was called a hearing. They took me to La Seine Court where a flunky, Joseph Drioux, introduced himself as the preliminary magistrate. Turned out they couldn't quite grasp what I was about. For two and a half weeks stupid Drioux repeatedly asked me the same questions.

"Why did you kill Jaurès?"

"When did you start planning the assassination?"

He called it an assassination. You don't assassinate swine.

"Do you regret killing him?"

What? Did I regret the greatest moment of my life? Was the fellow insane?

"Where did you purchase the guns?"

Find out yourself, my man, I answered in my head.

"How many times did you fire the gun?"

I almost broke my silence with a sarcastic remark. Check Jaurès' head. Honestly, there were times when I had to hold back laughter.

Then the trick question. "Did you fire both shots or did the other man fire the second?"

It would have been so easy to respond with a sarcastic, "What other man?" or enter into an argument in which I might have said something I regretted. Instead I maintained my stoic silence. By the end of this boring process, his only comment was that I gave no impression of regret. Well yes, he was correct. No regret whatsoever.

My warden friend, let's call him Pierre, warned me that they were watching my every move. That some low-order detectives were frustrated by my insistence that I acted alone. They had traced my clothes back to Rue St. Honore but friends there swore that I was alone, that I paid for the clothes in cash. The police discovered I had eaten at Eiffel's tower, but were disappointed when it turned out that I had eaten alone. Every metro ticket was purchased as a single journey. How clever of Theo, Maurice, and Action française. They said that I must take every possible opportunity to reinforce the claim that I acted alone. Find a way to put it in writing, but be extremely careful to talk only of Jaurès. It would be valuable one day. They planned everything with meticulous precision.

So I wrote to my brother. He had enlisted as a swanky aviator. Trust him. Took the easy way out. Flew around in the sky above the real action. Had I been free I would have served on the front line, pushing the Germans back to Berlin. He just wanted to be a hero, too. Like me.

Anyway, I wrote to him to confirm that I wiped out the greatest traitor of our time, the big mouth who tried to bury the hopes of those true Frenchmen who demanded the return of Alsace Lorraine; the traitor who voted down the three-year armed services law. My only regret? That I wasn't the first Frenchman to step into a liberated Alsace.

I punished him. I punished Jaurès absolutely. Me. In the name of France and our allies.

Do you think I made it clear enough?

12

August-September 1914 – Hope in a Time of Change

There were noisier morgues in Paris than the Tigers' Den at HQ. The previous night's jubilation had faded fast in the early morning certainty that everything had changed and no one knew exactly what that meant. Every man was at his desk by six A.M. though the commander hadn't summoned a meeting. Old Girard acknowledged each in turn as he arrived but was set on his own purpose. Mathieu watched him carefully put a large box on his desk and start to fill it as if he was wrapping precious memories to be carried off in private. He held up at a boxing medal and seemed on the point of speech when underneath he found an envelope. Girard withdrew a handwritten letter which drained his face of expression. He picked it up, looked at it, front and back, and visibly shrank before it. What secret lay inside? Which painful memory had been roused? He shivered, and Mathieu turned away lest he see him cry. Dubois, who had served with the captain from the day the Tigers had been established, rose to comfort him but hesitated when halfway to his feet. He had always found it difficult to capture the right words where emotions were concerned and was as likely to say something inappropriate. Whatever was inside, Girard had kept that letter close, though no one found out why.

Mathieu retreated behind the morning newspaper but couldn't read beyond the single word headline: WAR. It swam before his eyes and disarmed his focus. Yesterday's hope had gone, yet something remained. A different hope, as yet undefined. Guy Simon sat twirling a pencil as if he had no care in the world. He reclined in his chair, balancing himself, feet on desk, impervious to the anxiety of the others. This was the day he had dreamed of since he was a child at infant school in Sèvres, fighting the Germans—boys from a neighboring school—with his closest friends, setting traps for them on the way home, imagining victory and popular acclaim. The others had heard his stories over and again. Every moment of his military service had been focused on the day that war would be declared and he knew what he was about to do. So did Mathieu.

The commander banged open the door, looked around, and exploded. "What the hell is going on here? You look like mourners at a wake who've lost the recently deceased's body." He stood at the door and glowered. "So we're at war?" He opened his arms and shoulders and shrugged as if it was a regular occurrence. "We knew it was coming. We've known for weeks. So get your arses into gear. And start packing. We're on the move." That caught everyone by surprise.

The old captain followed the commander out into the corridor but had hardly stepped over the threshold before his objections were shot down. "You have to stay, Pascal, at least until this is over. I need you now more than ever." Roux's insistence was absolute.

Pascal Girard took one step forward and two back. "Christmas. I'll stay till then. But not one day after." He believed that would be sufficient time to drive the Germans back to Berlin. Most Frenchmen did.

Guy Simon brushed past the captain, clearly set on an early exit, and found his way blocked by the commander. "Don't waste your time, Sir. I'm returning to my army unit. Today." The unstoppable zealot met the immoveable pragmatist head on and blocked the corridor. Roux took a step back as if to let him pass but instead pushed Guy though his office door and slammed it shut.

"I make the decisions in this department."

The rest was a tirade of bitterness. Mathieu had never heard such anger rebound from the close confines of the Tigers' HQ, but neither man gave ground. The three remaining Tigers looked at each other in disbelief. Occasional sentences were formed from a legion of harsh words before Guy stormed out in anger, face burning with resentment.

"You will do as you are instructed," was the commander's final order.

Guy did not break step nor look round. "I will do what is necessary for France and return to my artillery brigade," came the retort.

And he was gone.

Mathieu knew what he was duty bound to do. He knocked on Bernard Roux's open door and, with some trepidation, explained his position. " Sir, I have to return to my unit, too. It's not that I want to leave Paris, but…" He got no further.

Bernard Roux did not even look up from his desk. He took one draw from his sturdy Gauloises and asked, "Have received your orders, Mathieu?"

"Well, no."

"Of course not. You have a problem, you see. You're dead. Have you forgotten?" Roux's abrupt reaction brought it all back. He was. He was dead.

Vincent had been buried in the Saint-Pierre Cemetery in Marseilles where a headstone commemorated his valor. Mathieu was the exile in Paris.

The commander blew out a calming smoke ring and called the others into his office. He stood in front of his desk and brought his anger to heel with deep breaths and timely silence. Once composed, he chose a quieter route.

"Look, I'm not sure that you all understand what's happening here. Last night Paris was celebrating the declaration of war against our old enemy. Today the whole backdrop to our lives has changed forever, and not one of us knows how that will end, believe me. This is going to be one hell of a long day and there will be many more to come." He parked his ample rear on the edge of the desk and tried to find a convincing smile. "Big changes will affect us all immediately. The prefect of police told me last week that he would have to step down when war broke out, but he has always had plans to reform and modernize the force. The Tigers will become part of counter-espionage in the Deuxième Bureau, with the responsibility to protect the head of state and nominated citizens, as well as keeping a close watch on anarchists, socialist dissidents, and the anti-war brigade. Stamping down on major organized crime will still be important to us, and I am to be the chief superintendent." He paused for effect, shrugged, and hauled out a packet of Gauloises.

Paul Dubois was truly impressed. "Congratulations, Chief."

Mathieu leaned forward to shake his hand.

"Yes, yes. Thank you for your loyalty and service. Etcetera." He had further news. "You will continue as a special unit, answerable only to the minister of the interior and me. For that reason we have another promotion to accommodate. I just hope you prove worthy of our confidence, Lieutenant Bertrand." Mathieu was taken aback, but said nothing.

Dubois beamed. Even Pascal looked happier. "A chief superintendent and a new lieutenant." Handshakes and backslapping lasted just as long as it took Roux to light up his next Gauloises.

"Start packing, we're on the move to number 36, Quai des Orfèvres."

It was the center of the known police universe situated close to the Palais de Justice on the famed Isle de la Cite, one of two natural islands as the Seine cut through Paris. Number 36 they called it for short, home to the Deuxième Bureau and the nerve center of police intelligence. They were on the move before the oldest clock in the city struck eight.

Mathieu was also trying to cope with equally important emotions which had stripped his innocence and left him wondering if he had found

113

hope. In the gathering dusk of the previous evening, he and Agnès had wandered out of the Café Cluny into the intoxicating warmth that wafted across the Seine and became entangled in their own moment.

"Do you have any more of those precious kisses?" Mathieu's voice quavered.

She looked up, the knowing accomplice, and teased him. "Perhaps, if and when I find a man worthy enough. I would never throw myself at any passing policeman, no matter how well connected he might be." Before he could stop himself, Mathieu drew her even closer so that they breathed in tandem and he could feel his heart pulsating close to explosion. This time their kiss was breathless, as if each was drawing strength from the other.

An old chapel door hung open beside them and they fumbled inside what was once an orchard, overgrown, even in summer, its strange dark recesses throwing their shadows deep against the historic walls. Agnès whispered encouragement to his eagerness. She tore at his shirt, and with one arm around his neck, unbuckled his belt and eased him closer. He raised her up and gently slipped into her. He wanted it to be right, to be perfect for Agnès, but nature took control and with unwarranted speed burst onto the scene, leaving him embarrassed and her disappointed.

Agnès could feel his dismay and said nothing of her own. "It's OK, really, it's fine, don't worry," she said softly. "Walk me home."

They checked the street for watching eyes and left the orchard to mind its own secrets. "You know, it wouldn't surprise me if my landlady was out," Agnès confessed with just enough emphasis to open a door of possibilities. It took Mathieu several minutes to realize that he had picked up the pace and was almost dragging her along the boulevard to a different promised land. Agnès was right. No landlady was there to greet them, and when she returned, Madame Labossière appeared to have company, too.

Late evening passed into sleepless night as the two lovers grew into each other. Outside, Paris took time to quiet down from the exhaustion of the day while indoors Mathieu and Agnès struggled against the sweat of their excitement. By three in the morning, they began to think of what might happen next. She talked for a while about the war and how she might make a contribution; he listened, but somewhere in the conversation a word—it may have been innocence—triggered an image of a child and its mother floating in a canal in Marseilles and he turned away as if to beg forgiveness. His old guilt rose up to haunt his new hope.

"Let's live for today," he murmured to himself, but Agnès heard him and agreed.

Today continued at a breakneck pace.

"Chaos at Saint-Lazare," Sergeant Toussaint, the gendarme at reception in no. 36 announced as they walked into the building with their personal belongings. He greeted Mathieu and Paul Dubois like long lost friends and looked at them expectantly as if they had the solution. He stood a burly five foot eight, too old for armed service, too proud to retire from police work. His enthusiasm for the aforementioned word *chaos* suggested that he embraced the idea with unbridled enthusiasm.

"And you want us to … ?" Dubois began.

"You've got a Panhard. Let's get over there. Better than melting in this mausoleum." Dubois elbowed his new lieutenant in the ribs and agreed. Toussaint helped them dump their boxes behind the reception desk, and with their unexpected ally in tow, clambered back into the car and headed towards the 8th arrondissement, past crowded avenues and swarming groups of excited men. There was a vibrancy in the air which they could touch, an unbridled expectation that this was the day of reckoning. Next stop—Berlin.

Mathieu had never seen the station in such ferment. Saint-Lazare's concourse throbbed with excitement. Thousands upon thousands of loyal Parisians clambered through the vast canopy, shouting, cheering, and waving at friends they had not seen for a while. Caps clung to most of the bobbing heads. Workers, pledged to *La Libertie*, carried the rest of their days in a single cloth bag. Straw hats and bowlers were also in evidence, but Mathieu was instantly struck by the predominance of the poorer classes. Farm hands from the surrounding districts must have risen before dawn. Had they given thought to a harvest as yet unfinished, he wondered. Shop assistants, factory workers, clerks and craftsmen, builders, joiners, and a troupe from the Medrano Circus joined with a battalion drawn from the municipal workforce. It was as if all Paris had heard a trumpet call and come running to a meeting point called Saint-Lazare. Years later Mathieu realized that it had been the prelude to a symphony called Armageddon.

Lines of willing conscripts and volunteers massed inside all the major stations to which they had been summoned. Saint-Lazare transformed itself into a drill hall. Though regular army troops were already stationed close to the German border, the reservists and territorials who stood ready for this moment were determined to have their revenge on the Boches. Some had lived their lives preparing for this dawn of retribution. France would be united; Alsace-Lorraine would be free. Some had given twenty-eight years of service from conscript to territorial reserve. Their time had come. The male population of Paris and its environs appeared to think they were going on a weekend tour, much as an all-conquering rugby team might. They had been assured of victory by a compliant press; a press owned by the merchants of war. That promise seduced even cautious men to march.

Pockets of impatience caused occasional flashpoints and tempers were strained where reservists and volunteers discovered that they had steadfastly joined a slow-moving column for the wrong train. Gendarmes had been stationed at the seven main front-arched entrances to help keep the throng moving, and regimental sergeants bellowed and cajoled the masses in front of them into a semblance of order. Both Mathieu and Dubois had to push back the more zealous as they threatened to break ranks; the sergeant reveled in the opportunity to punch them into line. Occasionally old antagonisms between the young bucks from different quarters of the city broke the mythical sense of a sacred union between all sections of French society which President Poincare so desperately wanted to promote. While the thrill of anticipation ran close to the surface of such excitement, a viper slithered through the unsuspecting ranks drunk on its own belief of invincibility, unaware that danger was ever present.

Dubois saw him first. "To the right, close by the fifth portico, hovering towards the back of that mob from the tramway company." He pointed towards a noisy collection of all ages drawn from the tram workers union, or so their banner claimed, who had waited patiently in a line which had ground to a halt for no obvious reason. Mathieu strained to see something suspicious, but the sheer volume in front blocked his view.

"Got him," Toussaint confirmed. "Clever bastard. Jumping around at the tail of the column, arms all over his half-drunk victim as if he's an old friend. Wait. See that? Quick dip into inside pocket and off. Let's get him." But they were not the only ones with sharp eyes.

"What a jerk. That asshole's swiped Martin's purse!" A tram-worker pointed towards the ragged thief who had been celebrating with them moments before. "Hey, you, stay where you are." The bedraggled pickpocket started to run, but the terminus was so overcrowded that he had nowhere to go. He struggled against the flow of outrage and was quickly grabbed from behind and disappeared from view.

Dubois realized what had happened. "That's the stairway to the station toilets. If they take him down we'll never see him again." Mathieu could feel alarm bells ringing as he pushed and shoved his way towards the toilet entrance. From the top of the stairwell they could hear squeals of panic rise from below despite the clamor around them. Word spread that a pickpocket had been caught stealing a worker's purse, and by the time this had passed through four different mouths, the story had grown into a case of grand theft and larceny and a crime against the unity of France. It was suggested that he must be a German agent, and low and behold, the thief's nationality was changed to meet the requirement of the damning accusation. Toussaint bellowed that everyone should stand aside, but no one was willing to move. He dealt with the issue like a plough would cut a furrow through a fallow field.

"No, no, no. It's all a misunderstanding," the ragged-trousered larcenist appealed as the first blow knocked him against a cubicle door, bursting his nose with spectacular effect. A second took all the wind from his thin frame. As he slumped to the sodden floor, part-flooded by the sheer volume of urine running through the station sewers, blood streamed down his filthy shirt and added color to the dismal surroundings. Dubois and Mathieu barged through and brought him momentary respite, but it was the sergeant who took control. "Police, stand back!" he yelled, asserting his authority over the vengeful mob. "We'll take it from here."

A couple of tram workers ignored him to their own cost. The first was cast into the urine filled slurry with one hand and the second had to be hauled out of the pissoir by his mates before he came to an ignominious end. Toussaint turned back to the half-conscious thief who had the wit to hold up the offended wallet in dejected submission so that it could be returned to its owner.

"Show's over, *mes amis*. Let's leave it at that." The sergeant did a double-take and leaned into the bleeding, urine-soaked figure who struggled to stand on his own accord. "*Mere de Dieu. Putain.* Moutie you are a sick, stupid, incompetent cretin. I mean," he was almost lost for words, "even for you this is pathetic."

"Shorry, Shergeant. Shorry." He spat out a tooth and put his hand gingerly to his face to wipe his nose. "Christ! It smells of pee."

"I've news for you, *mon ami*, you are totally covered in piss and it suits you." He laughed.

One thing was certain, none of the police officers had any intention of touching the sodden stinking offender who appeared to cry quietly at his fate. He stood looking at his wringing shirt and trousers, a cross between a pariah and a medieval leper and whimpered, "Look what they've done to me."

"Asshole, you did it to yourself." Toussaint caught a whiff of pungent urine and made matters clear. "I need you to walk one step ahead of us up

the stairs, and you can stop your pathetic attempt at amateur dramatics."
He turned to his colleagues. "Forgive me, gentlemen, but let me introduce
you to Moutie—thief, pickpocket, and bumbling idiot. If you graded the
entire criminal class in the city in terms of common sense, Moutie barely
makes it to the infant class. Now," he turned back to his captive, "when
you get to the top of the stairs fuck off and don't let me see you this side
of next year." The unsuspecting horde of reservists parted before him as
Moutie the fantasist rushed from the station to find solace in his own version of events.

The grand station clock struck loudly on the hour to assert its role as
master timekeeper for all travellers. "*Merde.* The chief will be wondering
where we are," Mathieu reasoned. "We'd better get back to no. 36. Sergeant, ehm, sorry we've not introduced ourselves, Dubois and Bertrand.
First day at the Deuxième under Bernard Roux. He'll not be impressed if
he hears what has happened."

"Ah, that explains a lot. Victor Toussaint at your service, reduced to
little more than the receptionist at 36 because of allegations from criminals that have never been fully proved. Just blame me. Say I misled you.
Everyone else does."

Mathieu cast a last look over his shoulder at the overexcited throng
still pushing its way through the vast concourse and shivered at the vi-
sion which took shape before him. Great clouds of steam billowed from
the mighty engines standing ready to take fresh battalions to the northern frontier. It cast a thick shroud over the platforms on the western side
of the station so that the volunteers and reservists disappeared like lost
souls in a fog-bound cemetery. Mathieu watched in dumb distraction as
the youths advanced fearlessly along the platform through the poisoned
haze to meet their ghost-like fate on the other side. One minute they were
drunk on their own bonhomie, the next they shrank into oblivion and
were gone. The constant clamor of station announcements, platform al-
terations, shrill whistles from beleaguered guards, and ear-splitting horns
from impatient engine drivers vied with the thunder of steam and the
grating of iron on iron. This was the sound of chaos, and for a moment
Mathieu felt he was in that dock in Marseilles, powerless to turn back the
tide of wrath which he knew had already been unleashed. He felt what
these young men couldn't—fear.

In truth the rest of the day was boring The team argued over desks,
filing cabinets, whether or not the telephone should be mounted on the
wall, and which of the well-worn seats they wanted. Mathieu thought of

Agnès, how serious the night before might be, whether or not they should have used a préservatif, did they really mean all the things they said to each other in the passion of the moment? Dare he tell her about Marseilles? Nothing would ever be the same.

13

AND LONG NIGHTS OF DARKNESS

One calendar month later Mathieu returned to Saint-Lazare to pick up the chief from a meeting on the outskirts of the city. He found himself in a strange world of altered images, absurd in its hollow promise to vainglorious youth. A presumption of easy victory had been undermined by the evidence of near disaster. Hordes of willing reservists had been replaced by nursing volunteers. In the space of half an hour, a queue of hospital trains pulled into the far corner of the through-line en route to Versailles-Chantiers where they would be cared for by a blessed legion from the Red Cross. Initially, injured French and Belgian soldiers were met with acclaim. Men and women cheered "Bravo!" and those depleted bodies that could walk or wave were filled with amazing resolve. Everyone on the concourse was moved by the sight of a one-legged infantryman, unsteady in his twisted gait, insisting, "We're just home for the weekend. Then it's back to give the Boches another taste of our bayonets."

But their bravado masked a harsh reality. Smiles hung from cigarettes as the maimed struggled towards a lifetime of misery. Gaslight from converted hospital carriages fell on others less fortunate, patched-up for public view but irrevocably broken. Mathieu shuddered at the thought of what lay inside the closed carriages with drawn blinds where the dying were administered to with desperation. The cheering faded, then stopped.

Despite their brazen early optimism, newspaper headlines began to reflect a cruel deception which Mathieu had always feared. French and British forces on the northwestern borders were pushed back by the German onslaught. In the east, the Russians were destroyed over a five day battle at Tannenberg which shattered their Second Army. The race to Berlin dissolved into an urban myth, as every Allied army was driven backwards across northern France. Instead, the German divisions indulged in their own alternative—the race to Paris. By the end of August, gunfire could be heard above the clamor of street noise on the outskirts; louder than the metro. The Boches were coming.

The chief's train ran twenty-five minutes late and he was angry and unforgiving, but not at the rail service. He nodded to Mathieu in recognition and relief, desperate to share his contempt. "They've decided to abandon Paris," he growled in disgust.

"What?" Mathieu's first reaction was embarrassment. His face stung at the insult those words implied.

"That meeting was supposed to coordinate the defense of the city, but I was ordered to organize the immediate evacuation of Poincaré's government and keep it secret. Can you believe this? They are going to run away from the Germans and leave the people to fend for themselves. And it's our job to protect them." Tears swelled in the older man's eyes. "It's dishonorable, Mathieu. The very person who engineered the war six weeks ago has turned tail and needs us to organize his secret escape from the City. The sly bastard. And the nation's gold reserves have already been sent to Brittany. In a worst case scenario, it'll be transferred to London or New York."

Mathieu couldn't take in the awesome betrayal..

"Classified works of art in the Louvre have been carefully selected and boxed so that they can be secretly transported out of the city." He drew a sharp intake of nicotine and spat on the platform floor. "We have to help those with power and money to run away while the ordinary man and woman is left to rot. *La Putain's union sacrée* didn't last too long did it? If the people knew what was happening…"

On later reflection, Mathieu considered this his most shameful task in the war years. The minister of the interior, Louis Malvy, was instructed to oversee the evacuation in a joint operation with the Deuxième Bureau, but his legendary need to compromise made clear-cut action impossible. Mathieu watched him scurry about like the proverbial headless chicken, in and out of Roux's office to offer advice which was instantly ignored. The minister of the interior had been instructed to organize a special presidential train from the Gard du Nord to Bordeaux which turned Roux apoplectic.

"Malvy, are you completely mad? Do you seriously think the president can sneak away from the people he serves through the busiest station in the country? You might as well call all the newspapers and ask them to send photographers. This is supposed to be a secret evacuation. There will be a riot." He turned to his own men. "For Christ's sake, find an alternative point of departure. Immediately."

The special train was hastily rerouted to allow President Poincaré's undignified retreat from Paris in complete secrecy. The governing class clambered over itself like cornered sewer rats as they scurried though the modest Gare d'Auteuil in the suburbs of the sixteenth arrondissement, scrambling over each other in their haste to abandon the capital. No military band trumpeted their withdrawal nor polished cavalry helmets sparkled in the dim gaslight, for a guard of honor was out of the question. *La Marseilles* was replaced by the silence of self-preservation. It was undoubtedly Bernard Roux's most embarrassing moment in a war of multiple embarrassments. Mathieu shared his disgust.

Ambassadors, civil servants, ministers of state, secretaries, wives, children, assorted pets, and overloaded baggage vied with each other for the best available space like refugees being carried to asylum on the last train to freedom. Just when it seemed impossible to make matters more embarrassing, the American ambassador, Myron Herrick, sauntered onto the platform with his wife to witness the debacle.

"Good evening, Chief Superintendent," he began with a smirk. "You'll be relieved that the citizens of your noble city have not turned out to jeer at the president." His assistant secretary, Bryson Hamilton, stood half a step behind him, smoking a trademark Gitane, taking notes and responding to requests. With every Allied embassy closed, the ambassador was to be saddled with the responsibility of representing their interests when the Germans marched into Paris.

Roux tried to bring a semblance of dignity to the chaos, but the more he urged calm, the higher the decibels. Though they were in no immediate danger, a sense of panic energized the assorted parties already on board. There were no first-class carriages. For those used to the privileges of State, it was a sad come-down. Just after eleven o'clock, as the train pulled away into the murky night, the ambassador's secretary turned to Mathieu and caught the moment perfectly. In his broad southern growl the American sneered, "They're like a band of gypsies."

Bernard Roux heard the throw-away line and shook his head. He agreed. Had an assassin appeared on the platform, he might have pointed to the president's compartment. And the final word from Poincaré to the citizens of Paris as his train steamed off to the safety of Bordeaux? "Fight and stand firm."

Bâtard.

Deserted by his own government, the formerly retired General Gallieni took military control of the capital. He gathered a dispirited force of army reservists, police, and citizens and swore to defend Paris against the invaders. Plans were drawn up to blow the bridges across the Seine. Gun positions were agreed and ammunition and stores taken to the barricades along the city boundaries. Boulevards were to have their trees cut down. Avenues with splendid villas and shops were scheduled for demolition. In the northern and eastern suburbs, whole sections of the city were emptied so that the defense would be unobstructed. Eiffel's tower was identified as a strategic communications link which would be razed to the ground. Nothing was more sacred than holding Paris at whatever the cost.

But the old Tigers knew there wasn't enough time for detailed preparations. Decisions were revised. Attack has long been the best form of defense. The chief superintendent summoned his reconstructed force to the old gymnasium under their headquarters and spoke with absolute confidence.

"The general has decided that Paris will not wait for the Boches. We will march out to defeat them." Brave words, but somehow they were not hollow. Bernard Roux's sincerity brooked no doubters. "You, Messieurs, will organize the transportation of every volunteer, reservist, gun, and bullet to the front line. Starting today. You have the power to requisition any and all means of transport available. Do it." He drew heavily on his blessed Gauloises as if to reinforce the command. "Now."

14

SEPTEMBER 1914 – SECRETS

Armed with megaphones, standard rifles, and a squad of recently seconded gendarmes, Roux's men set about their mammoth task. Gendarmes and special police units in every prefecture did likewise. Any citizen who had a car, taxi, truck, or useable means of transport was explicitly ordered to assist in the movement of men to the front immediately.

"Slight problem." The chief looked uncomfortable at their mid-morning meeting. "The ministry has emptied the prisons. Given an amnesty to prisoners who have sworn to defend France." He made it clear that his advice had not been canvassed. "Just…" He was momentarily lost for words. "Just do your best. And before you ask, Lieutenant, Raoul Villain has not been released. Any worker with a gun in his hand would put a bullet in him. No. He's safer where he is."

Cars began to appear on the streets of central Paris heading for the city barracks. Mathieu teamed up with Paul Dubois, who claimed that in a previous life he had served in the first road transport unit and found himself manipulating the flow with a precision that the others had to admire. His hand, eye, and arm coordination was spectacular. "Like riding a bicycle," he exclaimed. "You don't lose it."

No one had ever seen Dubois near a bicycle, but he was clearly enjoying himself.

He stopped a delivery van driven by a loudmouthed socialist with whom they had crossed swords at a number of demonstrations. Dubois recognized the wizen-faced factory worker, a well-known trouble-maker with a sour attitude and sourer breath, and demanded he open the rear door. The two men scowled at each other in mutual distaste.

"Sacred union my arse," Dubois scoffed. "Let's see what anti-war propaganda this peasant is carrying to the front." Inside, eight armed reservists were engaged in emptying a third bottle of vin rouge. They looked none too pleased at this intervention.

"Are we there already?" The youngest cocked a snoot towards the intruder, emboldened by the wine.

"Fucking flics wants to check which side we're on." The driver stared at him, giving no quarter.

Dubois had the grace to apologize with a nod of the head and a quiet, "Good lad," to the driver.

It looked as if every vehicle in France had been summoned to the cause. Cars of all types, some deluxe models, had been requisitioned. Charabancs, too. An ancient horse-drawn omnibus still advertising the route between *Madeleine* and *Bastille,* toiled towards the Porte de Bagnolet, laden with soldiers. Taxi after taxi after taxi—some estimates claimed over 600 taxis, more used to carrying the bourgeoisies than the last of the Parisian guards—were filled with men and munitions.

A Renault coupe proudly displayed its pristine polished frame, an oak coffin securely fastened across the rear seat. The juxtaposition of a chauffeur driving a makeshift hearse was less ridiculous than the sight of the driver, coat collar raised to cover part of his instantly recognizable face. Moutie.

Mathieu strode into the coupe's path and the hapless thief beamed in recognition, bringing the hearse to a stop millimeters from the policeman's foot.

"Inspector Bertrand, a fine evening for a visit to the front. Are you headed this way? Or are you … ?"

"Yes, Moutie, I am, and thank you for the promotion," he replied and jumped into the front seat beside the driver. "I'm glad to find you better dressed, my friend. And your nose looks fine." The ignoble thief touched his sore point gently. "Sadly, the smell hasn't gone way. Still. Look on the bright side. This will be the most unexpected sacred union in France, my thieving friend. The president will be proud of us both, joining forces for the common good." Mathieu swung round to glance at the box behind them.

"Tell me, what are you carrying in that coffin?"

"C-c-c … coffin?" His voice trembled.

"Yes, my friend, the coffin strapped across the back seat. You don't often see these in posh cars."

Moutie paused for a moment, keeping his eyes directly ahead while his brain searched for an acceptable answer.

"Ammunition"

"Ammunition? Excellent, my friend. I'll inspect it shortly."

Moutie was nonplussed. Sweat broke over his oily-haired brow. Unshaven, his sallow face bore the map of poverty better than the soiled rags in which he was still clothed. Had they been washed since Saint Lazare? This was not what Moutie intended. Clearly. Self-pity deflated his early attempt at bluff. Mathieu enjoyed the thief's misery as far as the Porte. Unfortunately, the stench of the unwashed pervaded the "hearse." Perhaps it belonged to the coffin's occupant. Perhaps not.

"Pull in here, Moutie." Mathieu pointed to a gap on the route. "This is far enough. There's a police station across the road. But first, let me see inside the coffin."

Moutie opened the rear door, unwound the cheap imitation brass screws, lifted the lid, and stood back, head down. Mathieu slammed the coffin lid shut and turned on him. "OK, Moutie, what are you going to do with the body?"

The thief protested his innocence. "There's a body in there? Never! Honest to God, I thought it was empty."

"Liar, you said it was full of ammunition."

Mathieu was on the point of hauling him across the street when a chauffeured town car drove past. He recognized the passenger from the file in Roux's office. Basil Zaharoff, engrossed in a swathe of paperwork. Zaharoff! On his way to support the boys on the front line? Not likely. Zaharoff on private business using the exodus as a cover? Much more likely.

"Right, Moutie. Report to the police station. Over there." Mathieu left him stranded by the roadside, unsure of his next move. Moral dilemmas were not his forte, so the thief stole away into the comfort of the shadows. Had he taken a glance inside the coffin before he stole the motorcar, he would have known that Mathieu had set him up. It was empty.

Mathieu gave chase in Moutie's stolen Renault, but the crowded streets limited everyone's progress, and breaking into the flow of traffic slowed him down. Zaharoff's beautiful blue town car blinked in the dying sunlight, but catching up proved impossible. From a distance, Mathieu could see it turn off the boulevard into a side street, but by the time he had maneuvered the hearse into position to follow, the avenue was empty. He found himself driving through a strange world, deserted, lifeless—semi-dark, boarded-up and locked down. These homes had been abandoned. The whole locality systematically emptied so that Paris could be defended. Looking north, Mathieu could see the flash of occasional gunfire across the darkening horizon, attended some seconds later by the dull pounding of distant anger. The ancient Greeks would have concluded that the Gods were mightily displeased.

He drove carefully along the unlit street. An elderly couple, arm in arm, bowed respectfully towards him. He duly returned the compliment. Three buildings from the end, he found Zaharoff's car parked outside a once state-ly mansion where the chauffeur, cigarette in hand, doubled as the first line of security. Other vehicles straddled the curbside in a display of wealth and power which underlined the French dominance in European car manufac-ture. Mathieu looked straight ahead, ignoring the guard's attention, aware that a hearse commanded unspoken respect. What he hadn't expected was the cloak of near invisibility that accompanied the driver. What could be less remarkable than a car carrying a coffin in a dying city? Mathieu drove on, crossed the next junction, and turned into yet another deserted byway.

He doubled back on foot through the empty backyards and found a suitable vantage point in a neighboring garden. He could see the flaking conservatory where Zaharoff and his associates were engaged in animated conversation. Faces he almost recognized but could not name peopled an otherwise empty room. Whatever was said annoyed the international arms dealer. He was adamant, but about what? Two of the men around him were representatives in the National Assembly. But who? Was that Wendel from the Iron and Steel Committee? *Merde*. He realized that the uniformed offi-cer, with whom Zaharoff examined what appeared to be a map, was one of General Joffre's personal staff whom he had met in Durfort's office. They had spoken once at the Quai d'Orsay. A figure turned towards the arma-ments tsar and in the half-light, the obsequious face of Benoit Durfort beamed towards his master, head half bowed like a no-necked toad.

A slight movement disturbed his concentration. "Ah Monsieur, would you kindly tell me what you are doing here?" It was Zaharoff's chauf-feur-guard, barely a foot away, pistol in hand, directly pointed at Mathieu.

With considerable authority he straightened up and answered, "I live here, Monsieur. This is my home." Mathieu indicated the villa behind them. "What are you doing on my property and why are you pointing a gun at me? Are you a Boches infiltrator?"

A flicker of doubt diverted the man's attention towards the house, and in that instant Mathieu lashed out with his right foot and parted his would-be assailant's groin with such force that the pistol dropped faster than the injured party. Dirty play? Yes, but he had a gun. A second sturdy kick to the chauffeur's head gave him time to dive into the bushes, side-step a row of pot-plants, run at full pace down an alley, start the car and drive off, heart pumping, mind racing. In the gloom of the deserted avenue he had to pick his way carefully around the debris which the former residents had left in their wake. Behind him the town car's broad beam swung into view. Having never driven such a top class Renault before, Mathieu struggled to get out of first gear. Zaharoff's man closed fast. Ahead, the exodus on the boulevard appeared to have come to a halt. Not good. Nowhere to turn; nowhere to hide. At which point a citizen, realizing that a coffin-carrier was waiting to cross against the current, stepped forward and parted the way. Moses would have been impressed. The rich man's town car, tried to follow and was met with a wall of angry rejection.

"I dare you."

An irritated mob appeared from both sides of the street, baying insults at the chauffeur-driven town car which stopped in its tracks.

Mathieu crossed the avenue to make his way back to number 36. The streets were thronged with the strangest column of fighting men in the history of French military advances, but the light was fading fast and in the semi-dark, Mathieu's vehicle was quickly absorbed into a counter stream flowing back to the center of the city. Only the back of the cars and taxis heading out towards the Front were lit and drivers were instructed to follow the lights ahead. This was history in action. The people's contribution. All hail the taxi drivers. Most of them returned to normal service after a few days but some remained at the front longer, to carry back wounded soldiers and stranded refugees. In accordance with city regulations, most taxis kept their meters running. Years later, Mathieu discovered that the French treasury reimbursed in full a claim for 70,012 francs lodged by the taxi companies. Altruism has always had limits.

A FLICKER OF DOUBT

The greatest sadness comes from love lost forever. Of all the consequences of my bravery, I had never considered the obscene destruction of my beautiful cathedral in Reims. I couldn't believe that the Boches targeted this most magnificent of churches. Its priceless presence was a symbol of our nation where once kings were anointed and crowned. How many times had I touched the wonderful masonry? Felt its history? Walked down the vaulted aisles? Stood in the wondrous reflection of the stain-glassed windows? Imagined myself at the coronation of King Louis the Fourteenth, the Sun-King; the most absolute of absolute monarchs. Of times when France spoke and the world trembled? This was their revenge. I was the keeper who let slip the dogs of war. I made sure that the enemies of France were rudderless so the Germans burned down Reims to punish me. But I will never apologize. Have you ever been punished for doing the right thing, my friend?

The warden let me read about the tragedy in great detail. Apparently, after continuous and deliberate shelling, the scaffolding around the north tower caught fire, spreading the blaze to all parts of the carpentry superstructure. In the brutal heat, the lead melted and spouted through the stone gargoyles, destroying the Bishop's Palace. Imagine the horror. The Cathedral fell stone by stone until there was little left save the west front and the pillars. My pillars. It is yet another heinous crime from the criminal Prussians. Warden says that all of the free world is appalled. They know that this is typical of the Boches mentality.

I had a visitor. Promised never to speak his name, but let me tell you he is still a very important person. The warden let him enter through the secret door in Rue Messier so no one knew. His news was bad. The war was not going well. Or not going as well as we hoped, but the Germans had been pushed back and once we had regained our strength, we would chase them all the way to Berlin.

There was more bad news. I was not to be put on trial, yet. I was very disappointed. When I talked with George and Theo, I was assured that if I was apprehended, there would be a quick trial, like Henriette Caillaux's, and I would be found not guilty, as she was. Suddenly there was a problem. The prime minister had decided that my trial had to be postponed because of fear that a public reminder of Jaurès' slaying would anger the left-wing troublemakers who might decide to desert the army. Apparently he believed that the sacred union of all Frenchmen would be endangered. They might even find me guilty if I was tried by a military court. They could execute me before an appeal was lodged. I had to take that into consideration. Certainly.

I could see that he, too, was sad. "I promise you this, young man, your bravery will not be forgotten. Your silence will be repaid. You will want for nothing." I almost blurted out that I didn't kill Jaurès for money, but thought better of that. Once I was a free man, I would need funds, and he would pro-vide for me. Good. He could afford it. I wondered if he might contact my father and ensure that he was well and understood why I did the deed. He said he would, though there was some doubt about the whereabouts of the civic administration for Reims because of the German invasion. Bastards. He would inquire, he promised.

I was quite comfortable and had to be patient. Are you patient, my friend? Comfortable in the sense that I was fed and treated as a special case, but that did not stop the waves of uncertainty. Couldn't shake them off. They are like the sea; unpredictable. Subject to laws we do not fully comprehend. But perhaps you do, my friend?

Personal doubt is also a cancer. It creeps into the mind and attaches itself to surprising memories, most often in those dark hours when secret fears blossom. Fortunately no one can share the moment. It is purely person-al. Black thoughts hidden in the shadows shout names from the past. Bad names. Cruel names. Names which undermine the confident person you want to be. Names which mock the hero. Names which strike at the core of self-belief and strip it of its dignity. Names you fear are true.

15

DECEMBER 1914 – THE LEGION OF DISHONOR

The chief superintendent listened carefully to his report. "Zaharoff, and, you think, Wendel, Joffre's man, and Benoit Durfort. Are you certain?" He stubbed out his Gauloises and pursed his lips. "Show me where they met."

Mathieu found the avenue on the wall map of the city.

"Yes, this part of town is being cleared to prepare a last ditch defense. Perfect for a clandestine meeting. But why?" Bernard Roux's antenna raised suspicion to conspiracy in one bound. "The munitions millionaire with the Grand Croix of the Legion of Honor, the chairman of the all-powerful committee of iron and steel owners, a representative from our commanding general, and the Quai d'Orsay's diplomatic eminence noir. What do they have in common? Armaments, power, military muscle, and diplomatic connections." The chief superintendent tapped his finger on the map. "Show me exactly where you think that house is."

Mathieu traced his fingers along the street map and hesitated. "Here, I think."

Roux nodded to himself and picked up the telephone. "Ah, Sergeant Toussaint, would you do me a favor. Check the address of Charles Laurent?" A flurry of invective followed. Toussaint clearly didn't like the named person. "Ah, that's what I thought, Sergeant. Yes, certainly, I'll bear that in mind." He returned to the wall map and chuckled. "Toussaint wants us to know that if we are going to arrest Laurent, he'd like to help. But that's who lives there, Mathieu. Charles Laurent, former civil servant with a finger in every pie, moved into banking and industry and often represents the Comité des Forges here in Paris. Add his name to the others and we are beginning to shape a notion of who *they* are. The people behind the curtain of power. The puppet masters." The chief pursed his lips and lit an inspirational cigarette in the hope of self-enlightenment. "What are they up to?" he mused.

Mathieu shrugged. "No good at the very least. What do we do? Have we enough evidence to take this further?"

"None at all. We don't know what they're doing and we don't know what they've done. We have to keep this entirely between us, Mathieu. These people don't want ordinary mortals snooping around. Put nothing on record. Nothing."

"But we are the Deuxième Bureau. It's our job to create a record," Mathieu protested.

"Of course it is, but there are some who are allowed to act above the state." Roux raised a finger to stop Mathieu's interruption. "Knowledge is power, and we now have the knowledge, you and I. We keep this to ourselves. Believe me, it is safer... for both of us."

* * *

Just how much credence was given to the story that Paris was saved and the German onslaught halted by the city's taxis and charabancs no one will know for sure, but the additional brigades from England, the reinforcements from Alsace-Lorraine, and the volunteers and reservists from the capital forced the overstretched German army to withdraw from the River Marne to the other side of the River Aisne in early September. Life slowly returned to the shaken old lady. Those who had taken refugee elsewhere began to slip back to their homes. Markets reappeared as if to herald normality. Some food and vegetables were available from local vendors, though prices had risen. Theaters and music halls slowly reopened, though the audiences were muted and the bonhomie of high summer had gone. Laughter found a more hollow tone, though the wine reserves remained constant by volume but dearer by the glass. Buses returned to their familiar routes. The metro ran a reduced service and the Sorbonne recommended classes in early December.

Each night Mathieu waited for Agnès to finish her work in the café, heart in mouth, knowing that she was determined to leave Paris. She had talked about it for two months and attended part-time classes at the Hotel-Dieu hospital so that she understood how to bandage minor wounds and apply clean dressings, though the message from the frontline field hospitals was that nothing could prepare volunteers for the chaos of the trenches. He found her sitting at the table in her apartment, small suitcase by her side, biting her lip, knowing he would be upset. Before he had time to react, Agnès kissed Mathieu passionately and drew away, prepared for his objections. She touched his lips and said, "You do your best every day to keep Paris safe, and I have to be involved, too. Young men have gone to war, the middle classes have boarded up their mansions and sneaked away in the night, and I'm still cleaning tables. No. When I see the injured and wounded on the streets I'm ashamed of myself. You know how I feel. So, I've decided. I am going to join the medical corps."

"But you're not a trained nurse yet," he protested hopelessly.

"No, but I can clean, cook, dig, wash, and learn to bind wounds. From what we see in the streets of Paris every day, I can help do something. Surely?" She kissed him again and smiled. "And for God's sake, change that shirt. You stink of Gauloises."

* * *

Next morning, sitting close to the entrance of Café Clichy, Paul Dubois and Mathieu were bemused to have their first coffee of the day delivered by the owner, Andre, a man more used to a late morning appearance than the frosty pre-dawn shift.

"Pardon, Messieurs." He placed the steaming coffee carefully before them and returned with a croissant for Mathieu, his face tripping him as if his life had been ruined.

"Five years, would you believe that? For five years I've paid Agnès well, helped her out when she had problems, and she comes in last night and bids me farewell. Walks out. What am I to do? I asked, but she was gone. Said something about doing her best for the war effort! Bloody war. Bloody women."

"Especially the ones who have joined the medical corps to look after the wounded at the front," Mathieu retorted sarcastically. He resented Andre's bitter self-interest, for his own sense of loss ran far, far deeper. He had reasoned with Agnès for weeks, but knew she was right and he had let her kiss his protests into a passionate *adieu*. He rose, dropped a solitary coin on the table, and said, "Let's go, Paul. Half the criminals in Paris may have been let out of prison to join the army, but whether they do or not is anyone's guess. The biggest criminal in town is on his way back from a short break, so we'd better go check he arrives safety."

"That's no way to speak about our dear president, Mathieu." Paul Dubois managed to make the word president sound like an insult. "I take it the whole political rat-pack are scuttling home from Bordeaux?"

Chief Superintendent Roux was visibly upset. He could see the cost of war standing in front of him, ranks thinned, the average age in the high forties, tired faces bearing the ravages of a troubled time. Many had lost sons, brothers, or friends within the first four months of a war that was supposed to be over by Christmas. Guy Simon for one. He had fallen on the second week of fighting, just south of Metz, as the conquering Germans swept all before them, his heart undiminished, his soul unrepentant, his wife a widow, his children fatherless. His sacrifice, like that of all such victims, however large or small, left bereft those who had to cope in the wake of death or injury. The women and families. And they were sacrificed on the altar of mammon. All of them.

"Gentlemen, I'm aware of the strains on the service and can promise you that in the short run, it won't get any better. Crime has apparently fallen, if we believe the statistics, but given the numbers who have left the city to good and bad purpose, we now face a different set of problems. I want you to stamp hard on the racketeers and black market scum you pick up on the streets. It is the new big business, and organized crime wants its share. I understand that the Corsicans have become more active in prostitution and trafficking of all kinds. Paris is coming back to life, believe me. Refugees from Belgium and the north continue to flood into our city. They need help and direction. With them will come spies and German sympathizers. I'm going to add a few men to the surveillance division. Obviously, anything we can do to assist the boys at the front comes first.

"Now that the president, prime minister, and Cabinet are due back, clearly our role in protection becomes as vital as our role in detection. Every group commander will report to me as always, but we will have to actively identify targets as you remain the first line of defense." He paused to give them time to absorb the shifting priorities they were expected to manage. "A word to the wise. Take care with tips; tips are for gamblers. We can't afford to gamble. And instinct can be very dangerous. Don't rely on instinct, that's how animals survive. We have to be more clinical. Aware of the dangers around us. The stakes are high. Stay sharp."

The assembly broke up. No cheering or clapping, but content that they had in Bernard Roux a leader who was also a policeman. "That's the longest I've known him speak between two drags at a Gauloises." Dubois was certain of that.

A clerk caught them on the stairs and redirected them to the chief superintendent's office. He wasted no time with unnecessary pleasantries. "I'm keeping you together because I trust you. The special division to monitor and protect named citizens and foreign delegates is now your responsibility, Captain Girard. I know it may be short-term because of your deferred retirement, but you are the senior man." Girard felt that his retirement date had become a fading illusion, like the rainbow's end sans the fabled pot of gold.

"Sit down, please." The chief ushered them to a mahogany table on which lay half a dozen sets of files. They sat. "We start with persons of significance, some political, some business, some dubiously wealthy and all free to move around the country at will. I have one question. What connects them?" He raised a blue file and said, "Basil Zaharoff, arms dealer and Legion of Honor. Recent allegations claim that he is being watched by foreign agents active in Paris. Handle with care. Connected to the Iron and Steel Combines. Personal friend of the president and high ranking military personnel."

Two red files covered the movements of the president and prime minister. "Clearly senior politicians will be protected by the military at all times, but we have to know if they are contacted by outside agencies, no matter the assumed innocence. But discreetly. Always discreetly."

Roux sifted through others and raised a brown, heavily marked file which had clearly been collated over a number of years. "Baron Édouard de Rothschild and family. Bankers to every crown head in Europe and connected by family ties across Europe. Manages important loans for the government. Of course he is above personal scrutiny, so take great care before any intervention by act or word." An orange file contained notes and cuttings on Alexander Isvolsky, the Russian Ambassador. "He is likely to be a target for a left-wing socialist assassin. Some of them believe he directly caused the war. Very close ties with the president."

Chief Superintendent Roux flicked through the remainder, stopping to advance his own thoughts on two particular names. "William Sharp, the new American ambassador. We know very little about him, and he knows nothing about France. But as President Wilson's man in Paris, he is immensely important. And watch this one." He pulled out an image of a stern-faced nobody staring coldly from a recent photograph, black fedora perched on his head, and tapped it twice with his left index finger. "Herbert Hoover. American mining engineer. Well-connected in London and Washington. Word has it that he will be in charge of a special relief program based in northern France and Belgium. We will see. Fifteen years ago the British money-power closed ranks behind him to cover his complicity in defrauding the Chinese, and he is a personal friend of their foreign secretary. Very close to the elite in London."

Roux picked up the remainder and tidied them into one careful lot. "These do not need immediate action. Our predecessors compiled a list of known left-wing and anti-war sympathizers who were to have been arrested and confined to prison when war was declared if there was trouble on the streets. Jean Jaurès was one of them, poor man. His murder isn't even mentioned here. Got to give Poincaré his due, the idea of a sacred union between workers and the state seems to have worked." He sighed and looked for a reaction. "So far."

"The connection, chief, is loose at best, but I can see that they can all move freely around France and leave the country at will," Mathieu observed.

Bernard Roux looked at his files again and flicked through the top two. "They are unlikely to be spies, but their interests may not always be ours. The foreigners have money behind them. Remember that."

"Captain, you allocate tasks and make sure that we keep tabs on them especially if and when they get together. But from a distance. They will make life awkward for us if the president and his entourage gets wind of this clandestine operation."

Mathieu was appointed to the Zaharoff file. He was in the best position to work on connections they did not as yet understand. Dubois was put in charge of the Americans and the Rothschilds, since they had already made connections to bankers in New York. Former allies from the old Deuxième Bureau were given lead roles in protecting the politicians and Ambassador Isvolsky, aided by the army of course. Each man was handed his allocated files. Mathieu pondered over his in detail and did not like what he saw. Money, power, armaments, international connections and political clout. He had been put in charge of monitoring a rag-tag bag of vipers. Where to begin?

"Moutie, *mon ami. Ca va?*" Poor Moutie almost defecated himself. Having just been dismissed from a charge of petty theft by a judge with much more on his mind, he was on the point of congratulating his good fortune when Mathieu appeared from behind a pillar. Moutie's legal representative had apparently misheard thirty as thirteen, misinformed the judge about previous convictions, and jail had been avoided yet again.

The thief protested. "There was hardly any money in the blind man's collection tin. And I didn't take it all…but you don't want to hear all this…" Then he remembered who he was speaking to.

"Monsieur Bertrand, how good to see you." He began to stammer. "I, I w-w-waited at the police station for t-two hours, but you never came back."

"We'll talk about that coffin later. I want to buy you a coffee."

The thief hesitated. "Somewhere discreet, Monsieur, please. I've a r-reputation to maintain."

"Of course you do. Lead on." Moutie didn't seem to understand sarcasm.

They entered a seedy, nondescript bar hidden between the canal and disused railway cuttings. Judged from the outside, it was derelict. A passerby might have thought that demolition workers had begun to pull it apart but stopped to join the army some five months ago. Window frames hung piteously from their sills and the corrugated iron door sat open to the elements, rusting in the damp which overlay the ruin. The sewers nearby ought to have run into the canal but were blocked. That was clear.

Once they had clambered over the natural debris, an inner room lay concealed amongst the rubble, wind and waterproofed. The tables and chairs came from different styles, ages, and localities, most likely stolen, Mathieu presumed. Conversation ceased as they entered the makeshift café-bar. Moutie spoke first to the bartender who looked over at Mathieu without apparent concern and nodded towards a table in the far corner where once a fireplace had warmed the surroundings. Miraculously, the room was warm and welcoming and the coffee hot, sharp and more than acceptable. Cheap, too. Five others sat around the bar-front engrossed in tales of their own misery. A mutilated soldier had been lifted onto a high stool from which his standing leg swung gaily of its own accord, his medal pinned directly on the front of his weathered jacket where once a button had kept it closed. It was the war, you see.

They sat in their own exclusion in the corner. Mathieu's opening words stunned the thief.

"I want your advice, Moutie." Paris's worst thief preened himself. This unexpected honor, he felt, was entirely justified. He leaned closer into the conversation so that he was the only one who could hear what came next. At which point Mathieu realized how clever Moutie had been. He'd brought his "friendly" policeman into the heart of this criminal underworld so that everyone could see them together. His fraternizing with the "enemy" was to be public knowledge, not a dirty secret. Unquestionably, Moutie's eventual account would embellish the truth but it gave him status inside a community which had no place for police informants.

From the corners of his eyes, Mathieu could see that the whole bar was watching the proceedings while pretending to ignore them. He handed Moutie a piece of paper with a flamboyance which ensured everyone saw it.

"OK, Moutie, put these names in order of untouchable. I mean, who would you least consider stealing from?"

"Oh I would never…"

"Just look and then tell me."

Moutie took hold of the list and dropped it on the well-soiled table as if he had been scalded. A small touch of drama to please the audience.

"*Mon Dieu*. They are all untouchable."

"Look, imagine that you had been caught stealing from them, which would be the most dangerous?"

"OK." He hesitated briefly, as if deliberating a ponderous point of law. "The president and Cabinet…ten years hard labor. Baron Rothschild, a sound whipping, so that you cannot walk for a week. The ambassadors, five to ten years." He stopped, turned the piece of paper over, and stared at the blank lines as if they hid a secret.

Mathieu waited until he raised his head. "And Zaharoff?"

Moutie eased himself closer and whispered with sufficient clarity to ensure that everyone heard, "Dead within the week."

"What?" Mathieu balked at the preposterous idea.

"My friend, Monsieur Zaharoff does not permit theft of property or personal possessions. Death. You'd end up in the canal, weighed down with bricks. Probably beaten beyond recognition. Have you seen his bodyguards?"

"No," Mathieu lied.

"Murderers. If Monsieur Zaharoff left all his doors and windows open and put a notice in *Le Parisien* that he would be away for a week, his property would be untouched. The last man in Paris to cross. Believe me."

"Tell me about the bodies in the canal, Moutie. Clearly Monsieur Zaharoff doesn't get his hands dirty on such unimportant matters as an opportunistic thief, but are these victims all thieves?"

"No. I mean, I don't know. I don't think so. I've heard they might have been journalists. But who knows?" Moutie knew immediately that he should not have spoken so freely. Honesty was never properly valued.

"Monsieur Bertrand," he began, placing his hand over Mathieu's. "You did not hear this from me."

Mathieu considered cutting off Moutie's hand at the wrist, but simply removed his own hand and replied, "Moutie, we were never here. Good day."

So. Even the Paris underworld feared Basil Zaharoff, and his bodyguards felt free to act above the law. Mathieu would have to take great care. He had blundered into their secret world and would be a target if identified. Bernard Roux had warned against reliance on instinct, but every instinct Mathieu possessed warned that this man Zaharoff was a danger; personally, and more importantly, a danger to France. And as for Moutie? That was a surprise. He was a pathetic thief but not a fool. Come to think of it, he could never have survived without being streetwise, and despite everything, he had friends and knew how to use them. Worth knowing.

As he drove back across the city Mathieu passed Montmartre and his thoughts turned again to Raoul Villain. Still no move to set a trial date. At the prime minister's insistence. Odd. Very odd. What else was hidden behind the convenience of his sacred union?

Raoul's Story

AN EMPTY CONFESSION

You know, my friend, I think that you are too trusting of people. Some might say naive . I was once, but managed to shed such damaging innocence. Perhaps it was because I was surrounded by dangerous and untrustworthy men in La Santé. Perhaps it was the product of many disappointments. I don't know.

Shortly after the war began I became aware that prison numbers were dwindling. Younger, fitter inmates disappeared into the ranks of army volunteers having sworn allegiance to the tricolor. I've no idea how many gave their lives to the cause and there was, most certainly, no role of honor in the prison chapel. Come to think of it, I doubt if many actually fulfilled their promise. And of course who were left? Elderly recidivists, suspected spies, child murderers and the grossly unfit and unhealthy flotsam of a disintegrating society. Even though it was a lonely existence, I knew that outside these cold bleak walls, I had friends. But could I really trust them?

It was hard to stay focused but the authorities let me write letters. I was obliged to let them read the contents but at least I didn't feel quite so isolated. I had planned at one stage to go back to Loughton in England and stay again with Mrs. Francis in her Rose Cottage, but more important matters intervened. She was a very nice woman, a widow whose husband had been an eminent architect. At that time I was a student of archeology at Ecole du Louvre and it was a real pleasure to live on the edge of Epping Forest and travel into London to visit its museums and historic buildings.

The only problem was the English. Not the language; the people. Mrs. Francis and her family were very pleasant, but travelling on the railways could be rough. People generally struggled to understand me, though my English was perfect. And rude? They probably thought that I didn't understand their insults when they called me "Froggie" or "Mister Frog." I remember being asked if I could recall the battle of Agincourt as if it marked their unbroken ascendency over France. One pub landlord had a brute of a mongrel called Bonaparte and he took great pleasure in calling the dog to heel when I visited his hostelry so that he had reason to insult the great Emperor's name. "Bonaparte, sit. Bonaparte do as you are bid. Bonaparte did you just fart?" Childish, don't you think?

Of course they were our allies in the struggle against the Bosches, and God bless them for that, but frankly the English army were badly prepared for the war. I mean, they didn't have iron helmets until half-way through! They charged bravely and blindly into the attack with no protection against shell fragments and it is said that their generals were even more stupid and stubborn than ours. Now that takes some believing.

I wrote to Monseigneur Richard at Saint Pierre de Montmartre and asked him if he might visit me to hear my confession. That was not why I wanted to speak to him, but I knew it would play to his ego if I made him feel like he was the only man who could save my soul. Huh! Of course he fell for it and came to La Santé within the week. It transpired that the prison Governor knew him personally and escorted the good Monseigneur to a secluded room in the special area close to the Rue Messier entrance. The Governor did not linger at the door, but bid the good priest farewell and asked him to come for a coffee in his office when his duties were finished.

We were alone, Monseigneur Richard and I and it was clear that he didn't intend to wait long. He sat on my chair, placed a purple stole around his neck and began to intone the Latin prayers. I coughed loudly, amused that he had thrown himself into the safety of his calling rather than indulging in at least some small talk. A greeting would have been nice, an inquiry about my wellbeing most welcome, perhaps a token of brotherly concern. Not so. His first act was to accentuate the importance of his office and avoid an interest in my person.

"Excuse me, Monseigneur. I would like to explain the conditions I must attach to this meeting so that you understand my intentions."

"Your intentions?" his vocal chords strained in disbelief, but it was his facial contortion which were most amusing. There he sat, the Parish Priest of Saint Pierre, barely a single step from the next vacant bishopric in France and the unconvicted prisoner had neither fallen to his knees nor shown any sign of proper deference. Worse still, said inmate intended to set conditions before he began his confession. Preposterous. Absurd. Unheard of. His eyes almost popped out of his face, its color adopting a deeper hue of purple than his stole. If one of us looked like Bozo the clown, it wasn't me.

"Let me explain. I wish to make a confession to cleanse my soul. I did indeed kill Jean Jaures and have never denied that fact, and I never will. I am happy to swear to you that I will not commit such an act again…but in this instance was my action a sin? Can you yet agree that one might kill for God? Kill to save my country from being overrun by Lutheran Germans? Do you recall once having this conversation with me outside Saint Pierre's?

I saw in his face a recognition. He knew who I was, and it discomforted him. He made to remove his stole as if to signify that our conversation was at an end, but I persisted. "I have decided that you are the only priest in the world to whom I am willing to admit my sin, if it be such, and express the necessary regret for absolution. You can save my soul or let it fall into the deepest hole in hell. I will let it be known that you and you alone have moved me to contrition and such goodness, such piety will undoubtedly have you confirmed as a bishop within the month. But…"

"There are no 'buts.'" He held his hands up in absolute horror. "You do this properly or not at all."

"But I need you to promise to help me. I have prepared a testament of absolute truth which I must ask you to hold for me in case something happens; something sinister. By that I mean my sudden death, unexplained disappearance or unusual accident. I have prepared this written confession and want to entrust it to you as part of my act of contrition. My faith in you is intertwined with my faith in God." I dropped to my knees and began to intone my confession before he had time to argue. "Bless me, father…"

By the time we finished I had lied my way through canonical dictates so that the Monseigneur accepted my apparent contrition. I said I was sorry for killing Jaurès but I wasn't. I couldn't be. He took my written testament and hid it deep in his cloak.

"I trust you won't ever have cause to use this mon père," I lied to him, trusting that he would ultimately open it read it and make sure that its contents were known inside the closed hierarchy of the French church. Why? Because news would reach Charles and Action française and they would believe in my utter dedication to this cause. Our cause, I mean.

The letter said nothing other than my singular responsibility for killing Jaurès because of his threat to France. Proof to them of my loyalty. I intended to pass a number of these to my visitors but one would be different. One would tell the truth.

Within the month Monseigneur Richard was appointed Bishop of Beauvais. Well, would you believe it? I smiled when the governor told me.

16

FEBRUARY 1915 – UNTOUCHABLES

New harsh words became part of the Parisian lexicon in those first six months of war. No one wanted to visit the ravaged *zone reserve* that lay beyond the city gates. Broken like a tarnished icon, no longer hailed as an example of style and grace, the area had been devastated by its transformation from residential refinement to trampled suburban disrepair. Disheveled residues of once-proud battalions limped back from the front, bloodied, bandaged, blinded and disillusioned through muddied streets which did not want to know them. Thousands of *mutiles* struggled for survival; limbless half-men condemned to prey on the conscience of those wise enough to avoid the misery of modern warfare, seeking that fine balance between survival on one leg or resignation to an early grave.

From time to time even they had to give way to the newest recruits with their artillery, ammunition, gleaming rifles and clean-cut uniforms, sometimes marching, sometimes on horseback or packed into motorized vehicles, eyes fixed ahead to avoid contact with reality. Broken walls, broken homes, broken dreams and broken promises littered the highway from hell. Isolated groups stood around fires fuelled by freshly cut trees, deep-set stares daring any local objection. Nature too was a disposable asset.

Inside the city there was much for the bourgeoisies to lament. Hotels which boasted luxury struggled to maintain their elite service. Laundry workers and cooks, dishwashers and chamber-maids, the essential bearers of quality provision went off to join the *replacantes* who were willing to exchange the routine of emptying piss-pots for a hundred more responsible jobs, once the exclusive preserve of man. In many smaller bars and restaurants the retired matron was obliged to return to the kitchen, clean tables and serve customers, while detailing the trials of her varicose veins. Within a relatively short period of time, even the rich were obliged to wait patiently for less than quality service.

Women manned the coal trucks; women learned to drive municipal tramcars. Basic street services like rubbish collection, gas-lighting and coal deliveries were given over to the fairer sex. They coped with the dead and dying as best their newfound talents would allow. Without the renewed reserve of feminine strength and purpose, the city would have shrunk beneath the Seine.

"This will all end badly," Dubois moaned, leaving Mathieu and Pascal Girard to guess what he was referring to. He flicked crumbs from their table in a riverside café, thoughtlessly left behind by the previous occupants. "How is your friend Monsieur Zaharoff? Living quietly?"

"So far," Mathieu grunted.

"Did you see the report I left on your desk? Apparently he and most of his household will be decanting to the Chateau Monthairons for a few days. They will let us know when they intend to return to Paris."

"Chateau Monthairons?"

"It's near Verdun. Inside the military zone. Zaharoff has permission to visit General Joffre."

Mathieu could read trouble crossing the captain's face. No one liked the suggestion that Papa Joffre was involved with these people. He chose another tack.

"Here's a strange question." Mathieu considered his words carefully. "Do you remember just before the war we had a series of bodies dragged from the canal, unrecognizable?"

"Of course." Paul Dubois almost sighed out loud at the memory of such blessed times.

"Has a body been fished from the canal in recent days? One that has been beaten so badly his mother wouldn't recognize him?"

"What's that got to do with anything?" Dubois could not see the connection. "But as it happens there was one reported yesterday," he admitted, "and d'you know how it had been weighed down?"

"Bricks in the pockets. Lots of them." Dubois straightened his back in surprise. Mathieu had struck gold with his first arrow. "Get the car. I'll explain everything en route to the morgue."

The body was wheeled before them by the coroner's assistant. She was new to the job, awkward with the gurney. Its wheels tried to take every direction at once, leaving her to maneuver like a novice dog-walker whose charges smelled her lack of confidence. When Mathieu pulled back the cover, she turned away, embarrassed. What had once been a face was crushed into red pulp, like raspberries pressed into hard earth. Ears, yes. Nose, probably. Eyes and teeth, cruelly mashed into the scull. Recognition, impossible. Mathieu lifted the right hand which hung limp. Three fingers remained. The rest had been torn from the flesh. He studied it closely. Held it gingerly. Let it fall back to rest lest he inflict any further pain. Poor guy. Well, this he knew for sure. It wasn't Moutie. The hand was much too clean, even after two days in the filthy canal. But it had some link, however tenuous, to Zaharoff, and he was about to leave Paris. Chief Superintendent Roux listened closely to Mathieu's request.

"We have to go there, even if it is only to find out what's happening. We need to know what game he's playing. No one in their right mind would visit a chateau so close to the front line. Secret meetings of clandestine organizations means something new is on their agenda."

Roux thought for a while, picked over the open file, drew fresh life from his Gauloises and coughed. "I'll write a confidential note to the general. Tell Joffre that the Bureau has reason to believe that Zaharoff's life is in danger. He'll say that his army is more than able to protect one Greek salesman, but the ace up our sleeves is that we will claim that you would recognize the would-be assassins. And they don't know anything different. Leave today so you have time to soak in the lie of the land."

Just before Basil Zaharoff's entourage set out from his villa in Avenue Hoche he was informed by Paul Dubois that his Deuxième Bureau minders would be travelling behind to protect him. At the same time, Mathieu was being introduced to Papa Joffre, as the General was affectionately known to his troops. The legend was unique. Mathieu immediately understood why Joffre was so popular. He exuded calm. As commander-in-chief on the Western Front, Joffre still basked in the glory of the victory which had saved Paris, but, unlike most of his contemporaries he lacked the conceit of military assuredness. Having waited in the grand entrance hall of Chateau Monthairons while three different ranks of military importance double-checked his credentials, Mathieu was ushered into the general's presence.

"How can I be of assistance, young man? I have heard well of you." Joffre shook Mathieu's hand with a strength that belied his years. Catching their general's tone, those around him gave due appreciation.

"You are aware, Sir, that we have concerns about Monsieur Zaharoff's safety, even here."

Eyebrows automatically lifted across the room at the absurdity of anyone daring to attack a visitor in the presence of Papa Joffre. "I have had previous dealings with one of the gang and would recognize him. May I have your permission to assume an army uniform and stay on the periphery during Monsieur Zaharoff's visit to keep watch, but remain incognito?"

If Mathieu had expected an objection, none was raised. Ten minutes later, he stood before a mirror dressed in the blue uniform of an aide de camp.

145

Night crept down upon the chateaux with the stealth of a seasoned ninja. Lights were doused and heavy satin blinds drawn over the great windows whose chandeliers would have, in better times, shone like beacons of wealth amidst the rural poverty. Mathieu needed to clear his mind and strolled outside. Darkness rested under the ample woods beyond the chateau but a clear sky and waxing moon spread strange shadows towards the right. Far off he could see the faint glow of a stellar pulse throwing reds and yellows into the night. There was no sound or self-explained explosions. That was what bothered him. Was the front line on fire?

"I would advise you stay inside the building, Sir."

Mathieu had not been aware that there was another night watchman breathing the outdoor air. Cold but pleasantly so, devoid of any wind to chill the bones. He turned to see a uniformed colleague, cigarette hidden from view but its presence confirmed by stale nicotine breath whipping into the ether.

"What's that? In the distance?" Mathieu pointed to the ghostly pulse, confused by its far presence. His colleague moved closer and looked round to confirm that no one else had come outside to smoke. They were alone.

"That's the glare from our blast furnaces at Briey. You don't normally see them, but it's cloudless tonight."

"Our blast furnaces?"

"Should be. Would have been until *someone*," he whispered, "decided that the Germans could keep the mines and smelters intact. Once produced ninety-percent of our iron and steel. Germans took them 1871 and have them still. Scandalous."

"What?" Mathieu failed to grasp what the officer meant. "Are you saying that we deliberately failed to protect the mines, furnaces, and smelters and left them intact for the Germans? That this is where they produce the materials for their heavy guns and munitions and … we let them?"

The stranger was uncomfortably hesitant, as if he had yet to decide if Mathieu could be trusted. "Yes," he conceded softly, with a hint of shame in his voice.

Mathieu couldn't see his unexpected informant clearly for a shadow crept across the grass like an incoming tide licking the edges of the ancient chateau walls, rising noiselessly to embrace them as a single cloud passed above.

"How do you know?"

"I was there." He double-checked that they were still alone. "In the first days of war, units were formed into a group known as the Army of Lorraine by our High Command, but for whatever reason, we didn't move. A full-blown army sat in the woods and waited for orders that never came. We were established on 19 August to take the mines, brought together on the 21st, and dissolved on the 25th without firing a shot. It would have been a great victory. There was no one to stop us. At the very least we would have ensured that the Germans couldn't use the coal, iron ore, and smelters."

"You must be mistaken, Sir, the records would show…" Mathieu protested.

"Check for yourself. You're Deuxième Bureau." He retorted. The stranger's assuredness hung in the cold, biting back contempt. "And why do you think that tonight's meeting has been called? Take great care." He stamped out his cigarette and slipped into the shadow, leaving Mathieu confused.

"Wait," he called, but no one was there.

A flurry of voices sounded from the front of the chateau capturing Mathieu's attention. Visitors had arrived. The guard of honor stood to attention and senior aides ushered the new arrivals into the great reception hall. While some were unknown, Mathieu recognized Wendel from the Iron and Steel Combine, Zaharoff, his minder deep in conversation, and several assemblymen. At a rough guess, it was basically the same group he had seen in the Paris suburbs three months previously. Simply more of them. Paul Dubois appeared a minute or so afterwards, straining to see if Mathieu was in the room. The hall doors, inlaid with amber to reflect the rich golden-brown excess of another epoch, were closed by Joffre's order. Zaharoff's man was not allowed into the meeting. No outsiders. Without exception. The proceedings were to be secret.

Dubois felt himself forcibly drawn out of the throng and into an ante-room by a uniformed officer. His protest fell short as he recognized his friend and colleague in the borrowed uniform.

"What has been going on? Zaharoff took his time, did he not? Where did Wendel come from?"

"Give me a chance to speak, Mathieu. We had to travel very slowly, lights off, and dozens of roadblocks to pass. Unscheduled stops, too. Thank God we were with Zaharoff. That made life easier. The closer we came to Monthairons, army units appear to have expected him."

Mathieu led Dubois into the garden, aware that a passerby could overhear their conversation.

"And Wendel?"

"Met him about two hours ago with the Assembly representatives and others I did not recognize. I've a list of names, as far as it goes." He patted the inside of his jacket. "About an hour ago they drove closer to the front, got out, and had a full-blown row about something. We had a problem with the car. It hit a rock and stalled. Timon came over to help us."

"Timon?"

"Zaharoff's doorman, his personal guard. The one who nearly caught you."

"Ah, that Timon."

"Still carries a limp, you know?"

"Stick to the story."

They walked on, outside the perimeter of light which spread from the chateau.

"Well, he said he knew about motor car engines, and after about twenty minutes it restarted. His driver brought over a flask of coffee and stayed to pass the time of day. He blocked us off from Zaharoff so I stretched my legs and saw that more men had joined the original group. They must have been there, waiting. Too far away to be sure. Some of them were speaking German, but they do in that neck of the woods."

"Did you hear the word *Briey*?"

"Hear it, no. But there was a road sign that pointed in its direction. *Briey 34 kilometers.*"

"So they were pointing towards Briey or the flashes in the sky?"

"Possibly."

"Very likely?"

"Yes."

"Do you know what Briey signifies? Treason." They sat in the sobering air while Mathieu explained its significance.

"Do either of you gentlemen have a light?" Mathieu instantly knew the voice but still turned around. Paul Dubois, more generously said, "Timon. How good…"

Zaharoff's man sprang at Mathieu, both arms extended towards his throat, his left leg kicking out at Dubois. Rule 1: never stand still. Rule 2: never play fair if a man intends to kill you. Mathieu feinted left and spun round to hit the angry bodyguard. One punch was seriously insufficient. Dubois lay still. The bastard must have caught him in the head. Concentrate. Keep moving. Both men circled each other like rabid dogs, aware that the first serious bite would poison their prey. They entered a strange dumb-show of silent movement. A dance macabre. Concentrate. The heavy

Timon snorted in the moonlight as if to clear his mind. He lashed out with his left foot but failed to make contact. If Joffre or Zaharoff or even one of the steel men saw them, Mathieu knew that he would be in trouble, but no one appeared to notice. No word was spoken. No threat, empty or real, was made. Again they circled each other, this time, in a counter-clockwise direction, eyes locked. They might have continued till dawn, but Mathieu's leg caught on a man-sized root and he fell over the sprawling body of the semi-conscious Dubois. Timon flew at him, but reeled back in mid-flight.

Two shots pierced the night with deafening consequences. Timon roared in pain. Movement on the left edge of the wood caught Mathieu's fleeting attention. Shaken by the noise, Dubois found life in his limbs and struggled to his feet. Armed soldiers rushed from the chateau, guns raised.

"Over there, about one hundred meters to the right," Mathieu pointed, sending a zealous troop of aides and clerks in the wrong direction. "Watch out, he's dangerous." That slowed the pursuers in their hasty tracks. He pointed to the fallen Greek.

"Get him to a field hospital immediately."

Timon lay wounded, unable to object. Blood was seeping from a hole close to his left shoulder. His thigh looked pink and wet in the moonlight. The second bullet had also struck home. Whoever the assailant, he was an excellent shot. Well, almost.

"I think you should get him to a field hospital quickly. he's lost a lot of blood. Are the general and his guests safe?" Mathieu brushed the dirt from his borrowed uniform and sought to confuse the issue by raising concerns in another direction.

"Yes, yes. Perfectly safe." Joffre's senior aide de camp led him back into the building where rumor of an attempted assassination became accepted fact before it reached the grand hall.

"Don't worry, Inspector, the general sends his apologies, but his guests left ten minutes ago, by a side exit in the east wing. As soon as the amber doors were shut, they passed through the hall, into a private office, had a brief conference, and were gone."

"What?" Mathieu was incredulous. Duped by his own military commander. Clever.

"They are on their way back to Paris as we speak. Perfectly safe."

"Are you telling me they came all the way here and there was no meeting?"

"No, no, Monsieur. They met. Indeed they did. I understood your man Dubois was with them."

"Paris."

Mathieu changed into his own clothes, grabbed his hat, and met the police Renault, its engine purring, all within two minutes.

"Don't know how much of this makes sense, Paul. A secret group meet in the forest with other unknown persons, then come to Monthairons as a blind, would you say? So we think that the meeting was with Joffre? We were allowed to see the people they wanted us to see."

"The question becomes who *didn't* they want us to see?"

Mathieu leaned forward in the passenger's seat. "You said you had a list." Dubois pulled out a small notebook and handed it to his lieutenant. The writing sprawled across the page, in parts illegible. Never easy to put down a list of names in a moving car on a rutted road. Mathieu read the names but failed to grasp what they meant. It said:

Francois de Wendel.
Henri de Wendel.
Basil Zaharoff + Timon+ 1 or 2

Édouard de Rothschild.

A banker from the Banque de France? Maybe.
Two Deputies from the National Assembly, names?
Charles somebody... it could have been another Wendel
An American or an Englishman.
Iron and steel men from Briey??
And?

Chief Superintendent Roux met them next morning with a cup of consolation coffee and a croissant.

"I'm glad you both survived the ordeal without permanent damage. You've kicked over a whole field of wasp hives. The darker corridors of power are swarming with stories of attempted assassination and secret evacuations. Brief me, please, but we have to keep this meeting short. I've to be at the Élysée in an hour." Roux checked the ornate Louis XIV gold-gilt clock on the mantelpiece, guarded as it seemed by cherubs and nymphs.

"Can we focus on what we know for sure. No guesswork, no intuition. Facts only."

"There is reason to believe that there is a scandal looming over Briey." Mathieu spoke first. God the coffee was wonderful.

"Not a fact. It is a statement we have yet to establish."

"Zaharoff and the Wendels are involved in an illegal... arrangement of some kind and Papa Joffre and President Poincaré know."

"Big list of assumptions there. Where's proof of wrongdoing?"

Mathieu tried again. "A relatively senior soldier, could be military intelligence, knows that orders were given to form an army unit which was disbanded before it could retake or blow up Briey in August."

"Can't accept that. At the moment it is simply a wild allegation. Where is the proof? Who is the soldier? Show me the orders."

Silence.

Mathieu found a fact. "Zaharoff's bodyguard, what is his name again, Dubois?"

"Timon."

"Timon knows who I am and tried to kill both of us last night."

"OK, I can accept that." A Gauloises was extracted and lit. "Carry on."

"Secret meetings have taken place, and the men involved don't want anyone to know what they are plotting."

"You're assuming a plot. What if they were simply fixing the international price for iron ore?"

"In a forest outside Briey in the dark of night?"

"Where better?"

"Chief, you know this stinks. You insist that nothing is written down to protect us from unnamed vested interests, but some kind of racket is going on here."

"So give me the facts."

Dubois dug deep into his pocket to find his notebook. He handed the list to the chief. Roux's face darkened. The Gauloises almost fell from his mouth. He rescued the perilous cigarette and stole a last drag of nicotine. To their amazement, Bernard Roux rose from his seat and dropped the list unceremoniously into the fire. Paul Dubois reached out to save the evidence before it disappeared, uncertain if Roux had made a mistake. The chief superintendent stopped him short and beckoned him to sit down.

"Both of you need to understand very clearly. There was no list. Nothing was ever put in writing. Nor will it be. Believe me, the people on that list are so powerful that they could have us killed within the day if they knew we had this information. You do know what it means?"

Neither man spoke. Dubois looked stunned by the boss's alarm. Bernard Roux placed his right hand on his moustache, stroked it as if it was a talisman, and made his decision.

"The names that didn't go all the way to Monthairons? Charles Wendel? Former member of the Reichstag? An American with a Rothschild? Isn't the Banque of France hosting J P Morgan from New York? You almost solved the conundrum yourselves. They are checking out our assets before agreeing to a massive international loan. These are the moneymen. These are the bankers of death and Briey is their major asset."

Mathieu protested his frustration. "This is all wrong. How can you say that Briey is their asset when it's held by the Germans. And why is it still operational? The smelters should have been destroyed. The mines, too. No, more than that. The whole area should have been blown apart. Wendel and the Iron and Steel combines must be colluding with Basil Zaharoff. That's treason, if it puts one Frenchman at risk."

"Of course, but we can't prove it." Bernard Roux needed him to calm down. "But the one question we're not asking is, who owns the entire complex?"

Dubois reasoned that since it lay in German hands, it must be Germany.

"But that's not what you found, did you?" Roux rose from his seat and wandered back and forth, understanding for the first time the enormity of their conclusion. "Your list, which never existed, contained the names of Frenchmen, Americans, Englishmen, and the mysterious Zaharoff. And who are they? Bankers, arms manufacturers, men who can move money across continents, and they think it's their asset, because it is. They own it no matter which country claims it."

"So what do we do?" Dubois rose from his chair and moved towards the nearest window, shaking his head. "Are you saying we can't do anything, chief superintendent?"

Bernard Roux reached back to his desk and grasped a packet of Gauloises. "No, I'm not saying that at all. We'll follow this up quietly. But we must resort to their tactics. We do it secretly and we share nothing, except with each other; not even within the Bureau. No records. Nothing that can be traced to us. We have to tread water until the time for retribution comes. Which reminds me, where did you put the files on Zaharoff when we moved into the building? I can't find them."

The telephone's shrill ring interrupted them. "Yes," he growled. His manner changed. "Very good, Sir. Yes, they're with me now." Long pause. "No. Nothing to report. Both are fine." Much longer pause. "Yes, certainly. Oh, that's … ehm … that's much appreciated."

He replaced the receiver and sat back. "Interesting. That was the minister of the interior. Called to congratulate you both on your sterling work last night. Sadly, the would-be assailant escaped, dressed as an officer. He wanted to know if we had learned anything about the goings on at the Chateau. Did I know who was there? You heard my response. We must never, ever let slip that we know what we know. Understood?"

They did and it frightened them.

"One more thing, Messieurs. Unfortunately the two bullets which hit this Timon thug missed his major organs. He lost a great deal of blood, but should recover. Monsieur Zaharoff thanks you most sincerely. Apparently one of you idiots told Joffre's men to take him to a field hospital." Spurred on by the loyalty of close friendship, Dubois pointed at Mathieu.

"Zaharoff will know for sure that we're on to him."

"He knows already. That's why he played you as fools at the Chateau. And if those files are in his hands, believe me, we now need to be smarter than ever.

Bad Memories

I felt less confident; less trusting. Had I done the right thing? Again doubt? Couldn't ever shake it off.

As a boy in Reims I would blame anyone I could. I needed to have the admiration of my father, my teachers, family friends, neighbors, and gullible adults. The gendarmes knew that I would tell them anything I knew if asked, but now certain persons believe that the truth could not be tortured from me. Well, it could. Usually. Except… not this truth. Not the truth which explodes in my dreams. I have watched reruns in my mind like newsreel in the cinema. A silent movie slinks around my mind, uncontrolled, like a venomous viper, poisoning sleep.

I stand alone in an orchard, waiting and watching. I hear their laughter before I see them. Loud whispers intermingle with calls for quiet. One, two, three small heads peer over the stone boundary wall, each carefully surveying the rows of apple and pear trees. Windfall litters the ground, but they don't want any old bruised discard. My brother leads them towards the center spot and they stand in awe at the foot of a great apple tree bearing awesome fruit. Lush and succulent. Near the top is the biggest, most perfectly formed Red Delicious ever seen. It hangs proud. An Emperor amongst the kings of apples. I follow them to the base, hypnotized by that apple.

"Go away, coward," says my brother without turning to face me. Did he see me out of the corner of his eye? Did he sense my presence? Did he smell my fear?

"Beat it, louse."

"Get lost, you toad." His friends treat me with equal disgust. I stand my ground a pace behind them, downhearted but unwilling to leave. They prowl round the base of the tree looking for a point from which to climb. The bark is gnarled and featureless. No matter how they try, there is no branch close enough to grasp nor foothold to step from. They leap, arms outstretched, but flailing hands fall far short of their objective.

"Piggy-back! Up on my shoulders." They try every possible combination without success. None is strong enough to let another stand on his shoulders.

"I can do it. I'm much lighter than anyone else. I can stand on your shoulders and reach the first branch." They look at me and consider the proposal.

"He could you know" my brother reckons. The others agree. It's worth trying, surely.

Eager to please, oh yes, always eager to please, I climb onto his back, and with assorted pushes and shoves, stand tall. I grasp the lowest limb and ease myself upwards. Here the branches are more plentiful and open onto a pathway to the clouds. I look back on their bemused faces. Is that a new-found respect I see? Above, the Holy Grail shines blood red, its perfection like unblemished skin on a beautiful girl. I reach up and touch the fruit. I look down and see three pygmies, mouths open in disbelief. One tug, firm and forceful. Nothing. I try again, wrapping my whole hand around the prize. Nothing. I hear a muffled snort from below.

"He can't even pick an apple from a tree" my brother is doubled over with laughter, his friends adding to the chorus of derision.

I spin round and grab the stubborn apple with both hands and pull hard. It gives. I fall backwards into oblivion and hear myself scream. Several branches break my fall before releasing me to mother earth, winded and sobbing.

"Stupid bastard." Pierre always had a dirty mouth.

"Someone's coming, quick."

They run. My brother stoops to pick up the flawless apple, and leaves me to face the consequences, heaving for each painful breath, unable to move.

A face appears above my own, quizzical, caught between concern and righteous anger. The farmer's eldest son, Jean-Paul peers at me, lying there in fear and pain.

"Are you all right?"

What a stupid question. Have you noticed how often people ask, "Are you all right?" when it is perfectly obvious that you are not? Does that happen to you? Half dead and helpless but all they ask is, "Are you all right, my friend?"

He helps me get to my feet. "What happened here then? Did you do it?"

"They made me."

"Oh, who made you?"

"Conrad, Theo, and Maurice." Oh no! I scream, "Not Conrad, Theo, and Maurice…other people."

"So Conrad, Theo, and Maurice made you shoot Jean Jaurès."

"No, NO, I did not say that…"

"How many times did you shoot Jaurès? You weren't on your own, were you?" He shouts at me, louder this time. "How many times did you shoot Jaurès? You weren't on your own, were you?"

"No not me. Them. No. That's wrong, it was me. It was."

"Them?" He looks left and right, walks as far as the stone wall, and checks for signs of intruders. "I don't see them. I see you."

"Yes, that's what I'm trying to tell you. It was me alone. Me."

He leads me to his father by my left ear and his father kicks my backside and sends me hobbling and sniveling down the orchard path. "Don't shoot Jaurès again. Not in my orchard."

You see how easy it is? Dreams confuse reality. Things that have happened change form. You make mistakes because you find yourself inside old memories. Bad memories. You have to be careful, Charles said.

17

MAY 1915-DECEMBER 1916 – SURVIVAL OF THE WEALTHIEST

The war continued to hemorrhage men and youths in epic numbers. Faced with the advisability of reorganizing the Deuxième. Chief-Superintendent Bernard Roux acted before any outsider could interfere. Mathieu continued his investigations into the international arms dealer but was obliged to keep a low profile, even when Basil Zaharoff went to England. Rumors about him rattled across tottering empires. He was a spy for the British. He was a spy for the Germans. He traded national secrets for gold. He was seen in Switzerland. He was seen in Athens. He was a Greek or a Turk or a Frenchman. The privileged air of diplomatic small talk grew thick with speculation but there was nothing which could definitively prove his war profiteering. Roux's inner ear heard it all, and for as long as the prince of darkness remained outside the borders of France, his department was impotent. The injured bodyguard, Timon, had been shipped off to a nursing home in the Bernese Alps. A unique perk in unique times.

He called his team together and shared his decision. "Pascal, I need you to stay on for a few more months." The old captain looked, listened, and refused.

"No. You said Christmas, then just a few weeks more, then Easter. I'll die on the bloody job, chief."

"You won't. I'm going to switch your responsibilities with Mathieu's. You can watch over Zaharoff and foreign visitors, and he can deal with the black market and criminal fraternity and do some real police work." Before Pascal Girard could reject his request outright, he added, "You'll be directing operations from here. The younger ones can tread the streets."

The team knew that Pascal's family had suffered their own bitter tragedy and teetered on the abyss of extinction. They admired him for accepting his fate with a stoicism which he and many like him endured on a daily basis. War is a wicked imposition. Pascal Girard had known Guy Simon as a friend and encouraged him to join the Tigers when the flying squad was set up. He felt his loss deeply in the first weeks of the war and agonized over his inability to convince Guy to stay in Paris. Worse followed. Pascal's youngest, Henri, was killed in a gas attack near Ypres during the second battle for the iconic debris which had once been an ancient Flemish town. The Girard family knew the misery of forlorn hope, believing at first that Henri was missing, then that he had been rescued and taken to a military hospital where he was recovering. All lies and conjecture. Henri had been dead for three months before official confirmation arrived via soulless telegram. Three months of useless prayer. No one knew what to say. Condolences are but words no matter how eloquently spoken and well-intended.

Pascal's devastation continued when his wife, Helene, died because living was no longer important. And, for the first time in his adult life, he was alone. His daughters were spread across the country, married with responsibilities of their own. Pascal's options were to stay in an empty house, no longer a home, replete with anguished memories, or keep working. He chose work for now.

Agnès, too, bore the marks of fatigue at close quarters. She was not easily given to complaint but when she stole time with Mathieu on a quick visit to Paris in the company of the broken, she unburdened herself in a torrent of welled-up emotion. No self-pity or indulgence passed her lips but she spent her days in hell and cruel images had been irreparably burned into her being. When Agnès left Paris in the first weeks of the war she broke free from the sarcasm and derision of men forever. Mathieu had been aware that some newspapers urged women to stay at home and serve their country by replacing men temporarily in offices, sew uniforms, and help out in childcare refuges so that the business of war could be left to the fighting man. The heroes. Behind the unbending determination which nurses had to instill in their own discipline, vicious stories claimed that female volunteers engaged in sexual activity with wounded men, were chasing officers, and had countless ulterior motives; that they wore their uniforms as the latest in fashion accoutrements. "Nursing should be left to nuns," the whispering bourgeoisie told each other in the safety of their middleclass tearooms.

Lying together on top of a patchwork quilt which Agnès felt was eiderdown, she kissed Mathieu's torso and stroked wisps of breast hair which might one day grow grey. He waited patiently for her to speak.

"Bad, eh? As bad as they say?"

Agnès inhaled the cold air in her apartment, appreciating its comparative purity, knowing that less than three hundred kilometers to the north, men were drowning in pitiless mud. She caught her breath, uncertain if she should speak.

"If I told you that our main enemy wasn't the Germans, what would you say?"

Mathieu leaned on his left elbow and looked directly into the eyes he had longed for, wondering what she meant.

"That France has many enemies who call themselves friends."

"Perhaps, because that's your world. In mine, war is a relentless succession of horror with the dead and the dying piled up and cast aside. It's backbreaking, heartbreaking and soul destroying. Living conditions are only tolerable because you have to sleep exhausted, but the round the clock bombardment, the rats, the mud, the bone-chilling winter wind, rotten food, and crass stupidity of the generals eventually wears you down. The non-stop triage of dressings, operations, and death become everyday companions. Depression sucks your spirit. And those boys, those poor, poor boys ... ."

Mathieu kissed her bare arm and pulled a cover from the floor. "You're here now, my darling. Safe, do you hear?" But Agnès did not.

"And then something happens, something ordinary and unexpected, and you can't take any more. Waiting for a letter which never comes can break the spirit. No water to wash underwear, which should have been cleaned three weeks before, crushes your sense of worth."

A single tear slipped down her cheek, but the very act of wiping it away enraged Agnès. She broke free of her protector and let rage have its way.

"But nothing, nothing, nothing compares to the madness and stupidity of our military authorities. Do you know what the first instruction is when a wounded man is brought in, eh? Never mind the severity of the wound, the pain, the hopelessness? We have to fill in form forty-six. Form forty-six. A must-do before treatment can even begin. You find yourself asking a man who cannot hear, who cannot see, who is tottering on the tightrope of life or death, what his personal details are. Form fucking forty-six." Her tears stormed from their own trenches and drowned the sickening memory.

Paris, Roux's Paris, was also in what felt like permanent decline, even to an in-comer like Mathieu. In the first six months of the war she had taken unexpectedly ill to the newfound limitations. Then she aged badly. Drained of her gaiety, the face of the old city became lined with grief. Her laughing eyes sagged, dragged down by darkening tears. Her lifeblood lacked oxygen. Like all the wounded she protected inside her boundaries,

Paris needed time to recover, but there was no time. Renewal was strained by the primacy of victory. All else had to give way.

By the third winter the city looked like an impoverished urchin; her former finery, torn and bedraggled, unkempt, neglected. Even sleaze in the Pigalle lost all semblance of sparkle. The Moulin Rouge stuttered to life haphazardly, unlit outside and unheated inside. Mathieu had heard that organized crime in the Milieu was scarcely able to make ends meet. In the underworld, war's cancerous calamity grew intense as the native population thinned through a plague of deprivation. Even the more affluent had to learn to do without. Metro and bus services no longer ran at night. Lamplights flickered, electricity cuts became more frequent and those who still kept candles dreaded the day these would be finally extinguished. Coal supplies for the ordinary citizen choked. People accepted that factories, especially those engaged in armaments and engineering, had to be fed first.

"It's the war, you know."

Color faded from the weather-beaten townscape. All was grey. Chilling Artic winds swept down from the north. Lonely citizens died in front of unlit stoves. The Seine froze from rutted bank to rutted bank, picturesque in watercolor, miserable in real life. Hoarding became an issue which divided neighbors, friends, and families. As the days shortened towards mid-winter, cafés, shops, and bakeries opened in the late morning and closed early. Food shortage accelerated towards crisis, except for the very rich and the black-marketeers.

In the midst of this pitiful sacrifice, Chief Superintendent Bernard Roux of the Deuxième was invited to the official celebration hosted by the Banque de Paris in the magnificently elegant Hotel Ritz. His invitation bore the pompous Latin inscription which claimed that the bank's fortunes might fluctuate but never sink, written in florid gold. How much did that alone cost? The fare was as sumptuous as ever, the guest list, less so. Any self-respecting man or woman might have asked what crime they had committed to be included in such a glitter of diamond-studded aristocrats, minor royalty, ancient title-holders, bankers, financiers, newspaper owners and editors, industrialists, former generals and part-time admirals, politicians and their glamorously coiffured wives and mistresses. This was no collection of the Great and the Good. Just the Great, as defined by themselves.

Obliged to sit at a table of his peers, Roux was far from impressed by the president's speech in praise of the war effort. Poincaré's fawning admiration for the support France was receiving from England and America, and beyond, left him colder than the bitter wind outside. No thought was given to the men in the trenches. Their wives and children made no fleeting appearance. This was money talking about money-making; a self-congratulatory indulgence.

But the food was divine. Bernard Roux had no stomach for the company, but…ah…the food. From a menu which dripped with descriptive pomposity, he could find no fault with the plates which were laid before him. After the third course, which had been mastered by chefs schooled in excellence, he thanked the attending waiter and asked, "How do they do that? It tasted like Atlantic salmon of old. Flawless."

"Thank you, Monsieur. I will pass your regards to the kitchen."

Good manners sometimes pays unintended dividends. As he cleared the venison dish, the waiter whispered in Roux's ear, "The chef thanks you for your kind words, Monsieur, and asks you to take this gift with you as a memento." He slipped something into Bernard's pocket and withdrew. Caught in mid-conversation with the minister of the interior, the chief superintendent neither touched the gift nor acknowledged what had happened.

Roux sat pondering an unopened tin lying at the center of his desk as Mathieu brought him a note of complaint from the mayor about drunken soldiers urinating on the exterior of public urinals. Remarkable what the middle classes thought important.

"Was at the Ritz last night. One of the disadvantages of office, might I say. Banque of France affair. Clearly while we desperately need millions of francs in war loans, the Banque is sufficiently liquid to splash out at the Ritz." He picked up the tin and reexamined it, turning it over to the base and back again.

"I was given this by a waiter."

He placed it carefully in Mathieu's right hand and sat back, reaching into his jacket for a Gauloises. It was a small tin of red salmon. Unopened. Images of a leaping fish wound round its side and on the top, a silver-stained salmon danced through blue and white-topped waves. *Best Quality Atlantic Salmon*, the bold print claimed. Mathieu carefully turned it over. On the back another label claimed that the contents hailed from Nova Scotia in Canada but that had been scored through and over-written with *Belgique*.

Mathieu appreciated the flaw. "You don't get Atlantic salmon from Belgium."

"Mmmmm," his boss mused, extinguishing the match with which he had lit his cigarette. "Not usually, no. But these are unusual times." They both nodded. "Why do you think a waiter in the Ritz slipped this into my pocket?"

"Bribery?"

"Don't think so. Doubt if I would recognize him again anyway."

"Then it has to be a message."

"Where would you buy Atlantic salmon, here, right now?"

"Black market? Would have to be."

"So tell me, what is the link between the Paris black market and occupied Belgium?"

"Finding a link between the Ritz and the black market would be easier. But Belgium? No. I mean these could have entered France from Brest, Bordeaux, Biarritz, or even Marseilles." He thought longer. "Switzerland, perhaps?"

"Possibly. Possibly even legally, for the top end of the market willing to pay exorbitant prices. But Belgium?" Roux had clearly thought this over.

"Could be a ploy to waste police time." Mathieu played Devil's advocate.

"Could be someone who wants us to investigate another black market scandal?"

"Or a rival? But where would we start?" Mathieu was far from sure that an inquiry into Atlantic salmon was worth the effort.

"Mmm. Let's not get sidetracked. It may mean nothing. Just be aware of Atlantic salmon. Pass the word. See what's out there."

18

In Search of Atlantic Salmon

See what's out there? Mathieu knew that the only service which was flourishing in the capital was prostitution. Without it, organized crime might have closed down. But no. At least forty brothels were licensed to practice the ancient art and God only knew how many abandoned women and war widows survived on a day by day basis because of it. Let the preachers rant about the wrath of God on loose women. You didn't see many starving clergy on the hungry streets of the capital. With thousands of soldiers passing through the city or taking advantage of a few days leave, the streetwalkers hardly had time to wash their faces. Sexual disease spread faster than rumor and hunger in this harsh reality. Petty crime was rife in the poorer quarters, but who could quantify the problem? People disappeared, returned to pre-war homes, sought refuge with relatives, or simply gave in and died; alone. Men and boys went off to war and if they did not return, great sadness prevailed. They had died for France. For civilization. Their memories were saluted in good wine. But women were disappearing, too, slipping under the surface of civilized society like ducklings sucked under the water by an unseen predator.

Madame Edithe Therbuet was a legend of the 10th Arrondissement. Even as a young woman, Dubois recalled a legendary status which had not diminished over the years. Now sixty-four, she draped the troubles of France across her bent and fragile frame. Only her tongue defied nature. Its muscle charged and recharged by constant exercise. Every conversation in which she engaged threatened to last an eternity. Topics ranged from the bizarre to the inappropriate. But essentially, every word was about her. She bore no illness nor suspected malaise without the neighborhood's knowledge. Nothing was secret and nothing was sacred. A boil on her inner thigh warranted public examination; a rash on her chest required a second and third opinion as she progressed along the Rue Rivay. Edithe Therbuet was not a gossip in the conventional sense, though she knew everyone else's business. She rarely listened to her neighbors' complaints because hers were far worse. It was not that she didn't care about others. She did. Unfortunately, by the time she had completed her own litany of sorrows, the listener had given up on conversation. Seen leaving her front door, Madame Therbuet had the effect of a debt collector in Pauper's Lane. Neighbors fled in the hope that she had not seen them. They hid behind curtains if watching from a window. It was widely believed that the local parish priest had reduced the penance for anyone who confessed that they had harbored thoughts of murdering her. He understood. God would, too.

She approached Paul Dubois and Mathieu from their blind side at the Café du Roc and sat down before they could escape. A waft of cheap perfume, so strong that it must have hidden a number of personal smells, accompanied her.

"Ah, Edithe, good morning to you." She was well known to Dubois's generation.

"Not so. The day is bleak and I need you to find my neighbor, Berthe." Her voice was curt and businesslike. It was not a request. "Berthe-Anna Heon. Disappeared."

"We are on important police business, Edithe. We haven't got time to look for missing persons. Why don't you get hold of the local gendarmes?"

"They don't care. I've been to them at least six times. They've done nothing. Not a thing."

Mathieu knew the dangers of a prolonged discussion but was surprised by her claim. "Six times! When did she disappear?"

"About a year ago."

Dubois shook his head in disbelief. What the hell did she expect them to do?

"I noticed that she had missed mass twice and knocked on her door. It was open so I went it, you know, to see if she was all right. Empty. Her best coat, red hat, and handbag were still there as well as her pots and pans. Odd, I thought. So…"

"A year ago. Edithe. There is a war on. There could be countless reasons why your neighbor left home and didn't tell you."

"She's not come back for a hat, coat, or handbag? Good quality, too. Not something a woman just leaves behind. And there was a man, you know."

"There you are. She met a man. They moved into his house and she forgot to tell you." Dubois offered a plausible solution.

"And left her best coat and red hat? I think not." What did men know about anything? She was on the point of giving up when her eyes rested on the tin Mathieu had taken from his overcoat. He had developed a habit of playing with it when distracted.

"You must be well paid to afford that? How much did it cost? Did you get a discount?"

Clearly Edithe knew black market value of a tin of salmon.

"No I didn't. In fact, it's not mine. But if you can tell me where I could buy a tin or two like it, I'd give you this one." Mathieu saw her eyes fix on the tin. The fate of Madame Berthe-Anna Heon no longer mattered.

"I'm not certain for sure," her tone switched to conspiratorial mode, "but I heard from a friend that there is a place in the Rue Rene Clair between Rue Poissonniers and the railway. They store stuff. You know. People."

That was unexpected. Mathieu looked into a face which told him nothing. Was she lying? Edithe walked the streets. Edithe talked the streets. Edithe drank in the streets and knew their secrets.

"I want you to take this tin and keep it for a week. If your information sends us on a fool's errand, I will come back for it and you will be very sorry."

She took the tin as if it were a gift from the Magi. "I do occasionally hear things which are true, you know. Second husband used to work on Poissonniers, for the Americans. Useless peasant."

She rushed off, tin tucked into bag, throwing, "And don't forget poor Berthe," over her shoulder as a parting jibe.

"There you are. Despite her reputation, Edithe occasionally listens. Who would have thought?" Dubois smiled generously. "We'll see." Then he realized to whom he had been talking.

"Edithe," he yelled, as she shuffled smartly away from the café. "Tell no one we gave you the tin. No one. Do you hear, Edithe?" He laughed at the stupidity of his own words. Half of the Rue would know within the hour.

"Second husband, indeed. Surely no two men could make the same mistake?"

Mathieu pondered the unexpected depth of her claim. "What's more interesting is the phrase she used. 'They store stuff.' So there are a number of these criminals in one place and a quantity of stolen goods."

"If she's telling the truth."

"True, but worth the effort to find out."

* * *

Before they left number 36 Mathieu that night issued instructions. "First car, with me; second, with Dubois, and number three with Jubert. Two additional men in each. Sergeant Toussaint has gallantly swapped his shift in order to be with us." Toussaint smiled at the others. He could smell trouble at fifty meters, and everyone knew he was a good man to have by your side in a fight. "Jacques-Francois Bernier here is the local contact." He pointed to a younger man, though none of them was under thirty. "He knows the area. Take us through it, please."

Jacques-Francois had been recommended to Pascal Girard as a detective with potential. No one was sure what that meant. Potential for what? He had been wounded on the Marne, and bore the scars of battle on his face. Shrapnel had bitten off his left ear and blinded him on that side in the passing. His upper jaw had been badly fractured but surgeons used a new technique to replace his broken bone with a steel rod. The skin around his temple was tightly drawn, giving his face an unbalanced appearance. Yet his wounds remained superficial. He was not a man who constantly looked in the mirror. He had charm and, as Mathieu quickly appreciated, a willingness to learn.

Jacques-Francois gave a no-nonsense explanation about the way Rue Rene Clair twisted along the track-side as the railway line snaked north from Gare du Nord.

"There are three possible buildings that could be used for storage on the front street and several smaller passages that run towards Poissonniers, each big enough for a medium-sized truck. We've had no reports of strangers or unusual business in the area, so if there is a depot, it must be for storage. We can't start a door-to-door search because there will be lookouts. And they will be armed. Especially if this is a serious criminal conspiracy. Strange thing is that the Corsican mafia who control the local hoods have never been seen in this part of Paris."

Sleet from the darkening skies turned cobbled streets into icy death-traps. Driving was awkward, but not perilous. Walking at pace was difficult. Running, an impossibility. It was a night to sit by a warm fire, but few were lit in the poorer quarters of Paris. Mathieu decided to place one car at either end of the street while he drove slowly in a circular motion round Poissonniers into the Rue Rene Clair, stopping regularly in the main thoroughfare lest their presence became blatantly obvious. The streets were deserted. Only a fool or a criminal would choose to be out on such a night. An occasional vehicle passed on the opposite side of the road, but in police terms, nothing suspicious broke the monotony. By 6:00 A.M. they admitted defeat. The two cars on Rene Clair were sent back to base. Toussaint was distraught. Out all night and not even a drink to comfort him. Mathieu felt embarrassed by the waste of good police time. He had put too much faith in an old woman's nonsense. And his tin of Artic salmon would be gone by now. *Merde.*

Jacques-Francois recommended a corner café on Poissonniers and insisted that Mathieu heat himself with freshly made coffee before Paris ran out of that lifeblood. Outside, commercial life roused itself sans enthusiasm. Dim lights were turned on in the Emporium across the street, but the window was so deeply frosted it might as well have been opaque. The first tram shook its way nervously down the line, uncertain of its own stability in the withering weather, the ping of its tin bell warning pedestrians to stay clear. Torn posters flapped helplessly in the growing daylight and the general gloom was deepened when the café owner announced that bread and croissants would not be on sale until nine. But the coffee was good enough for a refill. Two men entered and vigorously slammed shut the café door. Mathieu thought he recognized one of them, but let the notion pass.

A snap of the fingers was followed by, "Two coffees and four croissants, s'il vous plait." Words drawled across the room, the pronunciation as bad as the manners. Mathieu sat up but did not turn round. The voice. The drawl. It was American. He concentrated on the voice and raised his hand from the table to alert Jacques-Francois, who stopped speaking in mid-sentence.

"No croissants?" queried the voice at a volume which ensured that everyone in the room was aware of his displeasure. "My God, what's happening to this country?"

"Perhaps you could help us out with some flour, Monsieur?" came the retort from the café owner.

"Do you know these two, Jacques?" Mathieu whispered, keeping his voice as low as possible and switching into the broader Parisian patois which natives understood. He was intrigued.

"The one in the corner manages the Emporium across the street. The other, I've never seen before."

"I know his voice. The other one. I've met him … somewhere." Mathieu rapidly ran though the mental records still current in his head. The cold numbed his brain, too.

"What do they sell across there?"

Jacques shrugged nonchalantly. "All kinds of American imports, from clothes to phonographic records. Used to be a thriving business. Barely surviving now, I imagine."

The café owner joined them once the Americans had left, watching as they picked their way across the treacherous road.

"Two good coffees and not even a sou for a tip. Bloody typical. Waltz in here expecting the best and contributing nothing."

"Much happening across there these day?" Jacques asked, intimating a vague interest in the Emporium.

"They take deliveries on a regular basis, but the shop is closed for sales. Use it as a depot for goods that go all across France. That's the word anyway. If you hang on, the croissants will be here soon. Damned if the Americans deserve them."

Mathieu stood up, and at six foot, towered over the owner. "My friend, I guess you know we are police."

"Thought so." They both let their gaze stray across the empty street.

"What is happening over there? Tell me straight."

"Lorries come and go. I've plenty time to watch them. People don't eat out in these parts any more. As to what's in them? Can't say. I asked once and was told to mind my own business."

"But they have to carry the goods into the shop. You must have seen…" Jacques was cut short.

"No, no Monsieur, they don't park in the street. Their lorries turn down the lane to the left and disappear behind the high gates. If you walk past you'll see the gates. They've nailed a large American flag on the outside, and posted a notice saying *American Mission to France. Private. No Entry.* I assume they park in the yard or in the annex behind. Big storage hall behind the shop front."

The policemen looked at him intently.

"So what's going on? Your guess?" Mathieu wanted to hear the owner's suspicion.

He shrugged. "Might be stuff for the black market. Might just as well be embassy business."

Jacques touched the owner's shoulder and asked. "What makes you say that?"

"Well, a chauffeured Renault occasionally drops by. Maybe from the embassy."

"Blue? Was it a blue Renault?"

"I think it was."

Mathieu sat down, but changed the angle of his seat to give him a clearer view of the American property.

"Two more coffees, my friend, and two croissants as soon as you have them."

167

19

WINTER WONDERLAND

There was one serious blockage. Diplomatic Immunity. It was a minefield in war torn Paris. All allied and neutral personnel had to be treated with favored caution. Back at no.36, Bernard Roux's first words of advice were, "Take care. One complaint to the president's office and we'll all be transferred to the Spanish border."

"Do you think that the American ambassador knows about this?" Mathieu queried.

"Knows about what? Your suspicion based on an old wife's tale?" Roux regretted the put-down immediately. He had started the ball running with the tin of salmon, never expecting it to lead him back into rougher waters.

"No, no. I don't. Why would the ambassador be involved with anything which reflected badly on his country?" Mathieu remembered. From some far recess in his mind he recalled a voice. "The other American. I've just made the connection. He was with the ambassador and his wife on the night Poincaré and the government fled from Paris. I can hear him say, 'They're like a band of gypsies.' That's what he called them, gypsies."

"I remember, too." Roux picked up his phone and requested all information on American embassy staff. It was delivered within five minutes. Both he and Mathieu examined the contents.

"That's him." Mathieu extracted the photograph of Bryson Hamilton pinned to the inside cover of his file. He read aloud a very privileged CV.

"United States citizen. Career diplomat with banking contacts. Father a senior partner in Morgan Guaranty of New York. Mr. Hamilton served in London, Rome, and Paris. Has permission to travel at will throughout Europe. Recently in Switzerland, Luxembourg, Belgium, and Holland. Travels to Rotterdam on regular embassy business. Has a brother at Oxford University, a Rhodes Scholar currently working with the Commission for the Relief of Belgium at the personal request of Mr. Herbert Hoover."

"Look no further for the connection. It's Bryson Hamilton, but he is literally untouchable."

Mathieu appreciated the diplomatic nicety, but bristled at the thought of these Americans creating their own black market in Paris.

"What if…"

"Don't tell me. I mustn't know." Roux held up his hands in horror, the Gauloises trapped between his index and third finger of his right hand. "If you come up with an alternative way of stopping this you are ordered not to tell me. Am I making myself clear?"

"Chief, would you allow me to second Jacques-Francois to my squad to provide local intelligence should anything come up?"

He had a plan…

"Certainly."

…and Roux knew it.

* * *

"Jacques-Francois get that squad together again. This time we know what we're up against. Basically these American suppliers and French distributers are criminals who have cornered a market which we can't touch without all kinds of nasty repercussions. But what if another gang of French profiteers broke into their warehouse and stole the food? We know where they horde it."

"Lieutenant, what if it's not food. What if it's…I don't know…" Jacques's caution was understandable.

"Whatever it is, we are going to stop this rot. Tonight." Mathieu wanted action. The longer they waited the more chance someone would find out. "Be ready at 1:00 A.M. Have Commune lorries ready to move in behind us. Let's say, five. Tell your teams to cover anything that would identify them as commune vehicles, and above all, tell them not to shoot anyone, especially Toussaint. Make sure he knows there is a line he can't cross. I want no dead Americans. None."

"How will we know who is American?"

"Better fed, better dressed, and louder mouths."

At two in the morning the first lorry burst cleanly through the wooden gates and blew away the American flag, but the element of surprise was instantly lost. Jacques had instructed his men to shout in guttural patois, using names of any black marketeers they knew as they burst into the storage hall, shotguns in hand, cursing loudly and barking commands to surrender. Dressed in a rag-bag of assorted clothes, some deliberately soiled, they leaped from the lorries, faces masked, expecting stout resistance. Two men were on guard. Only two. They stood, open-mouthed in shock. How secure did they imagine they were, hiding behind the Stars and Stripes?

"Don't shoot, don't shoot! We're unarmed!" Their hands flew into the air. Frenchmen.

Shotgun in hand, Jacques-Francois barked violently at them like a sergeant major who had found new recruits asleep at their post.

"Turn around, walk into the recess over there, put your hands behind your back, and kneel down."

"Don't shoot us, please," the smaller of the two begged, his bladder betraying a loss of control.

Spellbound, the other police squads and city workers climbed from their vehicles and glared in awe at the riches before them. A mountain of precious grain stood six meters tall. Huge sacks distributed and guaranteed by the *International Milling Company of New Prague, Minnesota*, rose to the roof. Massive bags of dry rice stamped with the initials *CRB* stood shoulder to shoulder with the grain mountain, and stacked in the far corner, they could see a barricade of crates, all neatly piled one on top of the other. A note was attached to a box of clothes: *From the Children of Chicago.* Canned vegetables, soups, puddings, and fruit filled the remaining space. *Elk Brand Fancy Northern Apricots from San Francisco* sat comfortably beside *Libby's Food Products.* Some of the boxes had the letters *CNSA* stenciled across the side. Here was a feast for thousands while poorer Parisians shivered and starved in the streets around them. Large crates of *Columbia River Chinook Salmon* from Astoria, Oregon. Tea directly from India and Coffee from different parts of the British Empire had found their way to the self-named American Mission. Even chocolate beans. Where had all this come from? How could so much unreported food be stolen? It would have filled two railway trucks, never mind lorries. This was black-marketeering on a grand scale.

They might have stood in wonder for hours like tourists at Notre Dame looking upwards at the gift from heaven, but Mathieu bellowed, "Get to it. Now."

Every hand was needed to load the produce into trucks and out of the district before too many alarms were raised. But a further wonder confronted them. Behind the stacked crates on the left hand wall closest to the railway sidings, a second door lay hidden, crudely covered by a giant make-shift flag. It led to a much larger, cavernous building next door to the official Mission. Jean-Jacque's mouth fell open. He beckoned to Mathieu and started to shake his head. The hall must have been at least three times larger than its neighbor's with one essential difference. It was empty. Well, almost empty. At the far end the rear entrance appeared secure but on the floor, petrol spillage, burst packs of flour, discarded tins of dried fruit and damaged produce were spread around like abandoned waste.

" This was the main store and they've cleared it out. Somehow they knew we were coming but didn't have sufficient time to move it all. How? Who tipped them off? And if what we are left with is the smaller part of the entire haul?" Jacques was astounded. "what is going on?"

* * *

Unanswered questions had to be left till later. there was still a job to be done. For four hours the undercover policemen, security agents, and city workers did their utmost to clear the lesser hall. The five trucks were loaded and sent to five different depots across the city. More returned and guards were set on the main street to forewarn the team of the retaliation to come.

"I'm surprised. There's no reaction in the street." Jacques alerted the drivers to a possible barricade further along the rue. "What do you think these two know?" He thrust his head towards the confused captives. The two prisoners had not been arrested. In fact they were neither questioned nor cautioned. Blindfolded, hands roughly tied behind their backs, gagged, and double-bound back to back, they were dumped in an inlet on the far side of the hall. All they could do was listen to the noises around them. Mathieu remained close by as they whispered their confusions and an occasional threat.

"Who are these people?"

"Surely they know who they were dealing with?"

"Is that a Corsican accent? How many are there?"

Dozens of voices called across the emptying hall.

"How many lorries do they have?"

The larger of the two broke wind to the annoyance of his companion who had no option but to suffer. Both wore caps, one faded brown, and the other possibly green. Their long coats were thin and stained. Whatever their origins, they belonged to the lowest rung of this particular food chain. Unshaven, hair matted with the sweat, they were either recent recruits or army deserters. The smaller of the two shook violently. He whispered, "Remember the names. Serge, or was it Serge le grand? Fignan. Jeune JP."

"Remember the names."

"How dare they move in on the Americans?" The language that surrounded them was tough, gruff, and incomprehensible. Occasionally

Toussaint flashed a casual kick in their direction, adding to the tension of the moment. What next? Lorries came and went.

More bangs.

Doors slammed shut.

Engines powered into the night.

Silence.

Gone.

They thought they were alone. Mathieu watched as the two unfortunates squirmed in their wretched isolation, grunting undignified expletives. They wrestled and pulled at their bindings which made matters worse. They tried to stand up but the larger of the two failed to find strength in his legs. Condemned to a silent prison in a near silent world, they understood cold panic. The smaller began to retch in his own snot. Mathieu removed the gag on which his prisoner would have choked.

"Remember this," he grunted from behind his right hand side, "we know where you stay and where you come from. Do not move for ten minutes or I will have the guard on the door blast you with a shotgun. Whoever asks, you say nothing. We will be watching you." He cut their bonds with such a force that both whimpered.

"Ten minutes. Then take off your blindfolds and get out of Paris. You have till five o'clock before the Americans know your names."

Raoul's Story

THE SIN OF MADNESS

I was miserable. Depressed, probably. This should not have happened.

They said, yes, THEY said, I would be out of prison by Christmas, hailed as a national hero. And that was nearly three years ago. Do they appreciate how I languish in my misery? Doctors come and go, allegedly to assess my state of mind, which is, as ever, sharp. I'm nobody's fool. But you know that, don't you?

An unexpected hiatus shattered my routine. The door to my cell was thrown open by a swarthy unkempt moron of a jailor who was rude in the extreme. Squat and aggressive, always an unfortunate combination. To make matters worse he sported a cruelly-spread nose which had seen many battles and lost most. The acne from what must have been a tortuous adolescence scarred what could be seen of his skin but his hands were enormous. He threatened me with foul language, making it apparent that he believed I was a murderer and promised that there were dozens of other prisoners who would fight each other for the honor of slitting my throat.

"Pierre? Pierre? Who the fuck's Pierre," he laughed in my face when I asked where my faithful warder was. Only then did I remember that I called him Pierre without knowing his proper name. All these games we play.

"Warder Dupre, if that's who you mean, is ill. Could be influenza, so don't count on his return. Ever. Here's breakfast." He laid some tawdry mush on my table and said, "I'd check everything twice before I ate it. Especially the lumps."

The bread was stale. It must have been baked yesterday. I sat down, pushed the inedible offering to one side, and composed three letters of complaint. One to the prison governor, one to the doctor, and finally a stinging protest to my lawyers. I made sure that they understood the subtext: I wouldn't tolerate such treatment or keep my mouth shut for long. "Hunger and malnutrition weakens the strongest mind so that you may never be sure what you have just said," I wrote pointedly. Clever, eh?

During the two day torment, I revisited the worst of all dreams. I met my mother. Not for the first time, you see, but it was a dream which tormented me beyond pain. Guilt spilled from my grief and stripped the skin from my nakedness.

For some reason it always began in a classroom where one of the Jesuit fathers invited me to sit beside him. Beneath the gaze of the Virgin herself, he appeared an all-knowing visionary.

"Do you understand madness, petit Raoul?" His black soutane drained all the color from the room, afraid that it might be chastised for frivolity.

I shook my head, eyes fixed on the cross he wore as a badge of office. Permission to pontificate. It dared me to disagree.

"Madness is a sin. It is caused by the torture a soul goes through when it knows wrong but pretends that it does not. Do you understand?" He pointed to a blackboard on which was written in capital letters. MADNESS IS A SIN. "And you must remember your mother has confessed to me."

I wanted to shake my head and ask what kind of sin my mother committed, but I had absorbed enough catechism to know that a priest could not reveal such a thing. He would rather be slain or burned to death or eaten by lions than divulge the secret of the confessional. I've seen the holy pictures. I've heard the stories of the saints and their martyrdoms. He would not and could not disclose my mother's sin. It took me almost twenty more years to appreciate the convenience of the parameters set by the committed.

I nodded in compliance. I was a clever boy and therefore had to understand.

"We have decided, myself, Doctor Proal here, and your father, that your mother must be kept in the diocesan asylum."

"But why, Father? What has she done to deserve that?"

"Ah," he said, "we must not judge Madame Villain. What she has done lies between her conscience and God. You see, my boy, she is not fit at the moment to bring you up in the faith, to look after the spiritual integrity of your brother and you, and of course, your good father. Her mind has weakened. She needs help. She is safe in the special hospital at Chalons-sur-Marne. She will be looked after and provided for by the nuns and doctors. She will be happy there because she is surrounded by prayer and holiness. And do you know how you can help?"

I looked into his eyes for the answer, dumbfounded that he thought I could help.

"You can promise me that you will pray for her every day. Will you?"

"I do , Father, I do. I pray for mother every day and every night."

"Such a good boy." He touched my cheek and I shivered involuntarily.

Then I was with her. She was standing by a window looking out over the river. I went to her and touched her dress and all shivering desisted. She turned to acknowledge my presence, quite perfect in the fresh light. She took my hand and bent to kiss me, but faltered.

"He is lying, Raoul. Look at me. Look how I am dressed." Suddenly she was in rags, shredded and stained by injustice. "Where is my beautiful petticoat? They stole it from me Raoul, you know, to make robes for their priests."

Every time she said my name I felt a warmth possess my body.

"Raoul, listen to me. There's nothing wrong with me. Nothing. People said that your father's mother, your grandmother, Emelie, was weak in the head. She was not weak. She was a strong-minded woman, and they did not like that, the men who run everything. I'll tell you who's mad. He's mad. Your father. He has no soul. He does not love me, but he wants control of my inheritance."

"No, Mama, that's not true, please don't..."

"Believe me, he is a cold, deceitful, wicked man. But you saw him, didn't you. You saw what he did."

Confused, I started to cry, but she did not comfort me.

"I have to get out of here. Why does no one ever visit? Why do you and your brother stay away? Have you forgotten me?"

"No, Mama, never." But the strange fact was that while I could hear her, I couldn't see her face. It was shrouded from me. Her breath smelled sweet, but her words were bitter.

"Listen to the doctors, not the priests." Such a strange thing to say.

"Do they say you are…are…well, the doctors?"

"If you really love me you will get me out of here. Do you really love me, Raoul?"

"Of course, Mama."

"Then get me out. You are a clever boy. You can do this."

"But Mama…"

It was at that point that I broke down. Every time. I could not get past the fundamental fact that I had failed her. That the truth was, I did not know how to help her.

She painted a wicked landscape of betrayal in which everyone played their part. "They drugged me in the house and carried me off to this prison hospital. The nuns are corrupt. If I cry they shut me in a darkened room. They force me to take vile liquids, saying it will help me sleep. Why would I want to sleep, Raoul? There is no sleep."

I fell into memories which made me so sad, so unwanted…so alone. Who could I trust? You? Are you a man of your word, my friend?

We both began to cry but she was fading fast. "Stand up for me, Raoul. Stand up for France. You are a good boy. And clever, too." When I woke, my pillow was sodden. I had been left behind once more. She had gone.

Who to believe, eh? Dreams or harsh reality? Who would release me from my nightmare? They carried me into this prison and kept me here, but I never denied my so-called crime. It was not a sin to kill Jaurès. I'd stood up for France.

And then it came to me. I'd failed my mother.

No. No. Don't think like that. She failed me. Say it. Say it out loud. "She failed me." At the top of your voice. Shout. "SHE FAILED ME. SHE FAILED ME."

Liar.

Have you ever done that, my friend? You know, lied to yourself?

175

20

JANUARY-JUNE 1916

Chief Superintendent Roux gathered his senior officers in the Bureau gymnasium. The boxing ring had been replaced by trestle tables loaded with a cross sample of produce and foodstuffs taken from the American Mission. Such a sumptuous bounty. It was as if the Ritz had decided to sponsor a luxurious fete as a demonstration of excess.

"I want you to walk round and examine everything you see. Above all I want to know where it comes from and what it means. And I don't mean America. To add to the takings from early this morning, I received this. Left at the front door by a middle-aged woman, apparently."

He added another tin of Atlantic salmon to the pile. It had been wrapped in an old copy of a Belgian newspaper, *La Libre Belgique*. This time he turned the tin over so that everyone could see that the word *Belgique* had again been scrawled on the back.

"What is this Belgian woman, if she is a Belgian woman, trying to tell us?"

Jacques-Francois spun round and asked the company, "Does anyone know about this newspaper? *La Libre Belgique?*"

Julien Rioux, who had served in the Deuxième longer than anyone else in the room, cleared his throat. Quiet and unassuming, Rioux picked up the well-thumbed news sheet and held it aloft.

"Written by a hero of mine, Philippe Baucq. An architect to trade. Read by as many Belgians as can lay their hands on it. This is the free Belgian newspaper written to hearten the people trapped in Brussels by the German army. Brutally sarcastic about the German occupiers. Especially General von Bissing the military governor. A real morale-booster for the ordinary Belgians until..." He lowered the newspaper and continued in a voice quivering with emotion. "They rounded him up with a resistance group in mid-1915. Called it a spy ring, which arguably it was, and shot poor Philippe though he certainly wasn't a spy. They say that von Bissing ordered it. One other person was shot, and it still doesn't make sense. They arrested about seventy Belgians, tried half of them and shot two. The other was an English nurse, Edith Cavell."

"I remember now, Rioux. Didn't the Germans say she was a spy, too?" one of his colleagues asked.

"Yes. But there were a host of others arrested and tried, including minor royalty. But they shot the English nurse."

Roux asked the question that everyone was thinking. "Because she was English, do you think?"

"Could have been. But why would some as yet unknown person, presumably Belgian, wrap this tin of salmon in Baucq's newspaper?" Rioux looked around the company. "Anyone?" Silence. Some cast their eyes to the window, others, the floor, but no one answered.

Mathieu altered the approach. "Anyone know what the initials CRB and CNSA mean?"

Jubert knew. "In many ways they mean the same thing. The CRB is the Commission for Relief in Belgium under the leadership of the American Herbert Hoover. The CNSA is the Belgian wing of the same operation. Run by a ruthless banker, Émile Francqui. They literally supply Belgium and the occupied territory in northern France with food from all across the world."

"I thought it was called American Relief."

Roux interrupted. "It is. The funds come from America, we think, and are used to buy food from across the world. The Germans allow it to be unloaded in Rotterdam, transferred to barges, and taken to the occupied territories by river and canal. Apparently it is paid for by an immense system of fundraising in America."

"And our government and the English government allow this?" Mathieu wanted confirmation.

"Apparently."

"And the Germans, too? Why? Why does the Bureau not have all this on record. Or does it? Is it being suppressed?"

"It keeps the war going." Rioux's voice cracked with sarcasm.

"You could say that." Pascal Girard's tired reply made them realize that something was deeply wrong here.

"Thanks, gentlemen, that's helpful." Roux spoke for them all.

"We still don't know how all this found its way to Paris." Jacques-Francois had been invited to attend though he was not officially part of the Deuxième's squad. He scratched his forehead as if the complexity of this conundrum irritated his wound.

Paul Dubois moved around the table picking up items to explain his point. "Last night I thought this was absolutely random; pineapples, apricots, beans, salmon, soups, meat paste. Only the flour and rice seemed like basics.

But we are assuming that this haul was destined for the streets of Paris. What if it was purchased for the great hotels, casinos, embassies, and millionaires who can afford the outrageous prices? What if it was bought to order?"

"That crossed my mind," Mathieu admitted, looking for inspiration from his chief superintendent.

"One thing you should know," Jacques-Francois added. "There's not a murmur on the streets about the raid on the warehouse. It's business as usual. No complaint from the American embassy. It's as though nothing happened. Not even amongst low-level black-marketeers."

Odd.

"Right. I want you all to get back out there, call in favors from journalists; take embassy staff for a drink. Speak to Belgian refugees, there's plenty to choose from. Citizens who know the southern end of the river Meuse, or the canals that cross the borders. Do they know how this food-stuff gets to Paris or who it is for?"

"Give us a couple of days on this one, please." Mathieu was hopeful.

"Yes, two days. But be subtle. We don't want to be ordered to back off again. Where you suspect government connections, come straight to me. Any time, day or night. Be careful what you say to Americans." Roux needed space to think for himself. Out came the Gauloises.

Mathieu and Dubois took a quite remarkable decision. They went in search of Edithe Therbuet. She was out on the streets, red handbag over her arm, pinning back the ears of an unfortunate who had not seen her approach. The detectives from no. 36 sat in the café on the corner and let her come to them. Unsuspecting. She didn't see them until it was too late.

"Edithe," Mathieu called to her, but she blanked him and shuffled in the opposite direction. "Edithe, come and have a coffee, you can't run away from us. Be sensible."

She turned back. "I'm sorry but the salmon was too much of a temptation. It's gone." She almost managed to look apologetic. "Lovely supper, I had. Sorry." She limped her way back to their table.

"Glad to hear it, Edithe. What's news on the black market?"

"Gone quiet, it has." She sat herself down, placed her bag under the table, and remembered Berthe-Anna Heon. "Have you found Berthe yet?"

"Why? Are you desperate to return her handbag?"

She flinched and inadvertently grasped it closer to her sagging bosom.

Paul Dubois was not in the mood for her nonsense. "Edithe, you said your second husband used to work for the Americans on the Rue Pois-sonniers. Tell us about him. His work. What did he say about it?"

"Huh! Him. Wastrel. Drank himself to death. I blame the Americans. They paid him too much money. Not that I saw much of it."

"Why did they pay so well?"

"Not sure. He said that he worked on the trains for them from time to time, as well as in the Emporium. Went up there once but he was not pleased. All very hush-hush. Warned me never to go back. Fact is, as long as he brought the money home, I didn't mind. Then he started to drink seriously. Stopped coming home. Killed by a goods train." She sat back in her chair and in that moment of pained memory, aged visibly. Like hundreds of other widows, she was a reminder of what Paris had become. There was little time for sentiment.

"What did he do on the trains?"

"Don't know. Loaded and unloaded stuff. Shunted trucks from the Gare de l'Est across to the Rue Rene Clair siding in the Gare du Nord. Imports and exports, he said."

"Are you sure? That's not a normal route."

"It didn't make sense to me either. Apparently they stopped his train in one siding and transferred some trucks to another engine before they reached the mainline station."

"When did he die?"

"About a year, no, it must be fourteen months ago, I suppose."

"So he worked for them at the start of the war?" Mathieu felt that they were getting close. But to what?

She closed her eyes and tried not to remember better times. He had been a good man, really. She recalled how she felt on the night they told her that he had been killed on the tracks. Happened in a siding near the canal. They took her to see him in one of those new cars. His head and face looked perfect, like an alabaster statue under candlelight. From the chest down he had been crushed, trapped between two closing buffers. All life squeezed from him in an instant. No time to cry out. No second chance. The engine driver had apparently mistaken the guard's red lantern as it swung from left to right and reversed the trucks. It was over. From *is* to *was* at the snap of a finger. Wife to widow in the blink of an eye. Said he had been drinking heavily. Was drunk, seemingly. Couldn't argue. Her weeping; him dead.

"The Americans were very kind. I had money for a while." She shrugged apologetically. "It's gone now."

"Why would the Americans go to such lengths to cover their traces?" Mathieu was far from satisfied. "And you know they dealt in the black market. You told us that. You sent us looking in that direction."

"But you found nothing did you?" She either didn't know or was playing a very clever game. "I mean he would come home with a tin or two of some delicacy, occasionally. I suspected black market business, of course. But that was it."

"Where did the food come from?"

"America, I suppose."

"Yes, but where did the train come from?" Dubois tried not to be angry.

"Up north, close to the front. He once said that he could see the gunfire from the front lines. I thought he had been drinking. Trains from the Gare du Nord don't go to the front. Lying, as usual."

"And where did the produce go afterwards? When it left the Emporium?"

She could only guess. "Don't know, and he never said. When they were busy, he delivered orders to Parisian addresses. It never went onto the street. But it must have been illegal. All that secrecy."

21

Source of Wisdom

Mathieu had another source. Moutie. He thought it might add to Jacques-Francois's education to meet the hapless thief in person. Having heard nothing to the contrary, Mathieu assumed that the career-selfish burglar cum pickpocket, confidence trickster, and general wastrel had survived the worst so far. With little to offer in terms of bravery, honesty, duty, or loyalty, Moutie had always been particular about self-survival. He would steal from children and old people, lie to the gullible, pick pockets, and con the ill-advised, smell vulnerability like a true predator. He had no concept of truth. Come to think of it, he had no sense of smell. Despite all of these dubious capabilities, Moutie was not by any yardstick successful. He knew what to do and how to do it, badly.

They found him in good spirits, scavenging on the edge of the meat market at Les Halles.

"Ah, Commander," he began. "And, well, how nice, the Sergeant, from the Latin Quarter…" Moutie feigned a slight bow. He loved the pretense of fawning familiarity. It encouraged his self-confidence. Jacques was surprised to be recognized by a man he had never met so Mathieu cut across the conversation.

"Moutie, we don't have time for your nonsense. We want some help."

"Always pleased to help when I can, but not in public."

"Fine." Jacques took him by the arm. "I'm arresting you for—"

"For what?" Panic replaced cocky self-confidence. "Get your hands off."

"Doesn't matter. We'll find a reason in due course."

"Can we go somewhere less public?" he pleaded. There was a desperation in his voice that deserved consideration, so they retreated to a seedy bar behind the metro exit at the Gare du Nord. This time the coffee was hardly drinkable. The war, you see.

"How is business these days?" Mathieu smiled across at Jacques-Francois. As an opening gambit against the worst thief in Paris, it was hardly fair.

"Poor. Miserable, really. But I scrape by. Helping the wounded, supporting the old and doing my bit for the war effort."

"Helping yourself, robbing the blind and taking advantage of the disabled, more likely." Jacques had him summed up perfectly.

Mathieu got straight to the point. "Last time we had a conversation, you told me about Monsieur Zaharoff and his bodyguards. I must thank you for that. Proved very helpful. How is he these days, Monsieur Zaharoff and his man, Timon?"

"Eh, Timon? Never heard of him. Monsieur Zaharoff is not in Paris currently. But his people continue to work from there. Still not a place to visit uninvited."

Mathieu drew Moutie forward by the lapel and admitted, "I don't enjoy being so close to you, my friend, but I need to know what's been happening in the black market this week."

"Nothing…"

Mathieu tightened his grip on Moutie, his hands leaning perilously close to Moutie's throat.

"I need to know."

"Nothing's happening. Still the same gangs selling more or less the same things, in the same places. What is it you are looking for?"

"There's a depot at the American Mission in Rue Poissonniers. What do you know about that place?"

"Not for us poorer citizens. The best you might get there is the odd box, broken beyond use, for firewood. No, no, you do not mess with the Americans. Your lot won't touch them for a start. They sell whatever they import to monied and well-connected citizens. Don't tell me your boys in the 18th Arrondissement don't get a backhander to stay away."

Mathieu resisted the temptation to slap him hard. Jacques was astounded. Was that odor entirely his? It's how one imagined the living dead would smell if they had been locked inside the fish market.

* * *

It seemed that no one knew anything about the American connection. No reports of a robbery. No missing persons. Journalists shrugged off the question with a shake of the head, embassy staff were not forthcoming, and Belgian refugees wanted to share horror stories about which they had heard, but not themselves witnessed. Most had escaped to France in the first few months of 1914 at which point there was no American Relief. One Scottish Sergeant had an interesting story to tell, but it may have been confused by his alcohol consumption.

"During the fighting at Loos in '15, which was a bloody mess from start to finish, by the way, we came across a wee chateau a mile or so from Hulluch. Except it wasn't a real chateau. The Germans had turned it into a great store full of grain and foods from America that I had never seen before in my life. Can you believe it? Sacks-full stamped with names of American towns and companies. The Germans used the kitchens to prepare their meals. Imagine that. Real food in the trenches, or maybe just for the officers, anyway. The smell lingered on and it was wonderful. We just breathed it in. Nothing left, but. What freaked us out was enormous quantities of cement which filled room after room, must have been for their trenches, good trenches the Germans have, but the thing that really upset me was that the cement was from near Stirling in Scotland ... and so am I. How did cement from Scotland get into a chateau held by the Germans for over a year? It had a date from last May. I mean, I just stood there shouting at Malky, my pal, 'Malky, look, it's Cowie cement. Your father probably made it.' I mean, bugger the food, how did our cement find its way to the German front line?"

While the question was entirely valid, Dubois was more interested in the foodstuffs. "Can you give us any more information about the American food?"

"Naw," he answered. "I mean, I put a tin or two in my kitbag, but the fuckin' Germans began a counterattack so we had to withdraw. Pineapples, it was. Bloody good, too. Never tasted them before. Nor since, come to think o' it."

* * *

The second meeting with the chief should have been more enlightening. He had access to top secret information but he could not share it even within the safe confines of the 36.

"Let me try to explain what I can. At the political level, this whole business can be traced back to the first months of the war when we and the Allies pushed the Boches back north. Trouble was that over two millions French citizens were caught on the wrong side of the border. They couldn't leave and we couldn't feed them. Same problem for the Belgians in the occupied territories. Of course hundreds of thousands escaped to other parts of France and England, but the remainder had to be fed. Hence the American Relief, under the dictatorship of this Herbert Hoover. Now I use that word advisedly. As I understand it, he has insisted that since the money and the food come from America, he had to be in charge. Some of the Belgian bankers don't like it, but the powers that control this war, the men who operate above the governments, said Hoover … or no food. So, he is responsible for the vast amounts of food necessary to feed Belgium and the occupied area of France. According to him, it's his boats, carrying his food, insured by his banks which keep millions alive. Or so he claims. He's been here in Paris twice and our records show that he met the president and the minister of finance." He stopped to give the information time to register.

"The agreement is that the Americans can bring food for Belgium and France through one port. Rotterdam. From there it is taken to its destination by barge. The English press claim that the Germans are stealing the food for themselves. This is strongly denied by all parties. Our government hasn't complained and Mr. Hoover appears to be able to keep the food flowing despite objections. Since it is in the interest of our citizens caught inside the occupied zone, President Poincaré has ordered that Hoover and his people be given every assistance," he paused to look them all in the eye, "especially in Paris."

Jubert added, "Hoover is an amazingly arrogant man. I have watched him in meetings, and he refuses to listen to any other point of view. No one in France dares challenge him. He has the power of international banks behind him. He's like a messenger from the Gods."

Bernard Roux obliged the group to concentrate on what had been learned so far.

"Let's review what we now know. Captain Girard, please." He beckoned Pascal with a nod and slow drag on his Gauloises, to summarize the overall position. "We know that the black market inside the city is rife, but the American Mission, if I can call it that, is not aimed at feeding the ordinary citizen. There has been no noticeable reaction to our raid."

Jacques interrupted him. "Excuse me, Capitain, but there are whispers that three black market dealers have disappeared. One each from different arrondissements – 18th, 19th, 20th. Not been seen since yesterday. Might be coincidence. No bodies."

"But the trio is unlikely to have gone on holiday together," Roux surmised. Given that he was the boss, a low bout of laughter drifted from the assembled policemen.

"Keep an eye on that, Jacques. Do we know yet what happened to the men we caught at the mission?"

Apparently not. If they had disappeared, it was unlikely that any trace remained.

Mathieu found himself pacing across the floor. "So far we know that the raid on the *Mission* has not been reported by any agency. The prefecture, the minister of war, and Prime Minister Viviani either know nothing or are ignoring it for political reasons."

"They know nothing, and that's official," growled Roux.

"Our sources say that the food comes into Paris by train. It is switched from one route to a siding on Rue Rene Clair where it is unloaded and temporarily stored before being delivered to the rich, the very rich, and Five-Star hotels. We are going 'round in circles. We have clarified the Paris end of this scandal. Basically, the American Relief system, with the approval or tacit approval of our own leaders, is supplying goods to those with money to buy them. But where exactly does it come from?"

"And if someone is gaining, someone else is losing. Simple as that." Dubois was as frustrated as the others.

"Check every angle again." Roux ignored the groans as his senior officers trooped out to relay the instructions to foot soldiers who were expected to find the answers. He asked Mathieu to wait.

"There are men on both sides who don't want us to know what's going on behind the scenes. They pocket millions of francs every day. They move freely in ways you wouldn't believe, and if they thought we were on to them, we'd be in big trouble. The only way we can prove their complicity is to find irrefutable evidence. Right now, we have nothing. I want you to get as close as you can to the front. You'll be issued with the necessary papers, but be careful. Don't do anything stupid. Find out what you can. We need to know how this racket works. At the same time I will try to discover how far this scandal reaches into the heart of our government. Use local police knowledge. Check in with the gendarmerie wherever you go. Everyone knows that the Deuxième has responsibility for racketeers and black market fraud, but we must keep our suspicion about the American complicity to ourselves. Above all, no talk of government involvement."

"Can I take Jacques, Jacques-Francois with me?"

"No. Tell your team that you have a family emergency. I'll let it be known you've been given compassionate leave. Go today. Nothing must be traced to the department. Understand?"

"Yes." Mathieu realized that the chief was right. It would be less complicated if he only had himself to worry about. He stopped at the door and added, "We haven't replaced poor Guy yet. I'd like to recommend Jacques-Francois."

22

THE STRANGE HABITS OF ATLANTIC SALMON

Jacques was waiting in the quiet Café-bar St. Julienne. In truth, the venue had been prearranged before Roux's decision. Mathieu and he anticipated a debrief. It was how they worked these days. A cup of hot coffee sat in front of the empty chair.

"Where to start?"

Jacques had given considerable thought to this question.

"The key to this has to be the fact that the goods train was headed for Gare de l'Est but the trucks were diverted to the Gare du Nord. We had assumed that the flow was from the north, but if the key station is the Gare de l'Est, then the trucks have to be coming from the east. Why? This might make more sense if the source is Switzerland, but the chief's informant keeps insisting it's Belgium."

"So we have to ask ourselves, what starts in France and ends up in Belgium?" They looked at each other in agreement.

"It's coming by river."

"Or canal."

"Or both."

"Of course. Both. Sometimes it's difficult to see the obvious."

Jacques swirled the dregs of his coffee as if inspiration would naturally stem from there. "But if it comes from Belgium, how the hell can it get past the Belgian authorities, the German frontier guards, our own boys on the front line, and make its way here? And in the war zone, the canals are blown apart." He leapt to his feet. "We need a map."

Three sous on the table and they were off without a goodbye.

"Rue Richelieu, National Library. It's got every conceivable map."

"Saves any awkward questions from the war ministry, too."

Mathieu flashed his identity badge at the entrance and asked for the most up-to-date map of France.

"The Lieutenant will understand that the very latest maps are military and severely restricted." A pompous sneer was predicated on the librarian's belief that they were mere policemen.

"Deuxième Bureau," Jacques reminded the official, whose waxed moustache melted from the heat of his burning cheeks.

"Ah, yes indeed, Sir. Follow me please."

A general map of the country would have served their purpose, but the assistant was so intent on redeeming himself that he flustered and flitted between several drawers in the map room as if there was a special one, for their eyes only.

"This is the most recent we have in our possession. I have no doubt that the Ministry of War will have a more detailed map, but will this do?"

"Many thanks, Monsieur."

He bowed and waited.

"Leave us, please."

"Any man so obsequious must have a bad conscience," Mathieu mused as they unrolled the paper and placed it carefully on the central table. "Where would you start from? We need a railway line or junction which serves Paris directly. A main route to a town or city with a sizeable river."

"Or canal," Jacques reminded him.

"Find a railway timetable from l'Est. Even if it's pre-war, the destinations will give us some ideas."

Jacques returned almost immediately with the information. They studied both map and timetable, talking non-stop.

"Troyes? Too far south."

"Nancy? Perhaps."

What about Toul?"

"Toul?"

"Toul. Small city, but look at the river and canal interlink. The railway line is extensive. Direct to Paris."

They pushed the map and railway timetable around the desk.

"Look at the Meuse, it can take riverboats and barges. It's linked to the canal which goes all the way to Namur and into Belgium."

"As far as Verdun, I imagine."

That might be a serious obstacle given the battleground it crossed. Mathieu hadn't appreciated the extent of the northern canal system. There were thousands of kilometers of waterways in the north and northeast of the country; nearly 300 kilometers in the Canal de la Meuse alone.

"I have to start somewhere and Toul is as good as any. Roux wants me to go alone to cut the chance of leakages. But I need you to be my link to the Deuxième, Jacques. Be in the office at eight in the morning and six at night every day for the next seven. If I have anything urgent to report I'll phone you under the name of your cousin Henri."

"I don't have a cousin Henri."

He was joking of course, but Mathieu smacked his head for good form. "You do now."

* * *

His journey west was somber. If Paris had withered in the cold realism of an all-demanding war, the countryside bore the scars of ever deepening exhaustion with the resignation of despair. The train from Paris strained to share the weight of twenty-one coaches, mostly built to carry goods and livestock, filled with soldiers, provisions, water-pipes, electric cables, small canons, baled cloth, wooden pallets, and bedding which was surely once fresh. Two passenger coaches had been commandeered for officers, and Mathieu took advantage of rank to squeeze into a corner close to an open window. It was cold but bearable; dark with unlit lamps. Conversation which started chirpily in the Gare de l'Est lost the pretense of cheerful banter, kilometer by kilometer, until, by the time a crude gun-thunder could be heard somewhere ahead, it had dwindled to a whispered acknowledgement that the destination was close by. As the train snaked into Toul's crowded marshaling yard, a new-age nightmare loomed into view. Engineers were repairing water-supply piping in a far siding under makeshift lamps while work parties loaded pumping sets carefully into reinforced wagons. Horses and mules were lined up behind carts and wagons, willing the moment that their burden would be lifted from their shoulders onto the waiting rolling-stock. On an adjoining track, a damaged engine listed awkwardly to the left, its massive rear wheel ruined beyond repair. It would have to wait patiently for a replacement.

Mounds of freshly filled sandbags had been stored on Platform Four, according to the sign which hung tenuously from the station canopy, ready for service either in a mangled trench or, more optimistically, to protect newly won territory in the forthcoming advance. Important business was afoot. Transport officials, both military and civilian, walked purposefully along the track, checking wagons, inspecting the content to ensure that numbers, volume, weight, and loading instructions bore the correct stamp of officialdom gone mad.

Troops newly released from the front began to arrive on Platform Two as their train was signaled into the station, the engine wheezing like an asthmatic in the cold air. For the moment, their tour of duty had been placed on pause. Young lads leapt from the carriages before the engine had time to come to a standstill. Officers in the better quality coaches tried in vain to assert their authority, but to no purpose. They, too, wanted to bring on the wine and the dancing girls, but would probably have to make do with local ale and think themselves lucky. Toul was not the Pigalle of old, though neither was the Pigalle if truth be told.

The basic science of modern warfare challenged the historic rights of nature. At the far side of the marshaling yard lorries stood to attention awaiting tons of gravel and loose stone which would be used further up the line to create a temporary road to the front. Dirt tracks and country lanes were useless in a climate of relentless rain. Though the Romans would have shuddered at the prehistoric nature of these new highways, they served their purpose well. A stream of such routes supported by metaled reinforcement lead across torn fields and advanced on the trench system to enable tens of thousands of lorries and trucks, military hardware and ambulances to support the unfortunates at the front. Experienced engineers made daily checks on their condition because building the network across devastation required constant repair. Preparation for the next advance was essential, though no one yet knew when, and most had forgotten why.

The surreal nature of a world so far removed from previous experience shocked Mathieu. He'd considered himself immune to fresh horror. The human debris floating in Paris sewers, the flotsam and jetsam fished from the canals, the gruesome horror left behind by a child murderer or a vicious assault in a back street robbery ought to have hardened him. But this horror was shameful. The platform, so recently the scene of joyous release, was quickly emptied of high spirits. Expectation had been followed by resignation; anticipation, by dumb fear. A small group of shattered soldiers shuffled from the train, helped by nurses who shepherded them together for their own safety. They lived and breathed, but inside they were dead and gone, ghosts in broken husks masquerading as men. They looked with eyes that did not see. Some shook uncontrollably, others tried to communicate but could only grunt. They bore no visible wound, but their presence filled Mathieu with dread. These were once whole men. What hell did they carry now in their heads?

Under other circumstances Toul would have been an attractive city, with historic battlements and heavily fortified ramparts. Sitting by the river Moselle with canals and waterworks aplenty, its narrow streets and old cellars promised a respite from the misery further north. The ancient cathedral towers would serve as a perfect rangefinder if the Germans burst through the front lines but that was not his immediate concern. Such was the pressure for space in a town on the edge of insanity that Toul's main police station was housed on the ground floor of the Mairie. Mathieu's unheralded arrival raised interest. No one had met an officer from the Deuxième and the superintendent greeted him as a long-lost brother. His concerns about black market business were answered with shrugs of disinterest and replaced with questions about life in Paris. *Adapt and survive* had become Toul's new motto. Civil matters had to be given their appropriate place, but the military had such an iron grip on the community, that matters like the black market ranked low in the order of priorities.

"You must appreciate that everything changes on a daily basis. The constant flow of a population that is here today and may be dead tomorrow only adds to the confusion. You ask about the black market. I don't. If you want to know about drunken soldiers fighting outside our café-bars, I don't, as long as the fight is outside and the military police have been called. We survive by keeping the roads and railway open, the canals around us clear, and the troops moving. You inquire about trains between here and Paris. I don't. Our railway system is so overcrowded that no one knows for sure what is scheduled to go north, south, or west, no matter what a signature says on a bill of transfer. This is chaos unfettered. Unscripted. Beyond is the abyss. The seventh circle of Dante's *Inferno*. Take it from me." Stress weighed on the superintendent's shoulders till he could hardly lift his head.

"Look, if you get caught hoarding food, the law will stand on you. If you steal food from your neighbor and get caught, all hell will be let loose. If you can afford to buy extra food from a farmer, is that the black market? There is no black market, unless you are caught. And if someone has a source, do you imagine that they will share it? Quite honestly, I have neither the time nor resources to keep the black market under control." He paused, knowing that his remarks, though honestly given, reflected badly on his command.

"I do the best I can. If I was ordered to, I'd begin my inquiries at the canal." The superintendent's reticence made Mathieu suspect a shard of collusion. "

On the riverbank three battered old coal barges were berthed in formation beside the Bar du Port, an estaminet which had also known grander days. Their connecting ropes had possibly been spun in Napoleon's day, and like his famous Old Guard, blackened and bruised by sturdy service. Whether they were still watertight was a moot point. From midship to stern the empty black holds reeked of slag and dross with rot and red rust in attendance. Mounds of broken brick and stone sat on patchy decks which had been repaired so often that the original planks struggled to make themselves known. A washing line had been strung across the outer barge with two thin stained towels hanging grimly by their pegs like faded bunting from some long-forgotten celebration.

The tired drinking parlor was crowned by a buckled slate roof which defied physics, but the ivy wrapped around the adjoining beech tree served to hold it fast. Inside, standing against what appeared to be a series of coffins crafted into a serving bar, half a dozen cloth-capped bargemen sipped their beers slowly, talking privately, as if by excluding an outsider they could avoid the conflict around them. This was their private haunt. It smelled of their sweat mingled with a bitter tobacco and the low wooden ceiling had either been painted brown or permanently stained by smoke. Both perhaps. A selection of shovels were stacked close to the only door where, in more affluent quarters, parasols might have stood. They ignored Mathieu. He did not belong.

"Anyone going north in the morning? Got to get as close as I can to the front. Anyone able to help?" His question merited a slow turn of heads in his direction by two of the ancients but their eyes did not linger long.

Silence. No one appeared to have heard but Mathieu understood the process. His presence in the less-than-delicate Parisian underbelly was frequently greeted with similar disinterest, for if an informer was willing to sell information, he was unlikely to respond in public. The key was patience. It would be similar here. He emptied a glass of decent beer and strode briskly towards the first of the barges, prepared for a lengthy wait. From the field to his left, the sound of chomping betrayed the presence of barge horses. They ignored him too, their heads buried in fodder, but they offered a distraction as the evening darkened into twilight.

"You got money? You able to pay to go north?" It was the youngest bargeman, the one who had not even graced Mathieu's presence with a glance inside the alehouse. His approach belied his awkward stance. Mathieu placed him in his early sixties, legs and arms still strong. He had once been tall but his body was bent from a lifetime's toil lifting coal bags and emptying filthy barge holds. His enormous hands hung by his side ready for action as if he was a wrestling champion about to squeeze the life from an unwary opponent.

"Yes, I want to get as near as you dare go to the front. What's your price?"

"You French or Belgian"

"Cheeky bastard."

"As long as you're not German … or a spy … ten francs."

"I don't want to buy the fucking barge."

"Five then."

"Fuck's sake. If you thought I carried that much money you'd bend over backwards to take me north then smack me over the head with a spade when we're in the middle of nowhere and dump me into the canal."

A smile crackled across the big man's face and fought the dusty grief lines from his frown. "Great idea … why didn't I think of that?"

"I'll give you three francs. One now and the rest when we get there."

"Three francs and risk a firing squad if I'm caught? Do I look dumb?"

"What time do you leave?" The bargeman was offered a single franc and took it.

"Five in the morning. Be here. I won't wait."

Mathieu walked smartly back into town. Its lanes appeared empty, but shadows cast by the dimmed lamplight flattened across the cobbles to suggest another world open for business. A drunken soldier sat on the cathedral steps singing a plaintive song, slurred and choked with emotion. He had transformed it from ballad to dirge, though to his ears, it was so beautiful that the saints above him joined in the chorus. Life had slipped from the streets into the cellars, where drink and company were to be had, provided you had a couple of sous. No man wanted the space or time to think. Drinking to oblivion was warmer and more hopeful than another cold bitter night under the stars, frozen to a core so brittle it would willingly snap at the least tremor of gunfire.

He bought another beer and found a seat close to the door. Was this the civilization for which the world claimed to be fighting? Mothers would weep. Fathers would feign pride. Those who were about to die saluted their wine and drank deeply to dispel any thought other than survival. Simmering egos bubbled close to an unstable surface. Every instinct warned Mathieu to leave before the pressure gauge exploded, but having no home to go to, he stayed. Some locals pushed their way through the drunken horde, assuming territorial rights which made little sense under such conditions. Voices were raised. One push, a slip on the sodden floor, and mayhem ensued. Fists were flung at anyone stupid enough to invite, "Come on then."

"Out, outside. Get yourselves outside. Go on now. No fighting in here. The bar is closed."

The man and woman behind the counter removed all breakables as quickly as they could, refusing service and demanding order. The natural flow of disorderly violence emptied from the cellar into the narrow lane outside. Unfortunately, army units boasted champions whose duty was to prove themselves the most outrageous of alpha males, and within seconds, serious blows were thrown in all directions. Heads were split but whether that was caused by drunken attacks or the slippery cobbled surface, no one could tell. A full bottle of wine, lobbed blindly over the brawling mob, crashed into the butcher shop wall, wasting its dark red liquid over body and stone. The local lads were cornered, but had the wit to keep their backs to the shop fronts so the enemy lay ahead.

Though he had no intention of being drawn into the general melee, Mathieu recognized the bargeman. Fuck. He had to get him out of there. Shouting grew louder, sharp whistles rent the night. Angry guttural barks joined the free-for all.

"MPs" a voice sounded alarm.

"The dogs!" someone yelled.

At least one of the brawlers understood the merciless power of unleashed canine hoodlums. Whoever shouted, the warning was wasted. No one heard, or if they did, no one cared. Mathieu's bargeman slipped and landed on his shoulder, winded but not hurt. Two military Rottweilers snarled in his direction, forcing him hard against the wall. He lunged at the first and kicked it in the ribs and dragged the bargeman back into the fray. He was punched in the ear for his generosity but held onto his catch.

"Come on, we have to get out of here. You're my ticket north…"

He left the sentence unfinished in the expectation that the bargeman would recognize him, but instead found himself rolling on the cold cobbles. The older man was in a blind rage, fists clenched, face set in determined revenge, unaware that Mathieu rescued him from the dogs. One twist of his stronger torso and the bargeman was forced back so that they sat for a second, face to face.

"You."

"Yes, me. Trying to help. You oaf."

Explanations had to wait. Neither of them wanted to be arrested. They ran down a narrow lane, the bargeman first. Mathieu could see that his new companion had a curious limp, as if his foot had been broken and reset at the wrong angle. He panted, "Non," to two shadowy figures, while a third received a kinder, "Not now, Mirelle," before they slowed to walking pace. Only then did he realize that these had been ladies of the night.

No one followed. Dark unlit lanes invited not the unsuspecting. Military policemen were no strangers to the boundaries of law enforcement.

"I'm Mathieu."

"Bistrot," came the panting response. "Christ, I hate dogs. They freak me out. Sense my fear, but what can you do?" He drew breath and spat phlegm so black you could have set it on fire and lit a room for a night. Mathieu felt him wince more than saw his grimace. Bistrot bore inner scars from fifty years of coal dust. That stood to reason.

"Will you be ready to leave at five?"

"I'm ready to leave right now, but we have to wait until the lock system opens. Strict rules."

"Why don't I board now and save time?"

Bistrot considered the question. Mathieu could hardly overpower him if that was his intent, and, since he couldn't steer a barge, and probably didn't know which end of a horse to attach to the holster, he simply said, "Why not."

#

Raoul's Story

LAWYER'S LIES

Yet there were good days, too. I began to feel more positive, even though the daily routines were boring beyond belief. Had a visit from two lawyers. Two. At the same time. My lawyers, apparently. They were very apologetic that yet again the case has been judicially delayed. They repeated the story that even the president of the republic thought that I should wait so that true justice could be guaranteed.

"Better safe than sorry," one of them kept saying. "Better safe than sorry."

Well, I wasn't sorry about Jaurès. Never would be.

They told me that the war had gone through another bad phase. That both sides lost hundreds of thousands of men around the city of Verdun, but our army held its position and bled the Germans till they were forced back and all the forts around the city, regained. I've been to Verdun, you know. Very pretty, with a middle-ages-feel. Behind the stout walls and turrets, the earthen-works and half-moon defenses made it impenetrable. I remember sitting by the river, watching the working barges streaming north and south, dipping into the canals and inlets which surrounded the city. That's what surprised me. The large number of canals along which factories and warehouses plied their trade merged into a myriad of waterways. There was a sense of beauty and symmetry, a balance between nature and industry. I was happy there, seeking a spiritual link between my country and my God.

Do you believe in God, my friend? You should, you know. Of course it's difficult for you, but you should try. He loves you, you know. He loves everyone...except anarchists, socialists, Jews, and agnostics. And probably Protestants.

These lawyers had neither news of my father nor from my father. I asked repeatedly if he could be allowed to visit me. I wanted to explain to him why I killed the worthless Jaurès. He needed to hear it from me. They said Father could apply for a visitor's permit and they would respond. So far, nothing. They thought I knew that the civil government of Reims had been moved away from the city. No one had told me that. I asked if I could write again to my brother, and they said yes, I could, but they were convinced that he didn't want to hear from me. Of course that would be his answer to any of my requests. He never wanted to recognize my worth. Well, he would have to when my trial took place and everyone realized that I killed the socialist scum for the greater glory of France. Oh yes he would.

The lawyers said that he was one of those airmen who flew over the German lines and attacked the trenches or dropped bombs. Just like him. Always had to be in the limelight. Always had his circle of friends to fawn over his latest exploit. Well, one day he will be proud to tell everyone about his brother. The man who saved France from the socialist opposition to war against the Boches.

My lawyers, a Maitre Giraud and a Maitre Bourson, treated me like a child. I asked them where they came from. Who had sent them to visit me? When would the trial begin?

"You must be patient, Raoul. It is in your interest to stay here. Times change. Now is not good," Maitre Giraud snapped. He had what they used to call an aristocratic nose, pinned onto thin high boned cheeks. Colorless skin spread from colorless eyes as if he saw nothing of worth before him.

"You have friends, Raoul, and they will not disappoint you."

Yes, I knew that. But said nothing lest it was trap.

Bourson was drawn in a softer hue, placid in appearance, always proper in his demeanor, willing you to believe that he cared about you personally. They would have made a fine double-act at the Comedie-Francaise. I can see them dressed as vultures in court robes. Giraud with blood running from his beak; Bourson smiling by his side, head cocked, eyes alert, with a pretense of innocence, watching, prodding, waiting for a sign of weakness before he pounced.

Each time we met, they repeated the same questions.

"You know they will ask if you acted alone."

"Yes, I know they will. And I will say, Yes."

"They will ask if you were the only person who fired a gun."

"Yes, I know they will, and I will answer, you know I was."

Bourson sought to emphasize the need for eternal vigilance. "You must be careful. There are spies everywhere. You can trust no one."

Meeting after meeting, like a mantra, until I eventually added, "Yes, I know. That's why I have my own insurance."

"What? What do you mean, insurance?"

"My last will and testament. It's my final protection. Alive, I am a loyal son. Dead, well, there might be a story to tell. But don't worry, when this is all over…I'll alter my will. Eventually."

"But you trust us and those who sent us, surely?" Giraud's features lit up in animated shock. "You've left a will? Where?"

I paused to allow a smirk to pass across my face.

"With someone I truly trust. But have no fear. I don't expect that it will ever come to light."

"But…"

They left in flurry of insecurity. They needed instruction from a source they could trust.

But I can trust you, my friend. I do. I do trust you. I have to.

It was like a test in junior school. As if the teacher wanted to make sure that I understood the basic learning blocks. I did. I did. I knew that I must say these words in court. I knew that there could be no other answer or hesitation. I was a clever man. I would make sure that this is my message when the day came. Did they not realize how much I had to lose if I said anything else?

Monsieur Georges must not be compromised in any way. Ever. Or my beloved Action française. This I would never do. Yet I, too, needed insurance in case…

I did think about my father, and despite the beatings, I held no grudge against him. Life must have been difficult, bringing up two boys and running the civil court in Reims at the same time. I always tried to make him happy. My brother didn't care one way or the other. Father might have abandoned me in the difficult times when I was younger. I know that he was disappointed by my interest in mysticism, even though I stayed true to my faith. More than could be said of my brother.

I used to visit him at home once or twice a year but told him nothing about my involvement with Action française. It would only have enraged him more. He told me how dangerous and extreme these people were. Laughed at their ambitions to restore Alsace and Lorraine. Laughed!

"Where do you live?"

I didn't want him to know.

"How do you live?"

No, no. I did not want him to interfere. I only wanted him to understand.

But he knew how to hurt me. There was a phrase he kept by his side like a whip to cut me in mid-sentence. To touch the raw sore that could not be healed. To hurt.

"You're just like your mother, you know."

Oh, I was "just like my mother" was I? How I wanted to answer, "Yes, and you are just like your own." But I never did.

Did he beat my brother like he beat me? No. Never in my hearing. Marcel was his favorite, no matter how I tried to impress. He gave him a job in the courthouse. Wanted to groom him for higher things. Me? I was left on my own… just like my mother. Oh yes. We failed her. We all did. But as I grew older I realized that he failed her most of all. If only he had been capable of love. If only he had tried to understand her. But he did not understand love. I can't forgive him. And yet, I wanted to talk to him. I wanted to explain why I had been motivated by my love for France. So he understood. So he could see me in a new light. My light. As France would. It was hopeless. How could he have understood that without understanding love? Could you?

23

December 1916-January 1917
Bistrot's Barge

The seasons changed their purpose. Spring threatened fresh initiatives with the deception of firm terrain and untested reservists. Summer added slaughter to the treachery of trench warfare. Autumn drowned hope from the landscape as each new plan sank into the ubiquitous mud and murderous combinations of shell, gas, and bullets. Winter froze despair to the misery of trench-foot and fear of yet another year of conflict. War was free to destroy any and all that it could and choose the time that suited best. Generals on both sides rolled the dice in a game of rampant stupidity to decide who could lose the most men in a single gambit. Strangely, there was no winner.

Silence had fallen upon a countryside blanketed in winter frost. It was not yet the time for a full scale attack on the Western Front, though, without warning, an unplanned skirmish might break any day, anytime, anywhere. Long before daylight, Bistrot had tethered his nag to the barge. Even to an amateur eye it was clear he loved that animal more than himself. His sturdy draft horse stood over six foot high, smooth brown skin, attuned to his master's voice, impervious to the cold. It had been fed and groomed, stroked affectionately, and privately told the plan for the day.

"All set?" Mathieu shouted but Bistrot spun 'round in alarm and put his finger to his lips.

"No shouting. No unnecessary sound. This journey is dangerous enough without alerting the enemy." His half-whisper was a chilling reminder that they were about to travel on the edge of reason.

Bistrot's mare padded along the towpath, his barge noiselessly swishing through the untroubled waters. Everything was unnatural. Above a parapet of ice in fields fortunate enough to nurture wheat or barley, the hope of the earliest roots of spring had yet to show themselves. With luck these might make it to full term. Further north, in Flanders, the wind waves of summer had not blown over ripening crops for two harsh years, leaving winter to crush the life from rotting seed. As the canal merged into the river Meuse the landscape began to bear signs of recent devastation. The pale late-winter morning sky was shaded in a light-blue tint, washed out, drained of energy before the ninth hour. They came across a village where life had been suspended, forsaken for the moment by those who loved it most. Shards of trees hung beside skeletal roofs but there was no sign of the living. Too early yet for migrant birds, too late for native wildlife caught in the churning wrath of war. There was no movement near them. Eerie silence wrapped itself around the landscape in unnatural terror. Death had passed this way and would return.

Mathieu's imagination saw doom 'round every corner. A rustle in the wind took shape as a lone sniper, then bent away to form a thin-branched bush. Isolated vulnerability overwhelmed him and he took refuge in the hold, thankful for its dark protection. Climbing down wooden stairs which had only ever been washed by rain, he was aware that a different scent hung in the permadust. It was the smell of warmth; of woman. Someone else lived here. Unlike the rubbish-strewn deck, its scant debris suggesting better times, the hold concealed a tidy order. A rough worn woolen blanket marked out a well-defined territory bounded by the smell it masked and the stern. Soft light from above moved slowly as the barge progressed but between wooden casks and partly bound boxes he saw the outline of a woman busying herself beside a small stove.

"Sorry, I didn't realize anyone was down here," Mathieu apologized in a low voice.

She turned, saw him, smiled and nodded in one movement, and said nothing. Her hair flowed loosely, thick and on the cusp of turning white. It was neither fully brushed nor unkempt and she swept it behind her left ear as if she might hear him better. Her back was strong and muscled, more male than female in form, and she had wrapped a second faded blanket 'round her waist. Though he had caught a mere glimpse of her face, Mathieu was sure that she was embarrassed to meet him. Yet his appearance was clearly no surprise though he had not been aware of her on the previous night.

"I'm Mathieu." He offered to shake her hand but she pointed to a stool between the curve of the hold and the stove. A smile again. No words.

Several silent hours passed before Bistrot tied the barge to the riverbank and climbed aboard. He clambered down to the hold and kissed the nape of the woman's neck with a tenderness which surprised Mathieu. She offered them hot coffee in which yesterday's baguette had been soaked. It tasted sublime.

"Is she always so quiet, your woman?"

"Dumb, you see, from birth. But so alive in other ways. We're not married. No need. Been together for longer than I remember. Understands me and I understand her. Got lucky, I say. Margarite has always been my lucky charm."

She smiled again and Mathieu smiled back. How unexpectedly strange the world is.

"Very lucky."

"You got a wife?"

"No." Mathieu changed the subject. "Is it always so quiet on the river?"

"No," Bistrot assured him. "The closer we get to the front, the quieter it becomes. Look on the bright side. If there is a bored sniper out there waiting to loosen off a bullet, you won't hear it. In fact, if he's really good, you won't feel it either, so they say."

"Are there many refugees still?"

"Not any more. In the first months it was frightening, but worthwhile, too. They'd pay a sharp price for a trip down to Toul."

"Belgians?"

"At first, yes, but also our own farm workers and their families."

"What about contraband, that sort of thing? The black market?"

"In what? Coal? Stones? Trashed wooden roofs and tiles? Little else comes down the river. Do you Parisians imagine that we live in luxury here?" He shook his head in a way that made Mathieu think that he was the bumpkin. "By the way, you do realize that we can go no further than about a kilometer this side of Saint-Mihiel?"

"What? I thought…"

"Look, Monsieur, the front isn't a straight line neatly drawn across the land to divide the armies. I'll drop you off shortly. You need to make your way to Souilly. Army headquarters used to be there. Then around Verdun by land. But you are way off track if you think there is some black market running here. We survive. Just." Bistrot spoke with an authority born of experience.

"And keep your police and war office papers securely hidden. If the Germans catch you they'll shoot you as a spy. Our boys might shoot you for being a policeman."

"How'd you know?" Mathieu thought he had been discreet.

"You were asleep earlier. Snoring like a contented horse. Don't worry, though, I only took the two francs you owe me from your wallet. The rest is no business of mine." He paused and winked, smiling toothless approval. "Deuxième Bureau, eh?" When he dumped his passenger at a broken pier-head in the middle of what Mathieu took to be no-man's land, Bistrot said the he would be back in a couple of days, if a return journey was required. Mathieu thanked him, but thought it unlikely.

He braced himself for a long trudge across country lanes and nameless tracks, glad to put distance between the silence of the canal and his new found fear of unseen snipers. Normally the thirty kilometer walk would have taken five or six hours, but Mathieu was aware that he had to tread carefully. Within five minutes a road block stopped his progress. For the next half hour a dubious corporal checked his papers and used a field telephone to contact his sergeant at Headquarters. He was ordered to sit by the roadside and wait. One of them asked him questions about Paris in the hope of finding fault. Quite possibly they were bored and would welcome the summary execution of a spy posing as a Parisian policeman. When the telephone call was answered, Mathieu's credentials bore fruit. A lorry had been rerouted to pick him up, though it was evident that its occupants remained as suspicious as the first patrol. The countryside hardly changed, but there was less tension in the air and occasional bird-song broke the monotony.

"Where are we headed?" Mathieu was lost.

"Souilly."

The small town of Souilly, little more than a village with a crossroads, the compulsory church and an overfull cemetery, had witnessed one of the truly great treks of the war.

"They will remember this road, you know." One of the younger guards drew Mathieu's attention to the hard packed broad stone highway. "General Pétain brought all the men and ammunition from the railway halts by this road to save Verdun. Almost a year ago, every village had a repair depot along the seventy-five kilometers from Bar-le-Duc. Nothing was allowed to block the lifeline to the battle. Any breakdowns were hauled to the side and left there. Thousands upon thousands of lorries."

Mathieu was impressed. The journey was flawless. The road admirably smooth. A second soldier, young, perhaps eighteen, broke into the conversation. "There's the narrow-gauge single track railway." He pointed to the lines which ran parallel to the roadside, built to move vast supplies every day, including the bulk of the army's provisions and bring back the wounded that could be moved.

The small town hall had served as General Pétain's headquarters during the battle for Verdun. Mathieu was ushered inside, but first shook the hands of the young men who had escorted him. No false hope of good luck passed their lips.

201

Inside he was subjected to more questioning. His papers were in order, but his presence did not make sense. He could hear an officer talking on the phone to the 36. "Monsieur, according to your superiors, you are on leave. You must be lying. Either to us or to them." He turned to the nearest soldier. "Lock him up."

"Call them again. Ask for Sous-Lieutenant Bernier. I'm his cousin, Henri."

This was not what he had expected. There was no black market link from Belgium to Paris here. It was a myth. He had wasted valuable time and now he sat in a makeshift cell, friendless. How long would it take to convince them to contact Jacques-Francois or Bernard Roux? Would they even listen to his protestations? Fuck. Cold though it was, Mathieu sat alone in that sparse room for three valuable hours, sweating. He had rushed into this venture without considering what would happen if he was thwarted. A commotion outside drew him from self-pity. Some senior officer had arrived unexpectedly. Mathieu heard a deep voice resonate from the entrance.

"Where is he?"

"Inside, Sir. Locked up."

"So he should be. Bring him here."

"Would you like a coffee, Sir?"

"Nothing stronger?" A general sat himself comfortably in the center of the main room, an aide standing to his left. The prisoner was brought before him, dumbfounded.

General Messimy turned to face Mathieu. "You've been better dressed."

This was no place to justify his appearance. "Sir?"

"Do you remember my last words to you in Paris?"

"I think you said that you'd have me shot if I disobeyed your orders." The onlookers gasped.

"Correct. Bear that in mind always."

Messimy turned to the lieutenant. "I can vouch that he is whom he says he is. Release him into my custody immediately. I assure you that if he takes one step out of line, he will be shot." The general rose with imperial authority. He had what he wanted. With a curt word of thanks to the attendant military, he ushered Mathieu into an open-topped staff car. Barely two turns of the wheel later Messimy's driver stopped abruptly and reversed back to the Town Hall. The general stood up, looked at no one in particular, and advised, "This brief stop will not be mentioned in any report. You understand? Anyone who thinks otherwise will find himself before a court-martial. Proceed."

Barely five minutes later, the battle-hardened staff car turned into a lane and Mathieu was ushered to a second vehicle tucked behind an abandoned farm shed. Was this it? Mathieu had always found it difficult to determine which side the general supported. He was a pillar of the military establishment, yet the chief superintendent admired and trusted him.

"I understand from Bertrand Roux that you might think me one of the power-brokers behind the war. I am not. I am a loyal soldier of France, and yes, I wanted to put Germany in her place at the outbreak, but not on these terms. Not at this horrendous cost. Priorities have changed for the Bureau. You have to forget the black market for the moment. My good friend, Roux, who values your loyalty and ability, needs you to concentrate on other business. A certain French citizen called Basil Zaharoff is here about once again, protected by his old henchman. Apparently this man holds a grudge against you."

Mathieu said nothing but raised an eyebrow. Messimy read the physical sign as clear understanding. "We, and I include myself, believe that the failure to blow Briey to kingdom come in August 1914 was a grave mistake, but direct action was forbidden by the highest military command. And those above them. Roux and I agree that even now, disruption to the iron and steel foundries would shorten the war and save hundreds of thousands of lives. There are those who would stop us any way they can, so we have to be quick and we have to be careful. I am going to introduce you to colleagues who are determined to blow the steel plants to hell. They need protection. They don't know who can be trusted, because frankly, no one can be trusted. They don't know the Comité des Forges. They don't know Zaharoff's close associates, and Roux is confident you do. Keep them safe, Lieutenant."

Mathieu nodded but one thing puzzled him.

"How did you find me, Sir?"

"Ask Roux. I don't think you were ever far from his view. I should be asking how he knew where I was. When we reach headquarters get yourself cleaned up smartly. The army cannot abide a mess, unless of course it is of their own making. Then it becomes someone else's mess."

BLACK NIGHTS

I had a plan.

Bourson and Giraud said they would be coming back to see me regularly. The warder told me so. Apparently they were upset when they last left my cell and argued with each other all the way to the governor's office. Word was that they were most anxious to learn about an insurance policy I had. I laughed to myself. They thought themselves so clever, but my little exaggeration could not be easily dismissed. They demanded to know who I had been writing to after my arrest. There was only one letter, and that had been written on their instruction. Dictated, in fact. Now they wondered if I had written other epistles to my brother or bribed a guard to sneak one out of La Santé, perhaps? What joy! They had fallen for a half-truth and developed it into a full grown witch-hunt. Find the insurance policy was the new game in town…and there was none.

"Raoul," Bourson began in a gentle tone, "are you sure that you made a record of events before Jaurès' murder?"

"It wasn't murder. It was mercy-killing. I crushed him like a cockroach to stop him blocking the war. I saved France from the embarrassment…"

"Yes, yes, of course you did. We understand. And we will prove it was a just killing…at the trial…"

"You have a date?" I had their measure. I should have been an actor.

"No, not yet. You know we have to wait on the government."

Giraud barged into the conversation in a more menacing tone. "Stop your nonsense, Raoul, and answer the question. Are you sure you put plans on paper before you shot Jaurès? You were told not to do that…"

"Was I?" So they were in cahoots with Monsieur George at Action française. They reported back to him. Indeed.

"Well, as I explained before, I have taken out an insurance policy to make sure that no unforeseen circumstance impedes my acquittal…and my life afterwards.

"And where is this supposed document?"

"Let it be, Maitre Giraud. The word of Monsieur George is suffice, I do believe, but should anything happen to him, I have to…you know…protect myself"

"Did you send material to you brother, perhaps?"

"Perhaps, yes…but unlikely. He has disowned me. I have more loyal contacts."

I watched their eyes widen. Such a good word, contacts. "But don't worry. My mouth is shut. I will keep my promise. I will never betray Monsieur George. I promise. On my life."

"Indeed." Giraud turned on his heels and Bourson followed. Creeps. They made me feel small.

And the nightmare followed. I began to shrink. Very slowly at first. My clothes grew in size. They must have belonged to someone else. But no. They were mine. I felt diminished. I was speaking quite normally to the warder and I heard my voice lose volume. Strange. He noticed, too.

"Are you well, Raoul? Do you have a problem with your throat?"

It was like a child's fantasy; except it was happening to me. I began to fall though my shirt and pants and almost throttled myself on my undergarments. Did they really smell so bad? And the Warder had gone. I was physically disappearing and he had walked out on me? What discourtesy.

As all night fears do, they disappeared in the morning gloom leaving me depressed. So what had I learned? Bourson and Giraud were little more than agents for Monsieur George and Action française. They were spying on me, weren't they? Bastards. Presenting me with the illusion of care while they checked on my state of mind.

Dirty bastards, every last one…

24

TOUCHING THE UNTOUCHABLE

Within an hour Mathieu had bathed in warm water, shaved, put on his clothes which some unknown batman had attempted to clean, and swallowed a bowl of thick vegetable soup. Ah, the benefits of being fed by a general's cook. He was collected by Messimy's aide and taken down to a basement room. The smell of wine from ageing casks ached like a forlorn temptation. Messimy introduced him to yet another general, Guillaumat, who had served in Paris before the war began.

"Ah, here's young Lieutenant Bertrand. Now at the Deuxième, I understand." Guillaumat's smile was infectious and refused to hide behind a greying moustache.

If this is a conspiracy, Mathieu thought, *at least it's high-level.* He remembered them at the War Ministry in the last days of peace. Bernard Roux had been their close confidant. Of course. They had created the new structures before being transferred back into the military. These were the men who put Roux into number 36. He was amongst friends, which spoke volumes for the three others who were seated around a make-shift table. Dressed in officers' uniforms which bore the distinctive badge of the Service Aeronautique, they, too, shared a confidence of trust. He felt it instinctively.

The airmen were introduced as Pierre, Paul René, and Marcel, sous-lieutenant pilots based at Lemmes. Formalities over, General Messimy summarized the discussion.

"Pierre-Etienne Flandin and his comrades here want to bomb the blast furnaces at Briey and end the war within six months."

Mathieu recognized the name and then the face behind it. "You're Depute Flandin, are you not? From the Assembly. You worked with the generals before the war."

Flandin blushed. "And I've seen you somewhere else." Mathieu was sure of that...but where?

Guillaumat continued. "These gentlemen want me to authorize the attack on the German iron and steel foundries around the Briey basin, and take the flack if it goes badly." He was laughing at them. The meeting would not have been called if it did not have the blessing of both Generals. "Flandin knows the area intimately. These are his drawings." He pointed to a series of meticulous pencil-drawn sketches of the blast furnaces, mines, canals, factories, and railway sidings which were wrapped around the area.

"We all know that the entire Briey basin should have been wiped out in the first hours of the war. Without the iron and steel, Germany would have no guns by now. We have to stop them getting their raw materials in France. And we can. From the air."

"What do you know that we don't, Lieutenant?"

Mathieu looked at Messimy for permission before launching into the story of Zaharoff, his henchmen, the secret meetings with other Deputies, and a line of complicity which appeared to stretch beyond the president's office. Mathieu hesitated but had the courage to raise the issue which no one dared mention.

"It is important that you all know that this goes far beyond politicians and industrialists. The men who control Briey, the men of power, hide behind international companies and secret agreements. Do you imagine that key generals don't know what is going on? They pass on orders. They play the game."

"Name one," Paul René demanded, his indignation roused by disbelief.

"I know for a fact that Papa Joffre's aides attended their meeting in Paris…" Mathieu's words were cut short by a hiss of disgust.

"Never."

"Rubbish."

"That's treason. Papa Joffre would never…"

"I'm not pointing directly at Joffre, and I don't want to believe that he is part of the conspiracy. Honestly, I don't. But the company that Zaharoff keeps includes the president of France, the prime minister of England, and military leaders on the Allied side. Who knows if they stretch as far as Berlin? These people have immense power and money. I was removed from the Zaharoff case because my own boss wanted to protect me. Even the Deuxième has to take every precaution against these people." He stopped, lowered his voice, and added, "I've told you too much already. Once you have crossed their path, you will be in great danger. You have to know this."

They looked from one to the other. Even the generals were taken aback. Mathieu understood. They didn't believe him. They couldn't.

General Guillaumat turned to his own men. "Pierre-Etienne. You came to me with these plans. You were adamant, you all were. Briey had to be destroyed; wasted even. This and this alone could end the bloodletting within months. You asked me to risk my career. I am prepared to do that, though with General Messimy's support, I will survive. The government could not afford to have a public scandal. But the forge-masters and the industrialists will come after us if they can. The option is this. Do it to-night and face what comes … or forget it."

* * *

"*Merde, merde, merde, merde.* What am I doing here?"

Mathieu Bertrand was a detective, not an aviator. He kept his feet on the ground. Nature had not intended him to travel at over eighty miles an hour, two thousand feet above sea level, closer to the sun than he had ever been in his life. The story of Icarus flashed through his mind, but he wasn't so much afraid as terrified.

No sooner had the decision been taken to go ahead with the immediate bombing of the Briey basin than a major problem emerged. There were three pilots and a member of the Deuxième Bureau already involved, but the two Caudron G.4 twin-engine bombers available required a total of four airmen. If they tried to enlist another flyer from the base at Lemmes, time would be lost and the secret mission might be compromised. As the generals had pointed out, time was against them.

"Look, there's nothing to it. You hold the bombs out over the airplane and when I prod you, you let them fall." Mathieu had agreed to accompany Marcel, the other pilot. It sounded simple. Even he could release a twenty pound bomb. And a fully loaded Caudron G.4 carried a total of twelve. They had him kitted up with jacket and headgear, buoyed by his eagerness, delighted that the mission was underway. To his amazement, the bomber's seat was positioned out front of the twin-engine airplane. He had a fixed machine gun to play with, if necessary. Such was the extent of his training.

Mathieu had no regrets until the twin engines revved up and the entire world began to shake convulsively. Coherent speech was impossible from that moment onwards. He learned later that it was being phased out of service because of its high casualty rate, but blissful ignorance saved him unnecessary worry. Marcel swung the biplane onto the grass track and powered confidently forward. Mathieu watched the trees at the end of the field rush towards him until the Caudron raised its nose and headed into the clouds. He imagined that had happened but in fact he saw nothing. His eyes were firmly closed as he gripped the side of his seat and prayed that the belt which secured him to the mainframe had been properly attached. Why had he agreed to this stupidity?

The two Caudrons flew side by side. Paul René waved confidently across and pointed ahead to the sky. His antics appeared to indicate that Mathieu should be on the lookout for enemy airplanes and keep his hands on the machine gun in readiness for a sudden attack. No one had mentioned this when he agreed to be the fourth man. For thirty minutes the bombers flew eastward. Mathieu marveled at the world below with fields and towns, canals and rivers seemingly emptied of people. Verdun sat clearly to his left, its great defenses like a miniature model he once saw in the Parc Borely in Marseilles. He turned to see the pilot already engaged in complex navigation. They shouted to each other in vain. Communication was limited to lip reading and gesture. They flew over the front lines, pockmarked black and brown, as if smallpox had ravaged the world and disfigured the face of the earth for all time. Trench lines ran so close together that it was impossible to establish friend from foe. An occasional shot was fired from below, more for effect than real purpose. The airplanes began to lose height and Mathieu felt a sharp tap from behind.

The landscape had been turned into a vast industrialized complex colored by its own debris. Pierre-Etienne's plane circled over eight blast furnaces belching acrid smoke and brimstone into the sky. The second Caudron followed close behind so that, from the ground they must have looked like a pair of scavenging buzzards. Sulphur spat into Mathieu's eyes despite his protective goggles. He began to loosen the first bomb from its catch but it stuck fast. He pulled it free with both hands but it spun from his grasp and almost hit the floor. Jesus. That would have been a fitting epitaph. Blown up in midair over the blasted furnaces of hell. His heart rate raced faster than the engine's thrust.

Focus. Focus, you idiot, he told himself.

Ahead, Paul René began to drop his explosives at regular short intervals. Mathieu did likewise. He could feel the shockwaves from below but concentrated on his own delivery.

Surrounded by noise, the detective did his utmost to deliver destruction from the air. He could not imagine the surprise below. For the first time since August 1914, war reached over the border and smote the industrial complex on the Briey basin. Incredibly, this unexpected assault was the first attack on a crucial target which lay less than thirty miles from Verdun. The planes regained height quickly and turned back towards Lemmes.

"Keep your eyes open," the pilot must have yelled in Mathieu's ear because he thought he heard the instruction. Behind them the furnaces continued to flare wildly.

The return journey was uneventful. Save for the moment Mathieu realized that the Caudron was about to land, he enjoyed the experience. What damage had they inflicted? He was eager to know and was contemplating jubilant headlines when the plane descended rapidly and lost speed. Sitting out front it seemed impossible that anyone could control the landing. The wind buffeted the aircraft with increasing effect as it lost height. Unconsciously Mathieu prayed to his guardian angel for instant protection. Miraculously, the sturdy Caudron glided onto mother earth and trundled to a standstill. Inside his head Mathieu swore an oath. *Never again.*

He wanted to leap to the ground, do cartwheels and cerebrate a life preserved, but the others were so clearly nonchalant that he had to internalize his joy. He also had to extricate himself from the front of the Caudron and was last to reach the ground.

"How much damage did we do? Anyone see?" He tried to sound nonchalant.

"Reconnaissance will find out in the morning. Right now, we deserve a quality bottle of wine."

"Let's go."

Barely ten minutes and two kilometers later, the four "bombers" had uncorked a bottle of Cotes de Toul in an old auberge partially hidden from the adjoining road by a copse of trees.

"This Pinot Noir," Paul-Rene proclaimed, "is the king of the regional reds," before pouring a generous glass for each of his companions. "To victory... and an end to this slaughter."

"To the downfall of traitors who have protected the forges from hell," Marcel Villain replied.

Pierre-Etienne raised his glass in response. They toasted healthily on the rich-blooded red and ordered a rabbit stew for which the proprietress was famous. The detective in Mathieu obligated him to ask about black market tins of Atlantic salmon to the amusement of the others. Once more a blank. Sometime before the second bottle of Pinot Noir had been completely quaffed, an officer interrupted their repast. He saluted them with, "Excuse me, gentlemen. Have I the honor of addressing sous-Lieutenants Flandin, Dumer, et Villain? And Lieutenant Bertrand?"

The airmen nodded in unison, accepting the compliment with good grace. Mathieu cast his eye on the remains of the stew. Where had he seen this man? Think.

"General Guillaumat asks that you return to Headquarters. He expected a report from you earlier this evening, I understand. I have a car outside."

"Thank you, we will follow shortly." Pierre caught Mathieu's puzzled pose and waited for the emissary to leave. "What's troubling you?"

"Two points. The general did not want a report this evening. We agreed that nothing would be recorded on paper."

"True."

"And that officer," Mathieu gestured towards the door, "I've seen him before. In Paris. He was present at a meeting in the suburbs. The one which included Zaharoff. Is he not Joffre's aide de camp?"

"No, he's not. I'll tell you who he is…Levy's grandson. Levy of the Comité des Forges. He's a liaison officer on some committee or other attached to Papa Joffre's command. He belongs to the Comité des Forges. He is one of them. Not Papa Joffre's."

Relief shot down Mathieu's assumption. "Thank God for that," he said to himself, but there was no time to discuss the issue further. He rose from the table abandoning the succulent stew,

"We need to get out of here, now. These are the thugs Messimy warned us about."

Paul Dumer was already on his feet. He left a handful of coins on the table and shouted,

"Claire, we have to go immediately. Emergency."

A buxom young woman appeared from the kitchen. He kissed her cheek and put both hands on her shoulders.

"Ma Cherie, we need you to buy us time. Those men outside. Do what you can to distract them. We'll go out the back door."

Mathieu glanced out the front window, careful to avoid being seen. *Merde.* A charabanc was sitting on the far side of the road. Standing with his back to the auberge, Zaharoff's manservant listened attentively to the Levy messenger. There were at least six men waiting in total. Not a subtle murder squad.

Behind the inn lay a small wood which in summer might have offered better cover, but night had crept in while they celebrated, and darkness became an instant ally. They ran, but not blindly. Pierre led them across an open field and through a further thicket. Lights from a farmhouse guided them towards a hidden stream. Once over that hurdle they zigzagged across a withered vineyard and sat for a moment beside a family vault which stood at its center, camouflaged by receding vines. The consequence of rich earthy wine and thick rabbit stew weighed heavy on their stomachs.

"Bloody hell," Paul wheezed, stroking the terminally damaged fruit with immense delicacy. "These were pinot grapes. What a tragedy. South facing, too. This bloody war."

High cloud covered the moon with a distant fog which was a blessing when they reached the outskirts of Lemmes. The charabanc had stopped near the gates to the aerodrome, its lights dimmed. From a distance it appeared that the driver and occupants were in detailed conversation with the guards, but experience warned Mathieu that what they thought they saw, might be otherwise. He crouched in the ditch and was about to warn the others to keep low when the night exploded in raw violence.

"There's the bastard."

It was Timon, raging like a wounded hog. Revenge was all-consuming. There in the ditch was the cop whom he blamed for all the misery and pain he had suffered for the last three years. Zaharoff's bodyguard lashed out with his right foot, his target caught in the ditch. Mathieu parried the blow and tried to drag his assailant down from the grass verge. Pierre shouted for help towards the distant airfield, but no one heard. They were outnumbered, but riled by the unexpected attack, fought where they stood. Paul took his revolver in hand but his shot flew high and wide as he was tackled from behind. Pierre had reached the road before Timon emerged and the more even surface allowed him greater purchase. A right hand punch followed quickly by a jab from his left downed one of the assailants. Boxing lessons at his private school proved their worth. Mathieu had eyes only for the man who would be his nemesis.

The sturdy Greek lunged forwarded again, but slipped into the ditch. His greater weight cut through thin ice and rooted his front foot in cold slime which sucked him deeper into the mire. Blinded by anger he denied the logic of nature and thrust his rear leg down to free himself. The ditch began to collapse inwards. Mud spluttered up in protest, holding him fast, better than any vice. His profanities bore witness to his frustration. So close to Mathieu yet not within reach. Two of the attackers broke away to help Timon free himself, allowing the others time to regroup.

"Boches! Boches!"

It was a female cry, so surprising that heads were turned. The charabanc had reversed down the road at full throttle, swerving perilously close to the ditch. Two of the assailants leaped aside. The onrushing motor car thundered to a halt. Claire from the auberge stood at the wheel like a modern-day Joan of Arc, rallying her troops onwards. Unfortunately the strain of such unusual mechanical exertion killed the engine. Paul grabbed her hand and pulled Claire out of the stranded vehicle.

"Move." He raised his revolver to remind everyone he was armed. "Run," he urged.

Pierre had pulled Mathieu from the ditch and all five moved as fast as they could in the direction of the aerodrome. Ahead, two guards ran towards them, rifles in hand, confused by the commotion. Behind, the charabanc coughed back into life.

"Behind us," Pierre screamed at the guards as they closed in on the airmen and pointed down the road.

"What…?"

"No time. Explain later. You know who we are, surely." The first soldier saluted instinctively. It was time wasted. Further along the road they could hear the charabanc retreat. Its lights had been switched off but it was impossible to hide the engine's gruff whine as it disappeared in the direction of Souilly.

They were met at the gates by General Guillaumat's aide. Claire was not permitted entry, being both a local and a woman. Though her bravery in trying to delay the Forge's men by taking them wine, her refusal to give any information, and being bundled into the charabanc had bought valuables minutes, not to mention her intervention in the middle of the fracas, the best that Paul could organise was for one of his friends in the squadron to escort her back to the auberge. It was just as well, for the conversation with the general was highly sensitive. Once in the basement he dismissed his accustomed entourage and stood blocking the door.

"Firstly, congratulations. I don't think you caused too much damage, but we have certainly upset people in high places."

Mathieu noted the pronoun.

"I understand that the Forge's men, we have to believe that in the end that is who they are, got to you after the attack. Now do you appreciate how well connected and informed these people are? Imagine if we had waited. As it is, they will be furious at their failure. And," his face betrayed his own annoyance, "I have been given an official reprimand and ordered not to repeat the infraction, I think they called it."

"Ordered by whom, General?"

He didn't answer immediately.

"Whoever it is… there will be a day of reckoning, I promise you that." Brave words from Pierre, but Mathieu believed him. As Depute Flandin in the National Assembly, Pierre would be in a position to raise hell, once the war was won. When that would be, remained to be seen.

General Guillaumat continued, "Ordered directly by General Headquarters at Chantilly. Our mutual friend and colleague tells me that Joffre has been replaced by the rising star that is our new commander-in-chief,

Robert Nivelle. So we cannot blame Joffre for this. Indeed, General Messimy believes that once Papa Joffre works out that he has been totally sidelined, he will resign. Our president must be involved. He is the man connected to the armaments clique. Zaharoff is his personal associate. There are hints that the Americans are also behind the decision. American Trusts apparently own large shares in the French and German arms production. Whenever the Americans are cited, everyone bows the knee to the new world order. Mark my words. Until they decide to enter the war, Briey is safe from us."

Mathieu nodded. It was precisely as he and Bernard Roux surmised.

"But you have shown that the Briey furnaces can be destroyed. They know it can. That's why we've made them nervous."

General Guillaumat moved from the door, as ill at ease as everyone else. "We have to get the Lieutenant out of here. He is probably the most vulnerable target for these thugs. They have spies everywhere. Do you imagine your attackers chanced on the Auberge? You'll stay here under guard tonight. Tomorrow you have to go your own ways. I will personally apologize and give the impression that you have been dispersed to other units. We need them to believe that this will never happen again."

"A final glass of the best Pinot in the land to cement our small but hopefully significant victory today." Pierre withdrew a bottle from his satchel and found four usable glasses in the officers' mess. Since they had no idea who was trustworthy, they sat together in the corner under a picture of President Poincaré and the Czar of Russia. Paul René turned it to face the wall. He trusted neither. They might be listening. On further inspection, Pierre and Paul recognized an old companion seated on the other side of the mess, and excused themselves.

"It's Felix...look, he's back on his feet." Both strode across to greet an injured friend, delighted to find him back in uniform.

"How did you get mixed up with these two renegades?" Mathieu asked Marcel, his pilot for the day.

"Trained with the same escadrille earlier in the year. These boys are good flyers, believe me." He paused, looked deep into his untouched wine and said, "You've worked it out, haven't you?"

It would have been churlish to deny the fact. "Yes, I think so. You're related to Raoul in some way? A cousin?"

Marcel Villain exhaled deeply and bent his head. "Brother."

"Brother!" Mathieu was astounded. "Of course, his brother." He saw the shame in his new friend's face and tried to comfort him. "That's hardly your fault. We cannot choose our family. They are what they are. Friends, on the other hand, are the people we want to be with. Raoul Villain is not your fault."

"I know, I know, but I carry his guilt with me every day. The more you say it's not my fault, the more I think it must be." He sipped the wine, distaste overpowering his senses as if it had turned to red vinegar.

"It has ruined my father. Stripped him of the dignity of his senior years. Sometimes it's too much to live with. When I'm up there in the sky, I don't care for myself. If I get killed, what does it matter? Hundreds of thousands of better men are already dead. Probably gives me an edge, when you think about it."

Mathieu was disarmed by the revelation. "I was the one who arrested Raoul that night."

"You? You arrested him. Honestly, you?"

"Me."

Trapped by the coincidence, both men had to make a decision. They were not friends. They were definitely not family, yet fate had thrown them together. They lived in a blink of time where chance might pass in an instant. In the vagary of war, the word "later" was itself a risk.

"What was he like, you know, as a brother?"

"A leech. He hung around. Needy. He didn't understand the codes we lived by. Boys don't tell tales about other boys. He did. He never grasped that every time he dropped someone in the *merde*, he was making himself more of an outcast. When they took our mother away to hospital he withdrew into himself, at least socially. He was clever at school. Grasped ideas quickly, but then never saw anything, anything at all, through to a logical conclusion. He would start down one path, appear to have reached his goal, have success at his fingertips … and then change course. Rudderless, that's a good word. I thought at one stage he was going to be a priest, and it would have had to be a Jesuit, but religion wasn't enough. Nothing was ever enough." He drank again, emptying his glass and pulling the bottles towards a refill. "We weren't close. Ever."

Hearing the pain in his voice, Marcel wanted to accept that as fact rather than an excuse. "When did he get involved in politics?"

Mathieu Villain gestured helplessly. "Who knows. I heard him talking at our grandmother's funeral about the enemies within who were a threat to France, but hey, that's what he did. He flirted with so many ideas, so many new enthusiasms. He was troubled, of that I am sure, but we thought 'that's how he is.' It was like he never grew up."

215

"Do you think that he was on his own when he killed Jaurès? Can you imagine him shooting a man at point blank range? Do you think it was just his next idea?"

"No."

The certainty of sous-lieutenant Villain's reply surprised Mathieu.

"No?"

"No. He needed to be part of things. When he was left on his own, he backed away. Always. He had to be reassured at every turn. If he pulled the trigger, someone else must have loaded the gun and pointed it for him." Marcel Villain had no doubt. He looked up at Mathieu and asked, "Do *you* think he was a lone killer?"

The detective was obliged to answer. This conversation transcended confidentiality. "No, I don't. And he has very powerful friends, you know. They can provide the best of lawyers. They have bent the law to keep him out of court until they think it politic to have a trial. And you have to ask why?"

"He wrote to me shortly after his arrest. A strange letter. I had the feeling that it was written for the benefit of someone else. He repeated that he had been responsible for murdering Jean Jaurès as if it was in doubt."

"I've read it and I agree."

Marcel was taken aback. He had not considered that the police had read his private correspondence.

"We thought he, or rather his advisers, were trying to stop the inquiry going any further. When it comes to court, if it comes to court, the letter he sent you will be produced as evidence that he was unbalanced at the time, and acted alone."

Another moment of awkward silence left each man to his own thoughts.

"Evidence has been tampered with. In truth we don't know for sure if the prosecution has the right guns. Witnesses will come out of the woodwork. As long as your brother insists he was alone, no one can prove it a lie."

"And he thinks he started this damned war."

"Conceit?"

"Yes, he had plenty of that as a boy."

"Well, my friend, you do not. Don't throw your life away needlessly. You risk your life for France every day. You … I'm proud to know."

It was a fact. And on such a basis of honesty, they parted.

25

GREEKS BEARING GIFTS

Mathieu left the aerodrome in the early morning grey without saying goodbye. It was simpler that way. The officer in charge organized a car to take him to Souilly. The route down to the famous village was remarkably busy and they were obliged to sit behind a six-wheeled truck, commandeered for military purposes. The sky seemed to be permanently blotched with blackening cloud, but the rain had yet to make an appearance. Aware that he had to cover his tracks, Mathieu told the driver that he intended to make his way to Chalons-en-Champagne and onwards by train to Paris.

His antenna was on high alert. Anyone in his path might be an informer. Timon was unlikely to have gone far. Zaharoff's man had money, and money bought good information. Souilly was, as ever, the busiest crossroads in France. Few of the trucks showed any interest in stopping in the village, and when Mathieu's driver slowed to let him climb down, an irritated policeman shouted, "Keep moving. You can't stop in the village. Keep moving. We've got to clear this patch."

He barely had time to say thanks before the car had rejoined the flow. Mathieu headed back to the canal. With luck Bistrot might already have tied up his barge near Saint-Mihiel. If not, he would walk along the towpath towards Toul. Papers in hand, he approached the corner where the border patrol had previously been stationed, but no one was there. Deserted. Perhaps the soldiers had been positioned on a different corner? But as the road twisted towards the canal he realized that all was not as it should be. Mathieu stopped to listen. Nothing. Dead air. The silence of the grave. He was back inside the death zone. A high-pitched whine broke from the grey above, dropped an octave through an evil glissando and crashed to the ground half a kilometer away. He was thrown sideways as the world churned and spewed its innards high into the air, nauseating waves of indignation scattering indiscriminate stones and soil from order to chaos, ripping confusion through the unprotected field. Another mighty explosion followed within a second, emphasizing a power that could not be seen. Under the canopy of raining death Mathieu felt the horror of impotence. There was nowhere to run, nowhere to hide, nowhere to escape the monstrous contagion of an artillery bombardment. Lie still. Hide as best you can. Merge with mother earth. Seek her protection. Covered in soil and pulverized stone he watched death's shadow flirt with the skyline. He couldn't catch a breath. And so it would end.

But life resisted the temptation to give in so easily. He coughed a gasp of earthen air, shook free the clutches of defeat, and panting, trembling, realized that he had barely been touched. Within a beat of time a duller volley thundered its reply repaying shock in like kind. Still clinging to his newly defined mother, Mathieu pieced together what was happening. Here on the edge of lunacy one combatant had greeted the other with a morning wave as if to say, "Are you still there?" and the other, charged with a response, answered, "I'm well, as you can see." The target lay inside the minds of helpless soldiers whose sacrifice did not matter to the profiteers of war; the munitions men; the political class with warped ambition who ordained this waste in the name of civilization. He had seen them, and knew a few by name, but dared not speak … yet.

Mathieu crouched silently on one knee and drank in every possible alternative. Motionless. Guarded. Sensing danger close at hand, his brain defaulted to automatic. He had trained for such an eventuality in another life, years before he became a policeman. Slowly, he crawled onto the grass verge that laced the land-side of the tow-path and crept along the canal. Two painful miles down his pilgrim's way he found Bistrot's horse slurping on the wild grass, untethered. Behind, on the muddied track, his master lay prone, unmoving. Still no sound other than the hungry horse taking advantage of forbidden fruit. Mathieu moved towards man and beast with grave caution. There was no room for error. Unseen sniper? Hidden Greek? Dead friend? Anything was possible.

He checked Bistrot's pulse. Well, at least his heart was beating. An angry lump had grown over his left eye and forehead, but there was no external bleeding. The barge lay still; its deck littered with mounds of uncut stone so that the vessel sat low on the canal. Not wanting to draw attention to himself, Mathieu clambered on board quickly, keeping an eye on the surrounding hedgerow. The sound from below was muted but a guttural cry gave him sufficient warning. He leaped to his right as Timon threw himself from the hold, great coat fanned behind him as if he was a gigantic bat, renting the air with yet another roar. This time the Greek looked triumphant. This time he intended to end it all. This time the bloody policeman would get what he deserved.

In every man's life there comes a point where running away is eminently more sensible than standing up to fight. Trouble was, Mathieu had no option but to defend himself. The burly Greek towered above him, heavy coat open to the elements, lined, cut by a stylish outfitter, with special pockets sewn into the fabric like gun holsters. He laughed at his quarry's discomfort. The detective was trapped, his ankle twisted by his fall onto the stone.

"Well, Mathieu Bertrand, at last. I have waited a long time for my revenge. But I want you to know I will enjoy this. Every second of your pain brings me joy. Pure joy, do you hear?" He reached into the left hand pocket. "This is my gift to you."

"Ah, the classic touch," Mathieu said, anticipating his next move. "The brick to the face once the victim is helpless. Well, that won't work this time round. It may do for me, but we know who you are, and there's no hiding for a cop-killer."

The Greek leaned over and hissed in Mathieu's face, his breath strangely sweet from expensive mouthwash. "If anyone can find a cop's body amongst the thousands of mutilated dead in these fields, Bertrand, I will have lost my lucky touch forever."

"They will know that this is Zaharoff's doing," was the last card in his hand, but the game had swung in the Greek's favor.

He threw back his head in delight and laughed down at Mathieu's broken form. "You think I work for Monsieur Zaharoff? Well, yes I do, but it's not an exclusive contract. No, no, no...Vincent!" he laughed and spat in the same singular movement

Mathieu gasped audibly through his pain... He knew? Impossible.

"Oh that shocked you, eh? Yes indeed, they know all about you, Vincent. I can assure you your grandfather's name will not protect you forever. Believe me, I am paid in a number of currencies. And I haven't time to tell you which!"

With every gram of strength he could muster Mathieu crashed his forehead into the stooped Greek's face, rocking him back on his heels. Momentary respite allowed him time to raise himself up, unsteadily, so that he stood briefly toe-to-toe with his enemy. Timon feigned left and struck him down once more with a well-aimed blow to the head from the other side. Mathieu cried out in pain, not from the blow, but from his twisted ankle. It refused to bear weight.

"Beating you to pulp will be the best moment of my life."

The Greek took out the brick so that Mathieu would see what struck him, raised it high above his head, and with a swish and a crack, fell. Both men moaned in agony, prostrate, pain devouring but not overcoming them. Timon's body had broken Mathieu's leg in the fall, but the Greek seemed unable to rise from the wooden deck to take advantage of his double injury. Lying there, cheek by jowl, he grabbed at the detective's throat, entirely focused on murder. Timon began to throttle the injured foe lying prone beside him and raised his torso from the hip to gain more purchase.

Swish.

Timon's left hand reached to close the gaping hole that had been slashed under his jaw. He gasped. Blood spurted like an oil gusher in the desert. The Greek's head turned to look to his right. Incomprehension frozen on his face as the hole in his throat yawned open.

Bang. Definitely a metallic bang.

Timon's skull disintegrated as it flew to the side, but hung on grimly to his body, precariously attached by some sinew-like matter. For a moment the world stopped spinning. Nothing made sense. Mathieu could not understand why the near decapitated murderer collapsed in front of him, before sliding slowly over the side of the barge, his passage lubricated by his own dark blood. Heart pounding, he struggled to comprehend what had happened as Timon's lifeless body sank into the muddy canal, weighed down by its own special ballast.

A woman stood over him, coal shovel in hand, watching intently for any sign of life in the water. She grunted, her entire body animated by the adrenalin which surged through her veins. Mathieu recognized who it was as she slowly came into focus. Margarite. She was speaking to him in a series of noises which he could not decipher. Whatever, she was uttering, she had saved his life. Where did she come from? How? *How?* Shivering violently, he slipped into a coma of sorts, semi-conscious and confused. But he was determined not to die. Things to do, you know.

26

BONDS THAT BIND

nun. Mathieu didn't like nuns. A nun with a large starched wimple was leaning over him, her black wide-sleeved habit shielded by a grey apron. She made no effort to touch him, which was fine, but her disapproval marched before her. What was this layabout doing in the convent hospital? Her lip curled up towards a fine almost invisible moustache which would not have been so obvious had she kept her distance. He blinked. She drew herself up to her full five feet and left.

He was comfortable. His body was still sore in places, but the agony had passed. Mathieu knew that his ankle was held in a splint with his leg firmly bound and bandaged. Patches of memory returned, but not immediately.

"Can you say the Lord's Prayer?" asked Sister Glum later that afternoon.

He had decided on her name immediately.

"Hail Mary full of…"

"That's close enough," she assured him, before placing a bed pan by his side. He looked at it. She looked at him. "I advise you use this carefully, if you have to. You also need to wash, you know, beneath."

What was that woman talking about? Beneath what? The bed? A few minutes later the occupant in the next cot explained. "Beneath the waist. They don't like dealing with the lower parts of the male anatomy."

This made no sense.

"Your private parts. Nuns don't go there. Don't look. Don't touch. Don't wash."

"Ah."

That made sense. It was a fate worth avoiding, anyway.

Mathieu did not at first realize that his broken ribs were constricting his lungs. It hurt to laugh or sneeze. His midriff was also tightly bound and his left arm hung limp, held by a loosening sling.

He remembered Timon's head. Grotesque. Turned from human to misshapen to hang by a sliver in two mighty blows from old Grandmother Time. Scythe became spade. Spade became scythe, her height altered by his view from the deck. No she wasn't old it was…

Mathieu opened his eyes and there she was. Margarite, and beside her, Bistrot and Sister Glum.

"Your visitors can stay for ten minutes. Please impress upon them the need to keep the ward clean." One had to wonder if Glum disliked everyone.

"Margarite, you angel of mercy... and Bistrot... what happened?" Bistrot checked that no one was listening before divulging his secret story of *The Murder*.

"You won't arrest her will you?"

"What for?"

"She did it to save you."

"She did save me." Mathieu realized that he, too, had begun to speak in whispers as if they were involved in a conspiracy. "Bistrot. No one's getting arrested. In fact, unless you have reported finding a body in the canal, no one has died. Officially."

He looked blankly at Mathieu, unable to work out precisely what he meant. Behind him, Margarite gave a broad knowing smile. Uncomplicated. Thankful.

"So... what happened? How did he get into the barge."

"I was about to feed the horse when this huge foreigner appeared from the field. He was shouting angry words which I didn't understand and he slapped Hugo's arse."

"Hugo?"

"The horse."

"Ah... Hugo the horse."

"So Hugo reared up, caught me with his foreleg, and knocked me unconscious."

"Not Timon... the Greek? The horse kicked you."

"By mistake."

"Of course."

"Margarite saw the commotion and went to fetch a compress but this big guy leaped onto the barge and started to shout at her. She jumped down into the hold and hid. He lumbered about unable to find her, banging his head on the beams, his temper worsening by the second. He was about to leave when he saw you and waited in the shadows till you climbed onboard... then attacked."

Margarite mumbled excitedly. Bistrot translated. "She insists that he would have killed you, and she thought he had killed me, so she was... upset."

"Don't be, Margarite." Mathieu had rarely been so sincere. "He was a very bad man. But who taught you to use a spade like a scythe?"

Bistrot waxed lyrical about the properties of a spade in the hands of an expert. "If you know how, a spade can become a weapon in many different ways. Taught Margarite myself. She chopped his head off like Madame Guillotine. Apparently his body didn't float. It sank immediately, she claims."

Images flashed though Mathieu's mind. That was exactly how it happened as far as he could remember.

"Margarite." He beckoned her to his side and took her hand. "Margarite, thank you so much. If you hadn't been so brave, it would have been my body in the canal."

"No thanks needed," Bistrot the translator assured him. "Bloody man had assaulted Hugo, and Hugo is HER horse."

It may have felt like six months but within ten days Mathieu was deemed ready to transfer back to Paris on the hospital train. Sister Glum reinvented herself as Sister Happiness when she heard the news. "Wonderful. See what the power of prayer can do?" Mathieu wanted to point out that twenty-four hour nursing care and experienced doctors might have influenced his partial recovery, but it would have spoiled her moment.

"I have a very special present for you. Take this for your journey home. A treat. And pray for me." How do nuns manage to say "and pray for me" in a manner which sounds like their last day is upon them? What secret sins do they hide in their wimples? She handed him a small round package wrapped in cloth. He put it in his jacket which a second nun draped over his uninjured shoulder. This one was pretty... for a nun.

Bistrot and Margarite came to the convent hospital to say farewell to the one man on earth who knew she was a murderess... and blessed his good fortune because of it. "Are you sure you are fit to walk ?" Bistrot doubted.

Mathieu was adamant that he was, propped up by a crutch, breathing slowly. His step was painful but sure.

"Be careful, my friend," Bistrot began, just as Mathieu's jacket fell from his shoulder and the package hit the floor. Margarite bent to retrieve it for her injured compadre but the cloth tore and out spilled a tin of Atlantic salmon. They looked at that tin through different eyes.

"Salmon, from America. That'll be nice," said Bistrot, retrieving it at once.

"Wouldn't mind a taste of that!" mouthed Margarite, her emotions as discreet as ever.

"What! Where did that come from?" Mathieu could not believe what he was looking at. "This is the stuff I was asking you about, Bistrot. You said that nothing came down the canal from Belgium. Well, this is from Belgium, I can assure you."

"No, it's not."

"Don't tell me it's American. I know that, but this has come to Toul in a barge from Belgium."

"No, it hasn't. That's not where it came from. Nothing from Belgium gets this far south. It's from Germany."

"What? Atlantic salmon from Germany? Impossible. How?"

"If this is what you have been searching for, you've been looking in the wrong direction. You went up the wrong canal. This did not come down the River Meuse. Some detective you are." Local knowledge can make a fool out of a genius. Bistrot saw that Mathieu was struggling to understand what he meant and led him carefully to the far corner of the convent.

"There," he pointed to his right, "is the Meuse-Moselle canal, but over to our left is the Toul-Rhine canal. Those barges in the basin, the smaller ones, carry the American flag. That's their depot."

He pointed to a substantial red-brick building on two floors set on the far side of the tow-path. The word "Douane" had been inscribed on the Portico. Trust the Americans to have the best of everything. In the cold morning mist which hung lightly over the waterways, it was clear from the smoking chimneys that this Custom House was kept warm and welcoming.

"Their barges have to stop where the locks have been sabotaged near the French-German border, then they unload their cargo onto trucks and are allowed to pass freely as neutrals. Once the cargo has been checked, it is transferred onto the barges you see there on the other side of the unofficial border. Lots of the boxes are stamped Rotterdam, but that's in the Netherlands, not Belgium."

The enormity of the moment struck Mathieu physically and his legs buckled. "That's where Hoover's relief agency is based."

Bistrot caught him before he fell.

"Wait. Let me try to work this out. The Americans, as neutrals, are allowed to export to all nations. I know that. But the food they take to Rotterdam is for the Belgians…"

"Are you certain?" Bistrot was perplexed. For a senior detective, this lad didn't know much at all.

Barely able to stand, Mathieu grabbed Bistrot's shoulder and spun him round. Anger added to his unwillingness to accept what was being said. He wanted Bistrot to be wrong.

"How would they get the permits? Why would the Germans let food through to France? To Paris? It doesn't make sense."

"That depends on how much the Americans provide for the Germans. They do deals every day, these people. Where do you think Berlin gets its rich-man luxuries?"

Bistrot understood. Mathieu struggled with the facts before his very eyes. They were at war, but behind the scenes food which was supposedly earmarked for Belgium was sold down the Rhine. Supplied to both sides? Surely not. It wasn't just illegal—it was treasonable.

Mathieu tried to clear his confusion by repeating the question slowly. "Are you saying that the Americans are selling or supplying both sides? To Germany and Belgium and Northern France?"

"I suppose so, if you put it like that." Bistrot had never considered the matter as anything other than business. And war is a business.

The ambulance arrived to take Mathieu and the walking wounded to the station and onwards to recuperate in Paris.

"Bistrot." He handed the bargeman a piece of paper. "If anyone comes asking questions about the Greek I want you to take a note of what he looks like and contact me at this telephone number. Do the same if the Americans change their routines or do anything that looks wrong. In fact, go to the police station and ask them to contact Paris. Ask for me personally."

Though he felt like a fraud in the company of men who would never recover from the savage wounds inflicted by war, Mathieu was injured. Doctors had examined his foot and considered amputation. *Please God, no.* He knew that he would have to be patient until his infected ankle healed properly and the break in his leg had mended. His collar bone would heal. They had no doubt about that, but his ribs could bear no pressure at all. He understood now the sense of denial which wounded men experience. He knew his bones were broken. He knew that the pain would pass helped by the strong drugs they fed him. But he expected to be whole within days, not weeks.

Mathieu was a hopeless patient. Rest gave him too much time to think, and thinking brought its own frustrations. He was angry at himself. He hadn't trusted his own instinct at Saint-Mihiel. He had jumped to a conclusion about the canal system. He should have known that Timon was stalking him, not the other pilots. He was lucky to have survived thanks

225

to a dumb woman's anger. Perhaps he wasn't cut out to be a detective? He was hot, uncomfortably so. Possibly he was wearing too many clothes?

Mathieu was met at the Gare de l'Est by Dubois who had no inkling of what he had endured. Shocked by his friend's condition, Paul called for a porter and together they helped support him from the train into the waiting car. When the Renault reached no. 36. Toussaint was waiting at the front entrance, eager to carry the wounded man up the stairs on his own. Even in the discomfort of his injuries, Mathieu could smell Toussaint's early morning Cognac and prayed he was fit for the task. Jacques stood beaming at him at Roux's office door and saluted his friend as if he was his commanding officer.

Dubois laughed aloud and confessed' "I should have told you, Mathieu, things are so bad these days that the chief decided to keep this hanger-on and promoted him to Sous-Lieutenant. Can you imagine?"

Mathieu's smile said it all. "Excellent. At last I've got someone to make my coffee." but his attempt at good humor was superficial. Pain sharpened his breath though he was determined not to show it.

"Ah, the wandering minstrel." Roux rose to greet him and pointed to a comfortable chair with padded seat and armrest.

Where has that come from? Mathieu asked himself.

"Thank you, gentlemen, but I must speak with Mathieu in private."

It took Mathieu several seconds to recover his breathing, such was the effort needed to tolerate the pain. He began to outline his story, but even speaking at length took its toll.

"There is one unexplained factor, Mathieu, which we hope you can help clear up." Roux cut him off mid-sentence with an urgency which suggested that he already knew the answers to most of what he had been asking.

"What happened to your assailants after you were attacked at the Auberge?"

"They escaped in the motorcar towards Souilly."

"Thing is," Bertrand Roux squeezed a final intake of nicotine from his Gauloises, "most of the men who attacked you that evening... are dead."

Mathieu shrugged, not with indifference but with surprise. "Honestly?"

"Five bodies found in a wood on the other side of Souilly. Stripped naked. Clothes burned but still discernible. All shot in the back. Faces badly smashed but not beyond recognition. Looks like a rushed job. One was identified as Leon Levy, the liaison officer between the army and the Comité des Forges. Two were petty criminals from Souilly, presumably to add local knowledge, and two appear to have come from Corsica. The only one unaccounted for is the Greek."

Mathieu coughed again. His diaphragm constricted and he buckled forward. Color drained from his face and he shut his eyes for a second before finding a point of focus.

"Best you don't know, Chief. But don't worry about him."

"So, at a guess, I might think that Timon killed his accomplices and has disappeared."

"Yes, you might."

Still Roux prodded. "He wiped out his accomplices … even Leon Levy? He didn't spare the Forge-master's grandson?"

"Don't ever assume that grandfathers care more about their family than their position and wealth."

"But why kill them all?"

"Because they knew that he had failed? To save face? So the Greek couldn't be compromised by them? Because he was told to? I don't know. He was a murdering bastard …"

"So nothing could ever be traced back to him." Roux sat nodding to himself in reflective pose, convinced that his conclusion made most sense. "We are getting too close to the truth. We have to be doubly careful. It's the Icarus thing."

Mathieu drew deep from his bruised lungs and in a half whisper offered his own assessment. "There are personal vendettas mixed with corporate conspiracy. We don't need to worry about the Greek, believe me, but this whole war is an outrageous fraud. The Germans can only continue making enough guns and shells because we let them hold onto the iron ore and smelters just across the border. But that's a secret. The Comité des Forges let them replenish their armaments. Another secret. They are in collusion with the enemy, the Forge-masters, the president, and especially the Americans. Secret, secrets, and even more secrets."

Chief Superintendent Roux sat like the Sphinx, petrified that Mathieu's conclusion might be overheard. "Softer, Mathieu, softer." He moved closer to his injured colleague so that they could whisper their thoughts.

"We know that the American Relief is a fraud because it supplies both sides at the same time. That's a big secret. Rumors that Hoover's people allow vital food to be syphoned off to feed the Germans must be true. And the lunacy is that France has borrowed money on Hoover's behalf. In effect we are paying for their war against our own people. And that is also a secret so delicate that those who spin the web of intrigue must ensure it never comes to light."

Mathieu winced in pain, whether from the enormity of his confusions or the complexity of his fractures, he neither knew nor cared. It was uncomfortably hot. His head was sweating. Anxiety dripped from his troubled face. Too much thinking, he assumed.

They sat in silence. Both men looked away, unable to make eye contact, both trapped by a realization that they could do nothing about the situation. For they agreed on all counts. The Powers above them ruled on a completely different stratosphere of influence; it was the highest level of fraud imaginable.

Bernard Roux broke the spell. "Mathieu, you are ill. You have to rest until your body has healed. What happens if you get an infection and die? Eh? And all of these secrets are buried with you? I will not be able to pursue these people without you. We too need to have an insurance policy."

At which point Mathieu slid from the chair into oblivion.

27

January-June 1917 – A Slow Recovery

The next few months meant little to Mathieu. His injuries healed slowly. His ankle swiveled between amputation and survival as his body struggled to resist a potentially deadly infection. On the battle front and in field hospitals, pain and infection were countered by morphine and acriflavine, which was being widely used as a successful antiseptic on wounds far worse than Mathieu's. In truth, its most valuable contribution to quick recovery, which doctors and nurses in Paris knew well, was in the treatment of everything a soldier cursed, from gonorrhea to urinary infection. Such details meant nothing to the lieutenant from no. 36, as he hovered between semi-conscious absurdity and moments of uncomfortable clarity.

He was warm, too warm, burning. Burning but wet. Sweating. It felt like he was being roasted on a spit, then doused with cold water. He could see images from another time or another place which floated in and out of shape, talking to him in words he could not understand clearly. Too many covers on the bed. He tried to pull them off, but it seemed that he was strapped down, immovable. Timon was there.

"Timon? You're dead. I saw you die. I know you're still in the canal."

He could smell the dead man's breath but when he bent over to whisper in Mathieu's ear, it was scented, fresh, pure. No hint of the stink of stagnant black canal-water. He was cold. Too cold. Was he in the water, too? Had he drowned with Timon? Both dead?

Nothing.

Fitful sleep, voices and touch. Someone was patting his forehead, speaking softly, tenderly. He realized that his whole body was being cleaned. Born again? Was this his rebirth?

"Go to sleep, Mathieu. You must rest. You will..."

"I will what?" he tried to ask, but all he could muster was a jumbled monotone of sounds. Nothing again, until voices and touch. He felt good. He felt a rush of pleasure from deep within overpower all the pain for a fleeting moment and exhaust him. He was happy. Peace. A face. A smile.

"I know you," he said to the beautiful smile. "I know you," he told her in a sing-song voice which he thought might have been his once upon a time. "Once upon a time there were two dolls, floating in the water…" His heart stopped. He was in Marseilles. The storm clouds of uncontrollable fear crashed into a guilt he knew was his to bear no matter what the court of humanity ordained.

"And now there are none."

"I know, I know, I couldn't stop them. I should have…"

He was too hot again. Burning, again. Sweating profusely.

That's it. Had he been reborn as the Greek King Sisyphus to go through such punishment every day for the rest of eternity? He was strapped to his bed at dawn, burned in the midday sun, washed in the evening, and left to wallow in fear and self-loathing every night.

"Sleep now, Mathieu. I'm with you here."

His eyes half-opened like a camera shutter and he could see. He knew that face. He knew that smile. His pleasure grew and filled him with calm. He was being washed again. Still painful, though, that side, where Timon crushed into him on the barge. Yes, the barge. They'd been on a barge, not a sea-going ship.

Baby in the water.

No, body in the water. Bodies.

Spade like scythe. Margarite? Was this angel, Margarite? "I know you. I know you," he sang to himself. Something changed. He was not burning. He was more comfortable. Calm. In a bed.

Mathieu spent several minutes trying to analyze what he felt before the word came into his mind. *Happy.* He felt happy, but he could not work out why.

Pascal Girard was sitting smiling at him. That was strange. Was he dreaming again or did everyone smile constantly?

"Good morning, Mathieu. How are you feeling today?" Girard's words gave him a limited parameter within which to build a sense of where he was and what had been going on.

"Fine, thank you," he said slowly.

So it was morning. He was in a bed. Had he been ill? That was surely the sense of Girard's question. Yes, it was old Girard, Captain Girard, his colleague and friend. Before he could form a line of inquiry another person swept into the room.

Agnès. Agnès of the beatific smile. Agnès of his dreams. His Agnès.

"Ah, here's your personal nurse. She's kept us informed of your recovery, young man. No one did more to see you through your agonies than Agnès." He took her hand and kissed it, reverently, as only an old man could.

Of course he was in a hospital. But surely Agnès was at the front?

"Hello, Mathieu." She winked, a smile of real pleasure at seeing him and carefully propped him upright on the bed which she had been attending non-stop since she came back to Paris. "With us at last!" She tucked in his sheet and smoothed over a wrinkle as if it was of equal importance to his recovery.

"But how?" he began.

"Am I back in Paris?" She anticipated his confusion. "Quiet for now at the front, but plenty to be done here." She lowered her voice to a whisper and bent into his left side. "Actually, I came back to see you and found you in this state. What an imbecile," she mocked. "You have to stop trying to be a hero." The angel softly stroked his arm and asserted her authority. "You've doctors to see and questions to answer, but I'll give Pascal a few minutes more with you." And she was gone with a swish of curtain and a purposeful stride.

"What's…" He failed again to find the word. "How?"

"You've had a rough time, Mathieu. When you fell unconscious at the Chief's feet…"

"I did *what*?" Surely not. He'd have remembered that.

"He had you driven straight to the hospital here and transferred into this ward. You were delirious from your wounds and they discovered that you're allergic to penicillin. You needed constant nursing. Happily, Agnès heard what had happened and was transferred back to the Hotel-Dieu hospital. She more or less stayed by your side through your delirium. Said it was caused by the reaction your system took to some of the drugs. They hadn't realized how much morphine they'd given you in Toul and that complicated matters. She even washed and dried you every day."

Girard imparted these facts to underline her loyalty, as if to infer that no one else received such treatment. Mathieu's eyes opened in horror. Agnès had washed him all over. Even below, as the nuns would have said. Oh God. The pleasure? The relief? While she was washing him down and drying him. He must have… Oh the embarrassment. What would she think?

Pascal Girard knew in an instant that Mathieu was dumbfounded and admitted, "She didn't say that at all. Back in the office we decided that you both might have enjoyed the daily ablution. It made the story more interesting. Come on, we're detectives. If we don't have a solution, we make one up. Something was helping your recovery, so we decided it was Agnès and your daily wash."

Mathieu threw him a look which promised murder if the story was repeated.

"Anyway, I'll be back within the week to take you through what's been happening, Mathieu. Once you're fully fit, we need you back, pronto, because I am definitely, definitely, definitely going to retire." Girard rose to his feet and teased his friend who only needed time to recover. "Look on the bright side, Mathieu. Agnès knows you better than any other woman in Paris. There were no surprises in store." The pristine white pillow flew from Mathieu's bed and caught the captain in his midriff.

"Definitely getting better then. The chief will be pleased."

Recovery seemed painfully slow but Mathieu had his guardian angel by his side. She was a hard taskmaster, but her encouragement was endless. They reveled in the fact that the so-called best detectives in Paris hadn't worked out that they were lovers. It wasn't intentional. Life happens. Over a two month period Mathieu learned to walk again, and with the determination of Satan himself, relearned to run. He called it running; others might have described it as fast limping. On the day he was discharged he invited Agnès to a restaurant to thank her for looking after him but she insisted that they dine at home. She'd created a vegetable soup which could and should have graced the Ritz, but there was no miracle available for the paltry piece of pork that sat orphaned on the plate before him, camouflaged by a few green beans which had been so tired that Agnès had banned them from the broth. Hey, it was the war, but the wine was wonderful.

Being back with her was fulfillment in itself, but the demands of their jobs laid claim to precious time together. He, trapped in Paris. Her, ready to respond to the next offensive. Such a strange word, offensive. As an adjective, hurtful, wounding, repulsive; as a noun, a campaign of attack. Whichever you chose, it was hellish. Agnès proved to be a leader. A critical decision maker with a wonderful smile. Mathieu anguished about the relationship. He wanted them both to be happy and grab whatever time was left, but images of Marseilles lingered in reptilian recrimination, poised to strike when least expected. He wasn't ready to share his deepest guilt even with Agnès. It ran so deep that he could not bear to speak about the horror of the Mafia ambush. Even to himself. Despite which they laughed and sang and did things that lovers do. Carefully.

Whispers

Whispers. Be careful lest whispers, like half –truths, gnaw through your inner defenses and weaken your resolve, my friend.

Bourson and Giraud appeared unannounced, claiming that they thought it would do my morale some good to be visited by friends. Friends? I did not count them amongst my friends, though there was little competition in that sphere. Another less than subtle revision of the what I could and could not say? They sat down on chairs provided by the governor but failed to look comfortable. Apropos nothing in particular, Bourson began with small talk which startled me.

"France has changed since they threw you in here, Raoul. You wouldn't believe the number of rumors which circulate in the highest of quarters that the government is considering how a peace treaty with Germany might be constructed."

"What!" I leaped to my feet and spun round my chair to challenge the statement. "Peace? With the Boche?" I picked up the seat and slammed it on the stone floor. "You're lying. LYING," I screamed, pointing aggressively at them. "You are both liars. President Poincaré would never sue for peace."

"Of course not, but others might. There was a mutiny on the Front just after the disastrous Second Battle of the Aisle in April. A new Messiah appeared, General Robert Nivelle. He promised a decisive war-ending victory over the Germans within two days. Our troops were euphoric, confident in the coming miracle."

"But there was no miracle." Giraud grunted his displeasure. "Of course there was no miracle. Failure turned to a different kind of delusion. Men looked around at themselves and their plight and stopped in their tracks. Mutinies broke out in nearly half of the infantry divisions. Of course it was blamed on the socialist agitators and the communists who were attempting to undermine the war. But it had to be stopped. In great secret, over three thousand courts-martial were held."

"Three thousand?"

Bourson bowed his head like a suppliant pilgrim and added, "Very few people know this. Newspapers are censored. The new Messiah was yet another false God and has been replaced. They've brought in Pétain to soothe the storm. He has promised no more suicidal attacks. Exhausted units have been allowed to take home-leave and discipline has been moderated."

"But don't despair," Giraud urged. "America has declared war on the Kaiser."

"Alleluia. What are you worrying about? If the Americans are coming, victory is certain, surely. Good old Woodrow Wilson."

"What else could he do? If Germany wins the war millions of wealthy Americans will lose fortunes on the loans they have made to the Allies." Giraud, the cynic, was right. The American intervention was driven by practicality, not altruism. "Trouble is," he continued, "there is an expectation that the American army will join our troops in the trenches immediately. They can't. It will take months of organization."

"Worse still…" I thought for a moment that Bourson was about to break down in distress, "Pacifism stalks the mud and mayhem. Rumors abounded that Joseph Caillaux and his colleagues are engaged in talks with the Kaiser to bring the war to a close."

"Bastard. I should have shot him first."

"Ah, hindsight," Giraud sighed dismissively. "Makes geniuses of us all."

Disgust swept like nausea from the bile I nurtured for traitors. Victory spun like a coin tossed in the air. It might land on either side with entirely different consequences but fortune caught the wind.

Bourson raised his head and whispered, "But there is one glimmer of real hope. We hear that Georges Clemenceau may be the next prime minister."

The sun reappeared in the skies over France, but, whisper this softly. The evening sun does not always beckon a good day to come.

28

BACKWARDS AND FORWARDS, 1917-1918

When Mathieu was fully cleared to return to work in the last week of December 1917, he found himself in an ever changing world which had to adapt once more to danger and fear. Yet, his first question was the one he would never stop asking until the job was done.

"Any news of Raoul Villain?"

Roux shook his head sadly. "Leave it, Mathieu. He's in jail, going nowhere. Be patient."

They thought the Tiger might have the guts to see justice done. The former Flying Squad men always referred to their founder, Clemenceau with what they would call reverence, but never, of course in his hearing. "He never liked Jean Jaurès, but he is a man to be trusted in the fight against the criminal fraternity... in all of its shapes and sizes."

"And he will do the right thing when the time comes. Trust him."

"It's not the Tiger I distrust, it's the law."

The Chief exhaled his Gauloises through his nose and grunted. With Mathieu, he was able to tell it as it was, especially when the news was bad.

"We have a couple of problems on the horizon. Literally. Despite all I've done to keep him, Pascal has resigned. He stood down on Friday. Exhausted. He heard the news I'm about to tell to you and simply said, 'I'm leaving today. There's no more I can do. I'm too old. I'll do what I can for my neighbors and friends, but that's it. I'm finished.' He walked through that door without so much as a goodbye. After all these years."

"I wouldn't take it personally, Chief. Pascal has been running on empty since the war started." Mathieu knew they would both miss their friend. But it was the war, you see. "What else?"

"The Germans are planning a two pronged attack on the Capital. They've built squadrons of new bombers and we will have to deal with the fallout, literally. Military Intelligence, now confirmed by the Americans, claims that they have built a massive assault gun at Krupp's factory which can hit major targets from one hundred and twenty kilometers out."

"What? Impossible. That's sheer propaganda. It's nonsense."

"It's a fact." The matter was finished.

"And who will replace Pascal?"

"You, of course, Captain." He shook his prodigy firmly by the hand and Mathieu drew his six foot frame to attention to salute his chief. "Paul's too old. Wouldn't take the job."

"Does everyone know that Pascal has retired?"

"No. I'll let you tell the rest of the team. I'm also promoting Jacques to full lieutenant. It makes sense."

* * *

One month later hell descended from the heavens and Paris had no defense. Mathieu was working late at number 36 because Agnès was busy at the hospital and he had yet to master the range of duties which he was expected to cover. A shiver of fear ran down his spine when air raid sirens pierced the sleeping city and heralded the first wave of airborne attacks shortly before midnight. Up on the rooftops newly trained officers, some police, some army, unleashed the high-pitched scream from warning klaxons, but one followed the other without coordination or meaning. Below, citizens suffered the bewilderment of blind panic in dark streets and friendless neighborhoods. Where should they go? Where was safe? Four squadrons of German Gotha bombers, newly designed biplanes with a range of more than eight hundred kilometers, lumbered across the black sky. They were slow and cumbersome, but could not be seen in the late January night. No moon. No respite.

Mathieu covered the one hundred and forty-one wooden stairs from his office to the roof of 36 Quai des Orfevres at double time, testing both ankle and leg against the uneven worn floor. He quickly negotiated the tiny passage between offices crammed under the skylights, where windows filled with disordered files were harvesting generations of dust and cigarette ash, coffee stains, and the residue of stale croissant flakes and out onto the icy rooftop where two others were already pointing towards the north west of the city.

"Can you see them?" he shouted into the wind, but one of the gendarmes shook his head without turning back.

"Occasional flashes but not much else."

The Gotha engines grumbled towards them, growling from above like wild beasts foraging for their prey. An explosion much closer to the center caught them by surprise. Mathieu felt the force of the blast throw him to the side and learned that no matter how brave you might think it, standing unprotected when bombs were falling was stupid. All three climbed back into the building and headed for the ground floor, taking cover under a stout stairwell.

The first weak shaft of morning revealed the consequent damage. Across the river a house hung open, roof gaping, dust settling. The smell of fear became synonymous with the smell of the broken sewers. Scores of the living tried to reach out to the newly dead, crushed under the weight of vengeance from the angry skies. To the unarmed citizen, mainly the elderly and women with children, this was incomprehensible. Death in the midst of life is cruel; when life has hardly begun, it is sickening.

Those who could, screamed for help. An old woman, dazed and bleeding from her open skull, sat sobbing, "Christophe, Christophe, Christophe..." but no one answered. Her dress in tatters, her stockings shredded, she sat there on the broken rubble till dawn lit her death like a theatre spotlight slowly finding focus. Her blood had dried, coated in fine grey powder. She might once have been a cherub but she died petrified in dust, statuesque, noble but alone.

Chief Superintendent Roux held a mid-morning emergency meeting of all his specialist teams at 36.

"Captain Bertrand I need you to take over security around the prime minister. For as long as Clemenceau breathes, there will be no surrender, but we must keep a close watch on activists and these new Bolsheviks who are stirring trouble amongst the workers. We need the names of known agitators and we have to close down all talk of surrender or defeat."

"Or peace?" Dubois asked. The room fell quiet. Was talk of peace to become a crime against the state? Paul Dubois had not intended this hiatus, but where was the line to be drawn?

The chief solved the dilemma by asking for common sense at all times. "If activists are using promises of peace to undermine production or start a riot or convince soldiers on leave not to return to their posts, arrest them. In fact, arrest them anyway and we can let the courts decide whether it was lawful or otherwise."

Mathieu had found real comfort and companionship with Agnès, whose wisdom he greatly appreciated. He dared not call it love. He had not intended to move into her apartment, but it suited both of them to spend what little time they had, together. In bed, with the occasional moonlight washing her upper floor window, Agnès took care not to mention his past. She had seen men in every degree of distress try to cope with their fears. Those closest to death were often beset by their inner-torments as a last minute penance for a tortured conscience. She let him tell his tale in segments as he chose. Agnès had no need to know. Life was too precious and too short. She rarely shared her fears, either; what she had seen, what men did to men in the pursuit of some imagined victory. While vigilance, endless vigilance, was his stock-in-trade, her tireless work with the wounded and the dying gave her a greater appreciation both of what they had together and the possibility that it could end in the pulse of war. She liked to walk with him at night when the moon was high and the sky cloudless under the same stars which had blinked down on earth since the creation. Agnès didn't care if the creation was by dint of physics or by an act of God. The sky at night remained a wonder.

"Do you think anyone out there knows we are here, tearing ourselves apart for reasons we have already forgotten?" she mused. They sat huddled together on a park bench near Eiffel's tower, in love but afraid to say so, lest the fates heard and destroyed their chance of surviving together. It must end soon, they told themselves. The world is exhausted.

FEAR AND HOPE

I was very scared. Sirens first, then rumblings in the distance rolled into the city. The waves reminded me of that crushing sound when a storm takes hold. I will never forget the first time my cell shook violently without warning. Bombs. The Germans were bombing us. Bombing the city. What bastards. Obviously they didn't care what or who they hit, but the irony of being killed by a German bomb while my wonderful brother pisses about in the sky, made me shudder. Why weren't the famous espadrilles about which the newspapers write endless praise, up there, protecting Paris? This was the worst part of being locked in. There's nowhere else to go. My cell on the ground floor made secret visits easier, but you might think that the wardens would take us all down to the underground cells for our protection. It's not as if anyone would try to escape. Not during an air raid, anyway. Huh, they're probably down there now, looking after themselves.

These fucking heartless Boches. They'd do anything to win this war. Nothing is sacred to them. First they burn the great churches and libraries of Europe, then they commit all kinds of atrocities against Belgian civilians and unarmed soldiers. Their submarine attacks on allied shipping has backfired, though. What joy. It spurred the Americans to declare war. It was only a matter of time…assuming that we had time.

Looking back last year was disappointing. Sometimes I wonder just how poor our Allied Generals are? The Englishman Haig was unmoved by the loss of hundreds of thousands of his countrymen. He at least has back-bone born of privileged schooling, no doubt. The Italians have been sent packing. The Bolsheviks have seized power in Russia and rumors are rife that the bastard Joseph Caillaux has been secretly trying to find ways of making peace with Germany. Incredible. After the slaughter of millions how he could dare trade their gallant sacrifice for a so-called peace?

Each great new offensive ended in disaster dressed up as another "no gain." But let me tell you, my friend, I never doubted the wisdom of my action. Imagine where we would be had Herr Jaurès been allowed to live? Think how he and his German accomplices would have stirred the workers to lay down their arms. Instead they wander around headless, like ghosts from the guillotine, holding rabble-rousing meetings in the suburbs, producing shabby leaflets and feeding soldiers on leave fresh Bolshevik propaganda. But they have no commanding voice. No hero to rally round. Thanks to me. Yet there is promise of better to come. From the deepest recess in the darkest hour we have had the courage to turn to a politician who will steady those who might waver; a politician worthy of La France.

You probably will not have heard of George Clemenceau, my friend. He is a politician who also owns newspapers. Clemenceau understands. Right from the start he criticized the weakness in our government. They censored his paper, so he changed its name and kept going. They tried to seduce him with the offer of a ministry. He snubbed them. You see, on one vital point he is utterly inflexible. Like me, like all of us in Action française, he is a patriot who will not rest until Alsace and Lorraine are returned to their motherland. How they hated him at first, the government. His journal, La Libertie, created a slogan they repeated day after day. It simply said, "Gentlemen, the Germans are still in Noyons." It's up in the northwest, you see. Occupied. In other words, until Noyons is free, France will never stop fighting. Brilliant. Isn't it? It's like the Roman orator Cato the Elder, who ended every speech with the words "Delenda est Carthago" or Carthage had to be destroyed, until Carthage was razed to the ground. It's Latin, you see. I had the benefit of a Jesuit education.

I take it you've never met a Jesuit, my friend? Leave it that way. He'd break your back if he thought it would convert you. There is one concern, though. It was Clemenceau who created the mobile police, Les Tigres. That was his nickname, you see. Tiger Clemenceau. The mobile force was named after him. They were the ones who arrested me and tricked me all those years ago, after I had blown Jaurès' head from his shoulders. My lawyers have warned me so many times to say nothing to them or allow them to interview me unless they are present. Apparently, every six months these bastards object to the extension of my trial date and the judge ignores them. Will Clemenceau support them? Surely not. He hates all the left-wing activists. They hate him, too. Best the Tigers concentrate on keeping him safe.

But the sirens? I hated the whining. More frightening than the bombs, until they start to get too close. Fear ruled the streets, while above, unseen bombers ploughed death from the night sky. You could sense the panic outside and in. No one was safe. Death dropped from the heavens through the clouds and exploded mercilessly on boulevard or backstreet, on grand villa or crowded slum. No one was safe, even those who had taken shelter. They started on the outskirts of the city because the barrage began some time before the explosions could be heard. As the noises came closer, booming, crashing, shaking the building, the walls shivered with fright, the dust of a cruel century disturbed from its settled slumber. I tried to anticipate the line of attack by the noise outside and crouched in the corner beside the rats. Rats. Where do they come from?

"Jesus Christ let me out of this hell."

If you have heard stories of captives befriending vermin locked in with them, you didn't hear it from me. Light flashed from the street, followed by an explosive blast which tore the heart from the house across the road. Bricks smashed against the prison wall, thrown violently into a whirlwind of destruction. Within seconds a fire erupted from the severed gas main. We were all going to be burned to death.

"Help! Fire! Fire! I thumped the cell door. Others followed until the landing was alight with terror. "Let us out. We'll burn to death, you bastards!" Though I know it's nonsense, I convinced myself that death had knocked on our prison door and was waiting to be let in. Truth and logic melted in the heat of the air-raid and give vent to irrational behavior.

"It's ten times more dangerous outside, you ignorant peasants. Calm yourselves. You're safer inside," one of the warders screamed back from the far end of the corridor.

"Let me out, let me out."

But they didn't.

29

MARCH 1918 –
THE DEATH OF INNOCENCE

Paris was once more at the mercy of the skies. The powerful Gotha bombers brought nightly terror in March. People needed reassurance. Roux's command was straightforward. "Get out there and manage the mayhem as best you can."

Mathieu and Jacques went to the 19th Arrondissement because it had been hit several times as the blind bombers felt for the major Parisian railway stations beneath. Within thirty seconds of emerging from the metro, the streets were shaken by air-raid sirens. A throng emerged from the surrounding streets seeking safety where it could be found. Ahead, the entrance to a church crypt was quickly overwhelmed by desperate citizens and the great medieval doors to Christian charity closed abruptly.

"Full up. Use the cellars under the church of St Alphonse," a warden advised, pointing to the far corner of the square but the crowds pressed forward relentlessly.

Fights broke out. Innocents were injured. Few cared. "There are twice as many people inside than there should be already," Jacques pleaded.

"The sign says it's a shelter." A mother pointed urgently to the enormous banner above the door, barely able to control her anger.

"Use the metro," was the given advice.

Mathieu stood at the top of the steep entrance to the Bolivar metro, one of the city's safest and most cavernous stations, directing the crowd. "Take care, the steps are steep. Take your time, please." Reason was a breath wasted. Bolivar on Line 7 dived under the towering Maison Usse which lay between Rues Secrétan and Bolivar, a magnificent homage to the Third Republic. The classy bar-café with adverts for Biere De Maxeville and Tabac draped from the railings on the first floor, was a popular haunt for the local bourgeoisies. Six stories of expensive apartments layered above like a Japanese watchtower. A hand-painted banner proclaimed that the station below-ground was open to all. But the Gothas were upon them and bombs started to explode nearby.

Jacques, standing on the first landing, insisted that prams should be left behind. "No exceptions. People only. Carry the child, for god's sake, woman."

"It's alright for you, standing there giving directions. Help me," she pleaded.

He deserved the blistering scorn for the woman was terrified, but worse, she realized that she had lost control of her brood. "Justine." Her command turned to a scream. "Justine?" "Justine, WAIT!" Suddenly her feet gave way. Like dozens of others, she had not registered Mathieu's warning that the steps to the metro line were exceptionally steep. In the bare half-light of the weak electric lamps, both Jacques and Mathieu saw her disappear under the crush of human desperation.

She tried to catch her balance and hold onto her baby, her other children somewhere ahead. Strangers rushed past, ignoring her plight, motivated by that most friendless of instincts, self-preservation. The noise ahead was deafening. Cries of fright turned to screams of panic and torture. Behind the policemen, others continued to charge down in a rush to find safety. But they could no longer move freely. Something was very wrong. They were trapped.

"Back," an older woman shouted to no one in particular. "We have to go back!"

But reversing against the flow of desperate people, each believing that their survival depended on getting down the stairs safely, was impossible. "The gates, the gates…"

Screams of fear turned to screams of anger. "Back, back off…the gates."

The crush continued to force everyone forward. Mathieu and Jacques were caught in a human whirlpool, sucked downward yet physically unable to move. The electric light flickered as the bombs above struck close to the entrance, then failed, and darkness swallowed them all. They suffered the terror of entombment. Incomprehensibly, the log-jam broke and the iron platform gates below gave way from the center letting a wave of bruised humanity spew onto the platform. People continued to pour forward and fall. Even Mathieu failed to piece together the hell they had entered.

"Who were those idiots lying at the bottom of the stairs? What am I standing on? Get up you fool!" Though the station itself was modestly lit by older gas lamps, no one could change direction, stop for courtesy or make an allowance for a fallen citizen. The mother Jacques had ordered to hold her baby in her arms, lay close to the iron gates, crumpled like a discarded doll condemned to the rubbish heap. Her right arm clung to the wrought iron as if to claim sanctuary. There was none. Metro workers appeared from the opposite platform, yelling and waving.

"Take your time! Take your time. Stop for a moment..." Wasted words were drowned in wasted lives. "Come on, come on, slowly... slowly keep moving. The line isn't live. You can walk across safely." Gasping for air, Mathieu and Jacques tried to reassure the wounded, broken, lifeless, and seriously injured to pick up their beds and walk, but there was no biblical reprieve. Seven men, twenty-nine women and thirty children were declared dead on the platform. The injured went uncounted.

Her nose bloodied, her body bruised and trembling from fear, a child called Justine sat unattended, on top of an old man's body while all around the dead and dying lay as if scattered carelessly by an unseen force, some clearly broken in unnatural positions, some as if asleep. Many held themselves awkwardly, moaning in pain but glad to have breath in their lungs. It was the nightmare of Marseilles revisited on the underground. This time the child was alive but her mother was sprawled over the final step and the false safety of the Bolivar's platform.

"Mama... Mama," she cried through snot and tears. "Mama," she sobbed until she fell asleep exhausted, wrapped in cold comfort. An elderly couple passed by and the disheveled man lifted her gently in his arms. He turned to his shocked wife and said, "She must be lost. We'll take her home."

* * *

A pram stood buckled where it had been summarily abandoned at the top of the Bolivar entrance. Forever empty.

"How the hell?" Roux's sleep had been interrupted as he had instructed it must in an emergency, but the air raid had ended three hours before and he had just managed to turn over and go back to sleep. The body count from Bolivar made it the worst single incident in the war on Paris to date. So many women and children. Jacques flinched on the other end of the phone. He had asked himself repeatedly how they had failed to anticipate the problem. The death-trap which sat at the bottom of the steep entrance steps were gates which opened outwards towards the street. Once shut they had to be reopened from the platform.

"Sir, the bureau of information want to know what we should tell the press. How should I respond?"

"Give them the truth," was all that Roux said.

* * *

When Mathieu struggled home Agnès was able to update him. "The crush injuries are desperately dangerous. We ran out of x-rays and the best we could do was bandage those poor people and send them home if they could walk." The hopelessness of war engulfed them. They were both empty, emotionally; so far drained that the reservoir had dried. Mathieu wondered if he'd suffered a crush injury on the barge and was about to ask Agnès, but the moment passed. They fell asleep in each other's arms, a painful day had little promise of improving.

By early morning, reports had to come in from every part of the stricken city.

"Listen to this." Jacques held a written police complaint in his right hand, the froth of his anger almost choking his voice. "You couldn't make it up. While those poor women and children were being crushed to death in the Metro shelter, the audience at the Comedie-Française refused to budge and demanded that the performers continued to entertain them despite the air-raid. Bloody typical, eh? The innocents are slaughtered but the drunks and sloths that ignore all the rules of survival get away with it. The proprietor claims that he didn't hear the sirens for the laughter. Can we shut them down?"

"Probably not, but send the local gendarmes to threaten them anyway."

Chief Superintendent Roux called Mathieu to his office. "We've been given a special assignment. The prime minister wants to see the damage caused by the bombing."

Jacques, who was Clemenceau's designated driver, sat with a military aide by his side. The prime minister and chief superintendent were ensconced in the back seat with reinforced glass to protect them. Mathieu stood on the fender, alert to the many dangers which could arise. Clemenceau's rotund figure claimed most of the Renault's back seat. Roux had to squeeze himself into a limited space but appeared not to notice. The prime minister's reddened face boasted a white walrus moustache overhung by thick part-grey eyebrows. His cheeks, once full, were stretched by age and responsibility, so that his high jawbone was visible, as if to warn that behind the charm lay a no-nonsense predator. His forehead was lined but not with worry. Mathieu had never met a more positive, confident, and capable politician than the Tiger.

The morning-after syndrome lay over the Capital. Regret was mixed with the pain of visible hurt inflicted on a people close to the edge of toleration. The sin of the voyeur did not stop hundreds taking to the streets to see for themselves the destruction of their precious Paris. First stop was at the old cemetery at Vincennes in the eastern inner-suburbs. One explosive had transformed a row of marbled tombstones to crumbling rubble, with a single obelisk stubbornly rooted in its place as if to say that a mere bomb couldn't disrupt the eternal peace of those interred below. Two women had already begun to put back the broken marble from their family tomb, angry-voiced and frustrated. The prime minister doffed his hat and approached them cautiously lest he was disturbing a private grief, but they greeted him as a welcome visitor. Within a minute they were laughing heartily and shaking hands. He kissed both on their cheeks with the utmost propriety and returned still laughing to himself.

"Boys." He always addressed his Tigers that way when in private. "Never underestimate the capacity of strong women to catch the moment. When I offered my condolences, the elder said, 'Monsieur Prime Minister, the German bombs did not kill Alphonse. Absinthe was the cause of death on his certificate. He would have been the first to say that it was a far better way to go. Anyway, better the bombs fall on the dead and spare the living.' That's the spirit which will help Paris survive, no matter what they throw at us."

Clemenceau was forced to stop further along Rue de Lille where an enormous crater split the thoroughfare. A ladder pointed from the hole as if it was a natural entrance to the underworld, but the rank odor indicated that the sewers had been breached. They did not linger. A fine block of apartments in the Haussmann-style had suffered a direct hit. The partly demolished rooftop had been brutally caved in. Planks of wooden rafters hung limply from the top two floors where the cornices and domes once epitomized the sheer opulence of a Parisian boulevard. It looked as if a giant fist had punched the building from top to bottom. This time the damage spread to both sides of the street with windows blown out and shredded curtains hanging askew, open to the vagaries of the elements.

Every site which Clemenceau visited drew an appreciative crowd. His message of defiance was openly shared with those who would listen. Paris stood firm.

30

Late March 1918 – The Boches Gun

The team, which included Jubert, Jacques-Francois, Dubois, and Mathieu, had reported early for duty, aware that the prime minister intended to go to the war office. Two days previously, the Germans had launched yet another major offensive, earlier than anticipated. Logic argued that they were determined to win a quick victory before the bulk of the American army disembarked in France, and their projected line of advance between the British and the French forces pointed directly at Paris.

"A quick victory, indeed. After four years of failed quick victories, you might think the generals on both sides would concoct a better story than that." Dubois's sarcasm was entirely justified. The bombing raids had continued to inflict local damage in the center of the Capital and citizens had come to accept that when the sirens sounded, they took cover. The chief superintendent approached, the pungent smell of his customary Gauloises preceding him like incense might a prelate's procession. He had barely begun to outline the prime minister's agenda when a dull, deep blast interrupted his flow. Everyone in the room turned to the window, brows furrowed. A strange silence followed.

"Might have been a gas explosion." Jubert's suggestion rang false. It carried an essence of hope which was not realistically deserved. "It's, what, half past seven?"

"Air raid?"

"Couldn't be. No warning sirens. Out of a blue sky?" Mathieu stood at the nearest window and faced as clear a spring morning as he could remember. He turned to the chief and tried to read his inscrutable face.

"Anyone guess where that noise came from?" No one spoke. Jacques licked at suddenly dry lips.

Jubert shook his head in disbelief. "It can't be."

Roux sat down heavily. His seat squealed in protest, his temples thumping, his worst fears pushed from skepticism to certainty in a single shell burst. He blew his cheeks out and exhaled the words, "From one hundred and twenty kilometers."

Mathieu voiced what they all suspected. "The Boches gun."

"Right, gentlemen, to work. Firstly, we had best make sure that the prime minister is aware of the situation in person. Jubert, inform the president's office, then follow us over to the Ministry of War." Despite the urgency, Clemenceau was not immediately available. He had taken a call from Marshall Foch, the appointed head of all the allied armies in France. The British, under Haig, had been forced back by the German attack, and naturally the prime minister demanded regular updates.

As they waited in the ante-room, a second and third muffled eruption was audible through the enormous windows. A war ministry secretary handed Roux a press release. He despaired of official stupidity. It was almost pandemic.

"*NO, NO, NO,*" he boomed, deliberately increasing the volume in the hope that Clemenceau would hear him. He did.

"Monsieur Roux," he scolded when they were ushered into his private office, "what is the reason for your very vocal annoyance?"

"This, Sir." He handed him the sheet and waited for a reaction.

"So…what's the problem?"

"It's a falsehood. In fact, it's worse than a lie…it's an ignorant lie.'"

"You are about to explain." Clemenceau put the offending press release on the marble Louis Quinze table and fixed his stony eyes on Bernard Roux.

"That explosion, indeed, those explosions which you may or may not have heard, Sir, are not the product of an air raid. Furthermore, there were no German planes hovering over the Capital, and to make matters worse, according to the official statement which bears your name, no French squadrons ever took to the skies to chase them off. Paris is being bombarded from a range of one hundred and twenty kilometers away, and there is nothing we can do to stop the Boches. Nothing."

Georges Clemenceau froze, his mouth slightly ajar, his mind racing. "Would someone please explain this to me slowly?"

Roux nodded consent to Mathieu who began from the start. "Prime Minister, the explosions this morning come from German shells, fired from an enormous Krupp's gun one hundred and twenty kilometers away. I assumed that you have been informed about this."

Clemenceau's jaw dropped, his color changing hue as the enormity of the situation hit home. "I heard rumors, but they were never confirmed."

"The Germans appear to be firing randomly every fifteen to twenty minutes. But this official communiqué makes us all look foolish. There was no air-raid this morning. No bombs have fallen on the city. The story about our air squadrons chasing them back across their lines is pure fabrication. It started over an hour ago, and the sirens haven't gone off. People are walking around the city, coming and going to and from work was if it was a normal day."

"What!" Clemenceau exploded. The air was rent with a volley of expletives which would have barely been acceptable in an overcrowded brothel. He picked up his phone and instructed some unfortunate to put him through to the Paris fire service and ordered the alert. Within half a minute sirens wailed across the city. It had taken one hour and thirty five minutes to warn Parisians of the severe danger they faced. Only then did the trams stop on the boulevards and grand streets; only then did the buses pull into the side of the road so that their passengers could take appropriate cover; only then did the metro trains have their power cut so that the people could shelter on the broad platforms, the main line stations empty, the munitions factories close down. Only then. One thing was certain. The government would be blamed for the lies and the impossibly slow reaction from officials. Hundreds of thousands of working men and women had been put at risk as they made their way to work, exposed to the random chance of an unexpected explosion, let down by their own.

"We still don't know where the bloody gun is?" Clemenceau's tone betrayed the answer he expected.

"The Americans had a vague idea that the Boches were building a super-gun. Krupps, definitely, but they have worked hard to keep its location secret. Right now, with a full frontal attack across the north, I doubt our allies can do anything."

"I'll call an immediate Cabinet meeting. I want you there, Bernard, to spell this out clearly. If the people lose confidence in us, Paris will fall. No matter what … only the truth."

What Clemenceau meant was only the censured truth, but at his insistence a second communiqué was issued admitting that the Germans were bombarding Paris with a long-range gun, though, as always, the numbers killed or injured were watered down towards insignificance. From that day forth, shells were flung into Paris with wanton abandon until the populace learned to live with the possibility that one might hit them.

* * *

Agnès, beautiful Agnès of the beatific smile, was not by any means a hardline Catholic, but she went to mass, and confessed her sins in churches and chapels where she was unknown. Mathieu knew her faith in God did not waver in plain view of the misery of war's carnage for that was, in her mind, the work of the Devil. Her real passion was not religion, but religious music. She had described it to him several times, but Mathieu had long been unimpressed by religion and its trappings. Nightmare images of dead babies and slaughtered families sat ill at ease with a generous God. She, on the other hand, had been smitten in a very singular way.

The echoing tenor-bass of Gregorian chant which had survived the Middle Ages cast a spell of historic certainty around her own belief. The delicate joy of Palestrina filled her soul with sensual pleasure; aural and physical. A sung high mass was worth leaving Mathieu's bed because she was guaranteed to return filled with a holy spirit which he could more than amply quench; and she told him so. La grande theatre of Easter Week she found sublime with its stage-managed drama; the rubric from Maundy Thursday through to the rousing *Victimae paschali laudes* of the risen Lord on Easter Sunday thrilled her absolutely. Over the last two years she had managed to talk her way into Saint-Gervais for the Good Friday service, the most cherished of all. She was reduced to tears by the symbolism of Christ's death on the cross and the pageantry of the special mass. The people of Paris filled the church. Parishioners were guaranteed free entrance, but those who sought simply to enjoy the music were required to wait outside until the final third of the program. With due ceremony, the singers filed in from the North transept, and holy song reached up to heaven. Parishioners lined up to kiss the feet of Christ crucified, held reverentially by a surpliced acolyte on the edge of the altar steps. Divine. The choir paused to enjoy the silence of absolute approval. Applause was unthinkable. Agnès' contemplation was itself a thing of beauty.

As far as she could later recollect, she saw the Abbe Gauthier rise to intone the office of the day when a "thunderbolt" struck Saint-Gervais as if the Anti-Christ had been summoned to wreak havoc. The explosion hit the side of the church catching a weakened pillar which brought down the vaulted arch. Plaster, stone, wooden beams, and cornices rained from above. Acrid grey dust swept the aisles like a dry snowstorm. The central pillars were shaken, but did not stir. Death ran amok like a wild fox in a chicken coop, tossing bodies in the air, crushing the unsuspecting at prayer, burying parishioners and the paying congregation, choking life from the faithful and the faithless alike. Agnès fell, the inert body of the pious acolyte pinning her to the floor, the foot of the alabaster Christ-crucified left dangling over a smashed pew. She could hear groans and cries above her, but was blinded for some moments by the dust and powder. What a catastrophe. Had the roof given way, collapsed under the weight of the city's collective sorrow? That smell. Was that gunpowder? Agnès struggled to her feet, raised up by the black biretta-headed priest who simultaneously anointed the dying acolyte with the last rites of his church. It took several moments more for the awful sight to sink in. Saint-Gervais had been struck by a deadly shell hurled by the evil Kaiser some one hundred and twenty kilometers away. Well, that was how the newspapers would portray this escalation in modern warfare. She focused, controlled her breathing, let her professional training switch to automatic and turned to assist the twisted body beside her.

Jacques heard the blast first. He looked up but could see nothing. Strange. Toussaint, at the front door was shaken from his idleness and looking north saw a great cloud begin to rise from the church across the river. He screamed in horror, "They've hit Saint-Gervais… It's Saint-Gervais…look…look." A whispering pall of smoke and dust rose and thickened across the Seine through the ancient church roof as if it had been superimposed on a grumbling volcano.

"Saint-Gervais has been hit," Jacques echoed and grabbed his jacket which had been abandoned on the chair opposite. "Captain? Chief?…did you hear, Saint-Gervais has been hit."

Doors were flung open and policemen of all ranks, ages, and shapes scrambled down corridors and stairs to see what they could do. Jacques jumped into the Renault with Mathieu and the chief. He took off before the rear door was securely closed and within a minute they had crossed the Seine at the Point d'Arcole, driven by a mad-man along the bank of the river and into Rue de Brosse. The Gothic majesty of Saint-Gervais appeared almost untouched but the great door hung open at an unnatural angle and the historic painted glass windows had disappeared. Inside, a rescue of sorts had begun.

As was his way, Roux took command, dividing the ruined interior into sections and allocating police, ambulance men, firemen, and assorted volunteers as they materialized from the surrounding streets. The clergy were everywhere. Had none of them been hit? They appeared to concentrate on the dead and the dying, stoles over vestments, holy water sprinkled liberally over dust. Rarely, even in this horrendous war had the words "dust to dust" seemed so appropriate. Mathieu surveyed the sprawling corpses and bits of ragged bodies, searching for one whom he knew had been here, Agnès. He was not alone. Survivors wrestled with the horror in an attempt to find the loved one who had but seconds ago, been sitting or kneeling beside them. Dearth, injury, or survival was as random as any game of chance. Bernard Roux bowed his head towards the Countess Morand as she was carried on a stretcher to a taxi. She recognized him and smiled as if to say, *don't worry, I'm fine.* She died that night.

An American Red Cross model T staggered into the street laden with nurses and a doctor and all the medical paraphernalia that the modern ambulance could carry.

"Help me free my mother," a voice cried and Mathieu bent down to lift a heavy stone boulder from a crushed ribcage. As he looked back towards the door he saw three Red Cross nurses sitting immobile on the temporary chairs. Their uniforms were spotless. Their white skirts, perfectly starched. All dead. All three pierced by the explosion of wood-splinters when the vaulted ceiling crashed to the floor. He checked their lifeless faces again and again, but Agnès was not amongst them. Military stretcher-bearers in khaki loaded bodies into the first ambulances and bore them off to the Hotel Dieu.

Roux stiffened and half-whispered, "Fuck. Just when you least need them." President Poincaré had entered through the main entrance, top hat in hand, suit immaculate, face strained. He was clearly unused to such carnage, ill-at-ease with citizens so close, struggling to appear confident amongst the public. Behind him stood the more compassionate Clemenceau, a prime minister who had visited the trenches on several occasions; had seen death, and stared it down. Roux wiped his soiled hands and saluted both men. Poincaré did not appear to see him but Clemenceau strode up and took his arm.

"Despicable, my friend, truly despicable. How could the Kaiser allow this on Good Friday? Do we know yet how many have died here?"

Roux shook his head. Words failed him.

"Ah, Captain Bertrand," the prime minister swiveled towards Mathieu, "have we any idea of the numbers slain by the barbaric Boches?" He had clearly decided on the best headline before assessing the damage.

Mathieu saw her standing close to the door, instructing the stretcher bearers. Like all around who had survived the impact, Agnès was covered in the fine dust which settled like a smattering of late winter snow, not deep enough to last but washing color from the scene like a faded pastel. In that brief moment he realized that she was the female equivalent of Roux. In command. Orchestrating triage with the authority of a maestro.

"Agnès…you're all right?" His voice wavered between question and disbelief. There was no time for the slightest show of intimacy. No passionate hug. This was no romance novel.

"I'll direct every crush injury with a chance of survival to the Hotel-Dieu. If you can, help the ambulance drivers. Clear the routes to the hospital, and," with a nod to the politicians, "get rid of the sightseers."

Wonderful, Mathieu thought, his heart sinking. *I'll just order the president and prime minister to leave.*

He approached Raymond Poincaré, who recognized his presence but said nothing. "Sir, forgive my intrusion, but it would be safer if you were outside the building. The structure may not be secure, and it would be a horrendous coup for the Germans if you, too, were injured." President Poincaré took a step back. Clearly he had not considered that the church might be unsafe.

"Thank you, Captain. You are, of course, right," he conceded and with the slightest of bows retreated to the Rue de Brosse where he dutifully waved at the shocked onlookers.

Clemenceau required a more subtle approach. He had ventured deep into the ruins, stepping carefully over bodies and rubble and bending down from time to time to offer comfort to the dazed and partly injured. Priests ministered to the dead, dispensing pardon for sins committed and anointing the unfortunates. Mathieu drew Roux aside and told him that Agnès wanted the politicians to leave because they were a distraction.

"Oh, does she, indeed? I thought I was in charge," he mocked, glancing in her direction. "But I take her point. Come on then." The prime minister had stopped to talk to one of the priests, in fact the only one who remained seated in the third sanctuary choir stall, a hero of France, the Abbe Eugene Bernardin from Nancy. He had been taken hostage by the Germans at the start of the war but was later exchanged for German prisoners and sent back to France.

Clemenceau turned as they approached.

"He's stone dead."

Observed from afar, the Abbe looked as if caught in contemplation, his hood lowered over his receding hairline, untouched by the crush which surrounded him. When the shell burst through the wall a dozen arch-ribbed pieces of shrapnel flew harmlessly above the heads of the congregation and slammed into the ancient pillars. Save one. A solitary missile cannoned back across the nave and imbedded itself in the Abbe's skull. A ruby-red droplet of blood slid from his punctured brow and

253

stained his well-thumbed breviary. Its wafer-thin pages would never be opened again.

Clemenceau drew himself from his crouched stance and saluted the corpse. "My friends, the Abbe, too, died for France."

The three men stood together in admiration of the noble priest, but a sharp-voiced reprimand carried across the ill-strewn rubble.

"Will you get out of here and clear the streets so that the ambulances can get through?"

Agnès saw Clemenceau's surprise blossom into a wide grin. Few would have dared address him with such frankness, but this nurse clearly had style and confidence. It was clear that she knew what needed to be done.

He bowed towards her. "You've worked at the front, Mademoiselle, I can tell. What do you need us to do?"

"Please clear a passage for the ambulances," she repeated. "And if one of you could help with this poor lady." She went down on one knee and caressed an injured matron. "That would be most appreciated." Clemenceau was first to her side and lifted the old woman onto an upright pew. Her clothes must have weighed more than the emaciated body that lay underneath, for she was as light as a paper doll in a toy store. But she was alive. Roux ran down the front steps to instruct the gendarmes to clear a wider passage for three American Red Cross ambulances which had parked further down Rue de Brosse. Mathieu helped more stretcher-bearers step down onto the pavement and retraced his steps to Agnès. Clemenceau presumed that Mathieu was on protection duty and indicated that he would make his own way back to the War Ministry.

"I'll leave you here, Captain. Just do as the nurse bids." He smiled, gave a half salute, gloves in hand, and went to speak to a small group of journalists. Mathieu watched the professional politician work his message of shock and disbelief at the wicked German intrusion into Paris at prayer, knowing full well that he was witnessing the supreme headline-maker churn out stinging quotes for tomorrow's newspapers.

There was still much to do. He knew that stretcher-bearer. The one whom he helped out of the American Red Cross wagon.

"Mathieu, please, quickly." Agnès had found a body pinned to the floor. It was a child, curled underneath a smashed wooden pew. He or she was sobbing through a mucus-filled nose which had stopped bleeding, but which lay flattened against the small jaw, punched sideways by the flying debris. Agnès put her arms around the shivering body, not knowing whether the tremor was caused by cold or fear. Or both. While she tried to soothe the tiny victim by asking for a name and reassuring her—or was it a him?—that the nice man would lift the stones away, Mathieu pulled the great weight to one side, and was horrified to see that the left leg had been torn away by the awesome crush of the fallen vault.

Agnès called to the Americans, "Over here, now!" but help arrived from another quarter. A doctor and her assistant, both in their mid-twenties, ran over to help Agnès with the child. They were from the Scottish hospital and she struggled to understand their rich Edinburgh accents. But they were obviously used to dealing with trauma injuries and needed no instruction.

"Hotel-Dieu. Immediately." Agnès moved on. No time for pleasantries.

Something in the ruined church irritated Mathieu. What was wrong? Though the main aisle had taken the full force of the collapsed roof vault, the side chapels with their decorated altars remained untouched. There was not even a scratch on the wooden-canopied pulpit which protruded into the aisle. Had you stood in front of it, you might have chided the church cleaner for letting so much dust gather. A red sanctuary lamp swung gently in the light breeze, surprised to find that the wind was blowing through the smashed stained glass windows. The American Red Cross stretcher-bearers passed to his right carrying a crumpled body covered by a regulation blanket. The dead were beginning to smell already.

"Eh?"

It wasn't possible. That smell again. That smell? Mathieu swiveled 'round, drew his pistol, and pointed directly at the Americans.

"Stop where you are."

The two men ignored his instruction and broke into a run, but the floor was choked with debris. It was more like a disused quarry than a church aisle.

"I will shoot you first, Moutie."

Priests, police, nurses, and volunteers from every branch of the allied forces in Paris looked aghast as Mathieu steadied himself and took aim, his pistol grasped steady in both hands, his face twisted in fury. "Then I will shoot your friend. Put the stretcher down and your hands up. Now."

They stopped. There was no alternative.

"Now lay that stretcher down and turn round."

"This is a church. God is present," an exasperated clergyman protested. "Put that gun away, Monsieur."

The stretcher-bearers had the good sense to ignore the priest and do as Mathieu ordered. "Now step into that side chapel to your left. Be assured. I will shoot you dead if you try anything untoward."

255

Moutie started to shake." It's all a big mistake, Captain," he began.

"Yes, it is. On that matter, we are in agreement."

Several gendarmes, their capes flowing in anger, swarmed round the two men whose American Red Cross armbands reached upwards in surrender.

Toussaint sensed that Mathieu had cracked under the strain of such devastating mayhem, but could not fathom his anger at the stretchers-bearers. "What is it, Captain? What have they done?"

The parish priest sat on a large conical stone which once supported the ancient roof and tried to find a prayer. None would show itself.

Without moving his eyes from the target, Mathieu approached the two men with slow unfaltering steps. "Let's see what they have done."

With exaggerated caution, he raised the blanket from the bulging stretcher and unveiled his catch. Fine jackets, ornate handbags, expensive missals and prayer books, ladies hats with jeweled hatpins, umbrellas from La Gallerie Lafayette, a silver pocket watch, and initialed black leather wallets lay heavy on the stretcher, all purloined from the dead. The priest broke down, too tired to reach anger.

"Take them to the nearest barracks and shoot them." Toussaint spat on the floor in sheer disgust, then remembered to his embarrassment that he was still inside a church.

"Sorry, Father," he said to no one in particular.

"No. Take that one to the nearest precinct, lock him up, and if you like, throw the key in the Seine." Only then did Mathieu turn to face Moutie. "This one, I will deal with personally." He shoved the sorry thief into a latticed confessional, pushed him to his knees, put his pistol to his temple, and whispered, "Say your prayers."

Toussaint's face appeared on the other side of the structure begging Mathieu to think again.

"As one who knows the consequences, Sir, please don't shoot him inside the church. It'll be very difficult to cover-up." Such a practical mind.

Moutie's eyes darted from one policeman to the other unable to settle on his best chance of redemption. He felt the pistol hard against his temple and screwed his eyes shut.

"You will listen closely, do you hear. What I am about to say will happen, you fucking cretin."

Christ on the cross had heard worse, but Mathieu covered the thorn-crowned head with his left hand just in case.

"We are going back to 36 Quai des Orfevres and you will be locked up in the lowest dungeon. I am going to write up your charge sheet and have it confirmed and formally signed at every legal level. When this goes to court, you will disappear overseas for the rest of your life. Do you hear me? Overseas. Forever."

Moutie bowed his head and sniveled in rank self-pity. "I know. I am the worst person in the world. I know. But…" He got no further.

"No. You are the worst thief in the world. Probably the most despicable thief in France, but you are far from the worst person, even in Paris. From now on, I will be giving you instructions which you will follow to the letter. If you don't, you will disappear. Forever. Do you understand, Moutie? Do you understand… forever?"

Mathieu accepted the whimper as consent. He dragged the thief out of the confessional by his collar, through the side altars in the transept, down the ragged front steps of the church, threw him into a police wagon and drove him to no. 36.

Once Moutie had been manhandled inside, Mathieu instructed two gendarmes to take him to a bathroom. "Wash him as many times as it pleases you in carbolic soap, from head to foot and back again. I want to see his skin raw with cleanliness." Toussaint pulled rank and took personal charge.

"I'll get some old clothes." Mathieu found a pair of trousers and an oversized shirt in the basement storeroom and left them at the desk by the front office with a succinct note attached.

Forever.

Raoul's Story

Victory

Ecstasy. Now I could get on with the rest of my life.

I danced around my cell, joy unbounded. I did this. I, Raoul Villain, the man who paved the way to Victory by murdering the traitor Jean Jaurès, have lived to see the glorious day when the Boches were forced to fall on their swords, or bayonets or whatever. France has won. At last. They're calling it an Armistice.

I was attending one of those interminable sessions with the head-doctor, not the senior doctor as such, but a new-fangled doctor called a psychiatrist. He talked and talked and sought my opinion on many different topics. But I was careful. No matter the years or the fresh faces they shoved in front of me, I refused to answer. Again and again.

It had been foggy outside since the early morning, as if the mist had been unable to rouse itself against the weakening sun. Suddenly bells started ringing out across the city, and in that instant I knew. France had won. I could not help myself bursting into La Marseilles and everyone joined in, even the creepy new orderly who smelled of carbolic. He's very odd. Everybody agrees. Well, everybody I speak to. Been here since just after Easter. He is seriously weird. Like a character out of a book by that English novelist, Charles Dickens. I can't for the life of me remember his name. Wardens and Orderlies are basically low-level bullies who abuse their position every day. They push and shove, shout at everyone, show what big men they are, hit prisoners for no reason at all, but this one doesn't. He creeps about, fawning, as if he is the victim. I saw a couple of the others talking about him, but they don't speak to me. Huh.

Carbolic later disappeared and was gone for most of the day. He frequently came and went without purpose, but when he returned he had so much to tell. The center of the city suddenly housed the whole world. November skies were no longer foreboding. If nothing else the sheer force of exuberance lifted the mist which clung grimly to the church spires in defiance of the public mood. A huge banner was strung across a gigantic map, erected to show the allied progress day by day since the war turned in our favor in July. Now it proclaimed: "Victory. The War is won. Long Live France. Long live the Allies." Carbolic had never seen such vast crowds, he said, running, jumping for joy. Parisians hugging total strangers. And thousands of uniforms. Everyone appeared to have a uniform. American flags materialized out of the ether, or possibly the American Embassy, and men, women and boys vied with each other to carry them head high. Soldiers, former soldiers, would be soldiers, many who claimed to have been soldiers, wounded soldiers, some supported by their nurses, had flowers pressed upon them. Hotel bellboys, ladies with sashes, flat capped English officers, black American troopers, one sporting a delicate bone pipe, were surrounded by admirers. Sailors floated around the boulevards strangely separated from their mighty fleets, joining in the cacophony of celebrations. They took to organizing enormous conga-lines which zigzagged in front of news cameras, each clamped onto the dancer in front. Everyone was drunk with pent-up relief mixed with disbelief. It was all over. Never had a beer on the Rue de La Fayette tasted better, he said. Never had a bottle of Vin Rouge been more welcome. Victory at last. Sweet victory. How I wished I was free to join in.

Anthems were sung repeatedly. Colleges closed and students rushed to join the celebrations around the Place de la Concorde where a display of captured trench mortars and small cannon became symbols of surrender. Someone laid hands on an enemy flag and dragged it through the gutter. People blew tuneless horns; lorries and trucks responded with blaring klaxons. All was noise. It was at best organized mayhem, he said. A formal march-past with regimental bands swung down the Champs-Élysée to the Arc de Triomphe, barely able to hold ranks against the enthusiasm of celebrating onlookers. There were no boundaries, he told me. On the balcony of the grand hotels, residents and chambermaids, managers and kitchen staff waved gigantic flags which were usually kept for presidential processions. British, French, American, French, Italian, French. Along the first floor of the Drecoll fashion house on the exclusive Place de L'Opera, images of its Robes Lingerie range merged with a bevy of excited young ladies who abandoned their legendary disdain for public displays of emotion and waved and blew kisses to the rejoicing populace. Indeed hugs and kisses seemed to have been the order of the day. It was all so easy. Even Carbolic got a kiss.

"Such rich pickings," he mused.

I did not understand the comment. "What made rich pickings?"

"Pardon?" Carbolic was polite to a fault.

"You said it was all so easy."

"Ah, did I?" Carbolic thought for a moment and reworded his comment. "I meant…so easy to be happy…gay…ecstatic…so natural. And all those young ladies, all wanting to kiss a soldier…or a sailor…or," and he paused for effect, "a prison orderly…"

But I was still locked away.

One month on, nothing changed for me. Sometimes, in the pit of the night, I wondered if the authorities were playing games. They knew I was here. They occasionally sent a lawyer or warden to remind me that in theory I remain a favored son, but is it true? Have I imagined this? I will demand to meet with my legal team again. That's what they call themselves. My legal team, indeed. Bloody lawyers. I must confess that I thought Georges Clemenceau would have ordered my immediate release, given the disgust we share for socialists and anarchists.

Carbolic amused me, though I have not yet worked him out. He appeared to be a simple man, but knew many surprising things. He could be, what's the word…inappropriate. Yes, inappropriate. Sometimes he corrected me in a manner which made me feel that he is the educated man. On the previous day I had been talking about the end of the war and how the German surrender had been so sudden when he interrupted.

"The war has not ended, Sir. Only the fighting has stopped." He did not look at me when he said this but I could feel the smirk on his face. "Peace is an illusion. A lull between wars so that both sides can replenish their armies."

"Nonsense." I shuddered at the thought. "It is over. We have won."

I'd never heard him speak like this. Suddenly so certain, as if he was in the know. Who had he been listening to? I'd never seen him with a newspaper in his hand, so where did he get such ideas from?

"Have we, Sir? Have we really won? The north of our country right up beyond Flanders and into the heart of Belgium has been ripped out and left to rot. But look at Germany. Not a scratch on her great cities. Has her army been defeated? No. Did her navy suffer a single defeat over the last four years? No. Do the Germans feel remorse? No."

"But we won," I shouted back. It was self-evident. Everyone knew we had won the war.

"They have only signed a piece of paper called an Armistice. What does that mean? Do you know, Sir?"

"Yes, but Foch and Clemenceau and the English and the Americans will sort it out."

"Of course they will, Sir…but what does that mean?"

"We have Alsace and Lorraine back again. Restored to their former glory. French again. Germany will pay for the costs of this war. The Allies are all committed to that. Reparations. They will suffer."

"Of course, Sir." His slanted bow made me uncomfortable. I felt… patronized. How odd.

"Life in this city has changed beyond imagination. Not for the rich, of course. No, it never does for them, but the poor are poorer, the sick are sicker, and the hungry are still dying."

"For goodness sake, Carbolic, you sound like one of those whining anarchists or socialists."

"How many years is it since you walked down Haussmann or Avenue Hoche, Sir? What do you imagine Paris has become while you have been lying in here? Imprisoned, I mean."

It was a frightening thought. That out there is not what I imagine in my head. I had not considered a different Paris. Physical change has always alarmed me unless I can see for myself that all is well.

"And, Sir, stay well away from anyone with a fever. I've checked these corridors and we seem to be clear, for the moment."

Carbolic had reached the cell door and was at the point of leaving. I couldn't for the life of me understand what he was talking about.

"Clear of what, Carbolic?"

"Influenza…the flu…Don't you know thousands are dying all across Paris? It's far more deadly than the German shells ever were."

Of course I'd heard about the Spanish flu, but I thought it was confined to the destitute, the elderly, and the war-wounded. Possibly children, too. From the far end of the narrow corridor a racking cough echoed out towards us and added a new fear to my private collection. We looked at each other, and a shiver crossed from my shoulders to my spine and down to my shaking legs. In a second I would be alone again and I did not welcome the solitude.

"Wait a moment, my friend." I touched his arm but he gave an involuntary squirm. Carbolic was not to be persuaded to linger in the semi-dark where germs lurked in their multitudes.

"Do you think they have forgotten about me?" My words were so sincere that he found pity in his heart.

"Of course not, Sir. Believe me. Definitely not, definitely. Believe me, I know."

The door slammed and he was gone. It took me some seconds to think through his parting words. Believe me…I know.

"Hey, what do you know? What do you know, Carbolic? Come back. Come back right now. What do you mean?"

I sank back on the floor, confused. Was he really an orderly? Were they watching me? No, that would be ridiculous. He'd be the worst spy in the world if he were a spy.

What do you think my friend? Did you ever meet a spy who smelled of Carbolic soap?

Part 3

THE ICARUS STRAIN

31

1918-1919 Containing The Tiger

In no. 36 Rue des Orfevres, Bernard Roux discarded the newspapers which littered his desk, drew a final drag on his Gauloises, and extinguished it with vigor as if he was rubbing someone's nose in the vile ash. He walked through to the general office.

"Where do they get this from?"

Paul and Mathieu looked at each other, uncertain as to whom the question was addressed or what it was that the mysterious "they" had lain their hands on.

"The stories in today's press. Every newspaper."

"They print whatever suits them, Chief, you know that." Dubois shrugged it off.

"What story in particular, Chief?"

"The proposed Peace Conference," he retorted. "Where it's to be held. According to *Figaro,* the Americans have proposed Switzerland; Geneva or Lausanne." He grasped another journal. "*L'Humanite* has a full page on the Belgian government's aim to have it in Brussels, backed by the entire nation from Cardinal Mercier and the Catholic Church to King Albert." He threw it down in disgust. "*La Croix* claims that that Clemenceau is insistent that it be held in Paris, naturally, and is supported by *Le Monde* and *Le Parisien,* while according to *L'Opinion,* the British are happy with anywhere other than London."

"You can't fault Lloyd George there. Policing a bloody international peace conference will be a nightmare." Dubois knew the pitfalls and wished them elsewhere.

"My point, gentlemen, is that nothing has been agreed. These discussions are supposed to be secret. Officially no decision has been taken. When the Germans see the terms which the foreign office want to impose, they may not agree to anything. Someone inside our sacred government has leaked confidential information to the press. Deliberately."

Bernard Roux picked up the telephone and requested to speak with prime minister Clemenceau's private secretary, Henri Mordacq at the war office. They talked at some length but it was impossible to read the chief's inscrutable face as he paced up and down between the curtained windows, nodding from time to time, and grunting occasional but unrelated words. At length he finished, clearly satisfied.

"War Office doesn't know either. Our allies have already started to fight amongst themselves for prime position in the wonderful pecking order of the new era. President Wilson's minder, Edward House, has been in touch with both Lloyd George and Washington, saying that it would be better if a conference took place in neutral Switzerland. Don't ask how we know. But we do."

"Diplomatic telegrams … so easy to decipher." Mathieu nodded at Dubois.

"Well, we are going to upset that particular cozy applecart. The diplomatic caste will shortly give the Americans sight of secret information which shows that the Swiss aren't to be trusted. You know the drill. Full of spies and poisonous left-wing elements—possibly Bolsheviks—make them press their own panic button. Ambassador Sharp gets particularly agitated about Bolsheviks."

Mathieu was not surprised. "The Tiger is nobody's fool. He knows he will be in control if the peace conference is held in Paris. It's as simple as that."

"*Merde.*" Dubois hunched his shoulders, dropped his head, and spoke into his own lap. "He'll be in control of the politics but who will control the revolutionaries? It'll be murder to keep all those targets secure. It's an anarchist's dream."

"It'll be murder if we fail," Mathieu joked, but the witticism whipped past Dubois without registering.

There was an added worry.

"This isn't the place to hold an international conference." Mathieu was sure of that. "The bloody English and Americans imagine that they'll have a holiday. Look at the city. Where do we put everyone? Notre Dame will hardly make a great tourist attraction with its stained glass windows missing. Boulevards with shattered trees and great gaps where people have chopped them up for firewood. There are piles of rubble stored at every second corner and gaping bomb craters that haven't been filled in. Even the Tuileries gardens have been ruined by the huge hole that looks like it goes right to the center of the earth." He paused to change his angle of objection. "How do we feed the politicians and their hangers-on? We don't have enough basics, do we? Coal? Milk? Bread?"

"That'll be the least of our worries." Roux was halfway through another Gauloises. "The Americans will make sure that there are plenty luxuries.

But you're both right, it will be virtually impossible to police. However, the bottom line is that the Tiger has made up his mind. He won't contemplate its being held anywhere else, and frankly no one in France would either."

"I'll tell you what worries me most." Mathieu had lowered his voice to a half whisper so that his message carried more menace. "We've got so much unfinished business already. Raoul Villain is still being kept out of court and he is strangely confident that he will be rewarded for murdering Jean Jaurès."

"You know that for sure?" The question that the chief was really asking was, *How do you know that?* Mathieu did not answer, but continued to list his concerns. "There are so many unsolved crimes, unanswered accusations, victims who want payback … and I don't mean from Germany. The left wing, socialists, anarchists, and their numbers continue to grow, and don't forget, we walk a tightrope between revolution and loyalty. The irony is that the very man who could have kept them calm lies in his grave, murdered by the agents of the right."

"If only we could prove that." Roux dug deep into his jacket pocket, and with consummate ease, extracted yet another packet of Gauloises.

Mathieu nodded. "I think about it every day. Dream about it every night. Villain is an unexploded bomb and I can hear it ticking."

They were all aware that the scars which tore across French society lacerated the streets of Paris and every other major city in the land. Once initial celebrations had passed, victory flags hung limp from the lampposts. It was shameful to see the limbless veterans and newly de-mobbed soldiers in worn, faded uniforms add only to the ranks of the unemployed. There had never been so many beggars embarrassed by the desperation of their fate. Once, they sat in these same street cafés, heroes; guardians of the nation. Now they were superfluous. Their youth and their value spent in the extravagance of war. And the man who claimed that he had caused the war all on his own, slept safely in La Santé. And this was justice?

At no. 36, security became the overwhelming priority. International delegates began to invade Paris like sports teams in the oddest of Olympic meetings, with advisers, experts, academics, and secretaries all requiring special attention and the best of accommodation. Dubois had been passed the impossible baton. He had to assemble a team to monitor, support, and keep safe the hundreds of foreign representatives who flooded the city to no apparent useful purpose. And the paperwork. *Mon Dieu*, the paperwork.

"Do you think this is a mistake, Mathieu?" He held up a letter embossed with the stamp of the American State Department.

"What?"

"This missive from the Americans. They've asked for a vast number of facilities to be made available. I know they have the economic clout to move entire mountain ranges, but why would they need the Hôtel de Crillon and a second hotel on the Boissy d'Anglas, close to their prestigious embassy? And they want both to be staffed by their own countrymen."

Overkill? Who knows? They're American."

"But this letter is dated 30th October…and the Armistice wasn't signed until 11th November?"

"Really? Can I see that?" Mathieu was intrigued. How the hell did they know nearly two weeks in advance of the announcement of an Armistice? For the second time in his life he thought of the conspiracy inside a conspiracy, and shivered. "And the American Red Cross intend to use their premises on the Place de la Concorde to house US delegates."

"That organization has always been a front for the Americans in Europe, especially and increasingly, to cover their activities in Russia." Bernard Roux had been aware of this for six months, but the bureau was forbidden to interfere. Dubois's task was impossible. The best he could do was keep known troublemakers away from the delegates.

Mathieu's main concern was the Tiger's own security. Though Clemenceau was already in his mid-seventies and suffered from diabetes, his inner strength was legendary. He was said to have descended from a family of wolves, with all their cunning and lack of fear. The prime minister was, however, pestered by irritating eczema on this hands to the extent that he constantly wore gloves to cover the raw broken skin and had difficulty sleeping. His inner-circle of friends were much more important to him than any of the Allied leaders, yet even they were subject to close scrutiny.

"You've to organise a constant watch on Henri Mordacq, Andre Tardieu, and Louis Loucheur." Roux announced, shaking his head. These were the men that Clemenceau dined with virtually every evening, his trusted confidants.

"Are they under threat? What information do we have? Is it reliable?" Mathieu was intrigued.

"Well, yes, you could say that. Certainly reliable. We are required to collate a report on their activities and have it on the Tiger's desk by half past seven every morning."

"What? Did he say why? Is there a leak from his office?"

Roux inhaled a short burst of nicotine. "Not as far as anyone is aware. He intends to hand it to them so that they know they are being closely watched."

"What? Is he paranoid? His best friends?"

"I've thought about it. Clever idea. On the one hand they know they are being watched, the proof is there for them to read, and if it pleases them, check. In addition, if anyone is hanging about on the periphery with evil intentions, our boys are likely to become aware and take action."

"We don't have men to spare, Chief. It's nonsense."

"You tell him that," Roux laughed.

32

February 19th 1919 – The Blond Assassin

A s the weeks turned to months Mathieu Bertrand fell under the charm-spell which Clemenceau reserved for those he liked and trusted. Journeys back from Versailles became a constant source of laughter and scorn. Once he had ensconced himself in the back seat of the police Renault, the Tiger would remove his top hat, spread his ample rear across the well-padded fabric, and set to the task of ripping apart the characters of his so-called allied friends. He despised Woodrow Wilson.

"That priggish American thinks he can come over here and reorder Europe. He knows little of our language, even less about our culture, and positively nothing about our history. In fact, I don't think he's in charge at all. Firstly, he's not fully recovered from that flu bug which seems to be everywhere. He has been ill. Rumors of a stroke persist, but I think he's caught that flu which is killing thousands of the American troops before they even get to the battlefield. And most annoyingly, every single decision we agree upon is checked first with his dreadful sidekick, Colonel Mandel House, and then, and only then, do we proceed. And to cap it all, this House person is no colonel. Hasn't even got a military background,"

Mathieu was aware that Mandel House was the power behind the American president's office. A constant stream of diplomatic telegrams between House and government agencies in Washington was proof that he pulled the strings. What Colonel House suggested, became fact. What House disapproved of, was cast into the political waste bin.

"I was trapped between him and Lloyd George today. I tell you, it was like sitting beside Moses and Napoleon Bonaparte with his hemorrhoids down. The American clearly thinks that his ideas, all fourteen of them, are the new tablets of stone. And remember, Moses only brought ten commandments down from the mountain. Lloyd George never settles. He is the chameleon of truth. Telling one group what they want to hear, and another something completely different while all the time following his own agenda. Don't listen to Wilson; don't trust Lloyd George." Mathieu could tell by the way Clemenceau spoke that he disliked the American but had a modicum of cautious respect for the Welshman.

Another happy participant was Jacques-Francois. He admitted that he had the best job in the country. Each morning as he eased the prime minister's reinforced Renault RGA out of its special garage in the Pépinière barracks, he stroked the driving wheel as if it was an object of sexual gratification and breathed in the rich smell of fresh leather. It was his ritual, and to be fair, it made Mathieu smile, though little else did. First stop was at Rue Benjamin Franklin in the Sixteenth arrondissement to collect Clemenceau. The prime minister's morning mood, predicated on how little he had slept and whether or not the fencing routine with his masseur had been a success, was difficult to anticipate. Whichever way, he had a story to tell.

General Henri Mordacq drove with them, as did Clemenceau's son Albert. Jacques surmised that the Tiger probably wanted decent company before the dreary meeting ahead. As usual, an army brigadier sat in the front beside him while two other detectives stood on the fender, further protecting their precious cargo. Jacques-Francois had driven along this route so often that the car could feasibly have navigated the short drive on its own. He turned right into Rue Passy, left into Boulevard Delessert and swung slowly round the corner to avoid the tram lines which crossed the cobbled road at that junction. Jacques was aware of the crowd of well-wishers who waved and applauded the prime minister, but the Tiger was too busy discussing the business of the day to acknowledge them.

Crack.

Crack again.

The glass on the left hand side splintered. Instinct took over. Jacques accelerated at such a speed that the detectives on the fender clung to the hand grips in fear of their lives.

"Stop!" roared Clemenceau. "Stop and get him." The attacker began to run behind the car as it shuddered to a halt, still firing shots which pinged harmlessly from the bodywork. "Get him. I'm ordering you to stop. NOW!" the Tiger roared.

Both detectives and an army officer sprang into action, firing at the blond-haired target in the middle of the road. Having emptied his gun at the presidential car, the would-be-assassin raised his hands in surrender. In a blur of screams and yells of outrage from those who were still standing at the corner in shock and utter disbelief, a policeman threw himself at the assailant and downed him impressively with a side-tackle which

271

would have earned applause from rugby enthusiasts. The angry mob smelled blood. Realizing that it was safe to attack the unarmed assailant, they rounded on the dazed man with such ferocity that the gendarme had to stop them ripping his body apart. His clothes were torn from him and the detectives had difficultly pulling him to his feet.

"He's under arrest. Leave him." But punches and kicks continued unabated.

"Are you alright, Sir?" Jacques thought he saw blood seeping through the prime minister's waistcoat.

"Wounded, I think. Just a flesh wound." Henri Mordacq helped his friend into a more comfortable position and instructed Jacques to drive to the nearest hospital, the Boucicaut.

"You will do nothing of the sort," Tiger boomed. "Take me home. Now. I'm perfectly fine." Jacques-Francois looked at General Mordacq for reassurance.

"Rue Franklin, immediately." The prime minister was not to be crossed.

"You have to be examined, father. You need to go to hospital for a full examination." Albert Clemenceau tried to object but his father would have none of it.

"Do as you are told. Home. The doctor can come to see me." The old man was in control and not to be crossed.

Jacques drove back to Rue Franklin and while the others attended to the wounded leader, he called Mathieu at 36, where the news had already shaken the building like an earth tremor. He had little to add other than he thought one of the bullets had grazed his own arm.

"It's a blur. All happened so fast. Tiger's wounded, but I don't know how badly. He's playing it down."

"Nothing more dangerous than a wounded Tiger. Have your arm looked at by a medic and get back to Rue Franklin as fast as you can. We have to know exactly how he is."

In Rue Franklin, the prime minister's apartment became the most overstaffed hospital ward in France. A military surgeon was first on the scene. He had dealt with so many traumatic injuries that Clemenceau's small wound looked more like a scratch. He was joined within minutes by the eminent Professor Gosset who admitted that the patient was lucid and comfortable but his advice was "hospital."

"No," Tiger growled again. "Hospitals are full of seriously wounded heroes. This guy fired shots at me from point blank range and missed. Well, almost missed, he conceded. I hope to God he wasn't in the army. It'd derail the peace talks if the Germans thought that our men couldn't fire guns from point blank range. We've just won the most terrible war in history and this bloody useless Frenchman misses me six times out of seven."

But the doctor was having none of it. "He has to have an x-ray, no matter what he says. It's the seventh bullet I'm worried about."

Bernard Roux heard about the assassination attempt as his security meeting with British, American, and Italian intelligence officers in an ante room at the Palace de Justice was about to begin. He cancelled it and placed himself at the hub of the inquiry. Mathieu was already on his way to the commissariat in Rue Bas-le-Vent where an interrogation had begun. The officer in charge had slung the gunman's defiant figure, still half naked and clearly frightened, into a room devoid of charity.

"I think I have to start, Monsieur, with a word of caution to you. Normally when murderers are brought in here, we dish out the appropriate welcome, but beating you to a pulp would be a waste of time, and effort. The public appear to have got to you first. But let me assure you of this: should you try to be smart, lie to us, conceal anything, or fail to tell the whole truth first time, we will wait till your injuries have begun to heal and then beat you properly. Understood, Monsieur? And it will be a pleasure. The prime minister is a hero in these parts."

At which point, Mathieu burst into the room. All eyes turned to the captain from no. 36 and with a strange shiver of deja vu he remembered the night that the assistant commissioner had charged into Raoul Villain's interrogation and taken him away. Taken them off the case, or tried to.

"My apologies," he began. "I would like to sit in on this."

"You don't want to take charge, Captain? You are the senior officer."

"No, no. Please continue. You lads have done a terrific job in arresting the suspect so quickly and getting him safely into custody. I just want to hear what he has to say."

"By all means. Please have a seat."

"This is Emile Cottin, Sir." He turned to the confused and battered prisoner. "Monsieur Cottin, let me introduce Captain Bertrand from the Deuxième Bureau. He will be listening to your every word." Emile Cottin was clearly frightened. He glanced at Mathieu, but turned away lest the stony faced police officer had mystical powers which his folly had disturbed.

"You are Emile Cottin?"

"Louis Emile Cottin," he whimpered.

"So, Louis Emile Cottin, explain what happened this morning. Leave no detail out."

"I shot Clemenceau in his limousine on Boulevard Delessert."

There was a strange timbre of defiance in his voice, a mixture of fear and pride laced with quiet assuredness. He fixed his eyes on the blank wall behind his interrogators, hoping to distance himself from the proceedings. Mathieu grunted guttural disapproval as if to prepare the room for a change of approach. The interrogating officer understood.

"I think you should continue the interview, captain."

"Certainly." Mathieu turned to Cottin and said, "How many of you were there?" Louis Emile was lost. Completely perplexed by the people around him. He had not thought through what might happen because he didn't care. "Tell us what happened. How you did it. Who all was involved? Why did you try to kill the prime minister?" Before he could reply a change of plan was ordained from above.

Bernard Roux, having spoken to the prime minister's office, the president's office, and the Ministry of Justice ordered that Cottin be brought immediately to the Palaise de Justice for a formal interrogation. At every level of responsibility, desks were cleared and records examined to ensure that the finger of blame could not be directed at those in charge. The change of surroundings loosened Emil Cottin's reticence and his bowels.

"Clean him up and bring him straight to the upper corridor interview room. I'll continue in ten minutes. He speaks to no one other than me. Clear?" Roux was waiting for Mathieu with customary impatience, smoke rising with his blood pressure. He wanted to know how it could have happened. Here in Paris, with the whole world looking on.

"There were at least half a dozen gendarmes positioned around that stretch of road. How did he manage to avoid their suspicion?"

"Went for a piss. Simple as that."

"What?" Roux's Gauloises almost fell from his open mouth, but decades of practice allowed him to avoid the indignity of such an error.

"He sauntered into the street and went for a piss in the street urinal. No big deal. That's what urinals are for. Took his time and left by the rear exit when people began to cheer. He knew that Clemenceau's car always swung away from the tram lines, so he calmly stepped into the street and fired off three shots before anyone realized what was happening. When the car sped off he ran onto the road and emptied his gun chamber. Tiger ordered the protection team to stop and go for him, and ironically, if he hadn't, the crowd on Rue Delessert would have pulled him apart."

"Would have saved a great deal of paperwork if they had," the chief mused.

Cottin was grilled non-stop for two hours by the highest-paid assembly of inquisitors Mathieu had ever seen in one place. His actions and responses were dissected by the director of police judiciary, the procurator general, the state procurator, a judge, and a pack of lawyers.

"Where did you get the gun?"

"I bought it for thirty-five francs some months back, from a badly maimed former soldier."

"He was willing to part with a good solid Browning for thirty-five francs?"

"He was desperate and destitute. Have you the slightest idea what that means? To wander the streets of Paris, cap in hand, dragging a withered rump of a leg behind you? Thirty-five francs bought him enough drink to forget it all for a few hours."

The inquisitor reddened into unjustified anger. To hide his embarrassment he shouted in Cottin's face. "Who helped you? I see that you claim to be a well-known anarchist and member of the Communist Federation of the Seine?"

"It's not illegal now, is it?" Cottin's sarcasm bit deep. He had no intention of pleasing his audience.

"Why did you want to kill the prime minister?"

Emile Cottin slumped in his chair. His matted blond hair and facial contusions, torn vest, and thin bruised arms gave him the appearance of a third-rate boxer who had fought above his weight, and failed miserably to land a blow. He had almost begun to enjoy the exchanges with these bourgeoisie elitists who clearly had no idea about street poverty or living on the edge of destitution in a once glorious city. But they had touched a raw nerve. His hatred for Georges Clemenceau ran deep. He was the man who had prolonged the misery of the war; a war in which he had lost so many friends. He was the bastard who used the police and army to crush strikes and attack unions.

"Because I hate him and all that he stands for."

Mathieu drew a long breath in anticipation of a hard day ahead and a longer night beyond. Two months ago, no. 36 had received information about suspected Bolshevik activity loosely based in Switzerland aimed at destroying the unity of the allies in Europe. Stories abounded of arrests at the Swiss border, where suspected agitators had been turned back and refused entry to France. Agents raided the working man's lodging house in Montrouge where Cottin lived and found quantities of anarchist and communist literature. Emile did not smoke or drink, but he read profusely. While the right wing papers carried unsubstantiated reports of his association with a secret Bolshevik group in what they described as, "the more sordid quarters of Paris," Mathieu knew that the secret service had no factual evidence. It transpired that Cottin was a known activist who worked at the Caudron airplane factory after he had been invalided out of the army. There were hundreds like him. His police record included three sentences for inciting soldiers to disobey orders, and according to the report, his final arrest was because he shouted "Death to Clemenceau."

What disturbed Mathieu most was the web of unproven inferences which likened Villain's cowardly murder of Jean Jaurès, and the attempt on the prime minister's life by Emile Cottin. From nowhere newspapers reported that the police were looking for a "correctly dressed" youth who had allegedly called at Cottin's lodging on the evening before the attempt to kill Clemenceau. That was a lie. There was no such police activity. Not a single report. No one was looking for an accomplice, but there were men in high office who knew that Villain had accomplices. They were deliberately muddying the waters.

SMELL THE COFFEE

Then it happened. As naturally as the spring tides raise the river levels. Joy of joys. Wonder of wonders. They agreed a trial date. At last.

Maitre Giraud and Maitre Bourson had a plan. To be frank, I don't know for sure if it was their plan, for Monsieur Georges and Action française always had a plan. It was very simple.

"Wait." How Giraud loved to take the lead.

"Say nothing," echoed his witless friend.

"Mention no one." What? Did they imagine that I had forgotten the mantra?

"You will see. We will stand by you." Stupid Bourson never said anything of consequence.

"Unless…" But of course, there was no unless. For almost five years I had repeatedly said nothing other than I killed Jaures on my own.

"Trust your friends. Always." They nodded to each other. Just like…

"Remember that, my friend." Bourson smiled at me like a bemused Buddha. "Trust us," he insisted.

Really?

Carbolic brought me a bag of coffee beans which I had never seen before. He said that a manservant of "a friend" had delivered them to La Santé. They smelled divine. When I let him inhale the wonderful aroma, Carbolic's eyes opened wide and he said, "Very expensive, very. It's Blue Mountain, from Jamaica. Louis XIV brought it over to France, you know."

How could he have had such knowledge? The man couldn't tie shoelaces yet he made those ludicrous statements. "Only two men in Paris can afford such luxury…so who is your secret admirer, Sir?" I was intrigued by his interest. "Come now, Sir. You can tell me, surely?"

"It's forbidden. Need to cut out my tongue. Or rather, they would cut out my tongue if I told you."

I decided to play his game. "Let me offer you a few possible initials?"

Carbolic paused for a second and said slowly, "R or Z." Then I understood. It was more than a gift. It was a sign of things to come. Riches. Wealth. Fame and fortune. I knew who the Z was, and was fairly sure of the R. But I shook my head without comment.

"I hear that your trial date has been set." Carbolic smiled knowingly.

"You hear many things, Carbolic. Perhaps you should be more careful with such secrets. I understood that the date had not been made public. Have you been listening at my cell door?" I stared hard at him, watching for his reaction.

"Ah, my friend, the orderly who cleans the Governor's office might see a communication left carelessly on his desk." He bowed his head with theatrical precision as if he rehearsed such mannerisms in front of a mirror. "But if it is a secret, worry not. I am the keeper of secrets. You can trust me."

Putain, I thought. "My word," I said.

Carbolic donned his most obsequious stance. "Would you like me to make you a cup of coffee?"

The offer sounded generous, as if it were his bloody coffee beans. "I'm not sharing them with you, if that's what you think."

"Of course not," he said. "I'm not particularly fond of coffee anyway."

Liar. I knew a liar when I heard one. "Shame," I said. It wasn't really a shame, but I chose to be polite.

He procured a small pot of steaming water and within seconds the all-pervading smell of luxury transformed my little cell into a grand café deluxe. Slightly bitter for my taste, I considered asking if he could find some sugar to add to the coffee, but that would have betrayed a weakness I could not afford. Strong men drank strong coffee.

"And what do they say in the streets about Clemenceau? Will he die? I hope not. What will become of me if he dies?"

"No, Sir, it will take more than a bullet lodged in his lungs to kill the prime minister. Much more."

It was a terrible thing, to attempt to murder a great man in cold blood.

"I was shocked to hear about the anarchist who tried to assassinate Clemenceau. What won't these people do? How do they think it makes our country look when the eyes of the whole world are turned to Paris and everyone who has come to Versailles sees how these Bolsheviks and communists behave? I heard that bystanders ripped his clothes off and pasted his face black and blue. A butcher's boy landed the first blow, or so the papers say. Good on him, I say. He would have been killed in the street if the police had not intervened. They should have left the people to get on with it."

Carbolic's face twisted through a rainbow of expressions. He appeared to be on the point of speaking on several occasions, but failed to find the precise words. Was he having a heart attack? Was this how a stroke began? Was he laughing or choking? Was he in pain?

"Are you alright, Carbolic?"

Wide-eyed and speechless, it took him some time to recover his composure.

"You really must take care. Be a bad day if you survived all the influenza, pestilence, bombing and shelling, and choked to death in here. Do you suffer these fits often?"

He shook his head. "I think it was a fit of irony, Sir."

Strange man. I could never understand him. But I sought one more favor.

"Would you bring me a selection of quality newspapers, please? Le Figaro, Le Parisien would be appreciated." I went to offer him money, but to my surprise I couldn't find my purse. Could have sworn it was in my jacket.

He looked downcast, so I took him into my confidence. "You see, Carbolic…"

"Monsieur Villain, you do know that my name is Marti, or even Moutie, as my friends call me…this Carbolic has become monotonous. Boring, even."

"Oh, but I like it. I mean no harm. It's a compliment."

"Would the same remarks apply if I called you villain or assassin or murderer, Monsieur?" He was being rude. Offensive.

"No, it would not."

The cheek of the man. But I wanted to talk, share my good news with someone, so I swallowed my anger and began again.

"Marti," I said. It sounded wrong. "Wait till you read those newspapers. They are going to start an anti-Jaures campaign. He's to be revealed as a traitor to France. Isn't that clever?"

"Certainly would be, Monsieur. I'll tell my friends to watch out for it." He turned and left me to my thoughts. Now I had a future. My goodness. Where will I go when I get out of here? I need to see my father. I have to go back to Reims and show myself to those who made my life miserable. Oh yes, I would rub their noses in the merde.

33

March 1919 – The Ravaging Virus

Mathieu's world spun into an orbit of confusion. He needed to focus. An attempt on the prime minister's life, Emile Cottin, news of Villain's impending trial, a city full of political targets, newspapers spreading disinformation, journalists from every corner of the earth, anarchists, Bolsheviks, and now, Agnès. As he rushed towards the Saint-Antoine hospital on Rue Faubourg he revised the list. Agnès. Agnès of the blessed wonderful smile was his real concern. He was tempted to prayer, but resisted. How? Agnès had warned him repeatedly that this Spanish flu was lethal and everyone had to take precautions to avoid contact with a victim. One sneeze released half a million germs, she said. One cough could be equally as dangerous. She always wore her gauze mask in the hospital. She was protected, surely? Could it have happened the night before last? He had taken Agnès to the theatre to see Sarah Bernhardt, still a magnificent actress even if she only had one leg. That was the problem with this killer disease; it struck indiscriminately. Legs or no legs.

Matron Veronique Lore caught him at the main entrance of the Hotel-Dieu with its grand facade and famed central passage. Her stern face betrayed deep concern. Though barely forty years of age, her hair had turned prematurely grey and her lined face and sunken eyes reflected the agonies she had witnessed over the last four years. "You have to understand, captain, that Agnès is seriously unwell. Her temperature this morning was almost forty and she has trouble breathing. If pneumonia grips her…"

"Veronique." Mathieu had met the Matron several times when Agnès was in Paris. He took both of her weathered hands in his own and pleaded, "How? Yesterday morning she was perfectly normal. She is the strongest woman I know. She was in Etaples last weekend working in the military hospital…"

"And that is probably where she caught the virus. It's been around for months, and the government won't allow the newspapers to broadcast the extent of this epidemic. Professor Tuffier has been extensively studying victims brought to this hospital. They've called it Spanish flu, but it's not from Spain."

"No? But…"

"We're not certain but it appears to be rife in those overcrowded transit camps for American soldiers. And it's young adults who are most at risk. Agnès is strong, but *la grippe* has no respect for strength. When you see her, do not distress her by crying or overreacting. Put on this mask."

She handed him a simple, white gauze covering which he bound around his nose. Were it not so serious, he might have passed comment about looking like a horse with its snout in a bag, but levity had no place in his world. They passed through heavy swing-doors with rubber seals to retain any circulating spores and entered a universe of prim cleanliness. Rows of individual beds with cloth-tented coverings separating one from the other were draped in white sheets. Underneath lay sick and dying patients. Some lay prone, unmoving, while others coughed and squirmed in pain. Agnès was sleeping fitfully in the fifth cloth bay. She looked like the painting of ashen-faced Saint Odile which had graced the wall of his infant school in Marseilles. Translucent and vulnerable.

"Don't touch her or disturb her or I'll throw you out myself." Matron's warning was absolute.

"Thanks, Veronique. I'll be very quiet," he whispered. Mathieu Bertrand sat by his lover's side and dared himself to breathe. Agnès had been washed in cooling water and was visibly struggling in her fight against the inner enemy. He wanted to say, "I love you, Agnès," a hundred times over, but dared not. He wanted to kiss her pale rose lips, but dared not. Seeing her like this was agony. But he sat in the agony of hope for an hour.

Waiting, watching, seething at the fates who mocked this good woman who had dedicated her life to saving others and now sought to repay her with untimely death. He bowed his sorry head, exhausted, and fell asleep.

A nurse touched his elbow. Agnès was still … and was she more restful? "She's in a deeper sleep. That's usually good," she assured him. "By the way, there's an odd fellow at the door asking to speak with you. Smells of soap."

Moutie was agitated. The last time Mathieu had seen him pacing so uncomfortably back and forth was outside the police court before the onset of war. The man had certainly changed since his conversion, or was it conversation, in the Saint Gervais confessional. Moutie's clothes were fresh, perhaps not fully ironed, but clean. His addiction to carbolic soap, though welcome, was thought by his friends to have been caused by falling masonry in the shelled church. The word miracle had been used on occasion, but that was certainly stretching credibility. They moved swiftly to the nearby Auberge Saint Antoine though Moutie could not contain his excitement.

"They've opened discussions on Villain's trial."

"I thought they might."

"His lawyers, Giraud and Bourson, have concocted a plan to start abusing Jaurès' name in *Le Parisien*, and Villain is absolutely certain that he will be found not guilty. Could that be used as evidence that he has indeed lost his mind?" Moutie was as excited as a small boy with a new bicycle.

"What do you think of him, Moutie? How will he perform in court, do you think?"

"Arrogant. Truly believes that he murdered Jaurès on behalf of the nation. Not popular with other prisoners. Seems to call the tune with his lawyers... as if he is paying for their services himself. And stupid, too. Been too long on his own, probably."

"Does he appear rational or is he obviously feeble-minded?"

"As rational as me..." No sooner had the words slipped from Moutie's mouth than he realized what he had said... "And you," he added for effect.

"They certainly plan to do something. They've not kept him alive for the duration of the war simply to have him imprisoned for the rest of his life. He never mentions names?"

"Now, here's a thing." Moutie extracted a small bag from his pocket and handed it to Mathieu.

"What's inside?" His suspicion was understandable.

"Open it... and smell."

That was an invitation that would have previously been rejected out of hand. Moutie held the bag between his thumb and forefinger and offered it again. Mathieu took it from him without moving his eyes, opened it, and let the aroma from the luxury coffee beans take flight. "My oh my, that smells good. Do you know what this is?"

"Blue Mountain beans. From Jamaica. Costs a fortune."

"Perhaps. I couldn't have told you that, my friend. I was speaking metaphorically."

"Oh?"

"This is the smell of ultimate corruption. A reminder to Villain that he has very rich friends. Imprisoned and isolated, removed from reality and hemmed in by stone walls, they can provide him with the most exclusive of coffee beans. Everyone else has to put up with chicory, and this is what Villain has every day."

"Yessir, this is what our man in La Santé had with his breakfast this morning."

"Who brought him these?"

"He wouldn't say, but I tricked him by claiming that only two men in Paris could afford them. He still said nothing, so I offered him two initials… R and Z. When I said Z, his face lit up like Zaharoff's chandelier."

"Basil Zaharoff? Are you sure?"

"He didn't actually say so, but his reaction was electric. Do you know anyone else with a surname beginning with Z?"

"And the R?"

"Rothschild. He could afford it, but he didn't react to the R."

If Zaharoff was involved in any way, then financing Villain's trial was simplicity itself. Zaharoff? He mused to himself. That raised deeper concerns. Zaharoff and the president? Possibly. Zaharoff and Action française? Probably. Zaharoff and the Comité des Forges at Briey? Certainly.

Moutie's agitation interrupted his thought pattern.

"Are these coffee beans for me, or do you want them back?" Mathieu smiled innocently as his informer's face crumpled

"Well…" Moutie clearly did not want to part with them. "They were a gift, you know."

"I take it that Villain knows he gave you a gift?" Silence.

Mathieu's look was one of reproof; Moutie's, one of guilt. "You keep them, Moutie. You are doing well. Now, back to work."

Louis Emile Cottin, known to his friends as Milou, did not have to wait five and a half years before his trial. Indeed he did not have to linger five and a half weeks in jail. In comparison to Raoul Villain, Cottin was subjected to instant retribution. Bernard Roux first heard of the proposal to bring forward his trial at a joint service meeting on the first day of March. Not only had the judicial responsibility been passed to the military courts, but factions inside the Deuxième Bureau were actively involved in manufacturing the case against the anarchist, as the right-wing press would have it. A date was set. March 14th 1919.

The implications were transparent. While Raoul Villain was kept safely incarcerated until he could be tried for assassination by a civil court, Cottin was to be given a court-martial, though he was, of course, a civilian. The first would most likely impose a jail sentence; the second would order the death sentence. Mindful of the daily civilian disruption during Henriette Caillaux's appearance at the Palais de Justice in 1914, Roux despaired of common sense in French politics. "You have to ask who pulls the strings in this country? The president, the Assembly, the prime minister and his cabinet… or others?"

"Don't forget the Comité des Forges, Chief. They call the shots." Mathieu's sarcasm was evident.

"We'd better get the Paris gendarmerie and national police force to cancel all leave from mid-March onwards."

Jacques, who only knew parts of the conspiracy theory, couldn't understand. "If they can hold back on Raoul Villain, why not wait until the peace conference has finished and all these foreigners have gone home before dealing with Cottin? At all levels, this is crazy."

Crazy it was.

"But there will be a reason. Believe me, there is always a reason."

As predicted, Cottin became the victim of a St Valentine's day print massacre. The right-wing press splattered his defenseless reputation across their front pages and vied with each other to find the most villainous stories they could concoct to strip decency from him. At 1:00 P.M. the court-martial was convened in the Palais de Justice under the presidency of Colonel Hivert, with a Captain Mornet as government prosecutor and Maitre Oscar Bloch as defense counsel. Bernard Roux was thoroughly embarrassed that foreign journalists were allowed to witness the proceedings.

Though Jacques-Francois had not been present, he had to sit through the angry debrief led by Bernard Roux, discomfited by rising his blood pressure.

"I know he intended to kill the Tiger, but honestly, the trial was a travesty, even by military standards." He flicked his shaking right hand at Mathieu inviting him to continue.

"You are going to have to cut back on these cigarettes, Chief."

"I didn't ask for the obvious. Tell the Lieutenant what happened at the court-martial."

Roux's wheeze darkened the atmosphere further. Phlegm soiled the handkerchief he had drawn from his pocket. His lungs ached in protest and his faced turned purple.

Mathieu spelled it out. "They made a big fuss of his being an anarchist, and to prove it, cited the books he kept on the shelf in his boarding room. The works of Homer and Marcus Aurelius."

"Since when did either of those pen an anarchist tome?" Roux's ragged cough continued to strain his anger. "Followed by a book by Auguste Comte, father of French scientific philosophy? Incredible. How could any man call himself educated and claim that these world famous texts were the foodstuff of anarchists?"

They were genuinely affronted. Indeed, Roux was personally insulted. How they would laugh at the stupidity of the French court. But he was far from finished. "Then," he spat, almost swallowing his Gauloises in apoplexy, "they pulled out Flammarion's *Astronomy*, one of the most beautifully designed and important works of the last century, and concluded that all of these literary treasures added up to anarchism, Bolshevism, and rebellion. If Flammarion is an anarchist, I'm the King of Indo-China." His spluttering choked him to silence.

Mathieu intervened. "It was, as the Chief says, embarrassing. The prosecutor, Mornet, sporting his war medals to underline his importance, made a spurious comment about Cottin's intention to kill Clemenceau when the Germans were seventy kilometers from the gates of Paris. We couldn't understand what he was talking about. Germans at the gates of Paris? One of the court officials spoke to him and he corrected himself, claiming that Cottin had declared his intention to kill Clemenceau as far back as May of last year. Not last month. It became more and more absurd."

On a second telling it sounded so ridiculous that any fair person would have stopped the trial. But this was Paris. Bitter Paris. A Paris that had been terrorized. Paris that was determined to believe that it had won the war. And Emile Cottin was, in the eyes of even-minded citizens, a terrorist. Furthermore, the military court had to find a victory where it could. Stories had begun to circulate of courts-martial on the front line in 1917 where shell-shocked youths and men had been executed for refusing to fight as an example to others. Confused, shaken, ill, and enfeebled by months at the front, it made no difference to the comfortably uniformed upholders of military justice. The poor victims of harsh front line verdicts would have no place in the glory of France's victory. They were sentenced to be airbrushed from history.

"Cottin was the only one with a sense of dignity." Mathieu parted company with any pretense of impartiality. "His lawyers told the truth. Yes, he had tried to shoot the prime minister and failed. Yes, it was politically motivated, but given his youth and lack of guidance, the court should have consider a measure of clemency."

His coughing fit concluded, Bernard Roux finished the story. "It took ten minutes for the military court-martial to deliver its predicted judgment. Guilty. Unanimous decision. Death sentence passed. Long Live France." He threw up his arms in despair. Contempt rattled the room till the echo died in a silence of embarrassment.

Raoul's Story

THREATS

I fell to my knees and lifted my eyes to the high heavens. Blessed are those who hunger and thirst after righteousness, for they shall be satisfied. That was God's promise. And that was me. I thirsted for righteousness and slew the evil Jaurès. My grandmother was a mystic, you know. She claimed to have had a visitation from the Blessed Virgin Mary. It caused considerable interest and some annoyance. Had she not gathered a reputation for dabbling in astral nonsense, the Abbe might well have taken forward her claim, but they said there was no guarantee that she would behave appropriately. I always behaved appropriately. But you know that, my friend. Everything that Charles promised was falling into place. Everything in my life had meaning again. I was determined that when they announced that they wanted to build statues in my honor, I would say, no. At least, I would at the start. I knew that I would probably have to give way to such demands, eventually.

A court-martial condemned Emile Cottin to death. Quite so. You couldn't permit anarchists to take pot-shots at a prime minister. Seven shots. They say, he fired seven shots and failed to kill Clemenceau. Huh. Two shots and I blew off Jaurès' head.

Maîtres Giraud and Bourson came in person to give me the good news that my trial date had been set, but I already knew. Carbolic had alerted me. Must have read it on the governor's desk as he claimed. I was beginning to think that the governor left things on his desk so that Carbolic, I could not remember the name he preferred to be called, could let me know in advance. So it was to be March 24th. Splendid. But their attitude suddenly changed. I began to feel that this court case had more to do with them than me. Fifty-five months I'd been there. Fifty-five months of continuous instruction on what I must and must not say and then they began to treat me like a child.

"You will have your hair cut." Giraud's voice was harsh. Dogmatic. Unyielding, the bully

"You must grow a moustache, it will make you look softer," Bourson added as if I was to be a model for one of the fashion houses. The soft touch.

"You will be given a clean suit. Don't make a fuss, do you hear? It will be an ordinary suit. You will dress down for the court appearance. Do not ask answer questions about the clothes you were wearing when you killed Jaures."

What? My beautiful Hermes outfit? Surely I should look my best in court? A proud Frenchman of some means who would not tolerate the socialists and anarchists.

"Keep your eyes lowered until you are asked a question and then look directly at the judge or lawyer who is speaking to you." Did Giraud think I was a child-actor to be directed at every turn?

"You will be asked about your loyalty to France. Keep your head high and look proud to acknowledge that."

Well, obviously.

"Above all, do not call Jaures a traitor or bad-mouth him. Leave that to us." Giraud's conceit was obnoxious. I knew what to do and as the list of instructions became more and more repressive, I resented their inability to recognize that.

When they had gone I prepared a celebratory coffee. Its mouth-watering aroma drew Carbolic like a dog to the butcher's bone. God, what had I to call him, again? Moutie! Merde,.

But he knew things, and I liked talking to him…the way he held his head and nodded appreciatively did me good. He was crafty that one. He always managed to wheedle out my secret concerns.

"Did you know that I've been in prison without trial for nearly five years? That must be a record."

"Yes, Monsieur, I do. The government prosecutors have had to review your case every six months. They called it preventative detention." I swear he was on the point of salivating. His eyes never left my cup.

"Yes, my lawyers have managed to keep me out of court so that I couldn't be tried by the military. Good men. Know their job." On every count a lie.

"They must be costing you a fortune, Monsieur, such expensive lawyers." He smiled. Was that admiration or contempt? Or was it the needle to prick my resolve to silence. I almost told him that others were paying for my defense but caught myself in time.

"Only the best," I retorted, trying to mimic his pose.

"You do know that it was former Prime Minister Viviani, who asked the general prosecutor of the Seine to sign a postponement order on your original trial, and all of his successors have done likewise? Not your lawyers. The government was afraid that if your case went to court in 1914 it would put the sacred union between Frenchmen of all political inclinations at risk."

"Yes, of course." It's the way he spoke with such authority, as if he knew more than me that I always found annoying.

"The Human Rights League and some of Jaurès' friends have been clamoring for you to be brought to trial, Monsieur, claiming that it was unfair to you to be held in La Santé."

I had to put him in his place. "They don't give a sou about me. They think they can get their pound of flesh in revenge for the loss of the German-loving traitor, but they don't know…" I let the words drift towards the ceiling. Careful, Raoul.

"Don't know what, Monsieur?"

I was bored with the conversation but could not let him have the last word. "I have friends out there. They will look after me."

"You certainly have…but you also have enemies. You do realize that, surely?" He smiled again, that sly look on his face.

I laughed. Loudly. Scornfully. "Name them."

Without hesitation he rattled off a list of the riff-raff who had always been a danger to France.

"The left-wing press, L'Humanite in particular, the unions, the socialists, anarchists, the hundreds of thousands of ordinary people scarred by the war, and not just in France."

I had not considered this. Every time we spoke he managed to leave me feeling unsettled, but this was different. He was aggressive.

"I think you should go now. I have had enough of your impudence."

"You have had enough of MY impudence, you conceited nobody?" he retorted, his jaw set to intimidate. Carbolic came closer to me than he ever had, which was alarming on a number of levels. His breath smelled of the sour odor of decay. For the first time I realized that he had practically no teeth and his lips were stained with...was that nicotine? He was taller than I thought, and though his body bore the perma-smell of carbolic soap, his hair was matted and held in place by his own sweat.

"Go away. I don't want to see you again. Ever. Go, or I will call the warder." I was aware of the hesitation in my voice. Bastard knew how to upset me.

"You don't get it do you? You are a murderer. You killed an innocent old man in cold blood and you think you are going to get away with it. Well, you won't." HE was shouting at ME. "I make you this promise. I will make sure that you never rest easy."

"Help, help. Please, somebody help me." I couldn't stop myself shaking. The sheer effrontery of this pathetic ignorant man behaving like a thug overwhelmed me.

"Look for me at the Palais de Justice. Look for me in the streets. Be careful where you go at night. I will crawl into your head and invade your cozy conceited life, you bastard."

Stupid, I know, but when he slammed shut the cell door, I sank to the floor in relief. I'd see he lost his job. I would. My friends would. He'd be sorry. Then a deeper worry penetrated my soul like a burst dam which could no longer stem the river's flow. The statues? When they erected the statues? Would anarchists and no-good down-and-outs daub disgusting slogans along the base? Surely not.

34

24th March 1919 –
Blind Justice Mid-Morning

Although no. 36 literally abutted the Palais de Justice, Roux's special team decided to follow the old routine to celebrate the first day of Villain's trial. It would be the beginning of the end for Mathieu for whom the savage slaying of Jean Jaurès remained a crime in desperate need of punishment. They met for breakfast at the Café de Deux Ponts as they had for the entire week of Henriette Caillaux's trial five years before.

"It's like old times." Dubois rubbed his hands together in anticipation of the wonderful croissants which, as before, were already on their way from the kitchen, with just a world war in-between. "Remember how Guy used to say…" His words died as he spoke, drowned in a memory still too painful to talk about. They fell silent. That was the problem with war. The fighting might stop, but the hurt did not. Its victims lived on in the hearts and minds of those who cared and flitted into conversation uninvited, releasing pain and guilt, which though undeserved, broke ranks and asked, why me?

"Was that Guy Simon? I've seen his name on the role of honor, but never knew that he was part of this team." Jacques looked into their faces, croissant in hand, and realized that he was the only one to have touched his.

"Died in the first week of the war. We begged him not to go…but he insisted. Thought it would be over in a month." Mathieu picked up his coffee and let his eyes drift over the river. He'd not thought of Guy recently. So much had happened.

"It wasn't the only bad decision he made that week." The words were out before the chief realized that he had spoken. Dubois and Mathieu internalized the sentence and looked first at each other and then at Roux. Stunned. What did he mean? Three croissants cooled on the plate.

"I, ehm…I didn't mean… Yes…I'll explain later." He was clearly embarrassed.

"These croissants are superb." Jacques wiped his mouth with the napkin unaware of the tension. "Are you going to leave them? I'll help out if necessary," he joked, expecting a rude riposte. The silence hurt. They had not heard him.

"I will explain. In the office." Bernard Roux's pallor went even paler and markedly older eyes looked out from his tired face. "Later." He pushed the plate of croissants away and rose to smoke outside.

"I was only asking," Jacques tried to apologize as if he had made some gross error of judgment.

"It's the trial … and the memories we carry of the night of Jaurès' murder. They run deeper than we realize," Dubois said, knowing full well that there were unanswered questions which troubled those who had been present. He had forgotten that.

"This trial won't take long, will it? Be over in a day, surely. It's all very straightforward. He was caught in the act of murdering a man in cold blood in front of more witnesses than you could find in the Moulin Rouge on a Saturday night."

A deep and painful sigh wracked Mathieu's body as he rose to leave. His half-empty cup held no appeal. "French Justice is a lottery, my friend. You should know that, Jacques." His words drew pain. They left the café sad and somber. Three croissants turned cold on the table and hardened quickly, untouched, unwanted and quickly forgotten. Like the memories Mathieu wished could be forgotten.

NOTHING CAN GO WRONG

Special treatment is something that you should deserve. And I did. Most certainly.

The warden escorted me personally to the rear of the Palais de Justice and marched me through the glistening corridors towards a studded oak door which opened as if by magic into the inner chambers. In the shining marbled anteroom, normally the exclusive reserve of defense lawyers, Maîtres Giraud and Bourson were carefully dressing themselves in the robes of their office, glancing first at the wall length mirrors and then at the ribboned files which were neatly piled on the central space. They looked at me without uttering a word and continued their ritual transformation. Neither spoke until they were fully dressed.

"You've been carefully prepared, Raoul. Nothing can go wrong." Bourson, as ever, oozed optimism.

"Yet one can never be completely prepared for the twists and turns of such a public trial. Remember, if in doubt, say nothing," glowered Giraud, raising his index finger to emphasize his authority. God, I hated them both. In their black raised cap, gown, and white-laced neckpiece they picked at the documents which had been amassed over the last five years like magpies at the municipal rubbish-tip, touching this juicy morsel which, though unrelated to the case, might catch a headline or make the jury sit up and listen; picking up another, pecking over the content, then dropping it as if it were rat poison. Within two minutes the neat files were strewn haphazardly across the desk.

Bourson sat down and for a fleeting second I'm sure that he contemplated the consequence of failure. Untenable failure. But the doubt passed.

"You'll be exemplary, I know."

"Yes, you will," Giraud sneered contemptuously. "Too many have too much to lose if your case goes badly."

I was about to become the biggest celebrity in France at a time of celebrity overkill. The front pages of every newspaper had been filled for months with international politicians and generals whose names were known worldwide; names which commanded respect, not because it was deserved, but for what they now represented. Move over, President Wilson and his insufferable advisor, Mandell House; Lloyd George and his foreign secretary, Alfred Balfour; Marshalls Foch and Joffre, Georges Clemenceau and his finance minister, Klotz and many of the hangers-on who had filled the front pages for months. Now was my moment.

Giraud and Bourson preened themselves. They had completed the first stage in their task and been well paid. My lines had been rehearsed, my moves prepared, my gestures carefully directed. No time for stage fright. The jury had been handpicked; all male, all middle-class, all trusted and loyal.

At 12:30 the President of the Court, Boucart, entered the chamber, bowed to the legal fraternity, smiled towards the jury, and posed regally at his bench. The calm atmosphere offered no comparison to the near riot which accompanied Madame Caillaux's daily performances half a decade ago. A side door opened and the audience hushed. The curtain rose. Act One was about to begin. I entered the chamber slowly, hesitantly, almost deceitfully, aware of my audience and the task that lay before me.

35

24th March 1919 –
Blind Justice Mid-Afternoon

"*Merde*," Mathieu whispered to Dubois, "they've dressed him up like a bank clerk. Where are the expensive clothes he was wearing when we arrested him?"

"Christ Almighty," Dubois responded. "I think he's wearing women's make-up."

Mathieu looked at the thin pale figure at the dock, his blond hair neatly trimmed, his light moustache adorning a quivering upper lip.

"Moutie said that he had put himself on a diet of rich coffee, but this is ridiculous."

Villain appeared dazed by his circumstances.

"Look at the jury," Roux advised. "Look at them, they're smiling at him. He's taken them in already." The President of the Court leaned forward to hear Raoul Villain's soft-toned reply to the formal questions about his age and family history. To the astonishment of the few neutral observers in attendance, he proceeded to lead Villain through a list of personal tragedies for the benefit of the jury. Questions were asked which painted him as a lost soul who had never had a chance to develop normally.

"You never knew your mother?"

Through pouted lip he nodded. "I was aged four when they took her away to an asylum."

"Your grandmother had visions of the Blessed Virgin?"

He shrugged his shoulders and bent his head to the left as if the question was a mark of shame. "Yes, Sir. I have been told so."

"You were educated by the Jesuits?"

"Yes, Sir, for six years, and then at a High School."

This was not news to Mathieu, Dubois, or the Chief. They had read his files. Indeed they had helped fill out some of the detail. What followed astounded them. The President of the Court turned to Raoul Villain's military service and once more led him by the nose through what could have been an emotional minefield. "You had a bitter experience during your military service, did you not? You were happy at first to don the uniform of your regiment but you were shocked by the deception you found there."

"That's not even a question." Jacques began to understand that all was not as straightforward as he anticipated.

"You were mocked by others when you spoke of loyalty to France?"

"Yes indeed, Sir." There was a brief silence as if the judge was waiting for him to say more. Maitre Giraud came close to intervention.

"And in the barracks you were dismayed and offended by the outright disloyalty shown by your fellow soldiers?" Saved by the President of the Court.

"Yes, yes indeed." He cleared his throat to buy a second's grace. Then he remembered his lessons. "I *was* shocked, that's right, I was very shocked to hear the man who lay in the next bunk to mine ... who was in the guard of honor ... singing songs by the revolutionary jingoist, Montéhus ..."

He began to dry up, so the judge helped him again. "Do you mean communist anthems?"

"Yes, Monsieur, I do."

"Dreadful," Boucart said, loud enough for the jury to hear. Every effort was made to portray Raoul Villain as a fine Catholic boy who became a quiet respectful citizen. Testaments to his good behavior were read to the court. These apparently came from landlords he stayed with in Rues Fleurus and Duguay. Mathieu noted that the police had no such information.

Jacques nudged Mathieu gently and inquired whether he was to be called to give evidence.

"They know I'm here ... so are all the journalists from *L'Humanite* who were in the Café Croissant that night, but this is not about reminding the jury what actually happened."

The story, as repeated by everyone protecting Raoul Villain, became more ridiculous by the hour. Having spent time creating the image of a child who lacked all of the normal affections associated with motherhood, the judges then helped create the notion that he was a patriot.

Mathieu was livid. "If every motherless boy in France turned into an assassin claimed he was a patriot, we would have no politicians left."

"Good point," said Dubois. "Pity it's a piece of dog shit philosophy. What followed was a heart-warming picture of a young man, inspired by a visit to Alsace, to free the young people there. Allegedly he carried a photograph of the Kaiser in his pocket and had planned to kill him."

Roux turned to his men and shook his head slowly. "This is entirely bullshit. We had the records to disprove it all, but they've disappeared. Now we know why."

President Boucart continued the fantasy. "You were particularly upset by the action that Jean Jaurès was taking to stop the outbreak of war, were you not, and the idea to kill him replaced the idea you have previously had to kill the Kaiser?"

"Yes, Monsieur le President."

And you were at your grandmother's funeral in Reims when Jaurès and his colleagues from the socialist international went to Brussels to meet with the German delegates ... the same ones who went back to Berlin and voted for the finances for the war?"

"Yes, Monsieur le President."

"This is too much." Dubois was incensed. "They are twisting the facts into fiction. He went to Reims on 24 July. The Brussels international conference was on the 29th."

"And you came back to Paris determined to kill Jean Jaurès."

"Yes, Monsieur, but I did not know that he had a wife or children."

"Bloody hell. This is pathetic. Do you think anyone's going to tell the court that Jaurès' son Paul was killed fighting the Germans in Picardy last June?"

"And you did this out of patriotism?"

Mathieu and Bernard Roux pushed their way out of the courtroom. They could take no more. Dubois followed, blowing his nose into a frayed handkerchief. Jacques came running to catch up with them before they disappeared into a tavern on the left bank.

"You won't believe it but he ended his account by claiming that he shot Jean Jaurès on impulse."

Roux bought four brandies and told Jacques that if he didn't drink brandy, he'd transfer him to the customs office in the Pyrenees. Jacques usually avoided strong drink but if there was a moment to start, this was it.

"All this effort to turn Villain into a hero? I don't follow, I really don't. We arrested him, we had the murder weapons in our hands, he confessed, several times over. We had the evidence ... but they are rewriting it. Why?"

Mathieu smelled the dark promise of five-star Cognac and swilled it in its glass. "Why?" He looked for inspiration from Roux. Even after all that they had been through, the chief superintendent's secrets ran deeper than the city's metro system; deeper than the secret sewers under the city. Bernard Roux had grown into his senior years trusted by all sides of the political spectrum because he kept his counsel. In his elevated position at the Deuxième Bureau, he had access to many government departments, but not an inch beyond the closed file on those who owned France. Those who truly owned the nation, its politics and its people. Its wealth.

"He is the perfect whipping boy. He is able, but chooses at times to appear limited in his capacity to think for himself. He was active with Action française, and most likely he still is, and has powerful allies because of that. He has kept his secrets for five years and will not be broken now. His official records have been altered. And he is a beacon. With the war won, with victory on our side, he can be hailed as a hero. We all heard the judge. He will be declared a patriot by the right-wing parties. They have a champion. In five years' time he will be forgotten... and so will Jaurès."

"Why do we bother? Why do we spend our lives trying to bring criminals to justice when the system is corrupt?" Mathieu felt personally aggrieved; so too did Dubois.

"Because without us there would be anarchy. We have to make do in the knowledge that we do what we can... but we cannot always reach the real criminals."

"Like the men who made the war?" Jacques's question was unexpected but welcome.

"Like the men who made the war." Bernard Roux swallowed his Cognac and set his glass on the table with sufficient emphasis to indicate that he wanted another. Jacques rose to oblige.

Mathieu and Dubois turned to the chief. One question hung heavily over the table. It had to be answered.

"Guy Simon," Roux whispered. "You want to know why I said what I did about poor Guy." Neither flinched.

"Yes, Sir, we do," Dubois admitted.

He paused to seek comfort in a Gauloises and spoke in a quiet voice which confirmed the confidentiality of what he was about to impart.

"If I can take you back to the night Raoul Villain was arrested and brought to the precinct at Montmartre for a first interrogation. We were interrupted unceremoniously by the then Assistant Prefect Guichard who took him off our hands and bundled him into the back of a police wagon."

They nodded.

"You will remember that Guichard took everything from the table with him, but Mathieu's notes were on his lap and he kept them where they were. Guy was in the room, but had not been previously involved. Indeed I recall that he came in after we had begun. Next day Guichard knew all about it. Someone had informed on us. The assistant prefect wanted to have us disciplined for disobeying his instructions, but I had a friend at the prefecture at Ile de la Cite. A very high ranking friend who told me later that Guy Simon kept Guichard informed behind my back. Apparently they were both in the same branch of the masonic order. I didn't pursue the connection. But I knew then whose side Guy was on."

Jacques had started to put four glasses of fine Cognac on a tray at the café bar.

"But he kept the pistols, did he not? He could have handed them over."

"True, and that worried me. It worries me still. Just how many pistols were there that night? Did we ever establish that as a fact?"

"No," Mathieu conceded. "A world war got in the way and Guy never said goodbye."

"Bastard." Dubois gave the word real feeling. Then relented. "Poor bastard."

Jacques unloaded the tray onto the table, but the fact that his colleagues had suddenly stopped their conversation was not lost on him. He stood to attention and raised his glass.

"A toast, I think. To Guy Simon … because, gentlemen, he died for the France he believed in."

Simple words which cut across the pain they had unlocked. Clever Jacques. Intuitive genius. They rose as one and raised their swirling Cognacs. The amber nectar, darkened by its years encased in Limousin oak took on a lighter hue. Jacques looked 'round, waiting for someone to give a lead but they yielded place to him, the youngest, the only man who had not served with Guy.

"To Guy Simon, remembered by his friends for the good he did."

It wasn't Shakespeare; he wasn't Mark Antony, but the perfect simplicity of his sentiment moved them.

"Guy," they toasted in unison.

Raoul's Story

DAY OF JUSTICE

'm delighted with the first day of the trial. I gave a good account of myself. Of course I was nervous. All of those bearded faces watching my every move.

Have you ever wondered if everyone else in the room can read your mind and you're the only person who can't reciprocate? That everyone else knows what you're thinking? That's how it felt coming through the door into the chamber, dressed down like an apprentice accountant without two sous to rub together. Honestly, when I saw the suit they brought me, I was stunned. Henri Giraud explained that I mustn't appear wealthy or supported in any way. They wanted me to act as though I was in fear and trembling. That wasn't difficult. In fact at the start I was dumbstruck. Couldn't remember any of the cues I had been taught, but the President of the Court came to the rescue. He was wonderful. He looked at me encouragingly and nodded his head as if to say "trust me I'm on your side. I know what I'm doing."

And he did. Whenever I got tongue tied, he found the right phrase. At one point I stood like an elementary student under examination, hands clasped over my midriff, invited to explain how I felt on the night I blew Jaures' head off. I couldn't speak. My silence almost defeated me but the president stepped in.

"Let me rephrase that, did you act in a fit of patriotic anger?"

Perfect. I remembered my cue and replied, "That was exactly it, Monsieur, a blinding fit of patriotic anger." He provided my motive for slaying Jaures on a plate. Salome would have relished the moment. Patriotic anger. Amazing. What a man. He found the very words I had forgotten to explain my motive to the jury.

Then I had to suffer the indignity of hearing what three doctors thought of my mental health. The nerve of them. Doctors Claude, Briand, and Dupre. If their names suggest three clowns from Pinder's Circus, then nothing could've been more apt. I was described as...wait for it... "An incomplete human being...unbalanced and unfinished..."At which my trusty lawyers entered the fray. They jumped to their feet and shouted, "It was a crime of passion!"

Where had that come from? Brilliant, all the same.

"It was a noble passion...because what motivated him was a passion for his country...a passion for France. He did it for France." Giraud swirled his black cape like an ancient Senator of Rome might wrap himself in his toga to emphasize his family's importance.

Noble passion?

Magnificent.

I almost cheered myself.

One of the jury members clapped, as did a number of the lawyers and journalists.

298

"Noble in principle and disastrous in its consequences," added the advocate general, pursuing the theme as if the thought had just come to him. I kid you not. The advocate general weighed in on my side. In two short phrases he captured the case of the defense and the summed up the prosecution's line of attack. Incredibly, they did it without me. I knew at that moment it was all over for Jaures' apologists.

I enjoyed the summing up, which they eventually began on the fifth day of the trial. At last Maîtres Giraud and Bourson earned their coin, whomsoever paid for it. I confess there was a heart-stopping moment when a letter was read out in court which I had no recollection of writing. I must have, or was it written by my lawyers? Anyway, according to that letter it appeared that I was the person who requested the postponement of the original trial whose date was set for December 1914. As I remember it, in December 1914, we had only just stopped the Germans at the gates of Paris. Apparently, I suggested that the trial should be postponed on the grounds that national unity, the sacred union between political parties and unions, had to be protected at all costs, and that my trial would have dredged up old wounds between the right and left which would then have damaged the unity of France. In other words, I sacrificed my own chances of liberty in order to maintain the unity of the French people…

Magnificent. I really wish I had written it.

I mean, does that sound like me? Well, yes and no. Yes, if I am to be acknowledged as an important figure and no if you think that I am an imbecile…a lesser being…not a whole man…. incomplete, the bastards.

The prosecution had the damned cheek to raise the question of Emile Cottin who had been very properly condemned to death for the attempted assassination of the prime minister. I laughed internally when Maitre Bourson dismissed the name Cottin and reminded the court that in 1914, Madame Caillaux was found not guilty of murdering the editor of Figaro. He reminded the jury that there were two major differences between Cottin and myself. The doctors agreed that he was fully cognizant of all that he planned to do. There was no doubt about his mental health, whereas I had been described as unbalanced, a victim to a noble passion. He, in contrast, was motivated by anarchy and Bolshevism. Fantastic stuff.

Bourson turned directly to the men of the jury and spoke from his well-rehearsed script. It was a tour de force.

"Gentlemen, we know that Raoul's actions were legally wrong. But I appeal to you to find kindness in your hearts after all the years of death and destruction we have suffered together, to reach into your souls and find that precious word. Forgiveness. Pardon the boy. He has erred, but he did so for France."

Where is that little woman with the handkerchiefs when you need her? But the final line was mine. We'd rehearsed it many times over. As soon as Maitre Bourson had finished he bowed to me and I stood, straight-faced, and completed the charade.

"I humbly ask pardon for what I did to Jaurès and his family and for the shame I have brought on my own father and brother. I will never be able to shed the guilt of the misery I have caused a widow and her fatherless daughter. I will carry this with me always."

I don't know how many times they warned me not to mention the son who was killed at the front last year. Unlucky, that.

And then the verdict. I was lead into an anteroom and joined by Maîtres Giraud and Bourson. By that time they had earned my utmost respect, and we had coffee together. I was rambling on about their dramatic performances but they were keen to insist that I should take nothing for granted in case something went wrong and we had to go to appeal. That took me aback. No one had mentioned appeal at any stage over the last five years. Within minutes, and I mean within barely ten minutes, for the coffee was still hot, there was a knock on the door and we were summoned back into the chamber. The President of the Counsel asked the foreman of the jury, twelve honest Parisian gentlemen, if they had come to a conclusion and I began to shake.

"Is Villain guilty of voluntary homicide on the person of Jean Jaurès? Was this homicide committed with premeditation?" To each question he answered, "No." Loudly and proudly. The initial reaction from the Jaures camp was disbelief and their protests were slammed down by the judge. The court began to empty. I felt my legs give way and sat in the dock waiting; drawing breath. I waited for the hand of congratulation, the flow of praise to which I was surely due, the back-slapping and the shared euphoria of judicial victory, but no one rushed to shake my hand. The jury kept their eyes firmly rooted to the floor as they filed out. The chamber took on the mantle of guilt, as if a great wrong had been condoned by everyone in the court, but no one wanted to acknowledge it, be associated with it, or even see it.

I felt soiled. Used and abused by my co-conspirators. This was wrong. I ought to have been elated. Everyone associated with my struggle over the fifty-five month incarceration, ought to have headed to the Ritz for a champagne dinner. I should have been carried on their shoulders out of the Palais de Justice to fame and freedom. Maîtres Giraud and Bourson eventually realized that I had been left in splendid isolation and turned back to help me to my feet. No journalist waited for a comment; I felt … incomplete.

36

APRIL 1919 – IN PURSUIT OF PEACE

Mathieu's head was fit to burst. The world had surely spun off its axis. Cynicism had taken over a broken nation and twisted critical fact into ugly fiction. Artists had begun to experiment with nonsense such as irrational sculpture and painting. Nothing was real anymore. He was overwhelmed by emotional exhaustion, like the clergyman who discovers that there is no God. He was that man. The law enforcer who discovers that there is no law. The representative of justice who now knows there is no justice. He felt empty and useless.

Agnès was slowly recovering from the debilitating Spanish flu which almost took her life, but found herself in a much-changed world which expected women to retreat to subservient ways. She intended to return to nursing as soon as she was physically able. She had to be patient, but it was a lonely recovery because Mathieu seemed to hold himself responsible for every evil in the country. And that was dragging him down. He had been temporarily sidelined from responsibility for the prime minister's security because of the trial, but hankered to return.

At no. 36, gloom pervaded the building. Raoul Villain's verdict took the ridiculous to new levels of farce. Left-wing papers, the workers, unions, socialists, Republicans, and Democrats were outraged by the effrontery of the injustice to their former champion, Jean Jaurès. Few realized that it was also an effrontery to upholders of the law.

Chief Superintendent Roux anticipated the potential potholes in the road ahead.

"Before anyone else says it, I know that the consequences will reverberate around the nation and we will be expected to keep the city calm. I've been in touch with the prime minister's office and he wants to stay well away from any association with the verdict. His advisors think they can ride this out by doing and saying nothing. The Tiger does not want his name associated with anyone in the courtroom."

"It's not going to go away." Mathieu was convinced.

"I know, it's the Caillaux affair all over again," Roux agreed, "with no chance of an imminent war to make people forget. Everyone is consumed by it. If

Lloyd George, Clemenceau, and President Wilson agreed to dance the can-can at the Moulin Rouge, no one would turn up except the right-wing press looking for an indiscreet photograph. It's Villain they want to talk about."

Jacques spluttered his coffee over his trousers. "The very thought. But you're right, Chief. Trouble's ahead and if it's not a crime to blow Jaurès' head clean off his shoulders then how safe are the world's statesmen from all sorts of imbeciles who populate this city?"

"Precisely. We've alerted the embassies. I've asked that every incoming delegate and representative be advised of the likelihood of trouble on the streets." Roux was both somber and worried.

"There are so many different agendas running around at the present moment that we can hardly keep up with them. We're sitting on a powder keg in an arsenal and we don't know the length of the fuse."

Mathieu perked up and looked at them. "We've been here before, look-ing the wrong way when the real story is elsewhere. We may be missing something big. What else is going on?"

"Well, the so called peace talks, and some of the newspapers are begin-ning to ask if the war is really over. What if the Germans refuse to sign?" Dubois offered a worrying thought.

"Then they will probably starve to death, or Bolshevism takes over. I don't think they will refuse to sign a treaty of sorts … but is that the issue?" Jacques was intrigued.

"No, it would have to be happening right in front of our eyes, but hid-den by the Villain trial. If the people who pull the strings timed his court appearance to suit, this outrage will be covering something bigger."

Jacques felt that his mentor was taking matters too far, was seeing con-spiracy where none existed.

"You really believe that, Mathieu? That nameless people pull the strings? We would surely know, wouldn't we? Nothing gets passed no.36."

Whether Jacques believed that to be fact, Mathieu didn't know, but his eyes rested on the man behind the table. Was he hiding behind his Gauloises?

"Chief, you know my suspicions, and you have your own. Have we been drawn to the Villain case like mosquitoes to a lamp? The outcome was fixed for sure and Paris is completely absorbed by what will happen next. Half the country is focused on the insult to Jaurès' memory. Why now? Why not im-mediately the Armistice was signed? Why wait five months more?"

Roux scratched his ear, smoothed his moustache, and drew on his cig-arette. "Answer your own question. What else is going on in public but forced off the front pages?"

Dubois, Jacques, and Mathieu had nothing to offer.

The chief superintendent was surprised. "What's going on in the Assembly?"

"That stuff about the Comité des Forges? Those claims that they were working with the Germans?" Dubois asked.

"What!" Mathieu jumped to his feet. "How the hell did I miss that?" He was talking to himself, horrified that he had not picked this up. He had had Agnès, Clemenceau, and Villain on his mind. Little wonder it had passed him by. There was unfinished business there. Bitter, twisted business.

"Putain. They've covered one scandal by stirring another."

Raoul's Story

A Taste of Disappointment

I'm so disappointed I want to cry.

I feel used, like a brand new sponge specifically bought to clean the stains from a soiled nation which, job done, has been tossed aside, dirty, unwanted, of use to no one.

And I was promised so much.

When they drove me away from the Palais de Justice that evening, Maurice, Conrad, and Theo, I thought they had been sent to bring me to the inner core of the New France. Victorious France. France, where Alsace and Lorraine were once again reunited with the motherland. They were strangely tightlipped in the car.

"Keep your head down," I was advised. "Keep your head down!" Conrad's manner was aggressive. He almost pulled me to the floor of the car. That shook me. What was this? I had expected a Champagne reception.

"Why, why would I do that?" It made no sense.

"Because someone might blow it off," Theo quipped.

They started to laugh, not with me, but at me. They drove to a small auberge on the outskirts of the city. Because they forced me to the floor, I wasn't certain which district we were in but the word salubrious could not be attached. The building was distinctly third-rate. More of a hostel than a hotel. Paint had not been waved in its direction since the turn of the century and in the growing dusk it looked threadbare from the outside. Theo drew up in a side street and let the engine die. Maurice pulled out a bundle of notes and thrust them into my hand.

"This will cover your costs for a couple of days. We would advise you to leave Paris as soon as you can. Certain parties will be in touch about a bank account which will be opened in your name by a very generous benefactor." Their attitudes had certainly changed over the five years I was imprisoned. What had I done to offend them?

"How will you find me, if I leave Paris?"

"Don't worry about that, my friend. We will always know where you are. Always." There was menace in Conrad's promise.

Theo grabbed my arm and thrust his face into mine. His smile had morphed into an icy grimace, friendless, threatening violence from eyes that narrowed into contempt.

"You understand the conditions, Villain?"

"Wh...what conditions?" It made no sense.

"Your silence, idiot. One word about us and you will mysteriously disappear. Probably an angry anarchist or socialist who recognized you and took the law into his own hands."

"What are you talking about?" I simply did not understand.

"This is goodbye, Raoul. You have been spared the guillotine and rescued by your friends. Now you must remake your life elsewhere. We do not expect to see you again. Ever."

Theo got out of the Renault and from the rear, produced a small suitcase. "This is yours." It was, though I had not seen it for years.

"Good luck." Maurice had to push me out. I could not fathom what they meant and stood on the pavement in the darkness, lost like an orphaned refugee. A stranger in a strange land.

Paris looked so bleak when seen close up. Streets which backed away from the main thoroughfare hung jaded, exhausted by war. A cold spirit had descended over the entire arrondissement. Everything I had dreamt of turned to mockery. Inside, the lodging house offered little comfort. A sour-faced war widow glowered from behind the reception desk, her ancient mantilla drawn tight over her head and shoulders. She was thin. Painfully thin, and the black lace over her sparse hair held what was left in place. She looked quizzically as if she was unsure why I was standing there.

"Yes?" she croaked. No introduction. No manners. No interest.

"I need a room for tonight."

"Name?"

I hesitated. Who was I again?

"Name, Monsieur?

"Raoul…" Nothing followed. I choked on my own surname.

"Well, Monsieur Raoul, pay first and I will show you to your room."

This was not how it was supposed to be. I had stepped back in time to the squalor of a different age. I wandered around the streets next day, carefully avoiding the eyes of passing workmen. Paris had shrunk; lost its class. I saw the damage inflicted by the Germans. The trouble with modern warfare was that we all had to accept the consequence. It was unfortunate, but there you are.

I treated myself to a three course lunch at La Grand Véfour in the arcade of the Palais Royal. Before the war I had only ever peered through its majestic windows in awe of the ornate neo-classical interior, the chandeliers, and silver-decked, pure white linen-dressed tables, its walled mirrors with gold edging. I never imagined that I could afford to eat there. Maurice had pushed hundreds of francs into my hands. When I counted them at the auberge, there were almost one thousand francs in large denominations. I could afford their outrageous prices. Dressed in the clothes which I wore on that special day in 1914, I entered the restaurant and asked for a seat in the far corner. The doorman, in formal morning suit, permitted me a half bow while in the process assessed the class of my clothes, from toe to head. I sat with my back to the door, fit only for my own company, Duck liver pate was followed by a stunning lamb dish with all the trimmings. The silverware gleamed its reflection in the mirrors. A waiter looked twice in my direction and I bowed my head. Had he recognized me? Christ, he was coming over.

"Is monsieur ready for dessert? I would suggest the crème brûlée. It's the chef's specialty."

"Wonderful." I tried to sound confident. But suddenly I realized that fear was sitting at my shoulder. Every look in my direction frightened me. "Blow my head off." That's what Theo said. And he called me an idiot. Me.

When I recalled that moment, the crème brûlée soured in my mouth. I had more pleasant company in La Santé. No one suggested blowing my head off in prison.

Enough. Time to go. I paid a bill so large that I imagined I had been charged for every customer in the room. Once outside I breathed a purer air. A walk would do me good. A seat in the Luxembourg gardens. I purchased a copy of Figaro and to my surprise my acquittal failed to merit the banner-headline I surely deserved.

And there it was, on the front page, at the bottom of the sixth and last column. But it read like an apology. It was insulting. The nameless journalist wondered if the verdict had been occasioned by the jury's desire to bring harmony to the nation or perhaps in response to my lamentable background and sad pitiable life? What insolence. These were the very people who urged that Jaurès be silenced in the days before the war. I did it for them. I did it at their behest. I did it with their connivance. And apparently Madame Jaures had been awarded only one franc in damages by the court. One franc! Well. That would make these upstarts think twice about taking on the champions of France.

Then I saw him. Staring at me, shamelessly, across the glistening grass of the manicured formal garden. He stood motionless beside Leduc's magnificent bronze statue dominated as it is by the proud stag, head raised, ears pricked, his clan gathered for protection against an unseen enemy. But I could see my enemy standing defiantly in contempt. Carbolic.

"What do you want, scumbag?" I yelled. Did he imagine that I would run away? From him? He turned towards the garden exit closest to the metro and disappeared from view. Was this all that was left for me? To be spied upon by the underclass?

In the solitude of a second night in my shabby room, I decided to face my father. I had been informed that the civil administration of the city had been transferred to Auxerre, south of Paris. My father and the entire court had been forcibly evicted to the famous Yonne city for safety. Sadly, five months after the armistice, they, too, were still displaced citizens in their own country.

37

April 1919 – Careers to Protect

Mathieu wanted answers, and he knew a man who could help. He also realized that he would have to face some of his personal nightmares. Mention of Comité des Forges reminded him of Zaharoff and the terror that had introduced Timon to his night-sweats. Mathieu knew that Zaharoff was off limits—officially. But there were serious allegations about the manner in which these steel moguls across Europe and America had manipulated the war to their own advantage. No wonder Villain's trial had been scheduled to coincide with the formal inquiry into a malpractice which amounted to treason.

It took two phone calls to reconnect Mathieu with his former pilot friend, Pierre Flandin, who, having survived the war in the air, had taken his seat in the National Assembly. They met outside a café in the Rue de Lille close to the Palais Bourbon which housed the French parliament. Pierre looked slimmer and older, hair receding, moustache ample, and eyes burning with determination.

"Mathieu, or should I say Captain Bertrand," he grinned, gripping his hand firmly, "so good to see you. I assumed that you would be overwhelmed by the Villain affair. Bad business. Bad business, indeed." Pierre was as serious and straight-backed as Mathieu remembered. "What a tragedy for his family. I keep in touch with Marcel. He and his father are devastated."

"I'm sure, but so are a great many of us."

Rude though it might be, Mathieu had no time for small talk. "Pierre, what is happening here? Can you nail those bastards from the Comité des Forges for doing what they did…letting the Germans have control of all the forges, smelters, and mines at Briey?" To Mathieu's surprise, Pierre Flandin rose from his chair in the café and steered him outside. They crossed the boulevard to the river bank and walked towards the Quai d'Orsay.

"This is still a dirty convoluted business, but allegations of collusion run so far and so deep, that even I have to be careful about what is said and to whom it is whispered."

"How are they keeping the truth hidden? Why isn't it plastered across the headlines?"

"Because you are! Not you personally, but Villain and Jaurès and his family. Look, Mathieu, France believes that we won the war. Actually, we didn't. We managed not to lose it thanks to the Americans, but any politician who says so will be guillotined at the next election. The whole nation is trying to pick up the pieces and voters do not want to hear about military failures and bad news."

"But we know what was going on."

"Yes, we do. But are you listening to me? Back there," he pointed to the Assembly building, "even the socialists and republicans aren't focused on the facts. They are so insulted by what happened in the Palais de Justice that virtually all their time is spent planning a monumental march for Jaurès."

"It's no coincidence then? The parliamentary debate on Briey and Villain's trial?"

Flandin was hesitant. "We can't prove it. That's how clever it is. Oh, we are going through the motions, but the allegations aren't sticking. The Comité des Forges own more than half the newsprint in France, and they make our accusations sound like a left-wing attack on the government in response to Villain's acquittal."

Mathieu had to control his anger. Flandin was a politician. He might make it to the top someday. Surely he could do better than this?

"I remember three years ago a young flyer so fired by the injustice that the Germans had control of the Briey basin that he convinced his senior officer to let him and friends, one of whom still doesn't know the front-end of an aircraft from its arse, try to blow it apart? Do you remember that young man?"

Flandin sighed deeply. "Of course I do. It was ridiculous to put you in so much danger. I apologize for that. But these were desperate days. And it could have ended the war earlier."

"So tell them. Tell the Assembly. Bring the Comité des Forges to court."

"I've tried. I have told them about the military failure to take action. I told them that the war could have been brought to an end in 1915. I told them the whole story about the our attempt to bomb the bloody place and how we were crushed by the military high command. They don't want to know. People don't care. We won...and that is the only message the government, the prime minister, the president in particular, and the people want to hear. Not the truth."

He drew in a deep breath of early April air. Spring was threatening to burst through the winter miseries. Paris in spring was always special. With buds on the point of flowering, the boulevards assumed their first covering of leaves, days lengthened, and the city shook off the discontent of winter. People could reclaim the streets and pavements full of coffee drinkers, wine connoisseurs, and matrons, out to be seen in the coming fashions. Well, that's what it was before the war. But Paris had yet to recover. She, too, had been maimed by the ravages of war. It would take a decade to restore her former glories.

"There is another factor. You probably know this already at the Deuxième Bureau."

Mathieu's face darkened. "Another factor?"

"Are you aware that key evidence has been destroyed or removed?"

"I don't follow? What evidence?"

"Let me give you one example. When the Army High Command, and I mean the most important generals, were questioned by the Commission set up to investigate what happened at Briey, the generals shut down discussion by insisting that politicians knew nothing about the priorities of war and had no right to question the victor. It then emerged that in August 1914, when the decision was taken not to occupy the Briey basin and take or destroy all of the trappings of our industrial power, the orders were destroyed. Joffre issued a command that all documents were to be burned. There is no evidence against either our generals or those who gave them instructions, because these do not exist."

One thing was certain. Anyone who publicly criticized the army, the self-styled victorious and glorious army and a hero like General Joffre, would be pilloried. Of course Mathieu knew that there were no-go areas of inquiry, even at his level of security. Pierre Flandin was speaking from his heart, a rare thing in politicians.

"Barthe, the socialist leader, accused the iron and steel companies of being in cahoots with the Germans, but he was ripped apart by the right-wing press for peddling Bolshevik lies, and already this false news is being transformed into false history."

Flandin was close to tears. He grasped for words carefully, holding back emotions and memories which were encased in his soul.

"What truly disturbs me is that people don't care. They aren't interested in the facts. They want to pretend and move on. They're grasping at myths. Yes, Alsace and Lorraine have returned to the folds of our tricolor. But it's not enough. They want the peace treaty to crush Germany forever. France has moved from a theatre of war to a theatre of lies and half-truths."

Mathieu realized that his questioning had opened old wounds. Memories of friends less fortunate. Youth destroyed on the battlefield. Hope vanished in the war clouds. This was the reality of post-war survival. A name from the past could trigger yet more unguarded emotions. It wasn't over. Perhaps it never could be.

"Look, Pierre, I'm not here to question your commitment. I know what you have given for France. I know what you tried to do. I understand that you...no we, all of us, will have to live with the lies. But we can't give in. We have to find these people and deal with them."

"If we are allowed to. I mean, look what they have been able to do for Villain. He is free to lead his life while Jaurès is dead, his wife a broken widow, his daughter, traumatized. Do you know that his son Louis–"

"Was killed in June."

"Yes, Louis Jaurès fought with the tenth battalion in Artois, Verdun, the Marne, the Somme, the Ardennes, and Soissons. That is a list of regimental honor on its own. He gave his life even though his father was murdered in cold blood by an imbecile who stayed safely in jail and claims to have committed the deed for love of France. And there are people who believe that. Millions of them who want to believe that." Pierre Flandin's disgust was as deep as his.

"His time will come, believe me. He is no imbecile, remember that... but you mentioned evidence being removed...what else do you know?"

"Government documents, sensitive letters, records, and details of courts-martial have disappeared, and there must be more."

Years of experience had given Mathieu the ability to change the subject in a way which disarmed and surprised the person he was talking to. As a tactic, it had caught out many criminal liars.

"How honest is the prime minister?"

Pierre looked surprised. "You're asking me? I thought you worked with him. I'm not nearly as close to him as you are. Are you really asking if Clemenceau is part of a bigger conspiracy?"

"I suppose I am."

Flandin took a moment before replying. He stopped at the quayside and admitted, "I don't know. I don't think he is, but is Wilson or Lloyd George?"

"That's the problem. Who is? Who isn't? Who can we trust?"

"No one. But Clemenceau has one saving grace. He will listen to reason."

Villain might have been freed by a jury of his peers, but hundreds of thousands of Frenchmen were left betrayed. Justice itself had been debased to a point where the law stood unmasked, the scales weighed towards perversion. On Sunday April 6 three hundred thousand protestors crammed the Avenues and Boulevards around Place Victor Hugo, Place du Trocadéro, and Avenue Henri Martin in a triangle of solidarity outraged by the outcome of Villain's trial. To the relief of everyone at no.36, it was a dignified affair, led by literary and political figures, professors, senators, deputies, union leaders, and international representatives. Vast arrangements of magnificent flowers were delivered to Jaurès' wife and daughter at their house in the leafy Rue de la Tour but no gesture could bring back Jean Jaurès.

38

LANCING THE BOIL

Mathieu watched as Georges Clemenceau paced up and down his well-guarded apartment, ill at ease and uncomfortable with the fact that this political crisis had exploded on his watch, yet remained outside his control.

"Why did the stupid bastards at the Ministry of Justice rush Villain through the courts?" Mathieu tried to keep himself out of the firing line but Clemenceau caught sight of him on the lower stairwell.

"Captain Bertrand, a minute of your time, please." Mathieu skipped up the stairs, a veritable gazelle compared to the elderly statesman.

"What's happening on the streets? I mean, really happening."

"So far, so good. A couple of skirmishes on the outer fringes, but no rioting, burning, or looting."

"So far, you said." He turned to Mordacq. "Henri, what's the military view?"

"So far, so—"

"Right. I get it," he snapped abruptly. He was not a man given to patience. Once was enough. "But what can I do? I understand the public outcry. Not my fault. We're trying to keep the peace. Fine. But is it going to become a regular event? Will it escalate out of control? Disrupt the Conference? We cannot retry Villain. Where is he, by the way?"

"Immediately after the verdict, he was taken to a safe place by some interesting people. Members of Action française. First proof we have of their direct involvement." That was a fact. While Mathieu had always suspected their complicity, the Bureau had found no evidence up to that point.

"You must make sure that doesn't become public knowledge. A full-scale war between Right and Left would be catastrophic." Mordacq had a tendency to state the obvious.

Clemenceau stared at him with a sense of contempt. He knew that, too.

"There is one thing you could do, Sir." Mathieu surprised even himself, but the opportunity appeared and he took it.

"There is? What?"

"If you read the letters to newspapers from all kinds of citizens, hear discussions in café-bars and street corners, pick up what is being said in the Bureau canteen—"

"Spit it out, man. Tell me."

"It's the obvious injustice of Raoul Villain being found guilty of a crime he admitted, while Louis Cottin is condemned to death. Criminals with political clout are untouchable...those without have no protection. Least of all from the law."

"You mean, pardon Cottin? Come off it, man. I should definitely have him shot for missing me with so many bullets." This had become his standard comment, the ice-breaker for his fellow statesmen at the Conference. But it was no longer funny.

"Problem is, the president and half the Assembly want him shot as an example to others," Mordacq intervened.

"Just as they did with the traumatized front-line soldiers who had taken enough in the trenches by 1917?" Mathieu had no time for hypocrisy. "Hard line politics will break the nation in two. We need to compromise...Sir."

Mordacq did not disagree. Instead he closed the half open door and turned directly to the prime minister. "President Poincaré is, as we know, an utter asshole"

Mathieu did his best to show no surprise, but from the mouth of the prime minister's friend and confidant, it was unheard of. Of course the president was an asshole, but it was hardly politic to say so.

"You didn't hear that, Captain." Clemenceau's gaze never left Mordacq's face.

"He has had his war, won back Alsace and Lorraine, and is politically safe, for the present. But he has no understanding, not a clue about what life is like for our citizens." Mordacq's summary took Mathieu aback.

"The General is correct, Sir. If you decide to remove the death sentence from Cottin, people will know that you are listening to them. And they say that you do listen. You will be seen as the man who brought some balance back to French Justice."

"And it will piss off Poincaré." Mordacq certainly didn't like the president.

"But will it calm the streets?" Clemenceau wanted confirmation. He had already made his decision.

"Yes." Mathieu was adamant.

"I agree. And you can get back to running the Peace Conference. The others will see that you are the man in control." Mordacq knew how to deliver the coup de grâce. The tone of the prime minister's voice promised a decision.

"Fetch my secretary, Henri, please." Georges Clemenceau would reverse the findings of the court-martial. He began to laugh at the response he had concocted inside his head. *We cannot shoot him for missing me,* he would insist. *I won't allow it. Anyway as an old Republican and outspoken critic of the death penalty all my life I can hardly allow the misguided young man to be executed. He needs to learn to shoot properly.* It was a better line anyway.

Next morning, Louis Cottin's sentence was commuted to ten years of hard labor to the relief of his supporters. A fire was extinguished before it had the chance to burn Paris to a cinder. Peace talks continued unbroken.

Raoul's Story

A BRIEF REUNION

I knocked on the door of his nondescript house in Auxerre, half-way down a lane which narrowed into an ancient alleyway at the bottom, a stranger in a friendless land. Glancing around, there was little sign of activity. A few elderly citizens exchanged pleasantries with each other, but no one looked twice in my direction. The door was pulled open with some force and my father's voice barked the pained inquiry of a man who had been interrupted.

"Yes?" It was half question, half warning that peddlers would not be tolerated. "Yes?" he repeated but this time looked at the person in front of him. His eyes widened in surprise. Tension filled the space between us and burst into angry recognition.

"You!" He spat the word in my face as if it was a bullet, turned, and walked back into the house in silence, leaving the door behind him open. That was my father at his intimidating best. Personal rejection mixed with an unspoken invitation to follow him. I could never understand the complexity of his impulsive nature. The rage he bore; the blame he allotted; the guilt he never voiced. It seemed to me that everything he endured in life had been my fault...and still was. It wasn't Karl von Einem's third army that burned the Cathedral of Notre-Dame de Reims; it was me. And in still darker times I wonder whose face he saw at the door? Mine or my mother's?

What do you think, my friend?

"How could you do this to me? How could you insult your heritage by murdering an unarmed man, by shooting him in the back of the head. You coward," he screamed in my face. "Me, a guardian of the courts, a representative of our precious legal system. Marcel, risking his life in the skies for France...and you...a murderer...do you know what it's like to be father to a murderer?"

I refused to kowtow. "Not guilty. They found me not guilty, didn't they? If your precious legal system is so perfect, then you have to accept its perfect verdict." I drew breath and spat back in defiance, "Not guilty."

He sat on an armchair, put his hands on his head, and sobbed in self-pity. Him. He was the broken man. Him. "You murdered Jaurès. You and whomsoever put you up to it." His look promised a harsh interrogation. I was about to protest, but he raised himself up again and roared, "Don't lie to me. You're not capable of taking the decision to go to the toilet without a second opinion. I know you."

I had prepared myself for such a put down. "I did it myself and I did it for France." There was no place for half-hearted concessions.

"Stop it. Stop those lies. You prevented the one man who stood out against war from influencing the decision before it was too late."

"I stopped him weakening France. He was a traitor. A German-loving two-faced apologist for peace who would have ruined everything."

A woman whom I have never seen appeared from the kitchen and said that she had made a light lunch. "This is my son, Raoul," Father said without enthusiasm.

"I gathered that," she answered, "but you both have to eat, and I've prepared an omelet. I'm Marise, and I'm pleased to meet you."

The food smelled wonderful. Must have had cheese and spring onions with some mushrooms added to the basic eggs. We sat down with Marise between us. She talked of Auxerre, and asked about my experience in La Santé. It was not easy for him or for me, but Marise acted as a goodwill broker and blood pressures dropped accordingly.

Within twenty-four hours my suspicions were justified. My father rushed back from court after the morning session and slammed shut the front door.

"They know you're here. They know you are living with me…us."

"How?"

He shook his balding pate and confessed that he had not asked how. "One of the local Advocates came back from the Town Hall at about ten o'clock and told me there was a rumor circulating that you had fled Paris and come to Auxerre."

I knew I had been watched. Carbolic in the Luxembourg Gardens was no chance meeting, but I had not reckoned on being followed.

"The police know? That's good, isn't it? That means they can protect us here."

Marise went to the window, pushed the lace curtain aside, and looked up and down the street.

"I don't see anyone hanging about. Gendarme or anarchist."

She was a practical woman with a likeable nature. Forced out of Belgium in the first weeks of the conflict, age had filled her frame with ample sufficiency, and her plump cheeks had a tendency to hide her well lined face. But it was her eyes which promised levity, despite the burdens war had dumped on her. She told me she had been widowed in 1914. Her former husband had refused to leave Louvain once the German attack threatened to overwhelm the city. A librarian by profession, he had been with a group of his colleagues when the ancient repository was burned to the ground, and died with his books. I felt for her. And she did not blame me.

Who told the police? Why would the police be watching me, rather than watching out for me? I went for a walk next day through the medieval city with a clock tower at the heart of its culture, surrounded by old wooden houses in urgent need of restoration and narrowing cobbled streets which were not suited to modern transport. The Cathedral of Saint-Etienne beckoned and I dutifully made my way inside to admire the great renaissance edifice with its sumptuous stained-glass windows. A moment of calm reflection before the high altar restored my waning equilibrium. Closer to my God, I was home. A priest genuflected in the aisle beside me and spoke in quiet tones.

"Are you at peace, my son? Do you want to make your confession, Monsieur Villain?"

I felt propositioned. Had a price been mentioned, I might have been back in the Pigalle. Not that I frequented the Pigalle, mind you, save for occasional visits when my resolve is breached by temptation, apart. I looked at him, puzzled. Did I know him? Did he know me?

"Have we met, Father?" My politeness was forced upon me by upbringing.

"No, my son…"

"Then why do you presume to know me. Can I not speak to my maker without being harassed?"

He straightened to his full six foot frame, though his sallow appearance lent no threat to his action.

"Oh, forgive me, Monsieur Raoul…"

I whipped round in surprise. "How do you know my name?"

His voice softened as if to encourage some measure of confidentiality between us. "The street speaks of little else, my son."

"Then the street, and those who follow its frailties, should mind its own business." I turned back to my prayers, though they were not so much an act of devotion as an act of defiance.

But my presence in Auxerre gathered orchestrated hostility. My father became unnerved. He was unable to work properly, so he claimed. Marise was badgered in town when she went shopping. People began shouting obscenities towards me from outside the house. Each day more and more gathered in pathetic protest. Eventually the gendarmes appeared to move them along. But halfheartedly. Journalists knocked on the front door. Stories appeared in the local papers. Within a fortnight, my privacy became a myth. Though generally assumed to be a market town, Auxerre enjoyed its fair share of trades unionists and socialists and they were determined to hound me out of the city. A labor meeting became a department-wide rally against my presence. They gathered in the old town and marched to my father's home, chanting and booing. Normal life for all of us was impossible. Marise thought she should visit her sister in Valenciennes, leaving father on his own for the first time in years.

I gave in. It was my problem, not his. Without a by-your-leave, I slipped out of town and returned to Paris. Not pleasant. Not pleasant at all.

39

APRIL-MAY 1919 – THE NEW AMERICANS

The note had been placed on Mathieu's desk, as had quite a few since Moutie's time in the confessional at Saint-Gervais. His scrawl was thin and elongated, as if scratched with a sharp feathered nib. That was the only hint of elegance. If you were obliged to decipher the content, the task was decidedly harder, but Mathieu persisted and taught Moutie to leave readable cryptic messages.

The Tiger's life quickly returned to a more normal routine. He basked in the outpourings of goodwill after he reprieved Louis Cottin, though his clemency poisoned the already poor relationship he had with his own president. Roux reveled in the bad blood between the two elected leaders.

"Tiger outclasses that, and I use the word privately, gentlemen, pathetic cretin, Poincaré, any day of the week."

Mathieu pretended concern. "Careful, Chief. I've a career to protect."

"Definitely, Captain. I'll bear that in mind."

"The story about Sarah Bernhardt telling the Americans that 'Clemenceau is France' has riled our aforementioned president," Dubois added with relish.

"And every day one or two veterans leave their medals on his doorstep." Mathieu had had to deal with this growing demonstration of support for the prime minister personally. "If the gendarmes on guard outside find a war veteran laying down his medal, they are instructed to thank them on Tiger's behalf and take an address so that it can be returned, in due course."

It was one of those circumstances where friends vied with each other to recall the best story.

"I'll tell you what has really riled Poincaré." Roux had already begun to laugh in anticipation of his own contribution. "Pope Benedict sent him a blessing by telegram, so, old Tiger, who, as you know has always been a radical anti-cleric, responded by sending the Pope *his* blessing back."

But all was far from well. By early May the streets of Paris witnessed yet another afternoon of rioting which left two dead and hundreds of demonstrators injured and wounded. The prefecture had a serious problem to contend with given the frustration of workers and de-mobbed soldiers who filled the streets in protest. They wanted jobs. They wanted justice. They wanted to see the Germans pay for the war which the victors insisted was started by them. Anger and rage boiled over the central boulevards like hot tar, untouchable till cool. Lines of gendarmes, cavalry, even troops with fixed bayonets, enraged the crowds in the May Day parade. A fire engine was commandeered by the police to hose down the mob, participants and sight-seekers alike. With symbolic irony, the banner which fronted the union of maimed and disabled workers was washed away and trampled over by the guardians of the state. This was the cost of war. A fractured society mired in injustice. Paris was scared of its own many-shaped shadows.

Mathieu and Jacques witnessed the trouble in the Rue Royale and the Place de La Concorde.

"This is such a bloody awful job sometimes. You see people who've already lost it all, trying to make themselves heard, taking it out on the police and national guard who are only doing their job…some too violently, I'll concede."

"Jacques, we're in enough bother as it stands with our own job. The secret service boys say the German delegation to the Peace Conference are playing silly games."

That was news to them all. "They've been put in the Hotel des Reservoirs in Versailles," Roux explained. "Of course the main rooms have been bugged, but they've moved their team meetings to the basement, and play Tannhäuser at maximum volume on a gramophone so we cannot hear a thing during their meetings."

"Bloody unfair of them, don't you think?" Jacque's attempt at irony fell by the wayside.

"I take it we can listen to their phone calls?" Mathieu understood the nature of the diplomatic game in which they found themselves. Clemenceau wanted no more foul ups on his watch. But he didn't trust the Germans. Who did?

"They won't even admit that they caused the war!" Jacques the innocent knew only what the public knew. Roux looked for his next Gauloises while Mathieu turned away lest his face betrayed the truth.

"I hear that Tiger has ordered their heating to be turned off." Dubois laughed in approval. "Lets them know not to expect us to roll over."

When the peace conference stuttered to a start in January, it was assumed that an agreement would be signed within three weeks. Blind optimism has always been a soft option for a willing audience. Five months later the Allies still disagreed about priorities and President Wilson had fallen from the pinnacle of world savior to a pro-German lackey in the eyes of the press. Clemenceau wanted Germany crushed. That was the sole reason the British were involved, too. Woodrow Wilson wanted to bring eternal peace to the world through a concoction called the League of Nations. Eternal peace, indeed. How soft was he? The only man in the world who would've brought a bible to a poker game and expect to win the jackpot.

"Have you heard what's going on in the Quai d'Orsay? The fucking diplomats think they are dividing the spoils of victory to form a new world order." Mathieu had taken Clemenceau to a meeting there, and had spent some hours fascinated by the diplomatic caste and their cartographers. "I kid you not. They've transformed the Grand Dining Room. Even the Lienard mirrors have diagrams and notes stuck to the surface. It's like a giant board game where they move borders and boundaries every day on maps that cover the floor, the walls, and five of the doors. Benoit holds unreal conversations as if he is the master designer of this new world order. He gets so excited as if it is his decision, posing and strutting like the peacock he is. 'If we move that line to the river, the problem is, 50,000 nationals are left behind. Tricky business, I'll tell you.' They all want land. Every victorious nation wants a payback. To hell with the people who have lived there for a thousand years."

"Except the Americans." Roux spoke with that certainty which no one questioned.

"The Americans want money. Not President Wilson, but they're undermining him in Washington as we speak. After he sidelined his minder, Mandel House, who represented the money-power in the United States, the bankers are grooming a replacement."

"Really? That explains a great deal." Mathieu had not considered the American involvement except to assume that since the Germans signed the armistice in the belief that Wilson's ideas on fair play was their best option, Wilson would be the key player.

"We don't know the half of it yet." Roux rose to the mirror and adjusted his bowtie. The ashtray on his desk looked as if it would burst if one more Gauloises was extinguished in its bowl. "I've been watching the American delegates very carefully. Would it surprise you to learn that virtually every one is a banker, financier, or a lawyer associated with Wall Street?"

If it did, no one said. "We are currently accommodating about ten thousand diplomats, arms salesmen, and spies, but the bankers are American. They want their money back. Not just from Germany. From us. Believe me. And the most untrustworthy of them all is..." He paused for effect, and a reinforcement of nicotine, so Mathieu finished the sentence.

"Herbert Hoover, the untouchable, the racketeer...the United States Secretary for Food?"

"Precisely."

40

1919 – The Cover-Up

Mathieu returned to no. 36 with Americans on his mind. Toussaint saluted as he walked through the door and handed him three crumpled notes.

"They're from your man on the other side." Nothing got past Toussaint, and, truth told, his nosiness was sometimes helpful. Mathieu could smell the alcohol on his breath and was on the point of mentioning it when he glanced at the scrawl in his hand.

The first said, *Left Auxerre on Paris train. Expect.*

The second was equally as cryptic. *No. 7, Rue Jean-Lantier... calls himself Rene Alba.*

Moutie's final scrawl read, *Missing Window.* He was clearly taking cryptic messages to heart.

It was, to date, the clearest note which Moutie had ever scrawled. He was certainly trying, in more ways than one. Moutie was a natural. Not a natural thief. At that he was opportunistic at best, but in another life, he would have made a good assistant. Mathieu was far too busy with protection and surveillance of diplomatic visitors to involve himself with Villain directly, but Moutie was adept in keeping tabs on the wretched murderer. Little in the city's shadow world passed his notice. Mathieu picked up the envelope on which the note had been written and turned it in his hand. *Rene Alba.* Alba. That was Raoul Villain's mother's maiden name. Wow! The name had not been plucked from someone's gravestone or borrowed from the front door of an apartment. Rene Alba was a statement, a gesture of defiance. It said, *I am my mother's son, my grandmother was a visionary, so let the world know me as such.* There was something to be admired in that.

Before he had climbed to the first floor, a receptionist called after him. "There was a phone call for you, Captain, about half an hour ago. Would you please contact the Mairie at Toul?"

Mathieu took two slow strides forward and stopped. Toul? "Toul?" he shouted with a sense of alarm. "Was there a name?"

"No, Sir, but the superintendent of police sounded harassed."

"Right, will you call them back and transfer it to my office, please?" The telephone was ringing before Mathieu reached his desk. "Captain Bertrand speaking."

"Sorry to interrupt you day, Sir." Polite but not subservient. Mathieu remembered the superintendent's voice. "The bargeman who took you north…"

"Bistrot."

"Yes, that's him. He's been waiting for an hour or so to speak with you. Very agitated, I would say."

"Thanks. Put him on, please."

He could feel the telephone being dragged from the policeman's hand.

"Mathieu? Is that you?"

"Bistrot, what's wrong?"

"Mathieu, you have to come here today. You asked me to watch for activity in a certain area of the basin? Something's wrong. Very wrong. Can you come here. Now?" His alarm was obvious.

"Stay at the Town Hall and I will be with you as soon as I can. Are you or Margarite in danger?"

"Don't know."

"Ok. Stay where you are. Let me speak to the superintendent."

Bistrot did as was ordered and Mathieu issued clear instructions. "Don't let him out of your sight. Or his woman either, if she's with him."

He caught Dubois on the point of leaving no. 36 and rearranged his plans for the day

"Tell the chief there's an emergency in Toul. Ask Jacques to cover my shift with the prime minister, and if I need help, I'll call personally."

The Gare de l'Est always appeared neat and unruffled, like a small, groomed show dog who knows what elegance means. Its fifteen arched entrance was perfectly symmetrical with an ornate clock precisely placed at the center above the main portico. There was a train scheduled to leave for Toul at 10:03 A.M. so Mathieu took the metro from St. Michel directly to the station. Outside, buses waited patiently in the square, parked neatly in front of the tramlines. Inside the basilica-like chamber, platforms and railway lines were dwarfed by the spacious glass-bound dome which served as a roof. Pigeons loved that space.

He didn't stop to buy a ticket, but flashed his identity card at an officious guard and mounted the last wagon on the train as it pulled away in an impressive flurry of steam and grinding wheels. Mathieu settled at a window seat hoping that Bistrot's emergency would be quickly solved.

Time and steam sped him through a countryside in recovery, but as the train approached Toul, the landscape changed. Greenery appeared faded, but discernible. The temporary road surfaces had not been removed and in the marshaling yard, dozens of goods wagons lay empty and unused, the detritus of a more prosperous time. No troop transporters were in sight; no hospital trains either. Was this how it would be in Toul?

The peace dividend meant boarded up shops and an increase in poverty. Perhaps trade along the canal had improved? The Town Hall stood as it had, but now the square was all but empty as if lingering in a world of half-day openings. War, death, misery, and profit had given way to more peaceful, placid, safer poverty. Did the gods always punish humans this way?

He had hardly crossed the threshold before Bistrot was upon him. "You asked me to look out for them…just before you left, Mathieu."

"Captain Bertrand to you, bonehead," the superintendent snarled and made to smack the bargeman's head.

"No, no, Bistrot is a friend of some years' standing. He and Margarite, both. Where is she?"

Bistrot looked at the policeman behind the fading front desk before giving a cryptic reply.

"Safe and well. But they are back."

"They? Bistrot, the man who tried to kill us was dispatched to a watery grave. He cannot come back. And, unless you've told anyone, I assure you, no one knows or has reported the matter officially."

"No…of course not…it's the Americans. They're back."

"Americans? On the canal? Where they berthed their barges?"

"Yes. They've emptied the place. Stripped everything bare and disappeared."

"Show me."

Bistrot broke into a run towards the canal basin and the prim brick two-storied Custom House which had served as the American base at the canal junction three years before. Quite noticeably, the Stars and Stripes no longer fluttered from the flaking flagpole. Ownership had been severed. The arched entrance was boarded up in some haste and Mathieu pried open the wood covering on the east side. Breaking in was not difficult. It was illegal, but there was no time for niceties. He climbed through the broken window with a struggle, picking up a splinter from the cheap wooden frame for his troubles. Bistrot followed with an ease which suggested that he knew how to climb through windows. Inside, the cold darkness was accentuated by its utter emptiness. The bargeman's anger boiled over.

"They've stripped it bare." He kicked the bare wall and swore like the would-be mariner he thought he was. Had there been anything to rip from the walls, the room would have been further destroyed.

"Hold on, Bistrot, this has to be done properly. Good detective work might uncover something we can't see yet. We need help and a search warrant. Back to the Town Hall."

It took an hour to obtain a warrant. The local magistrate from whom they expected permission claimed that it was outside his jurisdiction and would have none of it. Mathieu phoned the chief.

"You know the power that the Americans have in Paris. If I ask, the American Embassy will be alerted. Go back to the magistrate and inform him that the Deuxième Bureau will be investigating him tomorrow if he fails to oblige. Turn the screw. Get that warrant locally."

Roux's advice encouraged the magistrate to have second thoughts. Mathieu made a mental note to open inquiries when time permitted. Detectives were short on the ground but the local superintendent grudgingly allowed three gendarmes to help in the search. By that time, Bistrot had described his confrontation with the Americans. They had simply driven up to the basin, gutted the Custom House in its entirety, and sped off in two army trucks without answering a question. The barges, too, floated high on the canal, empty.

"They were going to sink them as they stood, but we emptied the Bar du Port and faced them down. Can you imagine the arrogance? They thought nothing of blocking the canal because they had no need for the barges. Who are these people?"

Indeed.

It took less than five minutes to break open all the doors and windows of the old Custom House. The interior revealed a featureless shell of damp, blackened brick stripped back to maximize space. It was a shell that offered no comfort. A space to leave as quickly as possible.

"Have you used standard procedures in carrying out a formal criminal search before?" Mathieu asked the three gendarmes. The question was his error of judgment. No one appreciates being patronized as a country hick and the look he received was deserved.

"Sorry, of course you have. Just take great care and check with me before touching anything that might be evidence."

Though the building and its contents had been evacuated at high speed, little of consequence appeared to have been left behind. There was an odd iron or steel molding on the upper floor which had been broken into four unequal parts, no longer useable, but strangely out of place in its dank surroundings. Beside it, a small furnace, perhaps for making bread, was crammed with ashes. A gendarme called to Mathieu who was downstairs examining deep scratches on the floor.

"Captain, you should see this."

The ashes still retained some heat which suggested that whatever had been inside was the last to be destroyed. His instruction was to put the remains in a box and try to keep them in order, leaving the policeman to wonder how that could be done, given that there were no boxes. More importantly, perhaps, was that keeping ashes in order required more of a magician's sleight of hand than a policeman's balance. A crate was requisitioned from the bar and the gendarme painstakingly carted it downstairs like a precious prize-winning dish carried by a proud chef.

The barges offered some evidence of the trafficking in black market foods which had brought Mathieu to Toul. A row of canned peaches from Florida sat at the back of a broken cupboard, hidden by an upper shelf which had collapsed on top of them.

"Could you lift that cupboard, please?"

Instinct argued that if they had missed the peaches above, the Americans may have missed something below. And there it lay, blackened by dirt and dust, a ledger detailing border crossings on the Toul to Strasbourg section of the Canal de la Marne au Rhine. All in all, there were eleven pages of dates, arrows, and coded notes, border crossing permits, stamped and dated, French, German, and Dutch numbers and letters, so precisely annotated that it screamed *Prussian*.

"Perfect. I'll take this back to Paris in the morning."

Such was his excitement at the find that Mathieu almost called it a day.

"Excuse me, Captain, but we may have overlooked something back in the Customs House."

"What?" Mathieu Bertrand was tired. The day had been long but profitable. He had the evidence he came to find.

"It's those iron pieces on the first floor. Somebody went to a great deal of trouble to break them carefully."

Carefully? They seemed like four randomly smashed bits of metal but he let the gendarme lead him back inside. The metal still looked like four pieces of a larger machine which had served its purpose years ago and broken up so that no one else could use it.

"What do you think that was, then?" He turned to the youngest gendarme, hoping for an answer which wouldn't waste his time.

"Can I lift it, Captain? Feel its weight?"

Mathieu's grunt was such an exact imitation of Roux's usual means of approval, that he corrected himself and said, "Yes, certainly."

"It's heavy, maybe steel, or perhaps…" He lifted it to eye level and felt the weight once more. "Graphite?" The lad, for he had barely entered his twenties, reordered the broken pieces so that a hollowed brick-like shape took form.

"And what do you think it's for… eh, your name?"

"Barthel, Henri Barthel, Captain. I'd say it was a mold of some sort."

"What? A bread mold?"

"No." He looked closer. Everyone in the building gravitated towards the conversation, hoping to add a perceptive comment. But Henri held the floor.

"Can I take these outside? I need to see the central indent."

"Of course, Barthel, lead on." Mathieu had not the slightest idea what the boy meant, of course he should examine the central indent in a better light. The gendarmes carried the broken mold outside to the welcome daylight. The cool air smelled fresh and sharpened their spirits.

Henri was enjoying his moment. "Ah, it's an inverted stamp of some kind. Probably a hallmark, but I'd need a magnifying glass to identify it."

"A hallmark… isn't that used on…" Mathieu paused to make sure he was hearing properly.

"Silver or gold," said Henri Barthel in a very matter-of-fact voice.

"What makes you think that, Barthel?"

"Started a course on metallurgy before the war, Sir. It's definitely a crucible of some sort. Not French."

Yet another layer of mystery hovered over the canal basin like a swirling summer mist. Silver or gold? Atlantic salmon or peaches from Florida? What would be next?

"Ah," the elongated sing-song timbre of an educated American broke the moment. "Captain Bertrand of the Deuxième Bureau? You've got our property there, I see." Mathieu recognized the drawl before he spun round. Bistrot was wrong. The Americans were still in Toul in the person of Bryson Hamilton and at least six associates in US army uniforms. He had walked down the tow path and positioned himself squarely at the head of his posse like the sheriff of the county.

"Why, it's Mister Bryson Hamilton, as I recall, from the Paris embassy." You could see surprise register in his body language as Hamilton realized that Mathieu knew who he was. For a moment they stood facing each other like cowboys in a standoff. Who would blink first?

"Your property?" Forced politeness bordered on sarcasm. "I think that this ledger is German in origin, not American, and I have to ask why you would want some useless ashes and pieces of scrap metal?"

"They are American property, owned by the American Relief Agency, and we are here to reclaim them."

"Why? Are they valuable in some way? Clearly your people disposed of all the paperwork and broke the metal because it was useless…or perhaps you had another motive?" The conversation was in English which meant that Bistrot and the gendarmes did not understand the detail of the argument, but the grim faces required no translation.

"None of your damned business, Captain, but you have two options. Either hand over our property immediately or we will escort you to the Town Hall where our embassy and the president's office will instruct you in your obligation to France's most important ally." Bryson Hamilton was the embodiment of smug, the playground bully whose muscle was provided by the Headmaster himself. Mathieu turned away from him and spoke rapidly in the local patois, hoping to unsettle his American foe.

"Men, the loudmouth here has the backing of the American government and our president so defiance will be short lived. However, when we get back to the Mairie I want you to write detailed notes on what we found. And you, Henri, I need you to do drawings of the metal…and do your best to identify that hallmark. Put the evidence we have on the ground and go immediately. Bistrot, stay with me."

That said, he turned to Bryson Hamilton and conceded ownership to the American. "I would like to understand what has been going on here."

Hamilton beckoned his troopers to pick up the ledger, box, and scrap iron and brushed Mathieu's inquiry aside.

"As I've already said, it's none of your business, let me assure you. And don't imagine that you have greater influence here than I do. Without the food and aid which we provided during the war, you would have starved, Belgians would have perished by the hundreds of thousands, and Germany would have won the war."

With impulsive anger Mathieu retorted, "Because you also provided them with food and finance? Or was it gold and silver? Tell me."

Hamilton's demeanor changed instantly. His face sharpened in surprise before he rasped back, "You should be very careful of wild allegations, Vincent." A twisted smile crooked round Hamilton's lips. Mathieu stepped back inadvertently. That name. His name. The American knew who he was. How? Hamilton registered Mathieu's shock and smiled with victorious conceit, as if having the last word was the end of the matter.

"We still have a peace treaty to sign at Versailles. And you have a career to safeguard in the years ahead." He turned and strode off, hands swinging, fingers twitching. But Hamilton had made a mistake. He had played a card too early, out of sequence. Mathieu had never considered the likelihood that the Americans were watching him … and presumably the chief. Now he knew.

"Bistrot, I have to speak with the gendarmes and contact my department in Paris. I'd appreciate it if I can stay on your barge this evening. Please jot down all that you know about the Americans and the way they have behaved over the last four years. I'll read it before I leave. Is that all right?"

"Yes, if you want, but I'm not much of a writer." Then his face lit up. "And if you're not too late, we can empty a bottle of wine … or two."

"And tell Margarite I want to see her. She is in no danger … absolutely none at all. Make her understand?"

The three gendarmes reacted to the American's arrogance with defiance. Though their shift had finished they stayed on to help Mathieu understand what had been happening around Toul.

"When they first hoisted the American flag over the old Custom House we were taken aback that they could use the canal to get through, somehow, to the Rhine. But they could. They had special permits. They were the American Relief Agency, which made them popular at first. But very little was actually destined for Toul. A few scraps of tinned fruit or fish, a handful of rice, some old clothing. Nothing regular. We followed their lorries to find out where their cargo was heading, but the best we could establish was that they went towards Paris, which could mean anywhere."

The stoutest of them, Gregor, had worked in Toul all his life, and accepted over time that the "American" basin and Custom House were off limits, even to the police.

"What we couldn't work out was what their barges carried, or how far they were allowed to travel through German lines. We knew that a few locks were damaged but were the tunnels open? They wouldn't say. Cut themselves off from the town. Didn't drink with locals."

Henri added his concern. "What did they carry in the other direction? We hadn't a clue. It wasn't food. When I realized that the metal container could have been a crucible or mold something fell into place. The Custom House chimneys frequently belched black smoke over the canal, but I never imagined that they might be dealing in metals."

"Can I see your drawings, Henri?" Mathieu considered the outline of what appeared to be a brick-like mold but it meant little. "And what about the smashed centerpiece, the hallmarks you thought you could see?"

The young gendarme shrugged his shoulders. "I can't make it out, but if they could generate enough power to smelt small amounts of gold into the mold, the hallmark would indicate where the gold ingot was made, or allegedly made, in this case. That way the police wouldn't know where the gold came from."

"Truth is, we don't know if it was coming into the country or going out. And that's the point. They never wanted us to know. Ever. These Americans have a special agenda. With the unspoken approval of our president and his allies, they are stealing all the evidence of how the war was run from the earliest days of the fighting. They don't want anyone to know what was actually going on. Or who was making vast profits." Mathieu sat back solemnly. "If this is happening elsewhere in Europe, it's world class theft on an international scale."

They sat quietly as the evening sun cooled its ardor in the growing shade. Black languid shadow spread through the streets with a stealth which matched the darkness of their mood. Gregor stood and took two immense breaths, filling his lungs with the clear air that promised to return next day. He just couldn't comprehend what had been said.

"If we can't stop them, Captain, and the president and all his men encourage them, who governs France?"

"Who indeed? Tomorrow, I'll take all these notes and ideas back to Paris. The Deuxième Bureau may not be able to do much to stop this, but politicians change. Sometimes the only way to win is to outlive the buggers."

The gendarmes parted with a handshake and nod. Further words were unnecessary.

In all that had happened to him in Toul, the person whom Mathieu most appreciated was Margarite. Voiceless but priceless, she had saved his life with that expert stroke from her sharpened coal shovel. The blow which all but decapitated Timon, servant to the Lords of Darkness, one of whom was Basil Zaharoff, had imprinted itself on Mathieu's memory. He would have been dead. Instead, he was given another chance. Yet she lived in fear. Petrified that she would be charged with murder.

"It wasn't murder," he had told her a hundred times and more in his dreams and daydreams. He had to tell her once more. Reassure her. Hopefully. Bistrot had opened a bottle of local red and set in on the upper deck table. It looked like an offering to the gods, sitting on an old threadbare table cloth, a shard from the rising moon catching the ruby draught as if from a rose-window in a grand Basilica. He saw Mathieu from a distance and hailed him with a great yell.

"Welcome back, my policeman friend. Take care, the mare is loose!" He slowed his pace to a cautious stride but Margarite caught him unexpectedly from his right and they almost tumbled into the canal. She kissed his cheeks with frantic enthusiasm while Bistrot laughed his approval from the deck.

"Hurry up, you young lovers, or I'll drink this bottle myself." He certainly would have, for Bistrot was well practiced in the art of scoffing wine. They climbed aboard, Margarite first, attacking the bargeman's neck with renewed passion. Bistrot pretended to fend her off, but there was a euphoria in the air which bathed the three of them in a special warmth. Margarite poured the drink while Bistrot opened another bottle.

"Got to give it time to breathe." She sat on his knee and in her own fashion, talked furiously.

"She believes she's free now because you've come back to visit us. You haven't forgotten."

"For the last time, my darling Margarite, you committed no crime. You saved a life. A very important life. You should get a medal."

Three bottles later Bistrot and Mathieu sat with their legs dangling over the side of the barge as small boys would, though not carefree and innocent. Margarite was snoring in her bed below, released from the curse of her inner demons.

Bistrot looked over the edge of the barge and mused, "This mess at the Customs House, and the Americans…what does it all mean?"

"It means that powerful men were using war to make millions of dollars, pounds, and francs. I don't know any more than you do exactly how much food, which should have gone to Belgium, ended up in Germany or on the black market. I don't even understand why they went to so much trouble to smelt gold or silver and change the hallmarks. Whatever they were doing was a crime against the people. And now, with the apparent blessing of our government, the Americans are removing all the evidence and taking it somewhere? It's scandalous, but what can we do? I will try to find out more and make sense of it, and all the injustices around us. I'll try." Captain Mathieu Bertrand yawned once, leaned back ,and fell asleep on the spot where Timon's heart stopped beating.

331

41

June 1919 – Losing the Evidence

The chief's note said, *See me outside. Emergency meeting of Armed Forces, Diplomatic, and Bureau intelligence groups at 9.30. Quai d'Orsay. We were both invited to attend. And by* invited *they mean* ordered. R.

Mathieu found the chief pacing up and down on the quayside close to the car park.

"We'll take the Renault to the foreign ministry and you can update me on your latest exploit.

You realize that we shouldn't tell other agencies too much, but it's equally imperative that we don't lie. I have been asked to ensure that we bring all of our files on certain parties and events and we will, of course. Any copy will have to be surrendered or 'lost' for thirty years." He paused for reasons of his addiction. "So, what happened in Toul?"

Once in the Renault, Mathieu recounted the events at the old Custom House, the state of the building, what had been found there, and the American intervention.

"Bryson Hamilton, indeed," Roux found that a reason to light up once more even though the smoke choked out every inch of fresh air in the car. "We need to find out if other agencies have records on him."

"Do you have any idea what the Americans are doing with the documents they've already stolen?"

Roux raised his eyebrows and shook his head, " No, but I aim to find out."

"I would dearly like to know how Hamilton discovered that we were checking on their former premises on the canal bank?"

"Either the judge contacted their embassy here in Paris, or someone in Toul tipped them off."

"Or someone closer to home?" The very implication left them silenced. Mathieu twisted uncomfortably before confessing his deepest concern "There is one other factor. Hamilton dropped a bombshell as he was leaving. He called me Vincent, and I don't think he meant to. His big mouth couldn't hold it in."

Roux coughed deeply, his breath trapped in a clouded throat, his lungs struggling to meet the body's need.

"Someone has been checking up on me, clearly. Someone with serious connections"

"And me," Roux insisted. "But they don't know what we have already uncovered. No one does. For the moment they can only suspect. But we must be even more vigilant." They were waved through the police cordon at the Quai d'Orsay still immersed in their own concerns, already late, but evermore troubled. "These thugs and gangsters don't live by the rules. They think themselves above the law. Suspicion alone could be deadly. Remember to take care with what you say today. There is no such beast as a watertight Intelligence meeting."

Though Mathieu had visited the foreign ministry at Quai d'Orsay many times, he had never presumed to use the front entrance of the magnificent Second Empire Palace of Foreign Affairs. Sitting proudly on the banks of the Seine, specifically built in the mid-nineteenth century to impress royalty and diplomats from abroad, sculpted rather than constructed, its Doric order dominated the ground floor and Ionic grandeur filled the first and second levels, giving it the aura of a grand aristocratic mansion.

"Good morning, Messieurs. You are here to attend the special meeting with intelligence agencies?" You might sometimes wonder if the Revolution ever took place. The uniformed attendants looked as if he had stepped out of a picture from another century.

Roux acknowledged the question with a nod, and removed his bowler hat. Mathieu followed suit.

"The meeting will begin shortly. If you would go directly to the Rotunda Drawing Room upstairs, Chief Superintendent, the prime minister wishes to speak to you before the first session. Captain Bertrand, if you would please follow Alphonse here," he directed Mathieu to a lackey who looked like a cross between a waiter at the Ritz and a general's aide de camp, "you will be called to participate in due time."

Tiger Clemenceau chaired the intelligence meeting. That raised its importance considerably, Mathieu thought, as he was led to an anteroom which looked out to the gardens. Every corridor was designed to impress, from the bas reliefs over the formal entrance doors depicting the spirits of war and peace under an Imperial Crown to the tapestries and wall paintings of former French glory. Roux had taken some of the files upstairs, so Mathieu had time to remind himself about their suspicion of American wrongdoings from previous files. There were questions about Briey that he would have liked to examine in more minute detail, but it was neither the time nor place. He was summoned to the Rotunda just after eleven o'clock and stood to attention until Clemenceau, who had taken the chair, beckoned him to sit beside the chief.

"Good. Captain Bertrand, welcome."

He addressed the others. "Let me tell you gentlemen that this young man has displayed immense courage over the last five years in many policing and protection roles. Like Chief Superintendent Roux, I hold him in high esteem, and there are several of you around the table who can confirm that." A wave of approval washed over the company as Mathieu took his place.

"I will take this opportunity to reinforce the secrecy and security which attends every aspect of our discussions today." Mathieu wordlessly acknowledged the statement.

"No one outside this room will be briefed or advised on what is discussed. I turn now to item four, the Americans. They have been our allies in many ways since war began, but where do we stand with them right now? Jean-Jules, would you update your previous statement."

The French Ambassador at Washington Jean-Jules Jusserand, began to speak without any reference to notes, demonstrating his complete command of the topic. He had been appointed Ambassador sixteen years ago and was highly regarded by President Wilson. His bright eyes held his authority to the fore and his high receding forehead descended into a well-trimmed beard dominated by a thick handle-bar moustache. Jean-Jules looked every part a well-groomed aristocrat. His immaculate black jacket with velvet lapel, butterfly collar and dark blue tie, sharply creased striped trousers and highly polished shoes were not mere dressing. Jean-Jules possessed an accomplished mind. He understood best what was going on.

"Prime Minister, gentlemen, you will be aware that I traveled here from New York with President Wilson to be part of the signing ceremony for the Versailles Treaty. He is not well. I believe that several factors are currently undermining him. His health, of course, his declining influence and power in the USA, and his recent decision to sideline Colonel House, his administration's contact with the banking fraternity. He may think that he is the most influential man in America, but he is not. Both we and the English pay lip service to his fourteen points, but the English have no intention of giving up their dominance on the high seas, and we are not about to give in to German demands until they pay for the destruction in France. In full."

A high-pitched voice to Mathieu's right added, "Exactly." He turned to find Benoit Durfort glaring at him from a seat set behind the main table, but the obsequious diplomat's reaction marked a sea change in attitude. Durfort raised his pretentious head and studiously turned away from Mathieu in an act of visible rejection. He wondered fleetingly how he had offended the self-important toady, but there was little time for such irrelevance.

Clemenceau drummed his fingers on the glazed table and nodded Jusserand to continue. "There is a new breed of Americans whom we have to watch carefully. Bankers and industrialists. There are more Wall Street financiers travelling in President Wilson's entourage than can be imagined. They are here to make or collect money. I believe that there is a further tranche of Americans who want to undermine us and the English. This group has as its target the division of the former Ottoman Empire. On this topic no one can be trusted. Whatever the promises made to our foreign ministry during the war, the English do not share empires. They acquire them. And they have betrayed agreements with us, with the Arabs, and with the former Russian empire to have their chosen way in the middle and far east. Do not trust the English. We suspect that they have made a deal with the Americans to set up a mandate in the Arab State of Palestine, which the Zionists, this new and growing breed of politically driven Jewish nationalists, want as a homeland. If that is so, then they have made an agreement behind our backs."

"But the Zionists constitute a very small group, insignificant, in fact."

Mathieu could not see who made the observation, but other voices disputed the claim.

"Insignificant in number, perhaps, but significant in influence, believe me," the Ambassador continued. "Behind the scenes, here in Paris, influential groups are scheming to change the world to their own advantage."

"Thank you, Ambassador. Any questions or comments?" Clemenceau turned towards Mathieu. "Captain, I understand you also have concerns about the Americans."

That was Mathieu's cue.

"Thank you, Prime Minister. May I ask about the many roles which the US Food Controller, Herbert Hoover, currently plays inside and out with France?" The table twitched. Mathieu felt discomfort emanate from several sides of the room as if he had conjured an autumn wind to destroy the fragile mounds of fallen leaves so carefully swept to cover broken cracks and dangerous pot-holes.

"This man Hoover asserts his right to do what he likes without fear of contradiction. His power to direct food to whole nations appears to be unlimited. Governments fear him, and I don't believe that we know for sure what his intentions are."

Several pairs of eyes went into lock-down as if to disassociate themselves from the question.

Ambassador Jusserand did not flinch. "We must be alert to Hoover's activities, but do nothing about them for the moment," he advised.

"Really?" Clemenceau sat back amazed. "Why should we do nothing, Ambassador?"

"Hoover is the coming man. In ten years' time I expect him to be president of the United States. He is a cunning operator, favored by the establishment on both sides of the Atlantic. His agency was feeding the occupied territories, Belgium, and Germany during the war, blowing an enormous hole in the blockade against our enemy. If the full details of his Belgian Relief scandal are ever discovered, he will spend the rest of his life in prison. He has complete control of all foods coming into Europe today from the Americas. Big business has grown fat on his relief administration, but their devious game cannot be proved. And we should not be found trying to prove it."

Bernard Roux understood. Had this been a game of poker it was the moment when the stakes were doubled. But it was no bluff.

"Is that why his men are clearing every depot, office, custom's post, and dock-side warehouse of all records as we speak?"

"No doubt," Ambassador Jusserand said calmly. He was a master of his brief. "And it is worse than that. He has permission to take all of the official war records from every one of the defeated nations, and certain allies, believe me, to be stored in America at a university in California … for safety. For posterity, so he claims."

Roux gave vent to an exaggerated sigh fueled by either his disgust or his need for nicotine.

"Chief Superintendent, you have an observation to add?"

Roux nodded and pulled his chair closer to the table in order to keep eye contact with the assembled intelligence officers. "I can tell you that on the eleventh of this month, a Professor Ephraim Adams from Stanford University arrived in Paris and began to collect an unspecified amount of war-related material to be sent for safety to America. He was invited here by Herbert Hoover to complete this task on his behalf."

A couple of gasps and single word expletives escaped into the air.

"Our intelligence reports that Adams intended to keep a diary of whom he met and where, but after a visit from Bryson Hamilton, he gave up on the idea. Hamilton is one of Hoover's closest acolytes. He spent most of the war here in Paris at the American Embassy," the Ambassador added.

Before another word could be uttered, Marshal Pétain thumped the table and blurted,

"That must be why General Pershing informed me that he was releasing fifteen history professors from army duty immediately to assist some American professor from California. He said he had permission from the top men on all sides."

Clemenceau's brow darkened. "*I* know nothing about permissions, Marshal. No one asked *my* permission." He accentuated the *I* to disassociate himself completely with the claim.

Pétain cleared his throat and said quietly, "I imagine he meant President Poincaré."

Embarrassment fell from the rococo ceiling and added to the general discomfort. Clemenceau drummed his fingers even more rapidly on the table. It was as if a priest had pronounced, "let us pray," intoning a grace before a meal for which there was no food. Heads bowed. No one wished to be part of the uneasy revelation. In the pause Mathieu saw every piece of the jigsaw puzzle fall into place. Hoover had the president's approval to remove all the evidence of malpractice during the war. It was already disappearing over the horizon to that part of America furthest from France. They were robbing Europe of its historical heritage to save their own heads. How far did this go?

Clemenceau made an instant political judgment.

"I want all of you to search for remaining documents pertaining to the war and place them with the Ministry of War. These will then be secretly locked away for safety, with access denied to anyone of lesser rank than you, Gentlemen. When *we* are ready, we can assess what they tell us. That of course assumes that there is anything left. Do it immediately when we end this meeting."

"Are we free to investigate Hoover himself?" Mathieu was also convinced that the American would be the big player in the coming post-Versailles era.

"*No* ... I've said it already. Do not even think about it. We need to keep the Americans sweet." Ambassador Jusserand was obviously alarmed.

Clemenceau found a middle way. "So, gather all of the material we have on Hoover. This time send it to the Deuxième Bureau. Again, it will be placed in a secret vault. No entry without permission from the highest order. With the greatest respect, Ambassador, we have to build up a clear portfolio on a man who may yet lead our major ally. It is in the smallest of fragmentary detail that we may one day find the key to manipulate even the greatest of men."

Mathieu was excused from the secret intelligence meeting, but as he left the Rotunda, Ambassador Jusserand caught his sleeve and took him aside.

"Captain, you have a wonderful future ahead of you. Do not put it at risk because of a snake like Hoover. Whatever you discover, keep it secret. We still need the Americans. Absolutely."

Raoul's Story

FAMILY MADNESS

I was in hospital, surely, but why? Aaah the pain. What had happened? In a general ward with other patients. Men. Ordinary men. They recognized me. I could tell by the stares in my direction. Harsh looks. Friendless. The doctor was perfectly proper, coming as he did from a better class of people. The nurses were attentive and kind. Breathing was painful, and when they bound what seemed to be my wounds, I squirmed, gasping for relief.

"You are a very lucky man, Monsieur Villain. Very lucky." Was he a doctor?

I was on the point of arguing, but sheer exhaustion intervened. I slept on my back.

I am going to tell you a story, my friend, and you can decide whether or not I am lucky.

After I returned to Paris to stay in Rue Jean-Lantier, half way between the elegant Rue de Rivoli and Pont Neuf, my life began to unravel from the security of absolute certainty to the eternal doubt that wraps itself around paranoia. True, I was housed in a better quality lodging and I had a regular income paid into an account at the Banque de Paris, but none of the wealth that I was promised. You could not say I was well off. No. Those who previously claimed to be my friends warned me off. The consequences would be severe, they said. I was sufficiently knowledgeable about money and coins to realize that in the post-war turbulence there was profit to be made.

By sheer chance, I bumped into an old friend from La Santé, the warder I called Pierre. He was able to purchase silver coins from unknown sources, and I agreed to sell them on as an investment to citizens with cash. This secret arrangement continued for a couple of months and it was a profitable relationship, my fronting the business while Pierre sourced the silver. Sometimes it was the finest of silver tableware. He assured me that it came from clients who needed cash. I worked alone from a small café in Montreuil, at the corner of Rues Douy-Delcupe and de Vincennes. Close enough to lure greedy men, but otherwise anonymous. Pierre possessed not the personality to front a business. The patron accepted a few francs to turn a blind eye but someone reported us to the police and I was arrested for trafficking in silver. The ignominy. As they bundled me into the police wagon I heard one of the local patrons call me "murderer." The desk sergeant at the prefecture in Montreuil was as fat as he was evil-looking. He practically drooled at the prospect of my being in his jail and within ten minutes of the arrest he wobbled into my cell and proceeded to lecture me with a dog-breath reprimand.

"Have you ever stopped to think," he pontificated, "how much misery you have caused our nation? How many lives your cowardly act cost France? Do you have the slightest notion how many heads have been broken and police injured in the riots that follow you everywhere you go?"

But we won. We crushed Germany. We have Lorraine and Alsace back. And these rioters were asking for it. Anarchists and communists, I replied in my head, but said nothing. It always annoyed the guardians of the law if you said nothing.

His parting comment cut me deeply. "You are a nobody going nowhere. Do France a favor and kill yourself."

I sat inside the solitude of my mind and realized what he said was true. I was a nobody. Again. My life caused others pain. My family didn't want me. My friends from Action française wouldn't speak to me. Who would notice if I killed myself? No one. But how? I took a silk scarf which I occasionally wore for effect and attached one end to the grille on the cell door, placed it round my neck in a noose, and pulled as hard as I could. I felt dizzy and began to lose consciousness, but the silk slipped from my hand and I banged my head. I tried again, with no tangible result. On the third occasion, a guard heard my fall, opened the cell, and shouted for help. Sergeant dog-breath squeezed himself inside and whispered contemptuously, "Not on my watch, you stupid bastard."

By the time a doctor arrived to examine me I had fully recovered. They let me out four days later, but I had to appear at the 11th Criminal Chamber on 18 October. A lawyer appeared to defend me, so I must still have friends, and great play was made of my mental weaknesses. I hated that. A fine of one-hundred francs was the verdict of the court. The news triggered yet another round of Villain-baiting by the left-wing press which took every opportunity to lambast the fact that that I had escaped murdering Jean Jaures, but was found guilty of the petty crime of trafficking in silver. Their reports dripped sarcasm when they asked if that represented justice? Of course it did.

Then I thought the planets had realigned. I met a girl who accepted me as I was. Charlotte was a modest young woman who had lost her husband in the war. She didn't know where he died or precisely when, but there were hundreds of thousands who experienced such sadness and had to get on with life. Charlotte had long red hair which shone in the bright June sunlight, and her button-nose twitched in the pollen-filled fields of Villeneuve in the Hautes-Alpes in Provence. The small hilltop town clustered around the church tower in no particular order, its red-tiled roofs bearing the stains of centuries, its close-knit streets protecting the six hundred inhabitants from the heat of scorching summer days. Charlotte held fast to an old-fashioned attitude to family duty and responsibility and we shared the same values and traditions. Her father had fought in the war of 1870 and reviled the communards and socialists whom he blamed for our defeat.

I asked his permission to marry Charlotte and dutifully returned to Auxerre to seek my father's blessing. September rains arrived to wash the autumnal dust and clean the streets and I almost skipped up the courthouse steps to his office, certain that his pleasure at my proposal would overcome his previous disappointments.

He slapped my face so hard I was sent reeling from the room. No word spoken, not even in anger, just a colossal backhanded slap across my right cheek. The venom of his attack surpassed any previous beating but conjured a memory so deep and so painful that it had lain dormant inside a locked chamber of the mind. Until that moment. I lay stunned in the corridor, immobile. Head bowed. The pain and sound released a final image from my earliest days. Slap. Then slap again. A third slap, then sobbing. Deep, heartbroken sobbing.

They had been arguing loudly, father and mother, about someone whose name I did not recognize, and he threatened to send her back to the asylum. Back? Had she been there before? I closed off every other sight or sound to concentrate on the image he had released. She squared up to him in the parlor, hair tied behind her head, luminous in the sunlight of my recall. She called him "unworthy" and slapped him. He slapped her so viciously that she gave way at the knees and staggered to retain her dignity. Did she know I was there, behind her? He slapped her again and as she fell, he saw me silhouetted in the door-frame.

"Go to your bedroom, boy. Now!"

Hesitation betrayed my loyalty. He slammed shut the door so hard that the corridor shook at his violence. I looked at the hall lamp swinging in protest and hid lest it consumed me with its knowledge of what had come to pass.

Then they came to the house, doctor, priest and lawyer. I crawled slowly from my room and put my ear to the door. Father explained that mother—he called her Marie-Adele, refusing to dignify their years together by using her married name—had been committed to an asylum in Chalons-sur-Marne at his request by a Doctor Bonnet for hysteria and a complete loss of reason. AT MY FATHER'S REQUEST. He requested it? It was true. She had been initially committed but released shortly afterwards. So she had been condemned twice. I never knew that. I heard my father tell them that she had slapped him in front of the younger boy and accused him of immoral deeds. She was, he claimed, completely out of control and unreasonable and had become a danger to the children. My mother was never a danger to me. She loved me. I know that.

I heard the priest confirm that Marie-Adele—he spoke in honeyed tones, drunk with pathos and insincerity—had become paranoid with wild ideas of persecution. The doctor's opinion was that she was displaying chronic delirium.

"I've heard," whispered the fish-wife confessor, "that she claims someone accused her of poisoning the children." He was the font of local gossip. "And it's hereditary, you know." I could not see my father's reaction but the parish dipped its fingers in the chapel's font of all knowledge, blessed itself in purifying holy water and prayed for her soul.

Authorized by representatives of the courts, religion, and medical practice, the doctor signed papers in our parlor which justified my mother's commitment to the mental hospital. What I had not realized till that moment was my father's determination to condemn her to a life of medicated imprisonment. She would never slap him again. He made sure of that. She was a mere woman. I picked myself from the floor and strode into his office. What possessed me, I do not know, but I heard myself begin, "It's a long time since I've seen you slap a person so hard." He stared back at me, countering my defiance.

"What do you want?"

"I have some good news, father."

"You do! How marvelous. Is this you the coward-murderer, or you the convicted trafficker in stolen silver? My son the assassin or my son the convict? You are no son of mine. You are HER son. You should have been locked up in an asylum, too." His unjust rant dragged up every conceivable childhood misdemeanor he imagined I had committed. I watched his blood pressure rise with considerable interest. If he died now I would have the pleasure of witnessing it. He came to a stop or was it a pause? No matter.

"Calm down, Father. I've some good news. Honestly. I intend to get married to a wonderful girl and I'm here to seek your blessing."

He stared at me and covered his moustache and mouth with his left hand. I thought he was about to show tender emotion, too late for love; be pleased for me, realize I had turned a corner. But behind the mask which crossed his lower face, his sandstone eyes hardened to flashing marble. He banged his fist into the desk as if striking a gavel to bring the court to order.

"You will not be married. You will not. Don't you understand that you are enfeebled, vulnerable, mentally ill, possibly a danger to children. Like your mother? You cannot do this to an innocent woman."

"You did." My aggression took him by surprise.

"She was mad, not me," he protested.

"No. You are mad. You know it. Grandmere was mad. Your mother was mad, and so are you."

Despite my best intentions, I burst into tears, shamefaced and desolate.

He rose from his desk, shaking. Anger moved to apoplexy as he thumped his fist again on the hard wood, self-control disappearing in the red mist of furious contempt. He grabbed me by the lapels and thrust his face into mine.

"You have disgraced your family and yourself beyond forgiveness. You will not extend the family line into further disgrace. You will not." He dropped his hands and threw me backwards against the wall, knocking over a hat stand in the process. How I hated this man.

"There is no blessing. There will be no marriage. Do you understand?"

He was screaming at me, words tripping over themselves in a rush of garbled incoherence. He stood there, head bowed, trying to find his next sentence. He looked me up and down and nodded slowly. Had he finally come to terms with the fact that I was an independent man who deserved better? Finally come to his senses?

"I have a pistol in this desk." He pulled open the top drawer on the right-hand side and rummaged around before producing his old Modele 1873 with its checker-patterned grip. I didn't know he had kept his army service revolver. "And I invite you to use it."

He slammed it onto the desktop, turned his back, and picked up a handful of assorted files as if to indicate that the meeting had come to an end. I looked at the gun. It was a solution. I picked it up, hands shaking, and wondered how proud he might be if I shot him in the head? Like Jaures?

"You are the coward, Father. You. You beat my mother and condemned her to the asylum. You are the coward."

He turned to answer just as I pulled the trigger—and shot myself. Trembling hands fumbled around the trigger mechanism, but the gun exploded and pain shot into my abdomen. He looked at me contemptuously. I was on my knees, the gun on the floor in front. He walked across, picked up the revolver, and handed it back. "I believe you have barely scratched yourself. Try again."

I was bleeding. I had been shot…and all he could say was, "Try again."

"You bastard. You callous bastard," were to be my parting words as I turned the gun into myself and fired again. I'm not a bad shot but the angle and circumstances mitigated against accuracy. The second bullet also hit my abdomen, but well clear of any vital organ. As I slumped prone on the floor, his office door flew open and staff rushed in, thinking, no doubt that he had been the victim of an attack.

"Monsieur Villain…"

My fucking father pointed in my direction with a disregard which spoke volumes about his attitude toward me…and I woke up in that hospital.

So what would be your opinion about luck, my friend? How much luck did I have with a father like him? Eh?

42

PICKING AT SORES

Moutie slid into a seat in the back parlor of the Café Gabrielle in Montmartre, picked up a menu, and chose a croque monsieur. His loose association with Mathieu brought him increased respect in his twilight zone because it was neither secret nor a threat. The shadow-world of the impoverished underclass knew that Moutie had led Raoul Villain by the nose into a conviction for illegal trafficking in silver coins because he told them. Served the bastard right. There was no love for Villain inside the criminal fraternity. War had cost them dearly. If Raoul Villain thought that he was being watched, it was not paranoia. He had more enemies than he knew. Moutie saw to that and reported it to Mathieu who slipped into the chair beside him. He was running late and looked tired.

"Ah, Captain Bertrand, my friend, the pursuit of justice is starting to wear you down. I've ordered a croque monsieur. What would you like to eat?"

Mathieu waved away the offer. For a start, he wasn't sure who'd be paying for it.

"He's thinking about moving on again, our man Villain. Paris is far from safe. Would be so easy to stick a knife in his ribcage in an alleyway. No one would see it, I promise you."

"No, Moutie. Let justice take its own meandering course. If he's living in hell in his Paris hovel the prolonged pain is well deserved. Let him die by a hundred thousand disappointments. Let it rend his soul into shards of fear."

He called for a coffee and resisted the temptation to eat, though the smell of fresh baking was instantly attractive. Mathieu's resolve was further tested when Moutie's beautifully crafted dish was placed on the table. The soft sourdough, gruyère, smoked ham, and creamy mustard mayo tempted his taste buds.

"Are you sure you don't want to eat, Captain?" the waiter enquired hopefully. Business was slow.

"Thank you, but not at the present."

A mouthful of melted cheese and ham was no obstacle to continued conversation. Moutie's table manners had never been particularly refined. In a family of nine siblings, he or she who hesitated at the table went hungry. It was the primeval law of survival in every ghetto.

"Are you saying we should let Villain be? Stop torturing him?"

"Well, I don't ever recall the word torture, but now that the foreign hordes are preparing to leave France to return—"

"Foreign whores? Which foreign whores? Nothing's happening in the Pigalle is it?"

"Hordes, Moutie, lots of people, as in the vast crowds of foreign journalists, diplomats, bankers, advisers, and so forth."

Relief flooded color back in to his cheeks. "Ah, those whores."

"So, I was thinking that you have honorably fulfilled your promise to me, and I should release you from my previous threats."

Moutie put down his fork and let his lower lip pout. Tears came to his eyes, but he blinked them back. He had never considered this possibility. Once he had come to terms with his conscience in the rubble-strewn confessional in Saint-Gervais all those years ago, Moutie's life had changed. That's how he saw it. If it wasn't his conscience, it was the fear of final retribution which motivated his rebirth as a cleaner, healthier, more focused citizen … and occasional pickpocket and thief when temptation and opportunity collided. He prided himself as the Deuxième Bureau's man on the dark side of the Seine. He had been their contact inside La Santé, kept the captain informed on Villain's comings and goings, who came to see him and what they brought. He had lured him into the courts with stolen silver. Thanks entirely to him they knew about Villain's very changeable state of mind. He had used contacts in railway stations, newspaper kiosks, amongst vendors and doormen, on the highways and byways, in unlicensed auberge and dockside bar, amongst the ladies of the night and those who managed them. Even his own extended family were involved. He had no wish to be released from the threat which changed his life. He stood on the point of being dropped back into the cesspit of swirling nobodies. From trusted confidant to the worst thief in Paris. Again.

"You can't do that, Captain. You said to me, more than that, you swore an oath that the contract between us was for all time. You made me swear in the ruins of Saint-Gervais that I would have to change forever and do as you bid for all eternity."

Mathieu sighed inwardly. Though those were not the words he would have used, the sentiment was essentially true.

345

Moutie swung round on his chair and called across the room, "Chantal, come and meet my friend the captain." A dark-haired woman of some thirty years rose from her chair, shifted her pleated skirt, wiped the corner of her mouth, and gracefully stepped towards them, clear eyes sparkling in delight. She smiled at Mathieu and proffered her ungloved hand as he rose to greet her.

"Enchanté, Mademoiselle."

Moutie pulled a chair from the nearest table and she sat down with them.

"Allow me to introduce my second cousin's daughter, Chantal. She has been most helpful in using her trades union contacts across the land to keep tabs on Raoul Villain."

"It has been an honor, Monsieur." Chantal had the alluring style of a trained actress. She paused for a moment and lowered her eyes. "You did everything possible to save Jean Jaurès from the murdering bastards who supported Villain, and we, all of us, will never stop till justice is done." Then she swept back her hair and laughed again. "And you should know that our family is also grateful for everything you have done for our aging uncle. To call him a changed man does no justice to the truth."

"Did you know Jaurès, Mademoiselle?"

"He was my hero when I first joined the movement. I've seen him win over ten thousand men and women with a single speech on working class solidarity, Monsieur. We will never forgive or forget. Rest assured." She turned to Moutie who beamed in approval. "If you'll excuse me, mon oncle, I have an appointment." And with a wink in his direction, she walked out of the café.

"She's a terror, you know. Always involved in the next injustice. I like her. But she's too political, if you know what I mean." Mathieu watched Moutie's pride as the young woman disappeared. He had never considered that he had a family, no matter how distant.

"And I've done more than simply have Villain's every moved watched. You know that."

Mathieu agreed. "I know, and you've done it well, but I don't think that there will be much for you to do now that the Versailles business in finished. It'll be back to normal."

"Captain Bertrand, nothing is ever normal in Paris. Anyway, what have you done about the widows? I sent you a note about missing widows."

"Widows?" He leaned forward perplexed, then remembered. "No, you wrote missing windows. It said missing windows."

346

"Well that doesn't make any sense, missing windows, does it? You should alert one of your detective teams to look into the number of widows who have disappeared in recent times."

Mathieu was about to argue the futility of such time wasting when, from the back streets of his overstressed memory, he remembered the gossip – Edithe Therbuet and her widowed neighbor whose name definitely escaped him. She was a missing widow.

"OK, tell me more."

"We're still a team, then?" Moutie's hand shot across to shake his own. Again, it was not the word Mathieu would have chosen.

"We're still a team, but business may be slow. Now, tell me what you know about the missing widows."

* * *

Had Mathieu the gift of clairvoyance he would not have thought the Versailles business finished. The treaty was signed but its business was far from over. Everyone wanted to be at Versailles on 28 June 1919. War would officially be over. Peace and sunshine broke from the clouds to herald brighter days. Or so it was believed in Paris, London, and New York. Most of the senior officials at no. 36 were at their desks by four in the morning. If ever there was a perfect platform for assassination, this was the day. Chief Superintendent Roux had spent most of the previous week in close consultation with every branch of the police and armed forces allotting positions, reviewing intelligence, arresting some known anarchists who had travelled to Paris. Nothing was to be left to chance.

A brigade of sparkling motor cars carried the senior representatives from all of the allied nations represented at the talks with police and secret service agents close by. A formal honor guard of French cavalry stood motionless save for the occasional snort from bored horses, obliged to stay unnaturally still all along the mile long drive from the gates of Versailles to the palace. Each appeared to carry individual tricolors in blue uniform, red and white pennant flying from their lances. In the courtyard, where even more troops were visible, rifles gleamed, purpose clear, and the invited participants mounted the Grand Staircase bordered, left and right, by the shining silver helmets with brushed horse-hair of the Republican Guard.

Mathieu mused that this overwhelming show of force usually graced the streets of the city if there was a risk of a mob uprising. With the theatrical flourish of a grand stage manager, Clemenceau included a selection of Paris mutilés, handpicked to remind all present of the victims of war. He might just as well have stood at the top of the grand staircase and pointedly shouted, "Remember, we do this for them." On the journey out of Paris he waved heartily at the crowds and reminded them "This is a great day for France."

To the immense relief of everyone at the Deuxième Bureau, the day passed without assassination or injury to anyone of even minor importance. That said, the crowds in the formal gardens outside the Palace of Versailles lost any semblance of decorum and rushed blindly towards their heroes as they descended from the rear terrace after the document had been signed.

"Move in *now*," Mathieu shouted at a group of soldiers who grabbed Lloyd George from the clutches of his admirers before he disappeared under their acclaim. The British prime minister's secret lover, Frances Stevenson, watched on in alarm from the terrace, and hardly dared breathe until his trademark moustache reappeared in their midst. President Wilson was almost knocked into a fountain, but his secret service agents sprang forward to save him from the indignity. Cartoonists would have relished the opportunity to capture the unfortunate incident for posterity.

Afterwards, Paris decided to have a party. But not at the Deuxième. Mathieu was obliged to monitor the revelries. At the hotel Majestic the British delegation enjoyed free champagne and an elaborate dinner with extra courses. In the grand streets and Boulevards, the cafés and restaurants shone in a blaze of extravagant light. Some motorized jokers managed to attach captured German guns to the back of their Renaults and towed them through the streets to repeated cheering and applause. How these middle-class boys loved a good jape.

"Let it go," Mathieu ordered. "There will be no medals for enforcing the letter of the law tonight. It'll be sorted in the morning."

Sumptuous dining and drinking was the order of the day. And the night. But euphoria is a waning phenomenon. The leading foreigners, Wilson and Lloyd George, were uncomfortable. The Welshman turned his caustic sarcasm towards the tricolor and was heard to say, "Why, you'd almost think the French won the war on their own."

President Wilson caught the night train to Le Havre and set off hastily for America. He wouldn't have a headache in the morning. Europe would.

* * *

Moutie's intelligence network continued to outsmart the police in terms of speed and accuracy. Of course, it was not encumbered by niceties like the law. He had updated Mathieu with details of Villain's romance with Charlotte and the attempted suicide, both of which seemed unlikely until confirmed at a later date through official police channels.

"He's talking about moving away from Paris. For some reason, he has set his sights on Danzig."

"Why?"

"No idea…but he's being watched."

Mathieu was grateful, but gratitude alone did not merit Moutie's dedication to the job.

"I think we've gone was far as we can with him, Moutie. I honestly think you've become more fixated by Raoul Villain than me."

"Possibly, Captain, but then I knew him better than you. Conceited, arrogant bastard."

Mathieu considered the matter finished but Moutie had one more bombshell to drop into the conversation.

"Tell me, Captain, who have you upset recently?"

Strange.

"You tell me. Too many people for me to know where to begin. Why do you ask?"

"I was questioned about you yesterday by an American who works with the Corsicans. He wondered what I knew about some drama in Marseille, which was nothing, and then he turned to a raid on one of their missions during the war. I played dumb, but I don't know if he believed me. He left with a smug knowing look and a stark warning. 'Don't get carried away, my friend. Your man's being watched. And so are you. Should he prove to have been involved in the Marseilles affair, he won't be long for this earth. Remember, my friend, if you lie with the dogs, you'll rise with their fleas.'"

"Nice phrase. Did he say more?" Mathieu concealed his concern. Here it was again. Someone checking up on him.

Moutie shuddered uncomfortably. "Should he have?"

REFELCTIONS ONE

On reflection, I have lived a life unfulfilled, my talent unrecognized, my genius misunderstood. My bravery remains unappreciated, but one day, history will record the facts. Of that, I am confident.

Looking back, France never deserved my loyalty. France abandoned me; my father and brother denied me; Action française betrayed me. And yet here in sun-soaked Ibiza, I have dear friends, a new house, and status. I am respected, as I should be.

My journey to the sun and sand was an unusual one. But I have been happy. Oh, yes.

I looked at a world which had changed before my eyes because of the war I facilitated and hoped that all would be well. But like the great prophets of the Bible, like Christ himself, I was not welcome in my own land. It came to me in a flash of self-realization during a sermon in Saint-Pierre de Montmartre, still my favorite church. You know how often you might fall asleep during a sermon, but the Jesuits have a capacity to construct argument with such real intensity that falling asleep is out of the question. He was a visiting spiritual advisor from Rome and delivered an eye-opening homily on why the prophet is always rejected in his own land. I felt that he was talking to me, about me. I was to leave Paris and find a suitable community which would embrace me as I am.

But where? I spoke to him afterwards on the church steps and he told me about the free city of Danzig on the Baltic Sea. It was a new city-state and needed new citizens to help create a new era. The Prussians had been thrown out and it was one of the many small communities whose creation came about because of the victorious war. In other words, me.

I fell in love with the city when I stepped from the Paris to Berlin to Danzig train. The only thing more impressive than the Long Market with magnificent ancient buildings and the grand Town Hall in its midst was the massive church of St. Mary which positively dominated all around it. A strange mixture of Russian -Byzantine and late renaissance architecture proclaimed Catholicism as the dominant force for good. I was instantly comfortable, and found a job at the casino as a croupier. I've always been good with numbers, and of course, it was helpful to intone the litany of the Roulette Wheel in fluent French. "Faites von jeux" and "Rien ne va plus" sound so perfect in the Parisian patois. Naturally, I perfected an astonishment when a successful gambler decided to tip me as if I had brought luck to the table. A bow of the head and touch to the heart would accompany the practiced "Personnel? Merci, monsieur," as another mug parted with his winnings.

"You speak such good French," they would say.

The hours were long but profitable. The company opened a second casino across the bay in Lithuania, at Klaipeda, or Memel as the Germans used to call it. Naturally, given my success in Danzig, they promoted me and sent me across to ensure it was well run. They didn't call me manager, but I was the one who made the decisions and ensured instant profitability. Here was yet another small protectorate created by the Treaty of Versailles, thanks to me. France was nominally responsible for the region until a more permanent solution could be worked out, but honestly, my countrymen couldn't run a simple game of baccarat, never mind a protectorate.

Realizing that they had to take action, the Lithuanians decided to occupy the region by force, and present the Entente with a fait accompli. It was a good decision, and a formal agreement was signed in Paris in 1924, which gave Klaipeda similar status to Danzig. It energized me, and my savings grew. Even so, every now and again, a second look in my direction or a furrowed brow which could have indicated recognition, made me feel uneasy. Living so deeply inside that part of Poland and the former East-Prussia made me aware of the growing Nazi party and its bullying techniques. I understood bullying. You know that.

I had some funds saved, more than anyone else knew, in fact, and in addition I inherited a small but significant gift of money. From my mother or a well-wisher, I cannot say. I could go wherever I chose. But where? If you had the whole world to choose from, my friend, where would you go?

43

February 1921 Icarus – Flown

Mathieu found his friend slumped, head turned towards the window through which his beloved Paris was beginning to embrace its post war renaissance. Blood had seeped into the blue patterned carpet from his mouth, nose, and ears as if an internal convulsion had ripped through his body and splattered his life onto the floor. Chief Superintendent Bernard Roux was dead.

He must have tried to steady himself for the reports on which he had been working were strewn across the desk in a mayhem of panic; a last effort to retain control which had gone long before he fell. So much blood. Unusual. Had the chief coughed up his rotted lungs? Mathieu stood in shock, defying the stiff, lifeless body to rise. It made no sense. But death comes like the thief in the night. He'd heard that phrase so often from his maternal grandmother that it was no surprise when she was stolen away many years since, though they never found the thief. But Bernard Roux? His mentor. His friend. The invincible Chief.

"Mathieu, have you seen … ?" Jacques spoke words behind his back but they passed into the confusion and were lost. He stepped into the office and gasped in horror.

"Chief." He moved to see if there was any lingering sign of life, any chance to offer comfort.

"Stop." Mathieu pulled his arm back. "Don't touch him. Something's wrong, and I don't know what it is. Get Paul and find a doctor… but do not touch the body. And don't say anything to anyone. We need to buy time before the chaos begins."

Jacques closed the door firmly and Mathieu took one careful step forward, not wishing to disturb the dead. Why was he surprised? How many times had the chief been told he was smoking far too many cigarettes? For how long had his raucous cough warned of bursting lungs?

He reached over the body and dialed an internal number. Within two minutes the photographer, a recent appointment, typical of Roux's determination to keep the Deuxième at the cutting edge in the fight against crime, came running down the corridor.

"Prepare yourself, Dominic."

Mathieu let him squeeze past rather than open the door wide as if he was protecting Bernard Roux's dignity from gathering ghouls. Younger than the rest, Dominic Verlaine had learned his trade in aerial photography during the war, and served a difficult and dangerous apprenticeship. He appeared to have survived without so much as a scar on his still-lithe body, but wounds from that terrifying conflict ran deep inside everyone who witnessed the dark monster of trench hell, even from above. He found sleep very difficult. One day something or someone would trigger a memory and the beast would crawl forth and unleash itself.

"Oh, Sweet Jesus, no," he implored and hesitated for a moment before taking flash images of the prostrate man.

"A lot of blood," was his first comment, "though he is a big man." He paused to look again. Dominic circled the body, absorbing detail, cautious lest he misread the signs before him.

"This isn't an internal hemorrhage or a burst lung, Sir," was his next. "It's more like he's been smashed to the floor."

He continued to take photographs, tiptoeing carefully round Roux's body to avoid the congealed blood. Dominic straightened up and looked at Mathieu quizzically.

"Well, that's not likely, is it?" He pointed to Bernard Roux's right hand and bent forward to take yet another photograph.

Mathieu dropped his left knee and looked again at the cigarette in Roux's dead hand. It was as though he had surrendered his life but held fast to his addiction. It was lodged between his middle and ring fingers. Why? He used any combination of index, thumb, and middle fingers, but not the others. Certainly never his ring finger. The cigarette must have been placed there after he was dead to suggest...what? That he had smoked himself to death?

"If you were standing directly above the body, you might well make a mistake. Someone put that cigarette into his hand after he hit the floor." He took another close-up shot of Roux's right hand, and stood up, waiting for instructions.

"Dominic, take a couple of general shots of the room, the desk, and the door...then disappear. Tell no one. And I mean no one. Get back to me when you have developed your film."

Mathieu sat on the window seat and opened the casement to the elements. Grey skies hovered above the city with thickening cloud drawing rain from the west. An involuntary shudder accompanied his despair. His friend;

353

his mentor; his father figure was dead. No warning. His last words had been, "I'll see you in the morning. Early. I want you to read this. Take care."

Take care. The telephone rang.

"Yes?" Mathieu welcomed the distraction.

"The new assistant commissioner, Tembey is on his way up, Sir. Thought you might like to know."

He barely had time to mutter thanks before Gabriel Tembey stood at the door, eyes widening, face as shiny as the buttons on his newly pressed uniform. No moustache. Ah, these modern trends. Mathieu's presence surprised him as did his first question.

"Bad news travels quickly does it not?"

"Yes, indeed." He exhaled deeply through his nose and blessed himself.

"The chief superintendent is dead, Captain?" It was a stupid question from a man who had forgotten his prepared script.

"Very, Sir."

"What a shock, dear me. Are you certain?" He took a step forward but Mathieu extended his arm to halt his progress.

"Very, very dead, Sir. And I must ask you to wait until the doctor has inspected the body. This may be a crime scene."

"What? Heavens above. Do you imagine that Bernard Roux was murdered? Here? Inside the Deuxième Bureau?" His attempt at lighthearted laughter betrayed a nervous undertone.

"Had you an early appointment to meet the chief superintendent, Sir?"

"Yes, well, no. I just happened to be passing so I thought I'd call in to speak with him before the day got started."

"Of course," Mathieu began, but was cut short by Jacques, Paul Dubois, and a doctor they had commandeered outside the Hotel Dieu, racing down the corridor in the vain hope that something might be done to save the day. They stopped to let the doctor enter first and Mathieu asked Jacques to escort the assistant commissioner to the visitors' room and get him coffee.

The doctor bent in two, panting for breath for half a minute before standing upright to reveal a shock of grey hair you might not have expected in such a relatively young man. He clutched his left side as if he had pulled a muscle, but his attention was fully fixed on the dead body. He, too, knelt, gently pressed his fingers to Roux's neck and shook his head.

"As a Dodo. I'd guess he's been dead for at least six hours. Cause of death? Can't tell yet. Looks like internal and external injuries. Needs an autopsy to determine that."

354

"Foul play?" Mathieu wanted to have cause to start further inquiries. "I mean, he had a bad cough and occasional fits and spasms. Too much nicotine. Smoked continuously. But that didn't kill him, did it?"

"No. If you contact the mortuary over at the Hotel Dieu, I'll accompany the body. It may take some time."

Mathieu balked. "No, it will not. You or your colleagues will conduct the autopsy this morning. Before ten o'clock. This is a matter of state security. And report to me and only me." There was no time for nicety.

As it does, news of the chief superintendent's death passed by word of mouth through no. 36 like a virus. Bernard Roux's body was carried from the building to an ambulance with all the honor he deserved. Policemen, gendarmes, detectives, workers from every department lined the stairwell, hats and kepis removed, heads bowed, saluting their leader in rigid attention. Lips quivered, but silence reigned. Outside, men and women who heard about the tragedy as they arrived for work, lined the street and bowed again. Grief had yet to find its voice, but under the grey cloud, sadness enveloped part of central Paris.

Back in Roux's office, the team began to piece together what had happened. Mathieu realized someone was missing.

"Assistant Commissioner Tembey Where is he?"

Jacques had no answer. "He followed me along the corridor, charged down the stairs, and was out the door before I could object."

"So, Assistant Commissioner Tembey just happens to call in early to see the chief, probably expecting to find him dead and take control. He was considerably put out to find us here, and currently knows nothing about Dominic Verlaine's photographs. We keep it that way. He's bound to find out that the chief's body has been removed, so send an officer over to the Hotel Dieu to keep pressure on them. Once we get the medical report we should have a better idea of time and cause of death." There was an air of collective disbelief as the implications set in. "The chief was murdered." Mathieu spoke with an authority which brooked no doubt. "Right here, by a person or persons who consider themselves untouchable."

"Slow down Mathieu," Dubois insisted. "You're going too fast. One step at a time."

"The chief was working late last night. Something for the Ministry. Had a report to finish. For their eyes only. He asked me to come in early so I could read over it."

"What was it about?" Paul Dubois wanted to know. He wanted to understand why this had happened.

Jacques produced three cups of boiling hot coffee, hoping for the stimulation it might bring to their collective reasoning.

"He had the American file on his desk in the late afternoon. I don't see it here. Does he keep it locked away, Mathieu?" Jacques picked up an empty file cover from the floor and dropped it back onto the desk

"That depends on which file. He kept special files somewhere outside the office, but we'd need his master keys to open the safe."

"And they'd be in his pocket?" Jacques reasoned.

Silence.

"Paul, would you please get over to the mortuary before they strip Bernard Roux. Bring his clothes back here."

The corridor began to fill with officers still arriving for work, anxious for details.

"Please, everyone, can we clear the corridor. Get back to your desks. Right now we need space."

Minutes later Patrick Verlaine burst into the room with two enlarged photographs. He handed over the glossy images and patiently turned them around. They were focused on Bernard Roux's hands.

"Look at the cigarette."

Mathieu looked, gasped, half rose to his feet, then bent down on one knee and looked again. How had he missed it?

"That's not a Gauloises." He looked at the others standing dumb, unable to make sense of what he was saying. "It's a Gitane."

The others strained to see the image more clearly, knowing full well that the chief had never let a Gitane touch his lips. Ever. Jacques upended the wastebasket beside the stain-strewn desk and an empty packet of Gauloises fell to the floor.

"What was he doing when you last saw him?"

Mathieu closed his eyes and took them through his recollection.

"He's working late on a special report. Is interrupted. He must have known his assailant or assailants. They make demands. He'd be angry. Next thing he's on the floor. Struck down by apoplexy or violence. He's dead. They panic. Take what is relevant, make it look as if he was smoking when he collapsed, but there are no Gauloises. One of them substitutes a Gitane, sticks it between his fingers, to mislead detection and...leaves. The only people who can walk in and out of here without special permission are us. Or a very senior officer or minister, or ... who was on duty last night?"

Jacques exhaled deeply and lowered his eyes.

"Toussaint."

"He was" Mathieu agreed. "He said Good Night when I left. Very chirpy."

"Oh yes, you can be sure he was very chirpy." Jacque's sarcasm was clear and obvious.

"What do you mean?"

"Cleaners found him lying on the floor in the downstairs changing room, snoring like a pig, stinking of drink. He had an empty bottle of cheap brandy in one hand. He was incoherent. Claims that someone left the brandy on his chair while he made his usual rounds. The duty officer dismissed him on the spot."

For a moment no-one spoke as each man tried to work out what had happened.

Jacques stared at his captain. "Mathieu," he began, "there's something else, isn't there?"

"It must have been a set-up. Whoever did this knew Toussaint was on duty and knew that he couldn't resist the drink. Whoever organized it, wanted Roux's report and the evidence he alone had access to. And Bernard Roux was the keeper of one special file." Mathieu paused and looked again at the murder scene, the bloodstains, the paper-strewn desk, upturned chair. The emptiness was overwhelming. He turned over the file which Jacques had taken from the floor. Scrawled in Roux's handwriting was a single word. *Icarus.*

Time spun from its natural order and blew certainty into Mathieu's understanding. He slumped against the far wall, legs shaking as if he had run a marathon.

"Does that mean something to you … Icarus?"

"All I can say, Jacques, is that they killed Bernard Roux, they're ruthless, and they are protected."

Of course. It must have been the Americans, or someone working on their behalf. Roux had collected and collated the secret files on Herbert Hoover, who had recently been given a senior government post in the new American government. Roux had flown too close to their sun.

The telephone on the chief superintendent's desk had the effrontery to burst into life, rudely interrupting their misery. Jacques answered its call with a curt, "Yes!"

He gave a sharp intake of breath and passed the receiver to Mathieu. "It's Agnès."

"My darling, I–"

He got no further. "Mathieu, I can see that Bernard Roux is dead. The Matron and I are with the body as we speak, but they are trying to steal him. You have to get over here quickly."

357

"What? They? Steal the body? Hold tight. We're on our way." Mathieu turned to his colleagues. "Hotel-Dieu. Move."

They burst from the front door and ran up the Rue de la Cité in a cavalry charge of limbs and flowing jackets. Few residents or visitors were yet out and about in the relative peace of the early morning hour, but those who were, stood back in amazement. Despite the limitations set by his ankle, Mathieu led the way, through the classical entrance hall, looking in despair for directions to the mortuary. Vital seconds were lost in the dimly-lit corridors which seemed to have been designed to keep out the sun, before a clamor of raised voices and angry retorts lead them to the double-door entrance to the hospital mortuary. The detectives clambered through in time to see a covered gurney disappear in the opposite direction, attended by four uniformed soldiers. Between them and Mathieu's team, Matron Veronique, Agnès, and the mortuary assistant stood blocking Assistant Commissioner Tembey's retreat.

Agnès saw them and shouted, "Mathieu, they've taken Bernard Roux's body. On the gurney."

The assistant commissioner stood his ground and barked. "Keep your distance, all of you." He waved a piece of paper in their faces and declared, "This is a judicial order instructing the hospital to release the body into the care of the military authorities."

"Nonsense," Matron Veronique insisted. "That's illegal. In all my years I've never–"

"They stopped Doctor Lamelle performing the autopsy. Just burst into the mortuary and closed it down." Agnès was personally offended. She'd witnessed the stupidity of military intransigence on many occasions during the war, but this was a civil hospital dealing with a civilian death. Furthermore, she knew Bernard Roux, knew Mathieu would never permit this outrage, knew it was worse than wrong.

"This is a police affair." Mathieu stood defiant. "Do you imagine that you can simply walk out with the body of the Deuxième's chief superintendent?"

"Imagine?" Tembey roared. "IMAGINE? Do you imagine that I'm doing this on a whim? That I had nothing else to do today?" He pushed himself into Mathieu's face and whispered, "You have no idea how high up this goes … or how bleak your future is going to be."

Jacques had been standing at the rear of the group and when Tembey moved to threaten Mathieu, he ducked past and ran towards the door through which the gurney had disappeared. Nothing. An empty corridor spread before him, but he heard an engine start somewhere to the left. He was too late.

"Where have you taken the chief, Sir?" he asked politely, but Tembey simply curled his lip and ignored him.

He turned to the Matron and said, "Madam, as I have already told you the autopsy will be carried out by a military specialist in a military establishment. For the moment, the chief superintendent's untimely death is a matter of state concern which we will address formally. I understand your objections, but I have the authority to overrule them."

"*Bâtard.*" Agnès could not hold back her contempt. She looked at Mathieu and saw a broken man trying to control his emotions. "*Bâtard.*"

When they returned to their office at no. 36 they found Paul Dubois in possession of the chief's clothes. He had been given them before the assistant commissioner's intrusion and knew nothing about the incident. Roux's jacket, waistcoat, and trousers were empty. No money, no handkerchief, none of the detritus of everyday living that people unknowingly carry around. No cigarettes. No matches. And certainly no keys.

Mathieu sank his head into the curtains. They had murdered Bernard Roux and stolen the evidence. Again. His keys were missing, and assuming that they knew where he kept his secret safe, so had Herbert Hoover's special file. It was over. Clemenceau had retired from politics and Poincaré, though no longer president, was back as prime minister. The old order had not entirely changed but a new authority had just reasserted itself.

"Jacques, Paul, I think this is what they call the end game. These people, the men who operate above the elected government, are back in charge. They've probably never been away. You have your families to protect. We may still have careers. But we no longer have the protection of Bernard Roux. God help us."

Mathieu wanted to be with Agnès to share that moment of realization. He walked past the chief's office and opened the door for one last nostalgic look. The shock almost blew him from his feet. The room stood in pristine condition as if dressed for inspection. Everything was in its appointed position. The carpets had been replaced, the desk cleared. Every paper and file had been removed. The chief's chair stood in solitary affirmation that it no longer had a worthy occupant. Floors had been washed and polished. Not a stain in sight. A vase of flowers sat in the window closest to his desk, an alien presence in a room which had been dedicated to nicotine. The central window had been deliberately left open to encourage the circulation of fresh air. Roux was but a memory of its past.

As he left the building the concierge confirmed that someone had sent cleaners to clear up the mess. "Ah," Mathieu nodded. "Someone."

Within an hour, the late morning edition of *Le Parisien* carried a fulsome obituary for Bernard Roux. It said that he collapsed and died from a heart attack at work.

Heart attack? It broke Mathieu's.

Raoul's Story

REFLECTIONS TWO

I won't be long now, my friend. Please hear me out.

I yearned for the sun and the sea. Danzig and Klaipeda offered the sea, but the cold artic winds which circled the Baltic in winter ice chased any semblance of warmth from the sun. One met many different kinds of people as a croupier and it always paid dividends to flatter those with money. Remember that, my friend. A well-to-do-Spaniard who collected artworks from across the continent painted such a vivid picture of the Balearic Islands that I decided to make a permanent move in that direction. I didn't know where these islands were, but since they weren't too far adrift from Marseilles and Barcelona, thought it worthwhile investigating.

I don't know even now what I expected, my friend, but you live in a very beautiful island. The rocky bays and the soft white sand mesmerized me. I checked into a small family hotel in Santa Eulària and walked down to the beach. Sunset flickered its last flecks of red across a placid sea and the warmth of the day had yet to be dispersed by the soft Mediterranean wind. Once I decided to settle on the island, I started to look for the kind of locale in which I could embrace a spiritual and personal renaissance. The boy from the country learned to love the sound of the sea. The man from Paris who could not swim or settle in the water, adored the soft sand. The prisoner from La Santé could never have tired of the pastel light of an evening on Ibiza. A new freedom offered itself. Forget the sullied past. The stench of the abattoir whose blood had flowed through Europe gave way to the clean pure air of Cala Sant Vicenç with its tiny port and colorful fishing boats.

And the artistic milieu thrilled me. Many different kinds of painters, designers, craftsmen, and gifted sculptors come here, as you know. I'll wager you've been painted in your natural habitat many times over, my friend. Have you seen the works of Laurea Bunol from Barcelona? I'm in one of his beach scenes, posing as a fisherman. Look closely. You, too, may be there. His canvases are stunningly fresh.

We drank local white wine together in El Café Rosa, by the rocks, lapping up the atmosphere, talking of the new. Paul René Gauguin, the painter's grandson, was one of our companions. He was from Norway and the first graphic artist I met. He was more than that, too. Paul was young, gifted, with film-star good looks and the kind of smile which spread confidence through a room without his realizing it. He could sculpt, illustrate books, and design the most elaborate stage sets for the theatre. As Pola Gauguin's son, he might have been daunted by the legacy of fame, but, unlike many others, he did not let his famous grandfather cast a shadow on his own talents. We talked, drank, and smoked through the dark hours, designing, creating, imagining, and dreaming of a better world peopled by like-minded men and women. Outside of our little circle of intelligentsia there were precious few worthy of our time.

Inspired by our artistic mélange, I decided to build a new house which Gauguin and others helped me design. Backed by a wooded knoll, it sat beside the beach, a modern statement of style; a class above the ordinary. Two flat-roofed towers bordered a quasi-Arabic frontage with three arches in between. The basement was extensive because the road sloped steeply down to the left. It's not completely finished, yet. Perhaps it will never be. But then, that is the nature of art.

I'm well aware that behind my back the locals call me el boig, the madman, but why would I care? I didn't want to socialize with sweaty fishermen whose stubble could cut clams, or a herdsman whose arrival could be anticipated by the smell of the matted goats which preceded him. Let the fisherwomen sew and leather-faced ancients sit and smoke in the shadow of the church, playing occasion games of boule when their fancy took. If I barked at them it was to keep distance.

I decided to place a solid wooden cross on the hillside behind the house at a height where, from an angle, it might look as though it was attached to one of the towers; that's the artist in me. But my project backfired when a group of widowed fisher folk congregated around the makeshift cross to say the Rosary. When I found those women kneeling in my garden, I took a stick in my hand and rushed them from the greenery. How dare they? Start that kind of nonsense and the next thing is beggars and peddlers at your door pleading Christianity as a basis for constant handouts.

44

BURYING THE TRUTH

Chief Superintendent Bernard Roux was buried in a family plot at Père Lachaise amongst the Great, the unknown, and the once-famous. He had not been a statesman or a decorated general or a titan of industry. He had kowtowed to no man but tried to bring justice to a world that hardly deserved him. The Roux family owned a Romanesque vault with one of the original ancient stone atriums which stood at an angle on the cemetery's main cobbled thoroughfare. His funeral cortege was simple. Not for him the trappings of grandeur or horse-drawn black carriages. No bands preceded, no symphony orchestra attended. No massive wreaths beloved of the wealthy or mafia families adorned his final resting place. Yet hundreds of Frenchmen trooped behind his mourning family like a regiment of the worthy. Some he knew and liked. Some he knew. Clemenceau was there, head bare and bowed, his trusted friend Mordacq by his side. I caught the general's roving eye as he swept the landscape and he recognized me immediately. Mordacq pointed beyond the vault and indicated we should talk after the official proceedings. I nodded in agreement. Kind words were spoken by the graveside, whether meant or otherwise.

For most at the Deuxième, Bernard Roux's death was an untimely reminder of the fallibility of man. His loyal team—Paul, Jacques, Dominic Verlaine, and Mathieu—knew he had been murdered. So, too, did Agnès and Pascal who stood by their side. The assistant commissioner was complicit in some way, which argued that some of Poincaré's new ministers were also involved. Beyond that lay the Zaharoff's and Comité des Forges, the international bankers and the industrialists who manipulated continents to their own end. And the Americans, now so powerful that they acted as if they owned the world. The trouble was, they did.

As Mathieu filed past, deep in his own thoughts, he realized what was staring at him and gasped. The Roux family vault was protected by a marbled statue of St. Michael the Archangel, sword in one hand, the keys to the Kingdom of Heaven in the other, with wings outstretched to protect the family tomb. But on each side of the plinth on which St. Michael stood in all his glory, two urns balanced the frame with wooden drawers underneath. Each had a lock. This was the vault. This was Roux's vault. His secret hiding place. And those were the keys dangling from the statue. Hidden in plain view amongst the dead. His secret files had not been kept at no. 36. Ever.

Mordacq waited patiently under a cypress tree, a pipe pouting at his lips, his black heavy coat wrapped loosely round him. He bowed his bare head to Agnès and took Mathieu by the elbow.

"This is wrong, Mathieu," he acknowledged. "A heart attack brought on by ruined lungs and clotted arteries, I'm told."

Mathieu Bertrand looked directly into his eyes and flashed a scowl of pure scorn. "And vicious murdering bastards."

"We know, Mathieu. We know. Clemenceau thinks that the Americans did not mean to kill Roux."

"So you would single out the Americans?" Agnès asked.

"Pure conjecture, Mademoiselle," he said very softly, "you will understand."

Even tombstones might have ears.

"We also know that they didn't get hold of the Hoover file. All good. But we cannot protect our own as we always have. For the moment, everything changes. Pendulums swing so far and then retrace their path. In the meantime, we want you to consider a new career. Outside Paris."

A top-hat and dress coat broke away from a passing group of dignitaries and extended a gloved hand.

"You know Ambassador Jean-Jules Jusserand, Mathieu. He would like to speak to you. Good day, *mes amis.*"

Top-hats were tilted.

"Captain Bertrand, I am pleased to meet you again, though the circumstances are devastatingly sad."

Mathieu tried to clear his throat but failed. The ambassador extended his formal greeting to Agnès in a manner which suggested that he knew of their relationship.

"I would like you to consider a post as special assistant in our embassy in Indo-China, working directly from there. For three or four years. You are well considered at the Foreign Office, with the probable exception of Benoit Durfort, but that stands in your favor, and Clemenceau believes in you, as he believed in Roux. The current president will not have you in a senior post at the Deuxième. Certainly not as Roux's replacement. We believe that your appointment abroad will be in France's best interest.

Your knowledge, some would say unique knowledge, of many aspects of the diplomatic world is invaluable. Would you please consider this offer? I need to know by the weekend."

They nodded respectfully and parted.

Mathieu looked at Agnès and shrugged. "We can talk about this later." She shook her head and smiled. "You see, my beloved, that is your great weakness. You are so determined to be fair that you have to consider both sides of the equation even when the answer is staring you in the face. Of course we will go. Both of us. I've longed to see Hanoi since I was a child."

And that, he had to admit, was her great strength. Decision-making. You don't spend years at the front making instant decisions on who might live and for whom it was already too late, without developing an instinct for such matters.

* * *

Moutie was standing by the imperial entrance to the cemetery, more mock-Roman in style than French. The Latin inscription predicted that the true believers were guaranteed immortality. It struck Mathieu that Roux would have preferred a Gauloises. Moutie played his part well. He was such a skilled mourner; pained features, deep sighs, his eyes cast down to exclude personal contact.

Mathieu bowed his head slightly and spoke into Moutie's left ear. "Café du Cimiere. Twenty minutes. I have a job for you." He bowed and left immediately.

45

UNLESS YOU ARE IN DANGER

Mathieu disappeared. Indeed, Mathieu and Agnès disappeared overnight nine days after Moutie had completed his task in the cemetery. It was hardly a difficult task. The keys opened the lock on Roux's family vault and the files lay untouched in the top drawer—-just as he said they would. Their conversation had been brief and entirely one-sided. Moutie wasn't sure that he fully understood what it meant but it seemed that Mathieu would be transferred to another post for a couple of years and he was not to worry. It would not be forever. He was to leave the Villain business as it was and on no account was Moutie to try to find him. It wasn't safe. It could be that the Corsicans might try to kill him, so it was far safer for everyone if he couldn't be contacted.

"Unless" and Mathieu spoke softly, "you are in danger … or chance upon something extremely odd that I should know. In that case leave a message for me with the manager of the Cafe Cluny. He will see that it gets to a third party who in turn may or may not send it to me."

Moutie sat in shock, not fully understanding what he had heard. Mathieu grasped his hand, shook it, smiled, and said, "Adieu." And he was gone.

Letter from Paris, April 1926

My friend, this letter was dictated to me by my uncle, an unnecessarily clean fellow on whom you have had a most worthy influence. It should arrive through a channel which you trust. His story is as follows.

I was doing nothing in particular other than watching the world go by from a cafe on the corner of rue Croix-des-Petits-Champs, you know, across from the great iron gates of the Banque de France, when they sprang open and a figure from the past strode through as if he was the governor himself. He's slightly older than I remembered him, his eyes still sharp and menacing. He signaled down the rue with the self-important impatience of the doorman at the Ritz. I shrank into my newspaper—well, it wasn't exactly mine, but someone left it on the cafe table so I thought I'd borrow it for a while, and I didn't want him to see me.

He was dressed in an expensive suit, dark in tone but not black; almost formal, but not too formal… bespoke. He had a badge of some kind on his left lapel and held real leather gloves which he began to slip onto his large hands. I remember those hands for they were unkind and unforgiving, yet the gloves made them appear refined. A limousine glided into the reserved space immediately in front of the Banque and our friend spoke sharply to the chauffeur. Couldn't hear what was said, but the driver nodded seriously and turned his head to face the front as if he had been forbidden to cast an eye in the direction of a living God. Perhaps he was. Then, like a circus clown, the man drew out a huge umbrella which appeared to open on command and moved back inside the forbidding portal. Surely it was... but how? Why?

Barely two seconds later and he reappeared in the company of Governor Moreau, shielding him from the elements, though the rain was hardly in evidence. They appeared to be sharing a confidence, perhaps it was a joke, as the governor settled into his limousine, and with one shake of his powerful hand Toussaint closed the door and the umbrella, and took a seat beside the driver who continued to stare into the future as if no one was there. Toussaint. It was him, it was Toussaint. He sat, preened like a prize short-toed eagle, ready to strike any assailant. I was so taken aback I left without paying. I thought he had been dismissed from the Deuxième because of his unprofessional conduct on the night Bernard Roux was murdered. Am I wrong?

Everything that week was a blur. Nothing made complete sense. Not even having to recover those files from Père Lachaise. The pain you've put me through, my friend. But forget that. Toussaint? After those dreadful days I never heard of him again. Never even in cafes around the old haunts. Just gone. Disappeared. And now it appears that he is the personal bodyguard to the governor of the bank. How did he manage that?

I made it my business to find out. Hung around in a couple of different cafés until the limousine returned and drank in as much as I could. Toussaint got out of the car first and spoke into a machine whereupon the iron door began to open. He returned to fetch Governor Moreau and without much hesitation they both disappeared inside the fortification that is the Banque de France.

This time I paid greater attention to the limousine's driver. He had a story to tell, of that I was certain. I traced him through the garage where the splendid car was housed. Lives in rue Marc Seguin between the railway junctions, and drinks in the ill-named Café des Roses which stinks of old soot and fresh ash. Our man—I'll not give his name—was naturally reluctant to talk about his work but after a month of casual head nods and one-word greetings, we emptied a bottle of vin ordinaire to celebrate my alleged winnings at Longchamp, and I chanced to drop the name Toussaint into the conversation. I confessed that I knew he *was a pure bastard, bully, and cheat who I had once had dealings with. Cut a long story short, he unburdened his pent up venom.*

Yes monsieur, he hates said Toussaint with a vengeance.

The facts are as follows. Four or five years back Toussaint appeared at the Banque as the new depute chief of security. Word was that he had retired from the highest level of policing and had been recommended to the Banque by one of President Poincaré's senior advisors. Toussaint built his own inner circle of former policemen and literally ran the internal security. He has a talent for brutality and has dismissed anyone who disregards his instructions. He cultivated the governor's approval and presents this image of a trusted confidant. In truth he is a trusted confidant. When the chief of security retired, hey presto, Toussaint was the automatic choice.

From disgraced front-doorman of the Deuxième, sacked for dereliction of duty… to head of internal security of the Banque of France? How did that happen? Who did he bribe? Whose dirty-work did he cover-up? I know it means something, but I don't know what that is. You will. That's why I asked my niece to write this down clearly. Take care, my friend, and trust me when I say, I have your back covered here in Paris. Well, in certain quarters of lesser known Paris.

I'm sorry about the ramblings, but uncle is extremely agitated about this discovery. I say, *once a cop, always a cop*, and there's nothing new about that. My uncle had some other stories which don't add up to much. Apparently Toussaint keeps mouthwash and eaux de cologne in the car so that he can have a sly Gitane when he is waiting for his boss, clean his breath, and disinfect his jacket. The governor hates cigarettes. Ah, the folly of the rich.

The former Captain from the Deuxième sat in the sultry Hanoi heat and began to absorb the news from Paris. Toussaint? Was it possible that he was the mole who stole files, leaked plans, diverted their attention, and murdered Bernard Roux? Had the team convinced itself that everything was the fault of the Americans and ignored the man literally standing in front of them? Or was it a combination? He had to go back to Paris. This was unfinished business and very personal.

Agnès read the letter slowly. Then she re-read it, taking in as much of the subtext as she could. She placed her hand on his shoulder and tightened her grip.

"The answer is NO. We can't uproot the family and go back to Paris without further evidence. This could be a trap, a hoax to lure you to your death. No. We don't even know for sure that it's from Moutie."

Agnès the wise.

REFLECTIONS 3

You know civil war broke out on mainland Spain with surprising intensity in mid-summer 1936. No, no of course you do, my friend. I presume so much of you.

Thank God we were isolated from the murder and chaos in the great cities from where there were regular reports of shameful atrocities. On the island, arguments raged on both sides with the short-lived intensity of a petty quarrel. It had nothing to do with me, but General Francisco Franco was hailed as the protector of decency and moral strength. I hoped he would crush the socialists and republicans, the anarchists and the revolutionaries who always spoiled the natural order. Envy, you see. That's what motivates them. They won't do a day's honest work, but want something for nothing. Wastrels. But worst of all, they were anti-clerics and murdered priests and nuns. Unforgivable. Murdering men and women of the cloth. It was no surprise that both the military garrison and the civil guard supported Franco.

I thought little of it. It seemed to me that the Spanish were set on tearing themselves apart, but we were safe in Cala, given that there was barely a track into the village. The locals had a saying: "Out of this world and into Cala." I made that mistake, you see. That's me at my best. Trusting and hopeful, expecting the best from everyone. The bastard Republicans in Barcelona sent an invasion squadron of two destroyers to take possession of the islands and vented their bile on an unsuspecting prey. They landed on Ibiza and a month later were followed by a column of nearly five hundred anarchists under a banner of Culture and Action. Culture mon cul. Their contribution to culture was to enforce a reign of terror in which nearly half of the parish priests were slaughtered. Bishop Cardona and his associates took to the hills and lived for a time in the caves around the coast. Almost every church was looted and burned. It was disgusting, but it did not go unnoticed.

Since I was French and clearly had no involvement in the troubles, I decided to visit my lady-friend Katerina in Santa Eulària, which I did from time to time to our mutual benefit. In truth, I wanted to see for myself what was going on, and she offered additional comfort. Taking a late lunch on the balcony of her rooms by the port, we were praising the bravery of the Sant Antoni townsfolk who rescued many of the ancient church relics from the pillaging Republicans, when a strange noise drew our attention to the skies.

"What's that?" Katerina asked, coffee cup in hand, eyes and ample breasts uplifted to the drone above our rooftop. Three airplanes appeared high above us, in slow methodical order, lining up to sweep over Ibiza town. As the noise from their engines faded a more ominous sound reverberated through the island.

"Bombs!" she screamed. "They're dropping bombs on Ibiza. Mother of God, we're all going to die!"

We ran into the street, as did the entire population, bewildered by the un-expected assault on the island. The harbor buzzed with the extravagant rumor that General Franco had come in person to rescue us. Nonsense of course. But a fisherman I knew insisted that a small detachment of anarchists had landed by boat on the beach in Cala San Vincent and were wreaking havoc on the un-armed populace. I had to return immediately. Though the house was not yet finished, I had moved in my belongings and some personal items which they were certain to steal.

A black pall hung over the village as a warning to all who might seek to in-tervene. I picked up my stride, anxious to protect my property from those scav-enging pigs. Looking back I could see clouds of billowing smoke and flames beyond Ibiza port. What was going on? The idyll was no more. As I reached the outskirts my next door neighbors approached me, clearly distressed.

"Raoul, stay away. There are angry and dangerous men stalking the streets. Came in by boat. Stay in the hills. Don't go down to the cove."

Not likely. Me? I ignored those idiots. I knew how to deal with soldiers. Huh, they weren't real soldiers anyway. From the road, I could see a figure on my roof, looking out to sea.

"Hey, you," I shouted, "get off immediately. It's not secure enough to take your weight."

The soldier turned and pointed a rifle towards me. It was a woman, but I knew the authority in my voice had unsettled her. She shouted at me, in Catalan, I assumed, but I marched onwards into the house.

"Stop where you are," a voice ordered from behind. He was an officer, of some dubious rank which I was unlikely to recognize, but his pistol deserved my attention. He was young, unshaven and nervous. His cloth cap was an unnecessary status symbol. You could see that his trousers were worn and patched and his hands were stained with black ink. A printer from Barcelona, perhaps?

"Who are you and where have you been?"

"Monsieur, I am a Frenchman, from Reims, and live here as a resident."

"This is your house?"

"Yes."

"You have papers? You can prove this?"

"Of course I have papers." Do they choose the particularly stupid ones as leaders to confuse the enemy?

He examined my credentials, unimpressed. I wondered if he could even read, but kept the thought unspoken. Most printers could read.

"You are Monsieur Villain?"

"I am."

"You have placed a crucifix outside, on the hill directly behind your house. Why?"

"Because I chose to."

"You are Catholic?"

"Yes, is that a crime? Most Frenchmen are Catholics." I stuck out my chest inviting him to back off.

"I know many Frenchmen," he retorted, "and none of them are Catholic. Do you favor Generalissimo Franco? Do you work for him? Perhaps you are a French fascist? Perhaps you are a Franco-spy." He poked my chest firmly and I took a step back. "Tell me again where you were earlier today. Did you see the airplanes?"

"Look, I was in Santa Eulària visiting a friend, and yes I saw them. Nothing to do with me."

"Did you tell anyone that we were here in Cala Sant Vicenç?"

"No. I didn't know you were here."

He had been joined by some others carrying loot of one type or another. A vintage clock that had long since given up telling the time. A saucepan, bedspread, and wall frame were piled in their arms. They looked like the gypsies and thieves I knew them to be. "We have to go back to the port now, but you will stay here in your house and await our return. Do you understand?"

"I've got business to do myself," I protested. "I'm not about to leave the village, am I?"

"What business? Franco-business ?"

"No. I've nothing in the house to cook tonight. I must buy some food."

"You will do as you are told, Monsieur Frenchman. Understand?"

He left me standing in the front room, looking out across the placid waves which lapped the coast, unaware of the trouble. I waited until they had disappeared from view, then gathered my valuables from the bedroom closet. It was hardly a fortune; two watches, a signet ring, and some cash in francs and pesetas. I would hide them six paces behind the cross in the garden, under the protruding roots of the palm tree. But he was back. He must have tiptoed into the house.

"And where do you think you are going with those?" he asked, brandishing his pistol.

"I'm taking them to a safe place," I began sarcastically, "but I don't think there are many left."

His face twisted into a sneer. Perhaps he had been drinking to bolster his confidence. "You will come with us, to the port. I need to know more about you."

"As you insist. Hopefully you will let me buy my food while we're there."

One of the underlings, a woman, appeared in some haste and spoke urgently to him. She looked dirty in her soiled black trousers, off-white blouse, and red-patterned neck-tie. Her short hair added to the masculinity of her demeanor and her eyes were hidden under a wide-brimmed straw hat. She carried a rifle which seemed to be at least as big as she was herself and an enamel can hung loosely from her waist. They reexamined my papers and their conversation became ever more animated. Then I distinctly heard the word Jaurès, mispronounced, as usual, but still recognizable. More pointing and excited insistence followed. They left the room to discuss me in private, so I took the chance to exit through the unfinished window by the side of the house. I ran across the road and onto the sand, picking up speed, not looking backwards. One minute was all I needed to get around the first rocks and they would not know where I had gone.

Slam. I fell as I ran, head first, down. Then the noise of gunshot carried forward past me into the soft beach. The shock of pain blasted through me and then subsided. The sand was warm and friendly. All these thoughts hit me as the bullet passed through my back and shattered my spine. I did not move because I could not. I heard my neighbors' shouts and the soldiers' replies, but it took some moments to understand.

"He's not dead, Sir. Should I shoot him in the head?" It was the woman again.

You coward, I thought. I'm unarmed and cannot move, yet you would shoot me in the head? You coward.

"No, don't waste another bullet, Chantal."

The officer stood over me. I recognized his battered brown boots. Wouldn't last another winter, for sure.

"You are a very stupid arrogant Frenchman. My colleague informed me that you have the same name as the murderer of the great socialist Jean Jaurès. Are you the bastard assassin?"

I chose not to answer. I had made that choice on many an occasion. My silence annoyed him further. He turned to the small crowd on the beach and warned them. "Leave him here. Do not move him. We will be back tomorrow, and if he is gone, every man, woman, and child in the street will be shot. Is that clear?"

From behind me someone said, "I'll stay."

So here I am, my friend. Still lying on the beautiful beach, but tired now. Very tired. Almost lifeless. Though I can't see you properly, you are the only one who has stayed loyal, day and night. I appreciate that. I do. I have sensed your presence. For two days you have listened to my every word. No interruption. Not once, my friend. Not once. I have shared my life story with you while you calmly smoked your pipe. Oh yes, I can smell it. I've shared secrets with you that no one else will ever know. And for that, I am grateful. Will you stay with me to the end, my friend? Please? It won't be long.

"I think you're right."

She was a woman. That woman who spoke French. Had she shot me in the back?

I wanted to see her face but she just sat there on a rock as she had for two days, cleaning and re-cleaning her rifle.

"Just to let you know," she added, "I'll be writing to my uncle shortly. You knew him once, I believe. In La Santé. You called him Carbolic."

And the sound of lapping waves gently seduced my being.

DENOUEMENT

A cutting slipped from the envelope. Postage stamp said Paris. With it was a two-word note in spidery scrawl.

At last.

The newspaper reported that the unarmed Raoul Villain had been shot in the back by Spanish Republicans on the island of Ibiza and died on the beach. Mathieu reread the piece without emotion.

"*C'est fini*," he said aloud, and turned back to the business at hand.

"Bernard, for the last time, will you do as your mother says."

ACKNOWLEDGMENTS

I have to begin by thanking Kris Milligan at TrineDay for his early enthusiasm for this novel. His faith energized my writing and he backed that up by introducing me to Todd Barselow, a literary editor with the patience and insight to help me bring Beyond Revanche to the page.

Previously I have written purely historical work in conjunction with my colleague, Jim Macgregor, whose dedication to detail was formidable. Switching genres from history to historical fiction was a challenge whose difficulties I didn't at first appreciate, and I am particularly indebted to the advice I received from a number of colleagues and friends.

I must thank Jo Bell, in particular, an up-and-coming Scottish writer and poet. Jo has presented her work at the Edinburgh International Book Festival and I am in admiration of her skills. Mark her name for the future. Louise Docherty and Lawrie Risk added helpful suggestions to the work-in-progress and guided me in areas that others might have been reluctant to criticize. Friends and family have been equally enthusiastic and I am grateful to them for reading tracts or earlier versions of the book.

Thanks also to my local expert on all things Corsican, Eddie Inglis.

Finally, a word of particular thanks to Jack Gibson for producing the front cover.